D0210632

THE BELL over the door in Steffie Wyler's ice-cream shop rang and Steffie glanced up as the latest group entered the small one-time crabber's shack that now served as Scoop's home, and her words died in her throat. Dallas MacGregor, a regular customer, came into the shop, trailed by her great-aunt and the tall, ridiculously handsome guy who'd been the object of Steffie's affection—and lust—since before she was old enough to know the difference between, well, affection and lust.

She tried to ignore the smile of recognition that spread across his face when he saw her. Tried just as unsuccessfully to keep her heart rate under control. Tried to push from her mind the scenes her imagination had conjured up of Wade walking into Scoop—like he just had, all nonchalant and gorgeous, smiling a special smile just for her—at which time she put the CLOSED sign on the door and they fell into each other's arms and frantically—

"I said two scoops of chocolate," the customer she was waiting on waved a hand in front of her face to get her attention. "That's pistachio."

ALSO BY MARIAH STEWART

Home Again
Coming Home

Acts of Mercy
Cry Mercy
Mercy Street

Last Breath
Last Words
Last Look

Final Truth
Dark Truth
Hard Truth
Cold Truth

Dead End
Dead Even
Dead Certain
Dead Wrong

Forgotten
Until Dark
The President's Daughter

Books published by The Random House Publishing Group are available at quantity discounts on bulk purchases for premium, educational, fund-raising, and special sales use. For details, please call 1-800-733-3000.

Almost Home

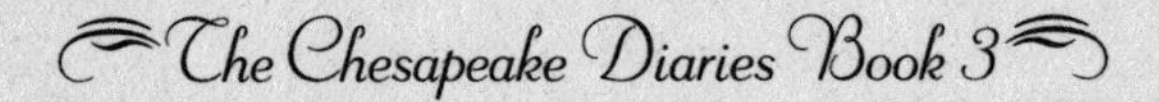
The Chesapeake Diaries Book 3

MARIAH STEWART

BALLANTINE BOOKS • NEW YORK

Sale of this book without a front cover may be unauthorized. If this book is coverless, it may have been reported to the publisher as "unsold or destroyed" and neither the author nor the publisher may have received payment for it.

Almost Home is a work of fiction. Names, characters, places, and incidents either are the product of the author's imagination or are used fictitiously. Any resemblance to actual persons, living or dead, events, or locales is entirely coincidental.

A Ballantine Books Mass Market Original

Copyright © 2011 by Marti Robb
Excerpt from *Coming Home* copyright © 2010 by Marti Robb
Excerpt from *Home Again* copyright © 2010 by Marti Robb

All rights reserved.

Published in the United States by Ballantine Books, an imprint of The Random House Publishing Group, a division of Random House, Inc., New York.

BALLANTINE and colophon are trademarks of Random House, Inc.

ISBN 978-0-345-52037-1

Printed in the United States of America

www.ballantinebooks.com

9 8 7 6 5 4 3 2 1

To Kate Collins—come what may

ACKNOWLEDGMENTS

As always, many thanks to the stellar team at Ballantine Books: Kate Collins, Linda Marrow, Scott Shannon, Libby McGuire, Kim Hovey, Gina Wachtel, Kelli Fillingim, Junessa Viloria, Scott Biel, Kirstin Fassler, and Quinne Rogers. (I hope I haven't forgotten anyone!)

Once again, the ADWOFF raffle benefitting the Nora Roberts Foundation resulted in a reader having won the right to have her name used for a character in one of my future books. Cindy Sims, the future is now! And thanks to Phyllis Lannik's kind heads up, Cindy's mother made a cameo appearance. I hope Helen Kay Hinson would have approved.

Thanks as always to my agent, Loretta Barrett, and the crew at Barrett Books.

Many thanks to the crew at the Borders Express, Springfield Mall, Springfield, PA, but especially to Maureen and Jenn. You guys most certainly do rock!

And last but God knows, never least—hugs to Chery Griffin aka Victoria Alexander for sharing some *extra* fine whine this time around.

Prologue

May, 1998

THE high school gym had been transformed into a fantasy in white. Small twinkling lights were draped everywhere, from the fake palm trees that lined the walls to the bandstand where the DJ hired for the occasion kept the music playing. Huge pots, spray-painted glossy white, sported arrangements of white flowers—roses, gladiola, hydrangea—all dusted with glitter. Here and there throughout the room, white helium balloons were gathered into bouquets that bobbled and floated. A silver glitter ball overhead spun continuously, a gaudy moon that cast a shimmering glow over the dancing couples beneath it.

The theme for Bayside High's senior prom, Candle in the Wind—no doubt inspired by the tragic death of England's Princess Diana—had been taken literally by the decorating committee, who'd planned for one thousand white candles to flicker throughout the gym all night long. Unfortunately, Principal Naylor—obviously a man without a single romantic bone in his portly body—had put the kibosh on that idea, citing the fire codes.

Steffie Wyler snuggled up to her date and swayed to

the music. Like so many of the other girls, she'd had her hair done that afternoon, and had her nails—fingers and toes—done as well. She spent hours in front of the mirror perfecting her makeup, then another few hours second-guessing her choice of gown. And like so many of the others, Steffie had chosen a white gown. But where most of her friends had picked white satin, Steffie's dress was white chiffon. She'd seen it in the window of a shop in Annapolis and begged her mother to let her try it on. Simple in design, it had a wide swath of chiffon over her left shoulder, a sweetheart neckline, and a skirt that flowed around her body when she moved.

Steffie had been on the fence about it when the saleswoman stepped into her dressing room and said, "Oh, my, you look like a Greek goddess in that dress." Which in itself would have been sufficient, but when she added, "So hard to believe you're only seventeen," Stef was sold. Ordinarily, her age wouldn't be an issue, but tonight, it was very much on her mind, since her date was four years older than she was.

Not that it bothered Stef—she couldn't have cared less how old he was. In her eyes, Wade MacGregor was the perfect man, or at the very least, the perfect man for her. She'd known him for as long as she could remember, so long that she had no recollection of ever having met him. He was part of her life in St. Dennis, or had been, until he left for college in Texas four years ago. Up until then, she'd seen him almost daily. He sailed with her brother, Grant, and in the summers, he worked painting houses with a couple guys in his class, Clay Madison and Cameron O'Connor. On any given day she could—and did—walk real slowly past whatever house they were painting just to look at him. Wade was always tall for his age, and in the summers, his sandy-blond hair lightened a few shades and his skin tanned nicely. Oh, yes—Wade MacGregor was the perfect guy.

The fact that he'd always had a girlfriend when he was in high school hadn't deterred Steffie one bit. She knew he was the guy for her, and once he figured that out, they'd live happily ever after.

She just wished he'd hurry up and see the light.

Tonight, she wasn't thinking of any of that. Prom night was supposed to be special—magical—and Stef was determined that she would have her share of special memories. The fact that she'd had to trick Wade into being her date—and trick her mother into letting her go with him—no longer mattered. She was certain that once he saw her in her goddess-gown, once he held her close enough to see that they fit together just right, once she kissed him—well, he'd feel the magic, too. He'd see that they were *Meant to Be.*

She did wish the magic would kick in soon, though. So far he'd seemed . . . indifferent wasn't exactly the right word. She'd seen the way he looked at her when she flowed down the steps in her goddess-gown. But so far, he'd kept his distance, thwarting every move she made to get closer.

Finally, the last dance was announced, and she rested her head on his shoulder, singing along with Shania that he was still the one, meaning every word. She could hardly wait to get into the auditorium, where they'd watch a movie compliments of the parents association—an event intended to keep the kids under their watchful eyes for as long as possible, though it was anyone's guess what was going on in the back rows once the lights went out. The movie—*Titanic*—was a love story for the ages. Surely that would put Wade—and every other guy in the auditorium—in a romantic mood.

Her first clue that the rest of the evening wasn't going to go the way she'd planned came when they filed into the room and Wade led her down the aisle to sit in the first row, pretending not to hear her protestations that they sit in the back. The second was the news that the film they'd received was defective, and instead of *Titanic,* they'd be watching *Men in Black,* an announcement that was met with cheers from most of the guys and boos from the girls.

The night's final insult came when Wade drove her home, walked her to her front door, and attempted to open it for her—without kissing her good night.

It wasn't as if he'd had to wonder if she wanted to kiss him. She'd stood in front of the door and wrapped her arms around his neck, closed her eyes, and puckered up.

"Ah, Stef . . . ," he'd said as he gently unwound her arms and held her hands in his. "That's not going to happen."

"Don't you like me, Wade?"

"I like you a lot, Stef. I really do. I always have."

"Then why don't you want to kiss me?"

"Stef, when do you turn eighteen?"

"In August. Why?"

"In October, I'll turn twenty-two."

"So?" It was all she could do to keep from sounding whiny.

"So, you are underage. I'm twenty-one."

"I repeat, so?"

"I'm too old for you, Stef. Next week, I'm flying back to Texas for graduation."

"I still don't understand what that has to do with you kissing me." She pouted.

"Some might think I was taking advantage of you."

"Yeah, like who?" she asked defiantly.

"Like, oh, your big brother, for one."

"You're not afraid of Grant, are you?"

"Whether or not I'm afraid isn't the point."

"Then what is?" She all but stamped her foot.

"Your brother is my friend, he's on my sailing team. I like and respect him. I would not want him to think I was toying with the affections of his little sister."

"*Younger* sister," she emphasized. "And you're not toying with me. And if you think I'm too young for you, why did you come with me tonight?"

"Look, I felt really bad about your date getting in that car accident and you being left without—" He stopped and stared down at her. "That didn't really happen, did it?"

"What difference would it make?" She avoided his eyes.

"You made that up, didn't you? The story about the guy flipping his car over and being in a coma . . ."

She shrugged. "It could have happened . . ."

Wade burst out laughing. "You did make it all up. Here I've been feeling sorry for a guy who doesn't even exist." He squeezed her hand. "Stef, why'd you do that?"

"Because I wanted to go to my prom with you. I told my mom and she said I couldn't ask you because you were in college and you were too much older." The whole sorry story spilled out. "So I told her I'd asked someone else, a guy from another school, and then three days ago I told her he was sick and he couldn't go but I'd find someone else to take me. I knew you'd be home this weekend because I heard Grant on the phone with you about six weeks ago talking about entering Sunday's race."

"So three weeks ago you knew this poor guy was going to be sick and/or in a coma and wouldn't be able to go, so you lined me up."

"Something like that."

"What would you have done if I'd said no?"

She shrugged. "Three weeks before the prom, I'd still be able to get a date." She paused, then asked, "If I'd told you the truth, would you have been my date tonight?"

"Probably not."

She pulled her hand away and turned toward the door. He grabbed her by the arm to stop her from bolting into the house.

"Stef, you are a beautiful girl . . ."

"Oh, please do not say, 'Someday you'll meet someone who's just right for you.' " She closed her eyes. "Tell me you weren't going to say that."

"I *was* going to say that. And it's true. Someday you will."

"I don't want anyone else." There. She'd said it.

She kept her eyes closed so that she wouldn't have to see his face.

"Stef, I'm going back to Texas in two weeks," he said gently, "and I'm staying there. I'm not coming back to St. Dennis."

"What? Not ever?" Her eyes flew open. "But I wanted you to come to my graduation party."

"I'll be here for that. And I'll be back to see my aunt Berry from time to time, but I'm going to be living and working in Texas."

"Why?"

"Because I have an opportunity to go into business with a friend, and it's what I want to do."

She could hardly speak. The thought that Wade would leave St. Dennis forever had never occurred to her.

"You're going to have a great life, Stef, I'm sure of it. Whether you're here in St. Dennis or somewhere else."

He leaned down and kissed her on the temple, then reached around her and pushed open the door.

"Good night, Stef. Thanks for sharing your prom night with me. It's been my pleasure."

He walked off the porch and down the front steps and went right to his car. Before he got into the driver's side, he raised his hand to wave good-bye. Pretending not to have seen, she turned her head and ran into the house.

Spring–Current Year

The wedding had been like a fairy tale, with a fairy-tale princess of a bride and her handsome groom exchanging their vows in the rose garden of a historic and stately inn overlooking the Chesapeake Bay. Steffie Wyler watched her best friend, Vanessa Keaton, march back down the aisle on the arm of one of the bride's brothers. The two of them looked like they could be the star attractions of the day, with Vanessa in her bridesmaid gown and Grady Shields, her escort, handsome in his tux.

Steffie stood at the bar. It had been a perfect day not only for the wedding couple, but for Vanessa and Grady, who were so indisputably perfect for each other. It had been one of those weddings that made you say "Ahhhhhh," one of those days so overflowing with love and romance that one could easily believe that there was indeed magic in the air.

"Hey, Steffie." A hand touched her bare upper arm as the soft male voice spoke her name.

She turned and looked into the eyes of the man she'd dreamed of since she was a teenager.

"Hey yourself, Wade." She smiled as she moved to one side to make room for him at the bar. "I didn't know you were coming home this weekend." Which, of course, was a lie. Vanessa, being the sister of the groom, had seen the guest list, and she'd clued Steffie in to the fact that her old crush, Wade MacGregor, would be back in town for the wedding.

"I wouldn't have missed Beck's wedding." Wade grinned as he signaled for the bartender. "Hell, Beck getting married is almost cause for a national holiday."

"There are some who did believe the day would never come"—she nodded—"but of course, that was before Mia Shields hit town."

Wade watched the bride and groom pose for photos on the lawn. "She seems like a really nice girl."

"She is. She's super. He's very much aware that he's a very lucky man."

"Good for him. He deserves to be happy. Beck's a heck of a guy."

"The best," Steffie agreed.

The bartender approached, and Wade turned to Steffie. "Another champagne?"

"Sure." She smiled. "Thanks."

Wade ordered the glass of champagne, then asked the bartender, "Do you have KenneMac beer on tap?"

"What kind of beer?" The bartender leaned forward as if he hadn't heard.

"KenneMac."

The bartender shook his head.

"I'll just have whatever you have on draft, then," Wade told him.

"What kind of beer did you ask for?" Stef wasn't sure she'd heard, either.

Wade grinned. "KenneMac. It's the beer I make back in Texas. KenneMac is the name of the company. I knew he didn't have it. We've barely moved into Oklahoma."

"Oh." She nodded. "You could probably get a few of your old cronies to ask for it. Start a trend."

The two glasses were served, and Wade handed Stef her champagne.

"Here's to the happy couple." Wade tilted his glass

in Steffie's direction, and they touched rims, drank from their glasses.

"You're looking good, Stef," Wade said, catching her off guard. "You always look good, but tonight you look especially pretty."

"Thanks, Wade," was all she could think of to say. Had he ever complimented her like that before?

It must be the dress, she thought, smoothing the skirt of water-colored silk that looked like one of Monet's gardens. She'd bought it at Vanessa's shop, Bling, because it had looked so damned good on her. And because it had looked so good, Ness had given her a really good discount. She'd hoped to catch Wade's eye tonight, and after having decided that she looked like a goddess in the dress, figured it was her best bet.

It was always so nice to be right about such things. Wade had gravitated toward her like a bee to a rose.

"I saw your aunt Berry at the ceremony," Stef said. "That's some hat she was wearing."

"You know Berry." He chuckled. "She likes to make an entrance."

Stef smiled and waved at one of her neighbors.

"So I hear your business is going well," Wade said.

"It's ice cream." She shrugged. "This is a tourist town now. How could I miss?"

"I hear it's more than just 'ice cream.' Berry went on and on about how it's her favorite place in town these days. She tells me you concoct some pretty fabulous flavors."

"Well, yes, I do," she said with no false modesty. "I work at it, though. I like the challenge of making things that no one else does. I like playing with flavors to—" She stopped. "Sorry. Ice cream is one of my favorite subjects. I was about to bore you straight into the ground."

"Not at all. I feel the same way about the beer that we brew. I really enjoy making unique flavors, too."

She watched his face to make sure he wasn't teasing her.

"You flavor your beer?" She frowned. "I thought beer's flavor was, well, beer."

He smiled. "I think that might be true of most of the beers from the big breweries. But microbrewing, ah, that's a whole 'nother story."

"What's the difference?"

"Think of the difference between the ice cream you make as opposed to buying prepackaged ice cream that's made in bigger batches by one of the big commercial ice-cream makers that's shipped to supermarkets all over the country."

She nodded. She got it. She knew every ingredient that went into every one of her batches and where it came from. She knew she made a superior product. Milk and cream from organically raised cows, fruits and spices organically raised. No additives, no preservatives.

"You make a better product than, say, the beer you're drinking here. Smaller batches, for starters." She nodded in the direction of his glass.

"That's right. And because I make it myself, I control what goes into it, so if I want a beer that has a hint of, say, ginger or some other spice or fruit or an herbal note, I can experiment until I hit on the right combination."

"I do that, too."

"I thought you might. I wandered past Scoop this afternoon, saw your sign, stopped in, but you weren't there."

"I was probably getting ready to come here. Stop in tomorrow, and I'll give you a tasting. A little of this, a little of that."

"That sounds like an offer I can't refuse."

There was more banter and the greeting of old friends whom Wade hadn't seen in a long time, lots of catching up, lots of reminiscing and laughter. When it was time to move into the ballroom for dinner, they wandered over to the table where the seating arrangements were displayed.

"Where are you sitting?" he asked.

"Table five." She held up the little card with her name on it.

"So am I."

"Really?"

"Well, I am now." Wade grinned. "I just switched cards with Ricky Davis. He'll never know the difference."

He took her arm, his fingers light as a whisper, and together they found their table. Throughout dinner they laughed and talked, their heads close together, and after, when the band began to play, they danced. Every slow dance, ever closer, ever slower . . . their bodies melting together until Stef could hear his heart beating, feel his breath against her cheek and against her neck. Visions of a long, slow, sweet, and sexy night of total magic danced in her brain, and she was all but drunk with the thought of what the night still held for them. Everything was going exactly the way she'd always dreamed it would. It took all her willpower not to pinch her arm to make sure it wasn't a dream.

Her body was so close to his that when his cell phone buzzed in his pocket, she could feel the vibration.

He held up the phone and looked at the number of the incoming call. Had it been her imagination, or had he blanched slightly? Whatever, he'd led her from the dance floor and back to her chair, and excused himself to take the call.

Must be business, she'd thought at the time, though what kind of business at almost midnight on a Saturday night . . .

And then he was back at her side, saying something like, "It's time to leave." She bit her bottom lip to conceal her smile, lest he realize how eager she was to get to her apartment and toss off the watercolor-silk dress that he'd admired, thinking, *Wait till he sees what's underneath. . . .*

He grabbed her by the hand, and after making short but sweet congratulations and good-byes to the happy couple, he all but ran out of the inn. Steffie's long legs hustled to keep up, and she was just about to ask, "Your car or mine?" when he pulled up abruptly at a gray sedan that was parked three cars away from her own.

"I'm sorry, but I have to leave," he was saying as he unlocked the car with the remote. "I need to get to the airport. . . ."

He mumbled something about flying standby but she didn't catch it.

"The airport?" Confused, she frowned. "Seriously? You're leaving *now*?"

"Look, I didn't want to say good-bye to you inside, but that phone call . . . something's come up," he said. "I'm really sorry. It was great to see you, Stef, great to catch up, and I wish I could stay. Maybe next time, when I'm in town . . ."

"Maybe not." She backed away from him. When he took a step toward her, she took another back. "Hey, don't let me keep you . . ."

"Stef . . ."

"No, don't, Wade. Just go."

She watched with disbelieving eyes as he got into the car and backed out of his parking space and sped off.

"Seriously?" she said aloud to the empty parking lot.

She growled and opened her driver's-side door and angled in behind the wheel. She jammed the key into the ignition, put the car in reverse—and found cars blocking hers. She banged on her steering wheel, took a deep breath, and set off for the inn, seeking the blood of the idiots who'd thought it was okay to park behind her, feeling humiliated, frustrated, and more disappointed than she'd ever felt before.

You led me on and then you let me down. Had your chance and you blew it. I don't know what you've got going on back in Texas that's so hot and heavy that it couldn't wait until tomorrow, but you just missed out on what could have been the best night of your life and you don't even know it.

It most certainly would have been the best night of hers, too . . . but that was something else he'd never know.

Diary ~

As much as I appreciate all the business the tourists bring to St. Dennis, I must admit that I do love it most when they leave and we townies have our little town by the Bay to ourselves again. Fall arrives and most of the summer people depart. Is any place more glorious in September than St. Dennis? The weather is perfect—what's not to love about cool nights and warm sunny days?—and the colors of summer and autumn blend in the foliage, if only for a few weeks. Yes, yes, of course I know that October is just around the bend, and the days will grow shorter and cooler, and cool leads to cold . . . I wasn't born yesterday. But I think that September just might be my favorite month of all—and not just because Daniel and I were married in September.

Dear me, that was so long ago . . . and he's been gone now for . . .

Well, I digress . . .

My point being that I look forward every year to reclaiming the town, to the changes that come when the tourists leave. The hustle is gone from the sidewalks, and the lines from the restaurants, and St. Dennis—the St. Dennis I grew up in and have loved all my life—reverts almost to the way it was before it was "discovered." Except, of course, for the day-trippers, but they arrive mostly on the weekends and are gone by Sunday afternoon. And I can't in good conscience complain about them, because they keep our inn full and keep our businesses open all year round. They're the reason we have the late-season sailboat races and fall festivals and special holiday events, which I have to admit I enjoy as much as the next person. The Christmas tour last year was just wonderful, and from what I hear, this year's will be even bigger. Oh, my, but the sight of all those old houses up off Old St. Mary's Church Square, decorated to the nines with wreaths and lights and . . . well, it was magic. And we all need a little magic in our lives, don't we?

I know I've had my share of magic over the years . . . oh, yes, indeed, I have. ~

~ Grace ~

Chapter 1

"THAT'S it, right there, ace. The house where I spent my happiest years. Number Twelve River Road."

Wade MacGregor hoisted the squirming child onto his shoulders. Delighted to be released from the car seat where he'd spent way too much time over the past few days, the little boy kicked his feet in the air, wanting *down* more than he wanted *up*. "Hasn't changed a whole heck of a lot since then."

Wade studied the exterior of the house for a long moment. "Looks like there have been a few changes in some of the trim color there around the porch. Aunt Berry always likes to keep up with the latest trends. Must always be on the cutting edge, you know?"

He paused momentarily to stare at the fence that ran across the front of the property. He wondered when the fence had been installed, and why. No one had mentioned it in recent phone calls.

Then again, there were things he hadn't mentioned, either.

"Let's go check out the river. See the water?" Wade crossed the broad lawn to the wooden pier in long strides, fully aware that he was procrastinating.

"Right down here is where I learned to fish and canoe and row and crab and do all kinds of fun things."

He looked up into the face of the dark-haired cherub whose heels kicked gleefully into his chest.

"Yeah, I suspect you'll be wanting to do those things one day, too. I'll teach you whenever you're ready," Wade told him. "I promised your mama that I'd raise you the best I could. I can't think of any better place for you to spend your summers than right here in St. Dennis, just like I did."

A sleek boat passed by, kicking up some wake as it headed toward the mouth of the New River, where it met the Chesapeake Bay.

"Someday soon, we'll go sailing out there. You'll like that. We'll have to get you a little life jacket first, though." Wade thought for a moment. "Your mama loved the water. That's one thing you'll want to know about her when you get older. She loved to swim and water-ski and dive. Maybe one day you'll want to do those things, too. She wanted to teach you herself, but that's not going to happen now." Wade swallowed the lump that threatened to close his throat. "I know you miss her, buddy. I miss her, too . . ."

Overhead a gull drifted, and attracted by something on the dock, dropped down onto one of the pilings to get a better look. It hopped to the deck, pecked at something solid for a moment, then took flight, the unexpected prize held in its beak. The bird changed direction, and angled back toward the Bay. Wade followed it with his eyes until it disappeared.

"Ring-billed gull," Wade said aloud. "Not to be confused with the herring gull. Someday you'll know the difference. Someday you'll know all the shorebirds."

Figuring he'd gotten about all he was going to get out of his efforts to put off the inevitable, he glanced over his shoulder at the house.

"Well, I guess it's time to face the music." He started back across the lawn. "You ready to meet your aunt Dallas and your cousin Cody and your great-great-aunt Berry?"

The back door opened and a golden retriever sped out, a fluffy white dog on its heels, both barking wildly at the intruders.

"Fleur!" A little boy of six or seven raced after the dogs. "Ally! Stop! Come back!"

The dogs continued to run toward Wade.

"See doggie!" The toddler demanded and struggled to get down. "Wanna see doggie!"

Wade stood stock-still, waiting to see just how close the dogs would come, if they'd continue to bark, and if they'd show signs of real aggression.

"Ally! Fleur!" The boy ran after them and caught up with them when they stopped about ten feet from Wade.

"Hi, Cody," Wade said. "Do you remember me?"

Cody narrowed his eyes and searched Wade's face momentarily before a smile appeared.

"You're my uncle Wade," he said. "You live in Texas."

"Not anymore." Wade gestured to the dogs, who had calmed down a little. "They don't bite, do they?"

"Nah." The boy shook his head. "They just act tough. Mom says they think they're Dobermans or rottweilers or something."

Wade laughed. "Where is your mom?"

"She's in the house. She didn't say you were coming

today." Cody pointed to Austin, who was trying to wiggle out of Wade's grasp to get to the ground. "Who's that?"

"Cody, this is Austin." Wade lifted the toddler in an arc over his head and placed him on his feet on the grass. "He's your cousin."

"Hi, Austin." Cody knelt down in front of Austin, who pointed a chubby finger at the dogs, who approached cautiously, wagging their tales. "Austin, this is Ally. She's Aunt Berry's dog. And this one"—he pointed to the white dog—"is Fleur. She's mine."

"Here, doggie!" Austin chortled as the golden retriever drew closer.

Cody glanced up at Wade. "My mom didn't tell me I had a little cousin."

"Your mom doesn't know."

"Boy, will she be surprised." Cody commanded the dogs to sit, then led Austin to them.

"Boy, will she ever," Wade muttered.

A woman started around the side of the house, her pale blond hair pulled back in a ponytail, her dark glasses obscuring half her face.

"Cody, who are you talking—" she began, then stopped in her tracks. "Wade?"

"Hey, Dallas." Wade walked to meet his sister as she started toward him. "We were just on our way up to the house when Cody and his furry friends came out to greet us."

"You stinker! You didn't tell us you were coming home this week!" Dallas MacGregor wrapped her arms around him and hugged tightly. "You're looking good, kiddo."

"You're looking even better." Wade hugged her in

return and spun her halfway around before setting her down. "St. Dennis agrees with you."

"Why didn't you let us know you were coming? And what's with the trailer?" She pointed to the drive, where Wade's Jeep sat with a trailer hooked up to the back. "You hauling your beer in there? Expanding your business to the Chesapeake?"

"Actually, I closed the business. I sold the equipment and the building."

Dallas's jaw dropped. When she recovered, she asked, "What happened? Your brewery was doing so well. All those awards you won . . . I thought you were really solid."

"We were. It's a long story, Dallas."

Wade looked away. He'd been dreading this conversation for weeks. He'd been so proud of KenneMac, the brewery he'd started from scratch with his best friend from college. He'd hated closing it down, but hated the idea of selling it even more. The company name—that had been his and Robin's. His brewing secrets had taken him years to perfect. KenneMac Brews had been the best part of his life for the past eight years. Giving it up was one thing. Selling it—allowing someone else to become KenneMac Brews—well, that just wasn't going to happen.

But then again, even giving up the brewery wasn't the worst thing that had happened over the past few months.

The back door opened and a woman of indeterminable age stepped out onto the porch.

"Dallas, who's that you're talking to? And what's that thing parked in my driveway?" Hands on her hips, Beryl Eberle—once known internationally as screen star Beryl Townsend—paused, appearing to study the scene. "Is that Wade?"

"Yes, Aunt Berry. It's me." Wade's smile was genuine. He adored his great-aunt. She'd been the indulgent grandmother he hadn't known and Auntie Mame all in one. He counted the years he'd lived with her as some of the best of his life.

She came down the porch steps, holding on, he noticed, to the railing all the way. She was always so spry, so clever and lively, he often forgot that she'd turned eighty-one on her last birthday and had another approaching. He quickened his step so that she wouldn't have to walk across the entire yard to greet him.

"You are a sight for these old eyes, Wade MacGregor." She hugged him fiercely. "How dare you stay away for so long."

"What was I thinking?" He embraced her gently.

"I'll be damned if I know." She stood back and held him at arm's length. "You look more and more like your father every year. And I don't mind saying that Ned was the best-looking young man I ever—"

"Stop feeding his ego with that stuff," Dallas admonished. "He's already got a big head."

"What is that thing in the driveway?" Berry asked again.

"It's a trailer," he explained. "Holds all my worldly goods."

"Does this mean you've come home? That you're staying?" Berry, clearly joyful at the very thought, grabbed Wade's hand and gave it a squeeze.

"I'm not staying, Aunt Berry," he said softly. "I'm just passing through St. Dennis on my way to Connecticut. I'm going to be working for another brewery."

"What happened to your brewery?" she demanded.

"We were just starting to talk about that, Berry," Dallas told her.

"Well, he's going to have to start from the beginning, because I want—" A squeal of laughter erupted from the lawn. "What on earth . . . ?"

Berry's eyes narrowed. "Is that a small child I see down there with Cody and the dogs?" She stretched out her arm, her thin finger pointing to the tangle of fur and human on the ground. "There. There's a little boy. Where did that child come from?"

"Ah, Berry, actually, he's mine." Wade's eyes glanced from his aunt's startled face to his sister's. "That's Austin."

"Did you say . . . he's yours?" Dallas's eyes widened, as if she wasn't quite sure she'd heard correctly.

"Yeah." Wade nodded again.

"Well, who . . . I mean, when . . ." Dallas sputtered.

"You've had a *child* and you didn't think to let us know about him?" Berry's face was deadly with accusation.

Wade started to mount a defense, then stopped. Of course he owed them an explanation. What had he been thinking, not telling them as soon as the whole thing started? It wasn't so much that he'd wanted to keep Austin a secret. It was simply that every time he thought about calling and telling them, he'd get cold feet. There were so many questions, and after the past six months, he was so depleted emotionally, it had been too difficult to think about having that conversation on the phone.

Wade sighed. "It's really complicated."

"Assume for a moment that your sister and I possess a certain degree of intelligence. Perhaps even enough to understand." Berry raised one eyebrow, her favored expression to convey sarcasm. "Provided you speak slowly and use only very small words, of course."

Feeling like a chastised twelve-year-old, Wade went to his son and picked him up.

"No!" Austin protested loudly. "Play doggie."

"The dogs are going to come with us, right, Cody?"

"Right." Cody ran ahead and both dogs followed. "They're following us, Austin. See?"

"Down." Austin continued to struggle all the way across the lawn.

"Austin, meet your aunt Dallas and your great-great-aunt Berry." Wade held the child in both arms.

Austin's attention momentarily distracted from Ally and Fleur, he giggled and pointed to Berry and proclaimed, "Berry!"

"You coached him to do that so I'd melt right here on this very spot," Berry accused. "And it worked. Hello, Austin."

Berry held out her hand and Austin giggled again.

"Let me have him." Dallas reached for the child, and Wade passed him over. "He is a darling little thing, isn't he?" She met her brother's eyes. "Who's his mother, Wade? And where is she?"

"That's the complicated part," he told her softly. "It's a really long story."

"I've got all day. Berry? You have plans for this afternoon?" Dallas shifted a squirming Austin in her arms, then let him get down.

"I do now. Into the house. All of you—kids, dogs,

everyone." Berry turned and started up the steps. "I can't have this conversation standing out in the hot sun without a cold glass of iced tea. It isn't civilized."

"She says march, we march." Dallas shrugged and followed in Berry's footsteps. She paused partway up and turned to Wade. "Wade, are you married to Austin's mother?"

"I was."

"When?"

"For almost three weeks, in July."

"Three weeks?" Dallas frowned. "You were only married for three weeks? Jeez, Wade, why bother?"

"Because she was dying," he said softly, "and I wanted her to die in peace."

For the second time in less than ten minutes, Dallas was momentarily stunned. When she recovered, she raised her hand and gently touched his face. "Oh, sweetie. What happened to you in Texas?"

"Like I said, it's a long story."

"Like I said, I have all day." Dallas took him by the hand and walked the rest of the way up the steps in silence. When they got to the deck, she paused and asked, "Is Austin your son?"

"He is now."

He opened the door for his sister, and waited while she entered the house, a million questions on her face and in her eyes.

He waited for the boys and the two dogs at the top of the stairs, and wondered where to begin to tell the story he should have told them months ago.

Chapter 2

THE bell over the door in Steffie Wyler's ice-cream shop, One Scoop or Two—known locally as "Scoop"—rang for what Steffie thought was probably the five hundred and fiftieth time in the past two hours.

"Top of the list of things to do as soon as the after-dinner rush dies down: deep-six that damned bell," she told Tina, one of two of her part-time employees who were working that night. "It was a cute idea when the shop first opened and I'd get a dozen customers in the morning and maybe twice as many in the afternoon. It's no longer cute. If I had a gun, I swear I'd shoot it off the door from here."

The bell rang again and she glanced up as the latest group entered the small onetime crabber's shack that now served as Scoop's home, and her words died in her throat. Dallas MacGregor, a regular customer, came into the shop, trailed by her great-aunt and the tall, ridiculously handsome guy who'd been the object of Steffie's affection—and lust—since before she was old enough to know the difference between, well, affection and lust.

The last time she'd seen Wade MacGregor, he was driving away from the inn at Sinclair's Point on the night of the local police chief's wedding—driving away and leaving a hurt, confused, and wildly frustrated Steffie standing alone in the parking lot after they'd danced away most of the night. No explanations. Just "Gotta go. Got a plane to catch. See ya." And just that fast, he'd disappeared.

Okay, maybe it wasn't quite that abrupt—there'd been some mumbling about something unexpected coming up—but Steffie's big plans for the rest of the night had faded into the moonlight along with the exhaust from Wade's rental car. That had been four months ago, and she hadn't heard a word from him since.

Jerk.

She tried to ignore the smile of recognition that spread across his face when he saw her. Tried just as unsuccessfully to keep her heart rate under control. Tried to push from her mind the scenes her imagination had conjured up of Wade walking into Scoop—like he just had, all nonchalant and gorgeous, smiling a special smile just for her—at which time she put the "Closed" sign on the door and they fell into each other's arms and frantically . . .

"I said two scoops of chocolate." The customer she was waiting on waved a hand in front of her face to get her attention. "That's pistachio."

"Oh. Sorry. I thought you said . . ." Steffie shook her head and forced herself to focus on the task at hand and hoped that no one noticed the red flush that she felt spreading from her neck to her hairline. "Sorry."

She returned the pistachio scoops to the container and remade the cone. "You can take it right over there to the cash register and Claire will ring you up," she told the customer, then nodded to the next person in the line that had formed in front of the glass-fronted case. "What would you like, ma'am?"

Seven customers later, Steffie looked over the counter and found Cody Blair, Dallas's son, waiting his turn. He held the hand of a little boy, a beautiful child who had dark curly hair and big brown eyes.

Neighbor's kid, I guess, Steffie thought. *Cute as a button.*

"What can I get for you, Cody?"

"I want two scoops of chocolate midnight madness," he told her solemnly, then added, "please."

"One scoop is plenty, Cody." Dallas tapped him on the head.

"Uh-uh." Cody turned to his mother. "I'm sharing with Austin." He leaned over and lifted the child. "Right, Austin? We're going to share."

Austin struggled to turn, and lifted his arms over his head.

"Daddy!" Austin reached up. "Daddy!"

"Right here, ace."

Steffie watched in dumb fascination as Wade reached over Cody and plucked Austin from his arms.

"Daddy's right here."

Daddy? *Daddy?*

"Stef, could you put two spoons in Cody's dish?" Dallas was asking from what seemed like another planet. "And maybe put a very small scoop of vanilla in there with it."

Steffie's hand clutched the scoop. For a moment she wished it was something more lethal.

Man attacked by crazed ice-cream lady wielding metal implement; film at eleven.

"And two spoons, if you would?" Dallas repeated. "Stef?"

"Right. Two spoons." Steffie focused on the cardboard containers of ice cream in the cooler. "Two chocolate midnight madness and one vanilla."

"Small scoops," Dallas added.

"Right. Small scoops." Steffie repeated softly as if reminding herself of something very important. "Two spoons."

She completed the order and held it over the counter to Cody, who stared into the dish.

"You forgot my chocolate sprinkles." He held up the dish for her to see.

"So I did." Steffie shook her head. "What was I thinking?"

She grabbed a spoon and sprinkled the tiny chocolate pieces over the ice cream and handed it to Cody.

"Better?" she asked.

He nodded. "Thank you, Steffie."

"You're welcome." She turned her attention to Dallas. "And what can I get for you?"

"I think some of whatever lemony thing you might have." Dallas's eyes scanned the cooler.

"Sorry. Nothing lemony tonight. I do have peach pecan deliciousness, though." Steffie kept her eyes on the contents of the freezer, as if seeing the flavors for the first time. Anything to keep from looking at Wade, or to let him think that she was even *thinking* of looking at him.

"The peach sounds great. Thanks. One scoop in a cone, please."

Stef prepared the cone and handed it over.

"Miss B, what would you like tonight?" Stef smiled at Berry.

"No lemon, you say?" Berry looked up and down the glass counter. "Oh, dear. I'd had my heart set on that lemon curd confection."

"I'll have some tomorrow, promise," Stef assured her. "But I think you'd like the plum tart." She put down the scoop and reached for a tasting spoon, loaded it with the plum ice cream, and offered it to Berry.

"Oh, my, that is tasty." Berry smiled broadly. "You never steer me wrong, Steffie. I'll have a scoop of that in a sugar cone."

"Coming right up." Steffie made the cone and passed it over.

That left one person in the party still waiting to be served. *Must not react,* she cautioned. *Must not let him know how rattled I am to see him. Must not act like it matters to me that that kid just called him Daddy.*

She took a deep breath and met Wade's eyes as he stepped up to the counter. "Wade?"

"How are you, Stef?"

"I'm good. Yourself?"

"Good." He nodded.

"Good. So, then, we're both good. Now what can I get for you?" she asked with all the nonchalance she could muster. *Just another customer,* she told herself. *He's just another customer.*

"I guess I'll have the same as you gave the boys. The chocolate stuff."

"Bowl? Cone?" she asked.

"Cone's good."

She kept her eyes averted from his until she completed his order and handed it to him. She lifted the cone over the counter and looked directly into his eyes without saying a word.

"Thanks."

"You're welcome." She looked away for a moment, then looked back.

He appeared about to say something else, but she didn't give him the chance. What was there to say, she reasoned, after the little guy said "Daddy"?

"Claire is at the cash register. She'll ring you up." She smiled her best smile then turned her attention to the man waiting in line behind Wade. "What can I get for you?"

Out of the corner of her eye, she saw Wade hesitate, then move on to the cash register. She concentrated on her customer, then on the next one, and the next, until Wade and his family made their way to the door. She didn't look up until she heard the bell ring, then stole a peek just in time to see his tanned arm pulling the door closed behind him.

She took a deep breath, ignored the stab to her heart, and fixed a smile. "I can help the next person in line . . ."

"He has a *what*?"

Vanessa Keaton sat back on the sofa cushion, a puzzled expression on her face. If she'd been perturbed by Steffie's late-night ringing of her doorbell, she gave no sign. After all, she and Stef were best friends, and as such, certain privileges were automatically granted.

Besides, Stef had brought ice cream, several cartons containing the little bits left over at the end of the day.

"A little boy. He looks like he's about two, maybe younger. Tough for me to tell. I'm not around kids very often." She dipped a spoon into the carton of pineapple macadamia fudge ripple. "Except, of course, the kids who come into the shop. But I never ask them how old they are."

"He has a son? Are you sure it's his?"

"Austin—that's the little boy's name—called Wade 'Daddy.' And when Wade picked him up, he said, 'Daddy's here,' or something like that. Anyway, it was pretty damned clear that *he's* the daddy."

"Who's the mommy?" Vanessa peered into the carton, found it empty, and tossed it into the plastic trash bag she'd brought into the room for just that purpose.

"That would be the big question." Steffie shook her head. "I have no idea. But do I feel like the biggest idiot on the planet."

"Why should you? You didn't do anything wrong."

"Oh, no. Just sort of crawled all over him at your brother's wedding a few months ago."

"I seem to recall he was doing an equal amount of crawling," Vanessa pointed out. "So if anyone should feel like a jerk, it should be him."

Steffie snorted. "Guys don't generally regret crawling."

"Seriously. Let's look at the facts." Vanessa repositioned herself on the sofa, her legs tucked under her. "Would you hand me the apple pecan if you're finished with it?"

Steffie passed the carton.

"He knew that he was . . ." Vanessa scooped up a spoonful of ice cream. "What is he? Is he married?" She licked the spoon. "You don't suppose he's been married all this time, do you?"

Steffie shook her head. "Wade can be a jerk, but I've never known him to be, you know, sneaky. Dishonest. Immoral." She paused. "I've never known him to be that kind of a jerk. The kind of jerk who'd romance one woman while being married to another." She took the carton back from Vanessa. "Then again . . . there is Austin."

"Maybe he and the baby's mother were married at some point but are divorced now. Or maybe they never married. Maybe the baby was an accident. Maybe she—whoever *she* is—got pregnant by accident and decided to keep the baby. Then Wade, being a jerk though not an *immoral one,* would want to do the right thing if he was the father. He'd want to, you know, be a real father, don't you think? He'd want to be part of the child's life, right?"

"I honestly don't know what to think. Except that he's known all along that he had this child and was obviously in a hitherto unknown-to-me relationship of some sort with someone else and yet spent hours priming me for a long night of bliss, which he then denied me of by leaving to catch a plane back to Texas." Steffie began to steam all over again. "Back to Austin and his mommy."

"What is Grant saying?"

"What?" Steffie frowned, her spoon stopped midway between her mouth and the carton.

"Grant? Your brother?" Vanessa's foot poked at Steffie's. "The guy who is hot and heavy with Wade's sister?"

Steffie reached into her pocket, took out her cell phone, and speed-dialed a number. "If he knew about this all along and he didn't tell me, I will kill him. What's the word for it? Fratricide?"

Steffie tapped impatient fingers on the phone.

"He's not picking up. Coward. I'll bet he knows that Wade is here with this baby and that I'm going to find out about it and that I'm going to be pissed off." She listened for a moment, then left a message for her brother. "All right, smart-ass. Want to tell *now* me why you didn't bother to tell me *before* that Wade has a son?" She ended the call.

"What's the baby look like?" Vanessa placed another empty carton into the bag. "Is he cute?"

"He is beyond cute," Stef admitted. "Dark curly hair, big dark eyes."

"Really? Huh, that's interesting," Vanessa noted. "The MacGregors are all so fair."

"Maybe the baby's mom is Italian or something. I'd be tempted to say Wade's 'baby mama,' but I really hate that expression." Steffie tossed her empty carton into the bag with Vanessa's.

"Me, too."

They sat in silence for a moment.

"I think maybe he married this baby's mother, Ness."

"Well, like I said before, they could be divorced. He didn't have anyone with him at Scoop, right?"

"She could have stayed back at the house. Oh, shit. Maybe she's here in St. Dennis." Stef picked up a throw pillow and held it over her face. "Everyone in town saw Wade and me together at Beck's wedding. Everyone knows I have had the hots for him all my natural life. This is so humiliating, I could just—"

Her pocket began to ring. She glanced at the caller ID before answering.

"Grant? Are you prepared to spill everything you know? Because if not, prepare to die."

"Stef, I have absolutely no idea what you are talking about," her brother told her. He sounded weary, but that wasn't going to stop her from interrogating him.

"Wade? Your honey's brother?"

"I know who Wade is, Stef."

"I want to know everything you know about this baby."

"What baby?"

"Wade's baby. Stop playing with me, Grant. It's not funny."

"Stef. I'm tired, I drove for twelve hours straight today to take my daughter back to her mother in Ohio. I just dropped her off a couple of hours ago, and right now I feel like the sky is falling, okay? So don't jerk me around. Just tell me what you're talking about because I swear I don't know."

"Oh, shit, that's right. You took Paige back today." Steffie winced. How could she have forgotten that he'd driven his daughter back to her mother—Grant's ex-wife, Krista—so that Paige could start the school year after having spent the entire summer in St. Dennis? "I'm sorry. I know how much you wanted to keep her here, and I know how badly she wanted to stay."

"Yeah, so have mercy, okay, and tell me what this is all about."

She told him.

"Are you sure the boy called Wade 'Daddy'?"

"Yes."

"Stef, I don't know anything about this. I swear."

"Dallas didn't tell you?"

"I haven't talked to her tonight. I left voice mail on her cell phone earlier, but you know her. Half the time she doesn't even look at her phone unless she's waiting for a business call. But Wade wasn't there when I left yesterday, and she didn't mention him at all last night, not even that he was coming home."

"Well, when you hear from her, will you find out what's going on so you can tell me?"

"Yeah, but I have a hard time believing that she wouldn't have told me if Wade had a son. I think there's some mistake."

"Yeah, well, when you figure out what it is, give me a call, okay?"

"Sure."

"And, Grant?" Stef bit her bottom lip. "I'm really sorry about Paige. Was she all right? About going back, I mean?"

"If you call not speaking to me once we crossed the Pennsylvania border into Ohio being 'all right,' then yeah, she's fine with it."

"I'm really sorry." She added, "I'll miss her, too."

"Anything else, Stef? 'Cause I'm beat, and I want to get some sleep before I start the drive back in the morning."

"No, that was it." She felt compelled to apologize one more time. "I'm sorry, Grant."

The call ended and she tossed the phone onto the sofa cushion and covered her face with her hands.

"I am shallow beyond all belief. I got so caught up in my own little drama that I forgot about Grant driving Paige back today. He should never speak to me again. I am a colossal . . . I can't even think of anything bad enough."

Vanessa rolled up a paper napkin and tossed it at Steffie, bouncing it off her head.

"Fine. You're the worst person ever born. Get over it." Vanessa went into the kitchen and retrieved another carton from the freezer. "Plum tart." She held up the carton. "I love it when you bring leftovers."

She took her seat again. "Look, Stef, if you'd realized that Grant was in Ohio and had just dropped off Paige and didn't care about anyone's feelings but your own, then yes, you would be a total bitch. But you didn't, and Grant knows that you didn't, so let it go."

"But I should have remembered something that important." Steffie picked up the napkin and dropped it into the bag with the empties. "I was only thinking about myself."

"You're allowed to do that sometimes, you know. Besides, you must have been really surprised when Wade came in with the kidlet."

"Shocked is more like it."

"I take it Grant didn't know about Wade's son, either."

Stef shook her head. "He said Dallas has never mentioned it—which is really odd, when you come to think about it. But he didn't talk to her today. He left voice mail for her but hasn't heard back yet."

"Strange that Dallas wouldn't have told Grant something like that." Vanessa appeared to ponder. "You'd almost think she didn't know, either. But nah, Wade wouldn't have kept something like that from his sister for two years, would he?"

"I don't know. I used to think I knew him pretty well. But now . . ." Steffie shrugged.

"You've known Wade for a long time, right?"

"Forever, it seems. He used to sail with Grant at the marina. They were on the same team for the races. I've had a crush on him since I was nine and he was thirteen." She picked at an invisible piece of lint on her denim shorts. "When I was fifteen, I was at a sleepover at a friend's house, and she had a Ouija board. We were playing around with it, asking it questions, like what were we going to be when we grew up, and who would we marry." Her mouth slid into a half smile. "My answers were always the same. I was going to own my own ice-cream shop and I was going to marry Wade MacGregor." She lowered her voice as if sharing her deepest, darkest secret. "That was my game plan. It's all I ever really wanted. Make ice cream. Marry Wade, have a family, live happily ever after right here in my little town."

She went into the kitchen and sorted through the cartons until she found what she was looking for. She came back into the living room, holding up the container.

"Peanut butter carob caramel. This was the test run. It's fabulous, if I do say so myself." She opened the carton and reached for her spoon. "So I got half of what I wished for. Some people never get that much. And I am grateful . . . why are you staring at me like that?"

"I'm sorry." Vanessa shook her head. "I'm still stuck back at the part where you said you wanted to marry Wade, have his babies, and live in St. Dennis forever."

"Doesn't make me a bad person." Steffie dug into the carton.

"What it makes you is one big fat liar."

"What d' you mean?" Steffie said indignantly.

"Didn't you tell me once that you'd die before you settled down like your sister did? That it was your worst nightmare to get married and settle into a routine?"

"Into my *sister's* routine. It's her life I wouldn't want to live. Her husband is Mr. Boredom. Evie is Mrs. Boredom." She paused. "I can't imagine life with Wade ever being boring."

"I'll bet your sister feels the same way about her guy."

Steffie rolled her eyes. "Trust me. My brother-in-law is boring. They live on a farm in Iowa and raise organic vegetables."

"There are worse ways to live."

"Yeah. Like spending your life alone while all your friends find their soul mates and they get to live happily ever after," Steffie grumbled. "Not that I'm not happy for you, finding Grady and falling in love."

Vanessa beamed. "Finding Grady was like . . . finding a gold bar in the bottom of a Cracker Jack box."

"Aw, Ness, that's so sweet." Steffie rolled her eyes again. "I'll be happy to sell your grandkids ice cream when I'm a lonely old spinster, living in my little place somewhere with a menagerie of pets, tending my garden. You and I can get together once a week for tea and talk about the good old days. Except, oh, right . . . I won't have had any."

Vanessa laughed.

"You go sell that 'poor lonely Stef the Spinster' tale to someone who'll buy it." Still laughing, Vanessa leaned over and patted Steffie on the knee. "Maybe we should ask the Ouija. See what it has to say now."

"That would necessitate finding one at this hour."

"Which would require traveling all the way to my kitchen." Vanessa stretched out the leg she'd been sitting on. "I found one in the attic when I moved in. I tried playing with it a little, but it doesn't seem to work very well."

"What do you mean?"

"Well, I read somewhere that before you ask it anything that you want to know, anything personal, you're supposed to ask it who your guide is. Your spirit guide. And it just kept spelling 'D-A-Z.' Who ever heard of a spirit named Daz?"

"You mean, like dazzle?"

"I guess."

"Who'd you do it with? Grady?" Without waiting for an answer, she grinned. "Maybe he was fooling with you."

Vanessa shook her head. "I had to do it by myself. Grady said it was a waste of time, so he wouldn't do it." Her eyes lit up. "Maybe I should run in and get it. You and I could—"

"Not tonight." Stef shook her head. "I need to get home and get to sleep. I'm back in the shop at five tomorrow to make ice cream. The stuff I sell isn't delivered by truck every day, like some people's merchandise is." She stood and stretched. "I promised Berry Eberle that I'd have something lemony for her tomorrow, and I have to get working on it."

"Think the way to a guy's heart is through his great-aunt's stomach?"

"I'm afraid someone else has won his heart, Ness." Stef shrugged and shoved her hands in her pockets.

"Well, if I can't sleep tonight, maybe I'll see if I can get 'Daz' to tell me who that someone is." Vanessa walked Stef to the front door and opened it. "If nothing else, you'll know who the competition is."

Steffie shook her head. "There's no competition. The game's over. Someone else won, and I lost."

Chapter 3

THE sun had barely started to burn off the early-morning fog when Wade slipped quietly through the front door for a run along River Road toward the center of town. Once he hit Charles Street, he passed the occasional vacant storefront and noted several shops that he was pretty sure hadn't been there during his last visit home: Sweetie Pies, a bakery, and The Checkered Cloth, which, according to the sign out front, closed every day at three. He slowed at the window of the upscale pet boutique, Bow-Wows and Meows.

Did someone really think that was a good name?

Only his need for exercise kept him from stopping and staring at the display. Galoshes. Hoodies. Party clothes. T-shirts with clever sayings.

Halloween costumes. For dogs.

Shaking his head, he continued on, the soles of his feet slapping softly on the concrete. Across the street, lined up like old friends, were places he remembered: the market, an art gallery, an antiques shop, a bookstore. Next came Bling, a relatively new classy women's clothing and accessory shop, and

Sips, which sold only beverages. On his right, Cuppachino, the coffee shop where the townies gathered every morning for news and gossip before going about their workday, had been the Coffee Corner when he was a kid, but served the same purpose. Upscale Café Lola was still owned by ninetysomething-year-old Lola, who continued to go to the docks every morning to select her fish for the day's entrées. Petals and Posies, the flower shop on the corner of Charles Street and Kelly's Point Road, was now run by the original owner's daughter. Wade turned right at the florist and headed toward the Bay.

The last of the mist was still rising off the pavement, the sun still not quite high enough to clear the trees and announce the new day. Bright lights illuminated the municipal building parking lot, where the police cruisers were lined up in their numbered spaces. The big public lot across the road was empty now, but by noon it would be filled to capacity as the day-trippers arrived for end-of-the-season shopping. Summer was over, and in leaving, it took most of the summer folks. The few who remained were mostly retirees, empty nesters, childless couples, or young marrieds. Soon they, too, would go back to wherever they'd come from once the weather turned cool and damp and the town lost some of its charm—well, to all but the residents. Those who were from St. Dennis loved her in each of her seasons.

Wade was partial to autumn. He loved the cool, crisp evenings and mornings that gave way to ample sunshine and warm afternoons. He especially liked mornings like this one, mornings with just a bit of snap to the air that hinted at the cool weather to come. The sky seemed bluer and the waves on the Bay—just a few hundred feet away—seemed to churn up whiter foam. At the end of Kelly's Point Road he jogged onto the boardwalk that ran along the waterline as far as the marina, where many of the slips were empty, the fishing boats having already made their way out onto the Chesapeake, the crabbers long gone. Only the pleasure boats remained at dock, their owners having the luxury of sleeping late should they choose to do so. Those who made their living on the Bay had no choice but to rise before the sun.

In his youth, Wade had sailed these waters in every season and in all kinds of weather. He'd been the youngest member of a team that had won more than their fair share of sailing awards. Ironic that one of his old teammates was now chief of police here in St. Dennis, and another was dating his sister. Their biggest threat every year had come from the team headed by Clay Madison, who was Wade's age but who was by far the best sailor in the bunch. Wade figured he'd run into Clay one of these days. Dallas mentioned he was living just outside of town on the farm that had been in his family for generations.

There was something comforting about being in a place where you could count on certain things staying the same, where the same families farmed the same fields or fished the same waters, where the names all had a familiar ring. Wade had liked Texas, enough to have stayed after grad school and build a business. He'd had some really good years there, but it was never home and he'd put down no roots. Sleeping beneath the roof of the old house his own family had called home for two hundred or so years had banished the restlessness that followed him since he left St. Dennis.

Funny to see Cody asleep in his old bed, though. Funnier still for Wade to have opened his eyes to find himself sleeping in his own father's room, with Austin's crib set up along the back wall. All in all, being back in St. Dennis soothed his battered heart and his weary soul, and he regretted that he wouldn't be staying longer. Being with his family filled those places inside him that had felt empty for months. He hoped that before he left town, he'd be able to soak up enough of that calm to last him through the coming year.

At the end of the dock, he paused to catch his breath. Though he'd once been a runner who'd never missed a day, it had been several months since he'd been out for a morning jog, and he found himself out of shape. With no one to watch late-sleeping Austin in the early hours, Wade had had to make adjustments to his schedule. That many parents would give anything for a child who slept late was an irony that wasn't lost on Wade. Only Dallas's promise to listen for his son should he awaken made this morning's run possible. Another early riser, Dallas had insisted that Wade tie on his running shoes and take off for a while.

"Cody did survive his babyhood, you know," she'd told him when at first he'd declined her offer. "Chances are I'll know what to do if Austin wakes up before you get back."

"It isn't that," he'd protested. "I just hate feeling like I'm taking advantage of you."

"Take advantage while you can." Dallas had unlocked the front door and opened it. "And take your time. I'll be here."

Dallas was a peach, and that was a fact. The rest of the world might know her as a screen icon, an award-winning beauty with pale blond hair and lavender eyes, but to Wade, she was the best sister any guy could have. She was thoughtful and fun and more understanding than even he had given her credit for. Hadn't she proved that last night?

She and Berry had been uncommonly understanding and nonjudgmental, under the circumstances. There'd been no jumping to conclusions where Austin had been concerned.

"As long as you're sure this is what you what." Dallas had reached across the table and taken his hand, and Berry had nodded her agreement.

"It is what I want," Wade had assured them. "It's the way it has to be."

It *was* what he wanted. There'd been no question that he'd step up to the plate as soon as Robin had laid out the facts for him. It wasn't how he'd imagined his life would play out, but there it was. Wade was okay with most of it—all of it, really, except for Robin dying.

As always, thinking about Robin made his heart ache.

It had been so strange last night, trying to explain everything to Berry and Dallas. So much was sheer emotion, so much was pain. Robin had been his best friend first, his business partner second. Hearing Dallas refer to Robin as his wife had given Wade a jolt. He'd never thought of her as his wife, didn't think of himself as a widower, but technically, that was the story. He'd married Robin, which made her his wife. She died, making him a widower. The fact that he'd married her *because* she was dying didn't change things.

But none of that mattered. What mattered was that Austin was safe, he'd always be safe now. He was Austin MacGregor, and so his mother could go to her rest without the torment of not knowing what was going to happen to her son.

Wade started back toward Kelly's Point Road, running alongside the water on the boardwalk. Up ahead he could see lights through the last remnants of mist, then realized he was looking at the interior lights of One Scoop or Two. As he drew closer, he saw movement inside, and he knew who was bustling about, preparing for the day. With the temperature projected to edge into the mideighties later, Steffie would be busy from the minute she opened her doors until closing that night.

He wanted to knock on her door and explain things to her. Not that he owed her an explanation—it wasn't like they were an item. They weren't even dating. Frankly, he didn't know what they were, so why, he asked himself, did he think he needed to explain anything to her? That he couldn't define the source of his conflict annoyed the hell out of him. All he did know was that he'd seen the look on her face, the confusion in her eyes, when she realized that *he* was the daddy Austin had been calling for.

Because of Beck's wedding, Wade admitted. That for a few hours that night, he'd allowed himself to put aside the drama that had been unfolding back in Texas and had responded to his attraction to Steffie without bothering to snap on the appropriate restraints. He'd left her standing confused and angry and hurt in the inn's parking lot while he raced to the airport to make his flight. There'd been no question that he'd be leaving that night—not after he'd received that phone call—as much as he'd wanted to stay with Stef in St. Dennis and try to figure out what it was that they had between them since she was seventeen and had asked him to her senior prom. He'd taken her, but had kept his distance. Even then, he knew he was attracted to her, but she was just too young.

And then the night of the wedding he'd left St. Dennis—and Steffie—because Robin had needed him. Wade would have walked through fire to get back to Texas that night, even though he knew the price he'd pay for going: He'd probably be ruining any chance he'd ever have with Stef, but he'd had to go.

In the dark, Wade hesitated near the side of the building and watched Steffie as she hustled around inside. He wondered if he should stop in for a moment, just to say hello. He could tap on the window and ask her to unlock the door.

She did keep the door locked when she was there alone, didn't she? Anyone could be prowling around at this early hour.

When he put his hand on the knob and turned it, he'd only thought to test it. To his surprise, it opened, the bell overhead ringing loudly and breaking the silence.

Behind the counter, Steffie jumped a mile.

"Wade?"

"Why is this door unlocked? Don't you know that anyone could just walk in here?"

"Obviously. *Anyone* just did." She stood with her hands on her hips, her honey-blond hair pulled back in a ponytail, a blue-and-white-checked apron covering her T-shirt and shorts. Her feet were bare, the toenails painted dark purple to match her fingernails. Across one cheek, there was a streak of something cream-colored that reached almost to her ear.

"What's up?"

"I just wanted to test the door. To see if it was unlocked."

"Why?"

"Because it isn't safe to leave the door open. The door should be locked when you're here alone."

"I'm not alone." She pointed behind him. "Tina is on her way in."

He turned as one of the women he'd seen in the shop the previous night came up the walk.

"So, while I do appreciate this sudden concern of yours—and if I weren't so busy, I'd ask what's up with that—but unless you're here for ice cream . . . and really, I'm not open, as you can see, but if you're having a sudden uncontrollable craving for some chocolate monster mash, maybe I could scrape something together. But if not—if you're just stopping by to say 'hey'—you said that last night. And besides, I'm really, really busy." Her hands still on her hips, Steffie met his gaze dead-on and raised one eyebrow. "Was there something you wanted, Wade?"

Before he could open his mouth, the bell over the door rang again and Tina came into the shop. She smiled at Wade and went past him.

"Morning, T." Stef still continued to stare him down, her expression unchanged.

"Morning, Stef," Tina replied as she headed toward the back room.

"Sorry," Wade mumbled. "I just thought that maybe . . . Sorry."

He watched her watch *him* as he backed out the door and into the snip of sunlight that spilled through the lifting clouds. He closed the door behind him sheepishly and headed up Kelly's Point, feeling like a complete ass all the way back to River Road.

By eight a.m., Steffie had made her day's worth of ice cream and the handmade cones she was becoming known for. She could make the generic flavors—chocolate, vanilla, strawberry—in her sleep. The specialties of the day, her own concoctions—lemon meringue, peach divinity, pecan fudge ripple, and in honor of Halloween coming up, chocolate monster mash—took a little more time. But she'd gotten her recipes worked out over the weekend, and all told, it took her only three hours to make all she planned to sell that day. When it was gone, it was gone, and that little bit of exclusivity had made Scoop a must-stop on many a tourist's agenda.

"Wow, I'm beat and the day has barely begun." She stretched both arms over her head.

"Want me to run up to Cuppachino and get you some coffee?" Tina asked.

"Thanks, sweetie, but I think I'll run up to Cuppachino and get my own. I need to stretch my legs." Stef untied her apron and hung it on a hook near the back door. "Can I bring something for you?"

Tina held up the travel cup she'd brought from home. "I'm still good."

"I won't be long." Stef grabbed her bag from under her desk, where she'd dropped it when she arrived a few hours earlier.

"Take your time," Tina told her. "Everything's under control here."

Stef went out the back door and crossed the sandy strip between the rear of her shop and the public parking lot. She was dying for a good cup of coffee almost as much as she was dying to hear some gossip about Wade. The same group met at Cuppachino every morning, and while Stef didn't join them every day, she made it there often enough to be considered a regular. Today, wild horses couldn't keep her away.

She walked briskly up Kelly's Point and rounded the corner at Petals and Posies onto Charles, calling a greeting to Olivia, the florist, who was setting pots of purple asters and orange mums on her steps. She went straight to Cuppachino, where the usual group was at their usual post—the big table close to the front window—and she waved to them through the glass before she went inside. Stepping directly to the counter, she gave her order to Carlo, the owner, who poured her coffee—light, one sugar—into the mug that bore the name of her shop. Carlo's wife, a potter, made mugs for each of the merchants who frequented the coffee shop on a regular basis. The chocolate-brown mug Carlo handed to Stef had SCOOP printed across the bowl in fat white letters, a pink ice-cream cone forming the *P*.

She paid for her coffee and turned toward the table, trying to decide where to sit, who was most likely to have the best gossip to share that morning. She hoped she hadn't missed the best of it. Then again, Vanessa was there, and of course, she'd share anything she'd heard in Steffie's absence.

Stef walked to the table, and pulled out the chair on the end, next to Grace Sinclair. If anyone knew anything, Stef was betting it would be Grace, who owned the town's only newspaper, and who, at seventysomething, knew everyone in St. Dennis.

". . . and I said to myself, that is one fine-looking young man." Barbara Noonan, who owned Book 'Em, the bookstore across the street, grinned before taking a sip of her coffee.

"For God's sake, Barbara, you're old enough to be that boy's mother," Grace admonished.

"Maybe so." Barbara nodded. "Doesn't mean I'm blind."

"Any idea who the mother is?" Nita Perry, owner of the antiques shop, looked around the table.

Steffie figured that someone—most likely Vanessa—had given Nita a swift kick to the shin under the table to shut her up, because Nita jumped slightly, then frowned.

"What? Everyone in town knows by now that Wade brought a little boy home with him. He certainly isn't hiding him. I figured maybe Stef has the inside scoop—pun intended—because of Grant and Dallas. What's wrong with asking?"

Barbara—who, like everyone else at the table, had witnessed Wade and Steffie's dance-floor romance unfold at Vanessa's brother's wedding—rolled her eyes.

"I don't know any more than any of you do." Stef

wore her best barely interested expression. "Grant's out of town, and as of last night, he had no idea."

"Dallas never said anything about it? Not ever?" Nita stared in disbelief.

"Apparently not." Stef shrugged it off as being unimportant.

"Doesn't that beat all?" Barbara shook her head and turned to Grace. "You're the investigative reporter here. I would think you'd have figured out a way to get the facts by now."

"From what I understand," Grace replied, "Wade only arrived in St. Dennis yesterday. But it's my guess that he's planning on staying for at least a little while."

"What makes you say that?" Steffie asked.

"I just happened to drive past Berry's house yesterday afternoon and I saw a car with Texas plates that had one of those trailer things hooked on the back. You know, the kind of trailer you rent when you've got more than a few suitcases to bring to wherever it is you're going."

The table fell silent for a moment.

"Of course," Grace added, "that could also mean he's on his way to someplace else."

"Maybe I should ask Daz," Vanessa mused.

"Who's Daz?" asked Barbara.

"My spirit guide on the Ouija board," Vanessa whispered as if sharing a mysterious secret.

Grace Sinclair choked on her tea.

"Sorry, dears." She waved a napkin in front of her face. "Went down the wrong way." Turning back to Vanessa, Grace asked, "What was that you were saying? Something about a Ouija board?"

"It's a joke, Miss Grace. I found one in the attic and brought it down to play with Grady. I was planning on asking it loaded questions and then spell out the answers, so I could drop little hints without looking like I was dropping hints." Vanessa smiled. "You know, things like, 'What size ring does Vanessa wear on her ring finger?' and then I'd have the board answer, 'Size five.' Just silly stuff like that."

"So what happened?" Nita prodded. "Did Grady fall for it?"

"We didn't get to play," Vanessa told them. "See, I'd read somewhere that before you ask it a question, you have to introduce yourself to your spirit guide. So I did that. 'Hi, I'm Vanessa, nice to meet you. What's your name?' But no matter what I asked it, it just kept spelling out 'D-A-Z.' Like it had been programmed or something."

"Maybe Grady was doing it on purpose," Barbara suggested. "Maybe he knew what you were up to."

"Grady wasn't even in the room. I was doing it by myself."

Grace cleared her throat, then took a long slow sip of tea before asking, "Found it in your attic, you say? I suppose it had belonged to Alice Ridgeway?"

Vanessa nodded. "It was there when I moved in, so I have to think it had been hers, since the contents came along with the house."

"Okay, you can admit now that you're doing it on purpose because you think it's amusing to say that you have a spirit guide named Daz." Nita laughed. "Whoever heard of a spirit named Daz, anyway?"

"But I'm not doing it, and I didn't make up Daz." Vanessa was beginning to sound slightly defensive.

"Maybe unconsciously you're moving the little triangle thing?"

"Stef, I swear, it moves itself."

"Maybe you're holding the board at a slant." Stef tried to think of some explanation that would allow her friend to save face.

Vanessa shook her head. "I wasn't holding it. I had it flat on the table."

"Maybe your floors are slanted and you don't realize it. Your house is pretty old," Stef reminded her.

"Maybe. Though Grady did hang some paintings for me, and he said the walls were plumb. Could the walls be plumb and the floors crooked?"

"Perhaps you could let me try," Grace said. "I used to use . . . that is, *play* with a board when I was younger."

"It's no big deal, Miss Grace. It's only a toy," Vanessa told her. "But you're welcome to have it. Since 'DAZ' isn't my ring size, I doubt it'll be of any use to me."

"Oh, look. Speaking of Grady." Barbara pointed out the window. "It looks like he's going into Bling, Ness."

Vanessa hastily downed the last of her coffee. "I left home a little early today, so he probably thinks I'm there. I'll see you all tomorrow."

Steffie grabbed Vanessa's empty mug from her friend's hand. It was customary to return one's cup directly to Carlo before leaving. "I'll take this back when I take back mine," she told Vanessa. "You go on."

"Thanks, Stef." Vanessa blew an air kiss in the general direction of the table before flying out the door.

Barbara leaned in the direction of the window. "Now, there's a match made in that place where all perfect matches are made."

"Oh, would you look at the way they just beam at each other. Anyone could tell they're madly in love." Nita sighed heavily. "Now, there is one very lucky girl."

"Not to mention one very lucky guy," Stef reminded them.

"True enough." Barbara nodded. "We should all be that lucky. We should all know what it's like to have someone love us like that."

"Amen," Steffie murmured. She turned her wrist to check her watch. "Look at the time. I have to get back."

She picked up Vanessa's mug along with her own and walked to the counter, where she handed them over to Carlo, then waved good-bye to the others before heading out the door and back to Scoop.

Stef waved to Vanessa and Grady across the street, but neither appeared to have seen her.

With Barbara's comment still ringing in her ears, Stef walked along Kelly's Point Road. She knew she'd never had that kind of love in her life. Oh, she'd had plenty of boyfriends, and she'd had a fling or two, but never anything serious. Never the kind of relationship where that over-the-moon feeling was mutual. Besides, in her experience, over-the-moon didn't last. She thought that might be the tricky part, getting it to last. The key to it all, of course, was finding the right person in the first place.

But what if you've found the person who makes your palms sweat and your heart beat faster, the person who filled your dreams for as long as you could remember—but that person didn't have a clue about you? What if the one person you knew you could love forever wasn't in love with you?

She thought back to Beck and Mia's wedding, of dancing so close to Wade that she could feel his heart beating right through the jacket he wore, of looking into his eyes and thinking, *Yeah, this is the one. This is what I've been waiting for all these years, this moment for him to look at me just this way.* The way their bodies had swayed together, as if they'd been made for each other.

And then, of course, there was the way Wade had abruptly left her standing there alone in the middle of the parking lot, wondering if everything else that night had been some horrible joke the gods had played on her for some petty thing she must have done at some point in her life.

She had so not deserved him dumping her that night.

She deserved someone who would love her forever, someone who'd look at her the way Grady looked at Ness and the way Grant looked at Dallas, not someone who got her all revved up and then walked away without explanation and was just *poof*—gone from her life.

And what was with that, anyway? She'd never understood his actions that night. Just as she'd never understood why she hadn't been able to find someone else who made her feel the way Wade did.

Annoyed with him all over again, she stepped over the weathered railroad tie that formed the boundary between the parking lot and the back of her shop, sighing as she opened the door. Well, his coming back here just served as a reminder—as if she'd needed one—of how alone she'd felt that night as she watched the tail lights of his rental car disappear down the inn's long driveway.

What she should do, she realized, is channel all this emotion into finding someone who *did* appreciate her, someone she could spend the rest of her life with. There had to be someone out there somewhere who could make Steffie Wyler numero uno in his life, someone who could love her forever. Since Beck's wedding, she'd made no effort to meet anyone else.

Well, that's going to change, as of right now, she told herself sternly. *From now on, I'm open to whatever the universe has to send my way. Wade MacGregor isn't the only fish in the Bay.*

Chapter 4

THE St. Dennis Historical Society held their monthly meetings at Old St. Mary's Church on Parish House Road. Once their business had been concluded, they adjourned to Captain Walt's down at the marina for a luncheon, followed by ice-cream sundaes at Scoop. Steffie usually prepared in advance for the onslaught by making sure she had sufficient staff so that no one would be waiting in line long enough to start complaining about it. Yesterday she'd been so distracted by Wade that she'd forgotten to prepare for the September meeting. Fortunately, Tina and her sister Claire, who pitched in occasionally now that her extra summer help was back in school, had been scheduled to work, so Stef had enough hands.

What she didn't have was the unique topping that the group's members had come to expect from their monthly visits to Scoop, the topping she'd create just for them.

It was almost ten in the morning when she realized her omission. The society's luncheon usually finished around one-thirty, which meant the first wave would arrive at Scoop around one forty-five. Three and a half hours to come up with something unusual, seasonal, and delicious.

She stood in front of her freezer and stared at the contents hoping for inspiration. When that didn't work, she asked Tina, "Quick. What fruit says 'early fall' to you?"

Without hesitating, Tina said, "Apples."

"Of course! Apples. Who has apples?"

"The markets all have them," Tina pointed out.

"I don't know where those apples come from. I don't know when they were picked or what they were sprayed with." Stef frowned. "I don't like not knowing. And yes, the irony that a junk-food aficionado such as myself would care about this is not lost on me."

"Madison's have apples," Tina reminded her. "I don't think they spray bad stuff on their trees."

"Right. Madison's." Stef grabbed the phone book and searched for the number, which she dialed on the wall phone. "Clay, it's Steffie Wyler. Yes, fine . . . Listen, I need apples. What do you have . . . ?"

Five minutes later, Tina was on her way to pick up a bushel of honey-crisp apples and Steffie was showing Claire how to make caramel. On the blackboard for the day, Stef wrote the special of the day: CARAMEL APPLE WALNUT SUNDAES. At one forty, she was scooping up the first of many bowls of vanilla ice cream swimming in warm caramel over chopped apples, topped with walnuts.

"Stephanie, do you think there will be any of that yummy topping left after the crowd disperses?"

At the sound of the familiar voice, Stef looked up and grinned from ear to ear.

"Mom! Why didn't you tell me you were coming today? Is Dad with you?" She tried to look over her mother's shoulder.

"I had some business to tend to that your father didn't have to bother with," her mother replied. "I thought I'd see if you and Grant had time for a quick bite of lunch, but Grant has a full schedule this afternoon. I stopped at the clinic on my way here but only had a few minutes to spend with him."

Shirley Wyler held up a bag that read THE CHECKERED CLOTH in black script across a red and white bag.

"I came prepared."

"Is that what I think it is?" Steffie asked hopefully. "Bleu-cheese burger on a brioche roll?"

"Would I bring my daughter anything but?"

"Give me ten minutes," Stef told her. "But you might want to start on yours now so it doesn't get cold."

"They triple-wrapped the sandwiches in heavy foil, so they should stay nice and warm. I'll just visit with a few old friends I saw outside. I'll be back when the crush is over."

"Great. Thanks, Mom." Stef turned her smile on the next person in the queue.

It was after two when Stef pulled up the chair next to her mother's at the corner table in the shop.

"Sorry, Mom. It's Historical Society day."

"I know. I saw Eliza Sherman and Peg Wordsworth outside a while ago, and I ran into Grace Sinclair when I first got here. Amazing that Grace is still running that paper." Shirley opened the bag and handed her daughter a foil packet. "I thought the *St. Dennis Gazette* was almost ready to fold when your father and I moved to Havre de Grace four years ago. Remarkable that she's been able to hold on all this time."

"It's the advertising that's keeping her going. All the town merchants advertise in the *Gazette* every week so the tourists and the weekenders know what shops are in town and what's on sale where." Stef unwrapped her sandwich. "Yum. The roll is still warm."

"Mine, too." Shirley smoothed out the foil wrapping.

"I'm so hungry today I could eat five of these." Stef took a bite of her sandwich. "Yum. Just . . . yum." She took another bite, then stood. "Would you like something to drink? I have bottled water and tap water, root-beer floats . . ."

Shirley held up a hand to stop Stef from running through the entire menu of drinks.

"Bottled water would be perfect."

Stef went to the cooler and grabbed two bottles and a couple of straws.

"So what's going on? What brought you to St. Dennis today?" She sat back down at the table.

"I had to meet with Cousin Horace's attorney," her mother told her. "About his will."

"Oh." Stef frowned. "I miss the old guy. Well, not like he's been the past few years, but before. Gosh, he was a fun guy. I owe this"—she gestured around the room—"to him. He taught me how to make ice cream when I was, like, twelve or thirteen. Remember that old ice-cream maker he used to have? The one with the handle that you had to turn?" She took another bite, chewed, and swallowed. "I wonder whatever happened to that."

"I imagine it's still somewhere in his house." Shirley put her sandwich down. "We'll know soon enough."

"What do you mean?"

Shirley reached into her pocket, pulled out a brass key, and handed it to Stef.

"I met with Jesse Enright this morning. Remember him? Mike and Patti's nephew who used to visit sometimes in the summer?"

"Sort of." Actually, Stef couldn't place the face though the name was vaguely familiar.

"Mike took over the law practice when his father—who would have been Berry's age—passed away. Since Mike and Patti have no children, everyone was delighted when Jesse agreed to join the firm," Shirley said. "They've represented my mother's family forever. Mike contacted me some time ago to come in to discuss the terms of Horace's will, since he'd made me executor, but since Mike and Patti are on a cruise this month, I met with Jesse." Shirley stopped and tapped her daughter on the arm. "You must remember him, Steffie. He's tall and very good-looking. He used to be really shy, but I think he might have outgrown that."

Stef shrugged. "He's not really ringing any bells, Mom."

"Well, anyway—to make a long story short: Horace left the house on Olive Street to you."

"Huh?" Stef's jaw dropped and hung open.

Shirley nodded. "It's all yours. Lock, stock, and cobwebs."

"But . . . but . . ." Steffie stared at the key that rested in the palm of her hand. "Why me?"

"Partly because he liked the fact that you were named after him. Stephen was his middle name, I'm sure you'll recall, since you used to call him H. Stephen, which always amused him." Shirley reached over and pushed a strand of loose hair behind Stef's ear. "And partly because of the ice-cream machine, I suppose. You were the only one of the kids who ever went over on your own to visit with him—at least, the only one who hadn't had to be dragged by the ear to go. No children of his own, no wife . . . I expect he was a lonely fellow. He often mentioned that he appreciated the time you spent with him because he knew you were there because you wanted to be."

"Are you kidding? I *loved* going there. I always felt like he was doing me a favor by spending time with *me,*" Stef said. "He was such a cool guy. He had all these fun things in the house and he let me play with anything I wanted. He never treated me like a little kid. He was more fun than any other grown-up I ever met."

"Well, there was more than a touch of the kid in Horace, we all knew that. And I suspect there will be lots more fun in store for you, since I doubt the house has changed much since you were a child. We closed it up when he went into the assisted living home, and I don't think anyone's been inside since. I always made sure there was someone to keep the grass cut and to shovel the walks if it snowed, but other than that, I haven't been inside since your dad and I moved, except to help Horace distribute some of the furnishings. Most of it went to Nita's antiques shop. I imagine she's sold almost all of it by now."

"Holy crap, he left me a house." Staring at the key once again, Stef shook her head. "I can't believe it." She looked up at her mother. "Are you sure you don't mind? Would you rather he'd left it to you?"

Shirley laughed. "What would I do with it? I already have one house here in town that I don't know what to do with. Why would I want another?"

"Well, he really was your cousin, not mine."

"No, he was my mother's cousin, remember? He and Gramma were first cousins."

Stef nodded. "I do remember that. But what about everyone else? Your cousin Kathleen, and your sister Betts and their kids. Are they going to be annoyed that I got the house?"

"I wouldn't worry about what anyone else thinks." Shirley dismissed Stef's concern. "For one thing, none of them ever bothered to send so much as a birthday or a Christmas card to Horace. Certainly no one other than you, Grant, and I visited him after he went into the home. Besides, he left everyone else cash."

"Including Grant? And Evie?" Stef hoped that her good fortune wasn't at the expense of her siblings.

"Both were well taken care of," Shirley assured her. "That was one of the reasons I stopped by the clinic. The copies of the will had to be distributed; which reminds me. I have your copy here in my bag." She leaned over and began to rummage in a tall green leather tote.

"I have a house. And not just any house. The house

on Olive Street is mine." Stef held up the key. "Is it mine now, officially?"

"There are some papers to be signed, which you can do over at Enright's office as soon as you get a chance." Shirley handed Stef a brown envelope that was addressed to her. "But Jesse said you can go on in and move in or sell it or—"

"Sell it?" Stef's eyes widened with horror. "Sell the house on Olive Street?"

"I told him that was most unlikely," Shirley assured her.

"I've been saving money since I opened this shop so that someday I could buy a house." Stef clutched the envelope containing the will to her chest. "I never thought I'd be able to afford one in that neighborhood, though. I never dreamed that someday I'd be living on Olive Street."

"I imagine the neighbors will be delighted to see you move in. The house has been vacant, and no one likes to have an empty house on their street."

"When can I move?"

"Whenever you want, though I think you're going to want to take advantage of the fact that the house is empty to do some updates. Nothing's been touched in many years, Stef. I'm sure the wiring and the plumbing and God knows what else needs to be brought into the twenty-first century."

"Let's go look at it." Stef's eyes were shining. "Can we go look at it now?"

"I don't see why not."

"Oh, boy."

They finished their lunches, and after assurance from Tina that she and Claire could handle the after-school crowd for a while if Stef wasn't back by the time the kids started pouring down Kelly's Point Road, Stef and her mother took off for Olive Street.

Four streets formed the second oldest section of St. Dennis: Parish House Road, St. James Street, Cannonball Road, and Olive Street. All the houses on these four streets had been built in time to see the British shell the town in 1814, during the War of 1812. Many of the houses were brick, but a good number were clapboard. Steffie had always thought that Olive Street was the prettiest street in town, because it had a nice mixture of both.

Stef stopped in front of the red-brick house that had the numeral "32" in black letters on one of the porch columns. Rhododendrons rose two stories high on either side of the porch, edging out what might have been hydrangeas and possibly a rosebush or two. Dead stalks of hosta lilies poked out from beneath a network of ivy, and ferns grew uncontrolled along the driveway. A white fence was missing some of its pickets and most of its paint.

"It is a bit overgrown," Shirley noted as they got out of the car. "Nothing that can't be cleared away."

"I think it's beautiful." Steffie stood at the front gate, her eyes glistening. "I think it's the most beautiful house in town."

"Let's go see what's going on inside, shall we?" Shirley reached around Stef and pushed the reluctant gate aside. "You have the key, sugar?"

"Right here." Stef paused on the front steps and studied the porch columns where the paint had weathered and peeled. "I guess it could use a little paint."

"Hmm, yes. A little."

"But paint is pretty cheap, right?" Stef said as she fitted the key into the lock and pushed open the wide oak door.

"Relatively speaking, yes." Shirley stepped into the foyer behind Stef.

"Oh." Steffie stood inside the door and gazed starry-eyed at her inheritance. "I'd forgotten how big the entry was, and how cool the steps were, the way they wind up to the second floor. And that chandelier . . . how beautiful that is."

"I imagine it could be cleaned up." Shirley assessed the finish on the overhead light fixture. "It looks a bit tarnished."

"I guess it wouldn't take much to pull that old peeling paper the rest of the way down the wall, right?"

"It looks like it will come right off with a good tug." To demonstrate, Shirley pulled on a strip that was hanging from the wall. It kicked up a bit of dust on its way down the wall, but it did in fact peel off with very little effort on her part.

"That'll be an easy job," Steffie assured her mother—and herself—as she followed the hall to the back of the house. "Oh. Looks like the kitchen could use a bit of paint, too."

Her mother stepped in behind her. "I think paint is the least of what this kitchen needs."

Stef quietly surveyed the room. "It's a big space, and the cabinets are fine. I like those big old doors. I'm just going to paint everything white." She nodded as she studied the space. "Maybe I'll put in an island. And maybe replace those counters with something really good, like granite, because I work at home a lot."

"The linoleum is older than I am," Shirley noted.

"I wonder what's underneath it." Stef went to the threshold and tried to peel up a bit of the flooring, but it cracked and pieces came off in her hand. "I'm betting it's wood. We just need to rip it up."

"Maybe you should wait until you know for certain what's under there," her mother cautioned.

"Too late." Steffie pulled a jagged strip of flooring off. "And it looks like pine. Super. I just need to peel this all off and refinish the floor and it'll be like new."

"Will that be before or after you paint all the cabinets, install the island, and replace the counters?" Shirley leaned her elbow on the counter and rested her chin in her palm.

"I guess I should slow down for minute." Stef felt an urge to pinch herself. "But, oh, Mom, it's just the way I remember it. The old stove—I'll bet that's still a good working stove, Mom—and the old refrigerator, though I will need to replace that for one with a bigger freezer." She reconsidered. "I could make more ice cream at home if I had a really big freezer."

"Horace cooked many a pot of soup on that old stove," Shirley remarked.

"He never married, did he?"

Shirley shook her head. "He always said there was only one girl he'd share his house with, but she'd never cross the threshold. Not sure what that meant, but that's what he used to say. I don't remember him ever bringing a lady friend to dinner, even for holidays, so who knows."

Stef unlocked the back door and went through an

unheated space to a second door that opened onto the back porch.

"Horace called this the shed." Shirley trailed behind Stef. "He used to store stuff out here in the winter. Potatoes, onions, things like that."

"Who did you say you hired to cut the grass?" Stef stood on the top step, her hands on her hips.

"One of the Anderson boys. Why?"

"It looks like that's all he did." Stef moved down to the next lower step when her mother came out the door.

"That's all I paid him to do." Shirley followed Stef's gaze around the yard. "Oh, you're looking at all the overgrowth? It does appear that things have gotten a bit out of hand, doesn't it?"

"Nothing that a good pair of shears can't handle. I've never pruned before, but I'm sure I can learn."

"If you get stuck, I'll give you a hand."

"I might take you up on that." Stef motioned for her mother to go back inside. "Let's check out the rest of the house."

They poked their heads into the butler's pantry, then went up the back stairs, past more peeling wallpaper and no small amount of crumbling plaster, to the second floor.

"The wallpaper is definitely early last century," Steffie observed after she'd gone through each of the corner bedrooms. "And the bathrooms are right out of *Psycho*."

She turned a faucet in one of the bathroom sinks. Dark water trickled out.

"I think you'll want to let that run for a time," her

mother said calmly. "Clean out the pipes, and all that."

Steffie nodded.

"I suppose I should make a list of everything that needs to be done, then decide which are the priorities."

"Good idea." Shirley started down the front stairwell. At the landing, where the steps turned, she looked back over her shoulder. "You might want to have someone go through the place and tell you what should be done first and how much it's all going to cost."

"Cameron O'Connor is a contractor. I can give him a call."

"Good idea." Shirley turned and went down the steps to the first floor, Stef behind her. "Cam did some work on our house about six years ago and he did a terrific job. He wasn't inexpensive, though."

"So the money I saved to buy a place will go for the repairs on this one."

"I'll bet you spend every penny of it." Shirley looked as if she was mentally tallying up the cost of the renovations.

"I remember that the dining room was so pretty," Stef said, her flip-flops flapping on the wooden floor from the foyer to the dining room. "Oh, and it still is."

"It looked different with the furniture in it, didn't it?" Her mother stood in the doorway.

"But it's still a pretty room." Stef ducked to avoid the crystals that dangled from the chandelier. "It has lovely leaded glass windows and the fireplace and all that nice wainscoting . . ." She stared at the walls. "Mom, that paper has to go."

Shirley laughed. "With any luck, it'll come off as easily as the paper in the front hall."

"I can deal with that," Steffie murmured.

"I'm sure you can, sweets, but don't fool yourself into thinking you can do everything at once. Go step-by-step, and by the time you're ready to move in—"

"I'm ready to move in now. As soon as I get back to the shop, I'm going to call Cam and see when he can meet me here. I know exactly what I want to do, and I want to get started as soon as possible. I can't wait to move in."

"You should call Jesse first, get all the papers signed. His card is in the envelope I gave you."

"I left that back at the shop." Stef glanced at her watch. "I need to get back there anyway. I don't feel right leaving Tina and Claire to deal with all those rowdy schoolkids on their own. Claire's only supposed to be working part-time this week."

She took one long look into the living room, and remembered there was a room off to the right that had glass windows on three sides—Horace had called it the "conservatory"—and a small library that they hadn't looked at. Well, she knew what the rooms looked like, and besides, she'd be back soon enough.

She turned the key to lock the door and took her mother's arm as they strolled back to the car. She looked over her shoulder as she went through the gate, and smiled.

Good-bye, my house, my very own wonderful, beautiful house. I'll be back soon.

Chapter 5

EARLY the following morning, a tap on Scoop's door sent Steffie's pulse racing.

"What is it with him and his early-morning visits?" she muttered. Clearly expecting Wade, she fixed her most bored and disinterested expression before venturing from the back room to the front of the shop.

She couldn't decide whether she was happy or disappointed to find her brother at the door.

"Oh, hi." She unlocked it and let him in.

"Great to see you, too." He leaned down to kiss her cheek.

"Sorry." She gave him a quick hug and closed the door behind him.

"Were you expecting someone else?"

"Not really." She shrugged. "Come on in the back room. I was just finishing up today's batch of lemon meringue."

"I was right about Cousin Horace, wasn't I?" He followed her into her workroom. "He did like you best."

"Well, of course he did. Why wouldn't he? Everyone else does." Stef teased. "Jealous?"

"Nah," he assured her. "Horace, bless his big heart,

left me cash. Enough to finish the renovations on my house, so I'm happy." Grant paused. "Are you happy?"

"Are you kidding? I'm delirious." She broke into a huge grin. "You know, I have always loved that house. If anyone had given me a choice of any house in St. Dennis, I'd have picked that one. I spent half the night last night over there, just sitting on the living-room floor, thinking about how I'm going to do every room, and pinching myself. It's a dream come true for me, Grant."

"Well, if you're happy, I'm happy." Grant pulled over a stool and sat at the end of the worktable.

"Thanks, bro. But are you sure you wouldn't have rather have had—" Stef looked up from the lemon rinds she was grating.

"Nope." He held up a hand to stop her. "I'm exactly where I want to be. Don't give it another thought."

"It was nice of Horace to remember us, don't you think?" she said softly.

"Damned nice," he agreed. "By the way, where's your helper this morning?"

"Tina will be in by eleven." She glanced up at Grant. "Is something wrong?"

He shook his head. "I have a surgical appointment in about an hour—a boxer with a tumor on its leg—but I thought I'd just take a few minutes to stop in and say hi before I headed into the clinic."

She stopped what she was doing and studied his face. "You okay? I mean, with Paige gone, and all."

"I hate that I can't have my kid with me, I'm not going to lie." He watched her dip a tasting spoon into the thick yellow froth in the machine.

She grabbed another spoon, filled it, and passed it over to him.

He tasted it, then nodded. "Nice, Stef."

"Thanks." Steffie rested her forearms on the tabletop. "I guess Krista would say the same thing, though, don't you think? Her mom would miss Paige just as much as you do."

"Well, that's the thing with divorce where kids are involved. One person is probably going to be unhappy at any given time. Sometimes it's me, sometimes it's Krista. Sometimes, it's Paige." He made a face. "During the school year, it's me *and* Paige."

"You know that she would rather be here than in Ohio, Grant. She told me she wanted to stay here, oh, at least five hundred times over the summer. She doesn't understand why what she wants shouldn't take precedence over what her mother wants." She debated for a moment before adding, "I think she wishes you'd fight harder for her."

"If I were one hundred percent certain that it was in Paige's best interests for her to be living in St. Dennis year-round, I would, in a heartbeat." Grant shook his head. "I just don't know, though. Krista insists that Paige is better off staying in the school where she started kindergarten, where she has lots of friends, knows the routine and all the teachers. She really believes that it's best for Paige to stay in the town where she's always lived, that it's better to keep at least that much consistent in her life."

"You don't sound convinced."

"Is it better for her to be there during the school year than here? Better here for the summer than there?" He shrugged. "And if she were to spend the school year here, she'd have to give up summers here to go to her mom's for those three months, and I doubt very much that Paige would like that. The bottom line? I don't pretend to know what's best." The circles under Grant's eyes were clear evidence that he'd been losing sleep over the situation. "I just know that when she's here, Paige is a happy and seemingly normal almost-thirteen-year-old. As soon as we cross the Ohio state line, she turns into a moody, miserable caricature of herself."

"Krista hasn't noticed this?" Stef checked the progress of the ice-cream maker.

"Krista says that's the way Paige always acts. That it's normal behavior for her age group. I tried to tell her that it isn't normal for Paige—at least, it isn't when she's here—but Krista doesn't believe it. She thinks I'm just saying it because I don't want to bring her back."

"Maybe you could request another custody hearing, maybe have Paige testify this time. She didn't last time, right?"

"I'm thinking that's where we're probably headed. I know the courts seem to favor the mother a lot, but I'm just as good a parent as Krista."

"You're a terrific parent," Stef assured him. "The fact that Paige would rather be here with you should mean something to the court."

"I'll have to think about it." He handed back the spoon. "This was really tasty. And brings me to the main reason for my stopping in. Besides congratulating you on your new address, of course."

"What's up?" She scooped out a spoonful of ice cream for herself. "Perfect." She turned off the machine and proceeded to fill a large round cardboard container with the lemony confection.

"Dallas has a birthday coming up. She's going to be thirty-eight in a couple of weeks."

"Really? She wears it well. I hope I look that good when I'm her age." She paused to consider. "Actually, I'd be happy if I looked that good *now.*"

"You're okay, kid."

"So what about Dallas's birthday? You're going to have a party and want ice cream?"

"Yes, but not just any ice cream," he told her. "I want something special. You know, she could celebrate anywhere in the world, but she wants to do it here. So I've been trying to think of something that we could do for her, something that would be really special and totally St. Dennis."

"And . . . ?" She gestured for him to continue.

"I want you to make an ice-cream flavor just for her. Make enough for her party, then destroy the recipe and never make it again."

Steffie stared at him.

"Pretty cool idea, huh?" He grinned.

"You thought of that all by yourself?"

"Yeah." He nodded, obviously pleased with himself.

"What if I made a special Dallas flavor and she wanted me to make it again? Then what?"

"Then I guess you'd have to do it, but you could only make it for her." He shook his head. "I can't think of anything else, Stef. She's the woman who has everything. She can buy anything she wants." He lowered his voice to a confessional tone. "I want to propose to her, but I can't buy a ring as big as what she could buy herself, even if I used my savings plus the money Horace left me."

"Perhaps we should have beeen discussing why men are so stupid instead of ice cream."

"What's that supposed to mean?"

"Of course Dallas can afford to buy herself the biggest ring on the planet. She's a huge movie star and makes millions of dollars every time she makes a film. You're a veterinarian, you don't make Hollywood bucks. I'm pretty sure she's figured that out, and I don't think she cares a fig about how big a diamond you could buy her. She has plenty of her own diamonds. Maybe what she wants from you is something that money can't buy."

"Like what?"

"Besides your undying love—though why she would want *that* is a discussion for another day—maybe something that has a deeper meaning. Something truly special. Something beyond a price tag. Something that no one else has."

"Like what?" He frowned.

"Like . . ." She paused to think for a minute, then snapped her fingers when it came to her. "Nana's wedding ring."

Grant stared blankly. She waved her hand in front of his face.

"You still in there?" she asked.

"You think she'd want that? Nana's ring?"

"I think it would mean the world to her. Dallas cares about stuff like that. If she didn't, she'd be commuting from Hollywood to St. Dennis once a month instead of the other way around. She values family connections, Grant. Hers, yours . . ." Steffie nodded. "If you're going to ask her to marry you, I think Nana's ring is definitely the way to go. Besides, it's a gorgeous ring. Platinum is very in these days, and the three stones in the band are quite lovely. And it was Nana's, so it means something."

"Hmm. Nana's ring . . . I'll think about it. Maybe I'll give Mom a call and see what she thinks. Thanks for the suggestion."

"I live to serve."

"So what do you think about the ice-cream flavor? Will you do it?"

"I'll play around and see what I can come up with. I know what flavors she's partial to," Stef said thoughtfully, "because she always orders ice cream in the same family. Peach. Lemon. Fruity but not too sweet."

"Thanks. I know you'll come up with just the right thing. You're a gem." Grant checked the time on the wall clock, then stood to give her a hug. "I gotta get over to the clinic."

"Here." She pointed to the back door. "Go out this way. It's closer to the parking lot."

She unlocked the door, but then blocked it with her body so he couldn't leave. "But first—what's the story with Wade and the little guy who calls him Daddy?"

"I thought maybe you'd forgotten."

"Not on your life." She closed the door, relocked it, and made a show of tucking the key into the palm of her hand before making a tightly clenched fist. "Spill."

"I can't."

"What do you mean, you can't?" She frowned.

"I promised I wouldn't tell anyone."

"I'm not anyone," she reminded him sweetly. "I'm your beloved sister."

He shook his head. "Sorry. I really mean that. I *am* sorry. But I gave my word."

"Who'd you give your word to?"

"Dallas," he told her.

Steffie bit the inside of her lip. "It's because you're sleeping with her, isn't it." It wasn't a question.

Grant sighed. "The guy's entitled to his privacy. If he wants to discuss his private affairs with you—or anyone else—he'll do it."

"This isn't fair. I knew you first. We grew up under the same roof. Your allegiance should be to me."

"You sound like a petulant eight-year-old."

Steffie stuck out her tongue.

"Make that a five-year-old."

Plan B, Stef told herself. *Maybe I can get Berry to spill over one of my special sundaes . . .*

"And don't be thinking you'll trick Miss B into telling you," he said as if reading her mind. "Her lips are sealed, too."

"Damn."

He wrestled the key from her hand and unlocked the door.

"Oh, and let me know what you come up with for Dallas's birthday flavor."

Steffie stood in the doorway for a moment watching her brother's long strides carry him across the lot to his car.

"Damn." She punched a fist into her other palm. "And I was so close . . ."

"I suppose haggis is out of the question."

"What's that?" Tina poked her head into the back room, where Stef had spent every possible moment that afternoon going over flavor possibilities for Dallas's birthday ice cream.

"I was just thinking out loud," Steffie told her.

She was thinking maybe she needed to come up with something that said "Scottish" to tie in with MacGregor, but the only two things that came to mind were haggis and heather. What did heather taste like, anyway?

She searched the shelves for the notebook containing the ice-cream recipes she'd started collecting when she was a teenager, and after spending an afternoon making ice cream with Horace, declared that she was going to make ice cream every day for the rest of her life. Over the years, she'd handwritten recipes she'd begged, borrowed, stolen, and later, made up, into the notebook. Through trial and error, testing and retesting, she'd come up with flavors that were all her own. Stef was the first to admit that some of her early attempts at creativity had in fact been duds. It had taken a while, but she'd developed an uncanny ability to blend flavors that others might not dream of putting together. Her ice cream had been written up in many local and regional periodicals, and her shop had landed on several of the must-see lists that appeared every summer in vacation guides and weekend getaway suggestions.

It had been a long time since she'd faced a challenge like this one, and she was enjoying it. She spent the entire rainy afternoon poring over her notebook, but she had yet to hit the right note.

She barely heard the ringing phone.

"Stef," Tina told her, "it's Cam. He wants to know what time to meet you tonight."

"Sometime between six and seven. Whichever works best for him," Stef said absently.

After she'd hung up the phone, Tina told her, "Cam said six-thirty is good."

"Thanks. Any chance you could work an extra hour or two tonight? We shouldn't be too busy with all this rain, and I'll be back before it's time to close."

Tina nodded, then reminded her, "I've got two kids in college. I'll take all the extra hours I can get."

Maybe something Scottish wasn't the way to go, Stef thought as she drove to Olive Street, the ice-cream flavor still on her mind. Maybe something that was more *Dallas* than *MacGregor.*

Maybe something with honey in it . . .

Yeah, honey seemed right for Dallas. But what with it? Dallas loved peaches. She almost always ordered whatever peach concoction Steffie had on the menu board. But she had the feeling that peach had been overdone that summer. Whatever she came up with for Dallas had to be special, something no one had done before. Well, no one in St. Dennis, anyway.

Yet delicious, she reminded herself as she parked in her driveway. *It has to be unique and fabulous, like Dallas herself, and incredibly tasty.*

She put Dallas's birthday ice cream from her mind as she walked from room to room with Cam, both of them taking notes on what they agreed should be done, and in what order.

Cam suggested they start by updating the mechanics—plumbing, electricity, the heating system.

"If you're going to put in a whole new system"—he looked up from his clipboard—"you might want to think about central air conditioning."

Stef nodded enthusiastically. "Definitely."

"And if we're doing over the plumbing, maybe you

should redo the bathrooms at the same time. You know, new fixtures, new tile. And maybe take some of that space from the back shed area and put in a powder room."

"Put a detailed estimate in there, and I'll think about it."

"Now, in the kitchen, you thinking about ripping out all those old cabinets?"

They stood in the kitchen doorway.

Stef shook her head. "I like the glass doors. I just thought I'd paint them."

Cam nodded. "I'd do the same. Now, about the floor . . ."

Two and a half hours later, with a promise from Cam that she'd have the estimate by the weekend, Stef went back up the steps to the second floor. The hall bath had been remodeled about thirty years ago, and was to her eyes, a fright. That one should be completely redone, definitely. But the master bathroom still had the old claw-foot tub and the delicate tiles with embossed flowers, and though a few of the tiles were crazed and others bore signs of age, she liked it just the way it was. Satisfied that she was on the right path where her house was concerned, she went from one room to the next, turning out the lights.

"Good night, house," she whispered as she locked the front door behind her. "I'll be back soon."

Honey.

She turned on her laptop and scrolled through her findings. There were more kinds than she'd ever imagined: orange blossom, wildflower, mint, Tupelo, lemon, heather, even chestnut and eucalyptus honey.

The possibilities made her head spin. There was blended honey—made from a mixture of honey that originated from different geographic origins, plants, and differing in color and taste. Polyfloral honey was made of the honey from several different flowers. Then there was monofloral honey, the honey from only one flower. And honey could be light in color and lightly flavored, like clover honey, or denser, darker, like buckwheat honey.

And who knew that honey came in so many different forms? There was liquid honey—that was what she was most familiar with—but there was also honey in the comb, as well as liquid honey in the comb, and something called "naturally crystallized honey." There was whipped honey and organic honey and kosher honey, raw honey and wild honey.

Flavor first, she decided, shaking her head to clear it. That should be the easiest decision.

She spent several hours going from one website to another. The sheer number of honey flavors was mind-boggling. With a groan, she saved what looked like the best locations, closed the laptop, stood, and stretched. She had time to figure it out, and once she did, after a test run or two, making the ice cream shouldn't be too difficult. She would need a guest count from Grant sooner or later so she'd know how much to make.

She turned off the lights, picked up her bag, and took it and the list she'd made with Cam into her bedroom. She left the list and a pen on her nightstand while she got ready for bed. Once in her oldest, most favorite sleep shirt, she crawled into bed, and reviewed her checklist and began to number things in order of priority, grateful that she had savings that would cover much of the cost. Where the funds once earmarked for a down payment fell short, she'd do the work herself or she'd postpone it. Hence the need for priorities.

First, of course, was to upgrade the electrical service and replace all the wiring and the outlets. Cam was right about that. It was boring and expensive, but necessary. Next would be the plumbing and replacing any lead pipes. After that, the heating and air-conditioning needed to be addressed. She could be painting the kitchen while all that was going on. A soft, dreamy white for the cabinets and granite for the counters. A sweet buttery yellow for the walls, or a dark cream? Maybe the very palest gray, like she'd seen in a magazine. She sighed with pleasure. She'd thought it would be years before she had such delicious decisions to make.

But should she wait until the floors were done to begin painting?

Tomorrow, she told herself. Dallas's ice cream and her plans for the house could all wait until tomorrow.

She hooked the pen onto the notebook and dropped both on the floor, then turned off the light, thinking of all the nights she'd spent in this apartment dreaming of the day when she'd have a pretty house to call her own. Of course, in *that* dream, she'd also had her own handsome guy to share it with.

Then again, all things considered, one out of two wasn't bad.

Chapter 6

STEFFIE hit the hardware store on Charles Street as soon as her daily supply of ice cream was in the cooler and Tina was behind the cash register. She'd awakened with a clear head and a definite vision for her house. She knew exactly what she wanted, and couldn't wait to get started. She bought the paint for the entire downstairs and the room she'd selected as her bedroom and bath, as well as all the supplies she needed: brushes, pails, rollers, and pans. It had taken two of the countermen to help her load it all into the back of her old Pathfinder.

"I'm a busy woman. I don't have a lot of time to waste," she'd explained as she paid the tab. "As long as I'm already here and I know what I want, I might as well take care of as much of my business right now as I can."

Later that afternoon, she met with Jesse Enright, from Horace's law firm. He had the papers all laid out for her on his conference-room table when she arrived.

"I know you're busy and don't have a lot of time to spare," he said when he finished explaining the terms of Horace's will and the legalities of the papers she was about to sign, "so I made sure everything was in order and ready to go. If you're satisfied, I'll show you where to sign."

He handed her a pen with the name of the law firm, Enright and Enright, in gold block letters, with his name underneath in script. After she'd worked her way through the stack, she handed him the pen.

"Thanks, Jesse." She couldn't help but grin.

"Keep the pen." He grinned back at her.

"Thanks," she said again.

"It's nice to see someone happy for a change," he told her as he packed up her copies of the deed and the tax records and everything else he was sending her home with. "So far today I've had two divorces and this morning I had to go to court with a very young client who was arrested for stealing his parents' car."

"How young is very young?" she asked.

"Eleven. I had to convince the judge it was a one-time thing to satisfy his curiosity and that he'd never do it again and that community service would be appreciated."

"Did the judge buy it?" She clutched the envelope tightly, still barely able to believe her good fortune and doing her best to keep from breaking into a happy dance.

"After he had his say, he agreed. But he did put the fear of God into that kid." Jesse walked her to the door, his hand lightly on her arm. "For which the boy's parents were grateful."

"I'm not even going to ask you who the kid is."

"Good. I wouldn't tell you."

"Right. Client confidentiality."

He nodded, his blue eyes dancing. "And probably a good customer of yours."

"Most of the kids in town are."

He opened the heavy wooden door and held it for her.

"Thanks again, Jesse." She stepped outside onto the brick walk that led from the sidewalk to the office building that was slightly set back from the street.

"Look, Steffie." He stepped out with her. "If you need help with anything—with the house, whatever—give me a call, okay? I'd be more than happy to give you a hand with . . . well, with whatever you need. I spent my summers working for a carpenter back when I was in school. I swing a mean hammer."

"Thanks." She smiled her prettiest smile. "I'll keep that in mind."

"Well, I guess I'll see you at the leukemia run next week."

"You signed up?" She paused on the walk. Steffie and Grant's parents had organized the first run years ago in honor of their deceased sister, Natalie, and since then, it had become an annual event.

Jesse nodded. "It's a good cause, and it seems like a good way to become involved in the community." He stepped out onto the walk, his hands in his pockets. "I haven't been in town long enough to get to know too many people, unless they've come into the office or they're friends of my uncle's. I figured it was time for me to get out and meet people on my own. All work and no play and all that."

"There are a lot of ways to become part of the community, so I'm glad you chose Natalie's Run. Obviously, it's a cause that's very important to my family and me." She shook his hand. "I'd be happy to introduce you to some of the people I know."

"That would be great, Steffie. I'd appreciate that."

"And you know, you don't have to run. You can walk," she told him. *He really does have nice eyes. And a terrific smile. Are those dimples? Sigh . . .*

"I already entered to run, but it's good to know I have an option." He walked her as far as the driveway. "So, I guess I'll see you there."

"Yes," she assured him. "You'll see me there."

Options, she repeated to herself as she returned to her shop. *Always good to know there are options . . .*

Jesse might be an option, she mused. *He's a really nice guy, he's cute as the devil—dimples!—and as far as I know, he's eligible.*

So you, Wade MacGregor, are not the only guy in town, she thought smugly.

"As a matter of fact, from this moment on, I'm immune to you. You have no hold over me," she mumbled as she entered Scoop through the back door. "You are so not worthy of me, and I'm happy to be looking elsewhere. I deserve better," she reminded herself.

"Are you talking to me?" Tina called from the front of the shop.

"What?" Steffie's face turned red. She hadn't realized she'd been talking out loud. "No, sorry."

She grabbed her apron from the rack and tied it on, and went out front to wait on her customers.

The paint was still in the back of the car when she pulled into the driveway around seven. She raised the back hatch of the car and tried to estimate how many trips it was going to take to get everything into the house. She decided to unlock the door first so at least she wouldn't have to wrestle with heavy boxes and the lock at the same time. On her way back to the car, she heard her name being called.

Wade. She pretended not to have heard.

"Hey, Stef." He crossed the street, jogging with Austin in his stroller. "Hey, great house. Congratulations. I heard the news."

"Oh, hi." She crossed her arms over her chest. *Immune,* she told herself. *I am immune.* "I guess you saw Grant."

"Nah, Berry heard from Grace Sinclair." He stopped on the other side of the fence. Austin peered around the awning of the stroller and smiled shyly before ducking back.

I remain immune to him, and his little boy, too.

"I wonder who told Grace?"

"I've no idea. She does just always seem to know things, though."

Austin struggled quietly to get out from his restraints.

"So, want to give us a tour?" Wade asked.

She'd been this close to him before, and really, she hadn't meant to stare, but it occurred to her how like his sister's eyes Wade's were. That odd shade of smoky lavender . . .

"Of course." She mentally slapped herself on the forehead. "Lavender. Lavender and honey. Lavender honey."

"What?" A puzzled Wade tilted his head to one side.

"Never mind." Steffie glanced down in time to see Austin escape. "Ah, Wade. Fugitive."

"Yeah, he's gotten pretty good at it." He turned to the little boy. "Austin, come say hi to Steffie."

Austin came closer, his eyes—so dark, she noted, so unlike his father's and his aunt's—studying her.

"This is Steffie, Austin. Daddy's friend. Can you say hi to Stef?"

Austin looked up at her and said, "Steppie."

"Wade, did he say 'Steffie'?" She smiled in spite of her vow to remain immune. "I think he said 'Steffie.' "

"Steppie," Austin repeated.

"There. He did. He said my name."

"He's pretty quick," Wade told her.

"He's really cute," she said. He *was* really cute. She could remain immune to Wade and still acknowledge the adorableness of his boy-child.

"Thanks."

It was on the tip of her tongue to ask who Austin looked like—maybe get some insight into Austin's mama—because clearly, the child looked nothing like Wade. Dark hair, big brown eyes, and, she thought, olive skin, though that could be tan. They had been living in Texas, and it is pretty hot there, right?

"Isn't it almost his bedtime?" She went through the gate and around to the back of her car to start unloading. With any luck, Wade would strap his son back into the stroller and stroll on home.

"It used to be. He's been staying up a little later since we came to St. Dennis because we take a walk after dinner every night, and then he likes to play with his cousin."

Before she realized what was happening, Wade had lifted the heaviest of the boxes of paint cans and started to walk toward the house. When she started to protest, he said simply, "I have it."

With Austin toddling behind, Wade set off for the house.

Steffie grabbed the bag with all the brushes and mixing sticks and the rollers and tried to catch up.

"You can put them down right here in the front hall." She trailed behind him. "Thanks, Wade, you don't have to . . ."

But he was out the door again, having passed her on the sidewalk, and at the car, hoisting another box and carrying it as if it were light as a feather.

"Wade, I appreciate your help, I really do. But don't feel as if you have to . . ."

"I don't, Stef." He lifted the last of the heaviest boxes. "Why would I?"

"I don't know." Stef gave up. She picked up the roller pans and went inside. Austin pulled tentatively at a strip of peeling wallpaper that hung almost to the floor.

"Step." He pointed to her when she came in.

"Austin, you are one smart cookie," she told him.

"Not a cookie." He giggled, and she fought the urge to ruffle those dark curls of his.

"Long as we're here, maybe you could give us a quick tour." Wade placed the last of the boxes on the floor.

"Sure." How could she not, after he'd carried in all the paint? She led them through one room into the next—Austin riding on Wade's shoulders—until they ended up in the kitchen.

"Nice cabinets, Stef." Wade stood Austin on the floor. "Are you going to make any changes in here?"

Fighting a sigh—why wouldn't he just say, "Nice house," and then leave?—she nodded and walked him through the remodeling she had in mind.

"It's going to be great," he told her enthusiastically. "I'm happy for you. You're going to have a terrific house."

"Thanks. I always loved this place." She could have told him more, like how she and Horace had spent so many hours making ice cream here in the kitchen, but she just couldn't bring herself to share any more of herself with him than she already had over the years. What would be the point?

Austin rubbed his eyes and leaned heavily against Wade.

"Someone's just about done for the night." Wade picked him up, and the child nestled against his chest and closed his eyes. "And I guess you have some things you wanted to do here."

She walked them to the door.

"Thanks again, Wade. I appreciate you giving me a hand."

"My pleasure. Anytime I can help out, give me a call. I'm pretty good at painting ceilings and doing the cutwork."

"Thanks. I'll keep that in mind," she said, knowing full well that she'd walk through fire before she asked for his help.

Wade walked down the uneven path to the gate, then turned suddenly. "Hey, do you have a ladder?"

"What?" She stepped outside.

"A ladder. You didn't have one in the car, and I

didn't see one in the house." He leaned over to place Austin in the stroller.

"I didn't think about needing one," she admitted. How could she have forgotten a ladder?

"Even as tall as you are, you'll still need one to reach the tops of the windows and the ceiling." He smiled. "I saw one in the carriage house the other day. I'll drop it off."

"No, Wade, it's okay. I can pick one up at the hardware store tomorrow."

"Why go to the trouble when we have one? As far as I know, Berry's not planning on doing any painting anytime soon, so you don't have to worry about returning it until you're finished."

"Really, Wade—"

"See you." He waved and started to jog down the street. Steffie walked to the end of the drive. He did look good in jogging shorts, she'd give him that. She thought back to the other morning, when he'd stopped at the shop wearing jogging shorts and a tank. Now, *that* was a nice picture to call up, she couldn't deny it.

She started to turn back to the house when Wade surprised her by looking back over his shoulder and waving just before he turned the corner onto Parish House Road, and her heart twirled around in her chest.

Now, why did he have to do that?

"Immune. Right." She snorted and jammed her hands into her pockets and walked back into the house. "Way to hang tough, Wyler."

* * *

"Did you try the new pumpkin spice latte?" Vanessa poked Steffie in the middle of her back. "Carlo is going seasonal this year."

Steffie shook her head. "I know this is a revolutionary thought, but how 'bout coffee that just tastes like coffee all year round? No need to change with the season, no need to be creative."

"You change your ice-cream flavors with the seasons," Vanessa reminded her.

"Ice cream is different. It has to have a flavor. Coffee already has one." Stef stirred her mug of breakfast blend. "Oddly enough, it's called 'coffee.' "

"You could just make vanilla."

"Boring."

"My point exactly."

"Nah, you can't compare." Stef took a chair at the table where Grace, Nita, and Barbara were already seated. "And you have to be seasonal because if you use fresh fruits, they have to be in season. Strawberries in early summer, peaches later, apples even later." She took a sip. "Other stuff in between."

"But strawberries seem to be in season all the time, somewhere." Nita looked up as Vanessa and Stef sat down.

"But I prefer stuff when it's in season here," Stef said.

"What do you do in February when you want to make strawberry ice cream?" asked Barbara.

"I use the berries I froze the June of the previous year."

"So, they're not really in season when you use them," Vanessa pointed out smugly.

"But they were in season when I froze them, so

technically, they count." Stef held up her mug. "And coffee is always in season."

The women debated the merits of flavored coffee over unflavored for another minute.

"Stef"—Nita leaned forward slightly to make eye contact—"was that Wade MacGregor I saw helping you unload your car last night?"

"I was unloading the car, and he just happened to be passing by on a walk with Austin." Stef raised an eyebrow. "Where were you?"

"I just happened to be driving by and I saw him getting something out of the back of your car," Nita explained.

"I bought paint," Stef told her.

"My, you're not letting any grass grow under your feet, are you?" Grace smiled.

"I want to move in as soon as possible," Stef explained. "Why should I keep paying rent when I have a house of my own?"

"And it's a lovely house, dear." Grace patted Steffie's hand. "I hope you'll be very happy there."

"Thank you, Miss Grace. I know I will be."

"So how much paint did you buy that Wade had to carry it for you?" Vanessa asked.

"I bought enough for the entire downstairs. And my bedroom. Oh, and my bath. And Wade didn't have to help carry it. He was just being kind. 'Cause of his sister and my brother, you know . . ."

"So tragic about his wife," Grace murmured. Every head at the table swiveled in her direction at the same time, as if on cue.

"What? What did you hear?"

"What tragedy?"

"Who told you . . . ?"

"I'm sorry," Grace said softly. "I thought everyone knew."

"Knew what?" Stef asked.

"Well, about Wade's wife dying." Grace looked somewhat chagrined to find out that she'd possibly be the source of gossip.

"What? She *died*? As in, DIED?" Vanessa gasped. "When? What happened to her?"

"And who told you?" Barbara asked.

Steffie sat mutely, taking it all in.

"Well, now, if I'd known that no one knew, I wouldn't have said anything." Grace was almost apologetic, but it was too late. The beans had been spilled, as Barbara was only too happy to remind her.

"Yes, but you did, so now you have to tell us everything you know," Barbara prodded.

"Well, it seems he was married to Austin's mother, who passed away from an illness. I didn't want to pry and ask Berry for too many details, you know." Grace glanced around the table. "Lest I appear insensitive."

"God forbid," Nita deadpanned.

"Who was she?" Steffie asked.

"She was his partner. The woman he went into business with. She got sick and died just recently."

"How recently?"

"I don't know for certain, Stef, but I believe it was over the summer," Grace told her. "Berry said he wrapped up all their business in Texas and closed up shop, then packed up that trailer he hauled up here. Just pulled up stakes and came on back."

"How long is he planning on staying, did she say?" Vanessa asked.

"It didn't occur to me to ask."

"Did anyone get the feeling that Berry and Dallas were as surprised as everyone else in town when Wade showed up with that little boy?" Nita looked from one face to the other. "Steffie, your brother is practically a member of the MacGregor family. Did Grant say if Dallas had mentioned that her brother had a child?"

Steffie shook her head, and her fingers began to tear tiny pieces off her paper napkin.

"Now, does that seem odd to anyone besides me?" Nita asked.

"It does." Barbara nodded. "That boy is what, a year and a half, maybe? Berry is, as you all know, a neighbor of mine. I see her several times a week, but she's never mentioned that Wade had a son. I can't imagine that she'd have known she had a great-grandnephew but didn't bother to mention it. It's not her style."

"Stef, at Beck's wedding, did Wade mention a wife?" Nita looked Stef right in the eye. No beating around the bush there. "You did spend a lot of time . . . *chatting* with him that night."

"Never said a word, Nita." Stef felt her cheeks flush. Leave it to Nita to come up with a clever euphemism for what Wade and Stef had been doing that night.

"Grace, did Berry say what the wife died from?" Barbara asked.

Grace shook her head. "No, and I didn't want to press her to find out what the circumstances were. All

I could think of was how sad for that little boy to lose his mama before he was old enough to really know her," Grace told them. "And how sad for Wade to be a widower so young."

Everyone nodded in agreement that it was sad, indeed. Except for Steffie, who, more confused than ever, downed the rest of her coffee. "Gotta run," she told the others. "I'm getting a late start today."

"When are you going on your new fall hours?" Grace appeared relieved to have the conversation moving in a different direction.

"As of next week, we'll be closing at seven, except for Friday and Saturday nights," Stef said. "With the kids back to school and the evenings getting cooler, there's no point in staying open later than that."

She gathered the shredded napkin and her mug.

"I'll see you all later." She started to walk away from the table.

"Stef, by the way, was that you I saw coming out of Enright's office today?" Barbara asked.

"The firm handled Horace's will. There were some papers I had to sign for the house." Stef smiled. These ladies didn't miss a trick. Between Nita, Barbara, and Grace, they pretty much had the whole town covered.

"That Enright boy can write my will any day." Barbara wiggled her eyebrows.

"He is a dear young man, isn't he?" Grace smiled. "I was glad to see one of the younger Enrights step in to keep the family practice going."

"Now, which of Mike's brothers is Jesse's father?" Nita asked.

"The oldest one. Craig. He used to be married to Delia Enright, the mystery writer," Grace told them.

"She and Craig divorced years ago, and he married Lainie, his current wife, Jesse's mother."

"I saw Jesse in the market the other day," Nita said. "He was picking up one of the flyers for Natalie's Run."

"He said he was going to run," Stef replied.

"I think it's so nice that the town gets behind that charity run every year," Grace said. "What a nice way to honor your late sister, Steffie."

"We are grateful to everyone who participates," Stef told her. "I hope I'll see you all there next Saturday."

Everyone at the table nodded.

"Great. Thank you. I appreciate it." Stef grabbed her purse from the back of her chair. "And this time, I'm really leaving."

She tossed the remains of the napkin into the trash and left her mug on the counter for Carlo. Walking back to Scoop, she thought about the good people of St. Dennis who were willing to donate their time and their money to run—or walk—to raise funds for childhood leukemia, the disease that had taken her sister, Natalie. Only eighteen months old—roughly Austin's age—when Natalie died, Stef had no memories of her sister, who'd been four when she passed away. There were photographs, but few of Stef and Natalie together. Natalie had been diagnosed when Stef was only five months old. Of the four Wyler siblings, Natalie had been the closest to Stef in age, and even though she'd never known her, Stef had always felt a connection to her. She wished Natalie had lived long enough for Stef to have some personal recollection of her, some memory that had been hers and hers alone.

She couldn't help but feel sick about Wade's wife. Had the woman been dying when she and Wade had been dancing the night away?

Uh-uh. Wade would never have left a dying wife.

But when was she his wife? And what if he hadn't known she was dying?

She shook her head almost imperceptibly as she walked along. Grace said the woman had been ill. He wouldn't have left her if he'd known she was on her deathbed, even for Beck's wedding. Which led to the question of whether or not he was married at Beck's wedding. But wouldn't Berry have referred to the woman as his *ex*-wife if he hadn't been?

Too many questions, far too few answers.

It must be so very difficult for Wade, Stef thought, to have had to bury someone he loved. And surely, he had loved her, if he'd married her, right?

And yet there was this . . . *something* between the two of them, some sort of fission that activated whenever she and Wade got within fifty feet of each other. She'd felt it last night at the house, and she was pretty damned sure that he'd felt it, too. Did that sound like a man who was mourning the loss of his true love?

And didn't it just suck for poor Austin to have lost his mom at so young an age? She viciously kicked a stone across the asphalt in the parking lot on his behalf. As tough as it was for her not to have known her sister, it was much sadder for Austin. All he'd know of his mother is what he'd hear from Wade or other people. He'd know her face from photographs, but he'd never know the sound of her voice or the way she smelled or the feel of her arms around him.

With the back of her hand, Stef wiped away tears for a dead woman whose name she didn't even know—a woman who'd won the love of the man she herself had wanted—but she couldn't wipe away her curiosity. Surely Wade had grieved for his wife, but somehow, Stef hadn't had a sense that his heart had been broken beyond repair, the way her parents' had been after Natalie's death. In Wade, she saw a deep sadness, but not the kind of grief that destroyed the soul.

What, she wondered, more confused than ever, was missing from this picture?

Diary ~

I heard the nicest bit of news—Horace Hinson has left his lovely old home on Olive Street to his cousin (twice removed, if I recall correctly), Steffie Wyler. And for my money, he couldn't have made a better choice. Steffie was always the old boy's favorite—why, I remember interviewing him for the paper once, right before he went to live in the home up in Ballard. He mentioned how he regretted never having married and having a family of his own, and how only his cousin Shirley Wyler's children came to visit him, and how, when she was just a little girl, he'd taught Steffie how to make ice cream on an old hand-crank number his mother used to use. So it's fitting that she should have the house where she learned her trade, I would think. Horace would be so proud of her.

I admit I have often wondered why Horace never married. Years and years ago, I heard my mother and one of her friends whispering some rumors that there'd been a love affair that was doomed from the start, but I never heard the name of the woman. Neither, apparently, had my mother or her friend, since I seem to recall that trying to guess who the lady in question might be was at the heart of their gossip.

Speaking of houses—I do not know what to make of this: Vanessa was chatting about having found a Ouija board in her attic, and how it claims to be guided by a spirit named Daz. Now, I find this strange, indeed—one would think that if any otherworldly spirit inhabited the old place, it would have been Alice Ridgeway, who'd lived in that house for ninety-some years and who, let's face it, knew her way around a Ouija board. I daresay the board Vanessa found had belonged to Alice, once upon a time.

Which just served to remind me that I must once again ask Vanessa to look in the attic for those journals of Alice's. And, of course, to let me know if she finds them. I shudder to think of what might happen to . . . well, certain reputations if those old books fell into the wrong hands! What a mess that would be!

And speaking of which, I certainly made one the other day in Cuppachino. We were discussing young Wade MacGregor and I lamented the fact that his poor young wife had died so recently. Well, how was I to know that no one else knew that he'd been married, to whom, and that he was now a widower?! Way to spill it, Gracie!

~ Grace ~

Chapter 7

STEF, you have to come now, right now," Vanessa demanded. "Whatever it is you're doing, drop it and come over *right now.*"

Steffie checked her cell phone for the time of her friend's call. Almost forty minutes ago. She was just about to hit return call when the phone rang.

"What's taking you so long? Why aren't you here? What about *right now* do you not understand?"

"Ness, I just got the message." Stef frowned. "Is something wrong? Are you all right?"

"I'm fine. But there's something you need to see."

"I'm on my way."

Stef grabbed her bag and locked the front door. She'd hoped to have gotten at least one of the kitchen windows painted that night, but apparently that was going to have to wait. Whatever was happening at Vanessa's must be really important, Stef thought as she locked the house behind her, because she sounded really fired up.

Less than four minutes later, Steffie was walking into Vanessa's cozy bungalow on Cherry Street.

"What is going on?" she asked as she came into the house.

"Come into the living room." Vanessa closed and locked the door behind her. "They're in there."

"Wait! Let me guess." Stef stopped in the foyer. "You were fooling around with the Ouija board and it told you that you there's a tall, dark, and handsome man in your future."

"I could remind you that I already have my tall, dark, and handsome man in my *present,* but some might consider that gloating." Vanessa led the way into the living room and sat on the sofa.

"What are those old books?" Stef stopped to check out the array of faded leather-bound volumes that were lined up one by one across the coffee table.

"That's what you need to see." Vanessa patted the sofa cushion next to hers. "Sit right here, and let me show you . . ."

She picked up the nearest book and opened it to a page she'd marked with a slip of paper.

"Remember I told you that old Miz Ridgeway left a ton of stuff in the attic?"

"Right." Steffie nodded and took a seat. "No surprise there, though. Her family built this house, and she lived here forever. She was ancient when she died. We knew that."

"Well, here's something you don't know." Vanessa lowered her voice. "Miz Ridgeway . . . dabbled."

"What do you mean, she dabbled?" Stef frowned. "You mean she painted?"

"No, I mean she *dabbled.*" Vanessa was almost whispering. "In *spells.*"

"What are you talking about?" Steffie laughed out

loud. "Are you saying that Alice Ridgeway was a wit—"

Vanessa clamped a hand across Steffie's mouth. "Don't say it!"

"Oh, for crying out loud, Ness." Stef slipped from Vanessa's light grasp. "You're talking about a woman who never left her house. She was agoraphobic."

"So?"

"So don't you think if she'd dabbled in spells that she'd have put a spell on herself to kick the agoraphobia so that she could go out into the world like a normal person and live her life?"

"Maybe it wasn't agoraphobia. Maybe it was a spell that someone else put on her."

"You make it sound as if St. Dennis was a hotbed of witchery." Stef was clearly amused.

"It was." Vanessa turned the book around and shoved it at Steffie. "Read."

Steffie leaned forward and began to read aloud but Vanessa stopped her. "Not out loud."

Steffie's eyes skimmed the page.

"Okay, so some of the local girls thought Miz Ridgeway knew some spells and they wanted her to teach them what she knew." Stef shrugged. "It sounds harmless enough. She was a lonely old woman and these kids probably thought she was more into it than she was because she never left the house and hardly anyone ever saw her."

"Did you read the names of the young girls who wanted to learn how to do spells?"

Stef looked back to the book and turned the page.

"Holy crap!" she exclaimed.

Vanessa pointed to the top of the page. "Beryl

Eberly." She looked up. "Do you think this is how she became a famous actress? By casting a spell to bring her fame and fortune?"

"Nah. Berry is naturally a great actress. I doubt she had to resort to magic. Besides," she pointed out, "according to Miz Ridgeway's own words here, all these girls wanted was to learn a love spell."

"Aren't you just a tiny bit curious as to why a woman like Berry would be interested in a love spell?"

"Maybe she was just going along with the crowd." Stef's eyes fixated on one name in particular. "Helen Kay Hinson. Huh. How about that?"

"Who's Helen Kay Hinson?"

"That's my nana Cummings's maiden name. My mother's mother. She would have been a little younger than Miz Ridgeway." She grinned. "I guess that's how she roped old Winston in."

Stef looked up. "Winston Cummings was my grandfather. They owned the house on Cullen Drive where we grew up. We moved in with Nana when I was just a baby, right after my grandfather died."

"Why didn't she move in with you?"

"Because she had the big house, and she was by herself, and my parents had a small house and four kids. It worked out better for everyone that way." Stef looked back at the page. "Anyway, I think it's sweet that she wanted to cast a love spell on him. I think it's sort of romantic; whether it was real or just so much hooey, it's sweet that she wanted him to notice her that much."

"I think the spell is for something more than 'notice me.' " Vanessa pointed to a name on the page. "Who's Elinda Esterhouse?"

"That's Mrs. Carlson. Reverend Carlson's wife."

"The minister's wife wanted to learn how to cast spells?"

"She wasn't a minister's wife back then. She was a bit younger than Nana, so she might have just been influenced by the older girls. You know, young and impressionable. She passed on a few years ago, or we could have asked her about it."

"Well, damn." Vanessa frowned. "We need to find someone who's still alive."

"Well, there's Berry. She's still very much alive."

Vanessa looked at Steffie as if she'd grown a second head. "Like a famous movie star is going to admit she had to resort to a love spell to make someone fall in love with her." She tapped her fingers on the page. "Wouldn't you love to know who Miz Berry had the hots for back then?"

"I'm betting it was Archer Callahan. He was her guy before she went to Hollywood."

"Then I guess whatever spell she used wasn't very effective, since she didn't marry him."

"But he asked her to, I'm pretty sure. And I'm pretty sure she said no."

"Hmm. Why put a love spell on someone and then turn them down when they propose?" Vanessa wondered.

Stef shook her head. "I don't know what was going on between them back in the day, but there were a lot of rumors."

"Like what?"

"Well, the big one was that Ned—that's Dallas and

Wade's father—was really Berry's son and not her sister's."

"What?" Vanessa's eyes grew round.

Steffie nodded. "Don't be repeating that, but that was what was going around for years. I remember overhearing my mom and dad talking about it once. Mom said that half the people in town thought it was nonsense, and the other half swore it was true."

"Wow. Talk about your basic bombshell. If it's true, that is." She fell silent for a moment, then said, "So what do you think the spell would have been about?"

"I don't believe in spells, Ness."

"I don't know if I do or not," Vanessa murmured. "But these ladies did."

"They were just girls back then. You know what it's like when you're fifteen or sixteen and someone gets something like this into their head. Didn't you play with tarot cards and stuff like that at pajama parties when you were in high school?"

"I never did sleepovers when I was in high school. I didn't have any girlfriends."

"Seriously? Not one time?"

"Nope. I was the girl from the wrong side of the tracks, you know?" Vanessa looked wistful. "I don't even know what girls did at those things."

"You ate junk food and listened to tapes and called boys, and if the parents weren't home, sometimes you all snuck out to meet the boys, who always knew where the pj parties were. Then the parents would find out or come home and the boys would scatter and the girls would come back inside and watch scary movies."

"Sounds like fun."

"It was." Stef knew that her friend had had an unconventional upbringing, but she hadn't known she'd been without friends. "Sleepovers were always fun. Next time Grady takes one of his wilderness groups into the wilds of the Montana mountains for a few days, I'm coming over to spend the night. I'll get some scary movies from the movie store out on the highway and we'll stay up all night watching them. We'll sleep here on the living-room floor and we'll eat ice cream and popcorn and stuff."

"Can we have s'mores?"

"Are they a favorite?"

Vanessa shrugged. "I never had them, but I heard they were treats that you eat when you're camping. Sleeping in the living room is sorta like camping."

"Good point." Stef pointed to the fireplace. "Does that work?"

"Sure. Hal told me to have a chimney sweep clean it out last year after I bought the place. We used it a couple of times last winter. Grady had some wood delivered so that it would be seasoned when the cold weather gets here."

"Then it's ice cream, popcorn, and s'mores for sure. I'll bring the goodies." Stef turned her attention back to the list. "Oh, but look! Grace Ellison's name is here."

"Who's Grace Ellison?"

"Miss Grace."

"Really? Well, that explains it," Vanessa told her. "Miss Grace asks me every other week if I've found any journals or diaries that Miz Ridgeway might have kept." Her eyes danced with mischief. "Now we know why. She's afraid I'll find these and tell everyone."

"We're not going to tell *any*one."

"Of course not. I suppose it could be embarrassing for a woman to have her sixty-year-old business put out there for everyone to know about," Vanessa agreed. "But I am going to let her know that I found the journals. I think she'd like to have them."

Vanessa's phone rang and she excused herself to take the call. Steffie continued reading the journals that had been written in Alice Ridgeway's delicate hand. When Vanessa returned, she apologized.

"Sorry. It was Maggie. She just wanted to know if I was all right with her staying at Hal's for a while. Which, of course, I am not."

"Not really your business, though."

"She made it my business by asking."

Vanessa was clearly unhappy that her mother, Maggie Turner, had come to St. Dennis seeking a relationship with not only her daughter, but her son, Beck, and Beck's father, Hal Garrity, as well. Everyone in town knew that Maggie and Hal had been in love once upon a time, and that Maggie, finding herself pregnant with Beck after Hal had deployed for Vietnam, had married another man. Until recently, though, no one—not Hal, or Beck, or Vanessa—had heard the real story—the whole story—that Maggie's parents had forced their very young, pregnant daughter to marry a man she didn't love. That marriage had been doomed from the beginning, as had all of Maggie's subsequent marriages. Vanessa still wasn't sure just how many trips to the altar her mother had taken, but lately, it was pretty clear that Maggie had her heart set on winning back Hal. For his part, Hal showed absolutely no signs of resisting her efforts, a fact that wasn't lost on her son or her daughter—or anyone else in St. Dennis.

"I hope to God Maggie never finds out about the love spells," Vanessa grumbled. "Hal would be a goner for sure."

"I hate to be the one to point this out, but Hal's already over the moon as far as your mother is concerned."

"Well, that just makes my night." Vanessa took back the book and closed it, sending a puff of dust into the air. They both sneezed.

"Hal loves her, Ness."

"God only knows why."

"She's pretty and she's charming when she wants to be, and she cares about him."

"She's charming because she wants something from him."

"What do you think she wants, Ness? You've said yourself that her last husband left her well off, so she isn't after his money." Stef took the book back from Vanessa. "I think she wants to be a family again."

"She waited long enough to do that."

"Better late than never."

"Not necessarily. Besides, Beck still doesn't want to have anything to do with her. After the way she dumped him on Hal's doorstep when he was fourteen, I can't say that I blame him."

"Ness, I know you had it hard growing up . . ."

"Hard?" Vanessa snorted. "We moved more times than I can remember, she was never without a man in her life, and she changed men as often as she changed our address. I didn't even know that I had a brother—well, half brother—until I was in my twenties and she told me to come to St. Dennis and meet him and his father."

"How many times have you said that was the best thing that ever happened to you?"

"Coming to St. Dennis *was* the best thing that ever happened to me. No one ever had a better big brother than Beck, or a finer father than Hal. Okay, so he isn't my real father, but he's the closest thing I've ever had to one. All that being true doesn't make everything else my mother did right or excusable."

"Hal is a good man, Ness. He has the biggest heart of anyone I've ever known. And besides, he never stopped loving her. He, of all the people I know, deserves to be happy."

When Vanessa started to protest, Stef said, "And has it ever occurred to you that maybe Maggie never stopped loving him, either? That maybe all those years, all that time, she was just trying to re-create what she'd had with Hal?"

"Well, I don't want her trying to re-create it with the help of this book."

"While you were on the phone, I read a few more pages. I think Miz Ridgeway was more amused by the girls than anything else. She says . . . where did I see it . . . ?" Steffie scanned the pages again.

"Oh, here. Listen to this." Stef began to read aloud.

"The girls were back at my door today, wanting to know if they could come in to visit. Well, my curiosity got the best of me and I did invite them in. One by one, I asked them to tell me their names. These chil-

dren . . . and they're all just children, I think Berry Eberle might be the oldest of the girls who have called on me but she wasn't with this bunch today. None more than sixteen or seventeen, I would guess. I served tea, as I would have done for their mothers or their aunts—all of whom are well known to me, which made the entire exchange that much more amusing."

"Amusing?" Vanessa asked. "She said 'amusing'?"

Stef nodded. "She goes on to say how these girls finally came right out and asked her about her magic, and would she teach them how to cast love spells, but she told them she thought they were a bit young and perhaps they could talk again when the girls were older. Then she adds, *I thought that would be the end of it, but two of the girls came back—alone—over the next few days, and since they were the older ones from the group, and seemed most sincere, I made up something on the spot and that seemed to satisfy them.*"

Stef looked up at Vanessa. "Don't you think that means that the whole thing was just sport to her? She said she 'made something up on the spot.' If she knew any 'real spells'—if there are such things—she wouldn't have had to make one up."

"I don't know. She has pages where she lists combinations of words, and then she has books where she talks about this combination of herbs or that." Vanessa pointed to another of the books on the table. "There. Open that one."

Stef did, and found page after page of herbal combinations, written in the same fine hand as the journal.

"These could be recipes for just about anything. Remedies to cure colds or fevers or keep ants out of the pantry."

"If they were recipes, wouldn't she have noted that? Wouldn't that say, 'Treat a cold with this' or something?"

"I have no idea." Stef sneezed. "Sorry. The dust is starting to get to me."

"I think they're herbs that she used with spells. I bet one of them is a love potion. Don't you remember, when I moved in, there were bunches of dried plant stuff over all the doors and window?" Vanessa folded her arms over her chest. "I bet they were herbs and she was using them to ward off evil spirits or evil spells."

Stef paged through the book slowly. Was there such a thing as a love potion? If so, was it in this book?

"I don't believe in love potions or love spells," she said aloud.

"But if there was one, wouldn't you want to know?" Vanessa poked at Stef. "Come on, wouldn't you want to slip a little something to a certain someone? Wouldn't you say the right combination of words if you thought it would—"

"No, I would not." Stef closed the book.

"Seriously?"

"I don't think it's love if you have to cast a spell on someone." Steffie added, "You didn't have to cast a spell on Grady, and he's head over heels in love with you."

"That's different. We're soul mates."

Stef rolled her eyes. "Well, would you have wanted him if the only way you could have gotten him was to use magic? Which I don't believe in, as well you know."

"If he hadn't fallen in love with me, would I have used magic to make him love me?" Vanessa pondered the question, then nodded. "Unapologetically, yes. And don't you try to act like you're all above the notion, missy."

Vanessa grabbed the book from Steffie's lap. She opened it to a page and began to read in a low voice.

"Vanessa, what are you doing?" Steffie asked, but her friend continued to read.

"There," Vanessa said a moment later, after she'd finished and closed the book.

"There what?"

"There, I did it for you." Vanessa smiled smugly.

"Did what for me?" Steffie's eyes narrowed. "What did you do?"

"I cast a spell so that your soul mate would find you. Don't worry, I didn't mention any names. I just sort of threw the idea out there. The universe will pick it up, and—"

"You realize I don't believe any of this, and I think you made up whatever it was that you were just muttering."

"Maybe I did, and maybe I didn't. In any case, we'll see what we see, won't we?"

"You're as crazy as Alice Ridgeway, you know that?" Steffie laughed. "I think you need to call Grace tomorrow and let her know that you found what she's been after." She yawned and rose. "I've had enough for tonight, Ness."

Vanessa stood also and walked her friend to the

door. "Maybe I'll ask Miss Grace which of these incantations she used."

"You do that." Yawning again, Stef opened the front door and stepped outside.

"Obviously it worked. She told me once that she and her Dan were married when she was eighteen after they'd dated for only three months." Vanessa leaned against the doorjamb. "They went through college together, as young marrieds. Isn't that the most romantic thing you ever heard?"

"They'd known each other all their lives, Ness. They grew up together. It hadn't taken a potion or a spell for them to fall in love."

"Maybe so, but then again . . . maybe not."

Stef laughed and hurried to her car. The air had grown crisp and cool while she'd been inside, and rain had started to fall. She debated on whether to go back to Olive Street, but knowing that she wasn't likely to get any painting done tonight, she headed back to her apartment. It was still early enough for her to experiment with yet one more batch of lavender honey ice cream. She'd found dozens of recipes online, and though so far she hadn't found one totally to her liking, she was certain she would find the one that, with a few additions of her own, would be perfect for Dallas's birthday gift.

She turned onto her street, still intrigued by Vanessa's reaction to finding the journals left in her home by the previous owner. Everyone in town knew Alice Ridgeway, and everyone knew that she never left that house. To Steffie's mind, Alice's "dabbling" was no more than a lonely woman's attempt to amuse herself and fill the many empty hours she spent locked inside her home. The curiosity of some of St. Dennis's teenage girls wasn't at all surprising, since many girls of that age are impressionable and might find the whole idea of casting a love spell dramatic and romantic, both of which would hold a certain appeal.

Vanessa, however, wasn't a teenager anymore, so for her to show interest in the very idea that such a thing was possible struck Steffie as a bit curious in its own right. Steffie smiled in the darkness as she pulled into her driveway. First the Ouija board, now a book of spells. What would Vanessa come up with next?

Of course, she could only be pretending to believe, Stef reminded herself. In which case, her casting a love spell on Stef's behalf into the—what had she said, the universe?—was sort of endearing. The sort of thing a best friend would do as a way of assuring you that the love of your life really was out there somewhere.

In which case, Stef thought as she unstrapped her seat belt and prepared to run through the rain, she hoped he'd hurry up. Despite her protests to the contrary, she could use some help with the painting.

"What are you doing, dear?" Berry peered through the doorway of the carriage house, Ally, as always, at her side.

"I'm looking for a ladder." Wade stood in the middle of the room, his hands on his hips, and surveyed the contents. "There used to be one in here. I told Steffie we had one she could borrow. She's painting the kitchen in her house."

"I imagine Grant would have one she could use," Berry pointed out.

"I told her I'd bring her one."

"I see," Berry said with that all-too-familiar tone that told Wade she understood there was more than a ladder at stake here. "Try over there on your right, dear. Nearer to the wall. Look around near the canoe."

"Why don't you come in here and give me a hand," he teased.

"Are you crazy?" Berry harrumphed. "I've seen those shows on TV where people have piles of things that reach close to the ceiling, sort of like the way things are stacked in here. I'm not giving that old sled an opportunity to jump off that pile and land on my head."

Wade laughed. "You're talking about hoarders."

"Anyone looking inside here would suspect me of doing just that."

"The place could use a good cleaning out." He found the ladder against the wall and carried it outside, where he tested it and found it slightly unstable and covered with cobwebs. "I guess I should hose this off and then pound in a nail here and there where I think it's a little weak. I doubt she'd appreciate me bringing a ladder that was covered with spiderwebs and likely to collapse."

"Who wouldn't appreciate you?" Berry appeared momentarily distracted.

"Steffie."

"Remind me. Why does Steffie need a ladder?" Berry asked.

"She's painting the kitchen in her house," he told her. "The house she inherited from her cousin Horace. It's on Olive Street."

"I remember Horace's house on Olive Street." Berry nodded. "I went to several parties there—years ago, of course."

"Well, it's Steffie's house now, and she's redoing it before she moves in. It's pretty dingy and dark inside and it hasn't been painted in a dog's age." He leaned over and patted Ally on the head. "No offense, girl."

"When were you at Steffie's?"

"Austin and I were walking past the house the other night when Stef was unloading paint from her car. I helped her carry everything inside, so she gave us the tour. It's a really nice house."

Berry smiled. "I always thought that house had charm. The arched doorways, the leaded windows, the wainscot, the tiles around the fireplace—it's just a lovely, warm, friendly house."

"I agree." Wade hooked the old hose up to an outside spigot and turned it on. Water sprayed through cracks in the hose, which leaked like a sieve. "I guess I should run out to the hardware store and get a new one. This one is beat. I can pick up some nails and just stabilize a rung here and there."

"What were you going to do with the hose?" Berry frowned.

"I was going to clean off the ladder." He stood and dropped the nozzle. He went to the spigot and turned off the water. "Berry, are you all right?"

"Of course I am." She appeared puzzled. "Why wouldn't I be?"

"That's the second time in this conversation that you seemed to miss a beat." He shook his head.

"What are you talking about?" Her eyes narrowed and shot a laser beam directly to his.

Well, he thought, *she hasn't forgotten The Look.*

"First you asked me why I needed a ladder, and I told you it was for Steffie, who's painting the kitchen in her house," he said gently. "Then a few minutes later, you asked me to remind you why Steffie needed a ladder."

Berry shrugged. "So?"

"So then I said I was going to wash the cobwebs off the ladder, and two minutes later you asked me why I needed a hose."

Berry waved a hand as if to dismiss him. "I'm a little distracted, and a little tired. I'm not used to having such a young one in the house. Not," she hastened to add, "that I'd have it any other way. I adore that boy, as I suspect you know."

Wade nodded. "I do know that, and I'm grateful that you're putting us up for a while."

"I'm not rushing you, of course I don't want you to go, but I'm just wondering when you're leaving for Connecticut."

"I was planning on leaving next week, but I think now I'll wait until after Dallas's birthday party."

"That's only the weekend after this one coming."

"I know."

She started across the yard, but the uneven terrain made Wade nervous that she might fall. She didn't seem as steady on her feet as she used to be. He left the ladder leaning against the carriage-house wall and locked the door, then took Berry's arm and together they started across the lawn. Ally ran ahead to chase a dozen or so Canada geese from the grass. The birds squawked as they scattered and sought refuge on the river.

"It's a lovely morning," she said. "Can you sit with me for a few minutes over there under the trees?"

"Sure." He glanced up at the house. Austin was still napping and Dallas was inside reading. She'd let him know if his son woke up.

There were several white Adirondack chairs, and Berry lowered herself into the closest one.

"Don't you love to watch the river on days like this?" She smiled and gazed out across the water. "I know that fall is in the air and I know what the calendar says, but on days like this, I just want to hold on to the very last threads of summer. The sky is always so blue this time of the year."

"It's a beauty of a day, Berry." Wade nodded and sat in the chair next to hers.

"So." Berry turned to him. "You've agreed to use your brewmaster talents to make someone else's beer. How do you feel about that?"

Wade shrugged. "It's not what I thought I'd be doing at this point in my life, but then again, a lot hasn't gone as I'd planned."

"You didn't answer the question, dear. I asked you how you felt about someone else using your expertise to make their beer."

He winced. "Do I like the thought of my beer being bottled under someone else's label? No. Not one damned bit."

"Then why did you agree to work for someone else?"

"I closed up shop and sold the building and all my equipment, Berry. There were a lot of debts to be paid. I don't have a business of my own anymore." Even though he'd thought he'd accepted this fact, he still found it hard to talk about. "But I do have to work. I agreed to work for someone else because I need a job."

"Forgive me if I sound dense, dear, but why don't you start another business? Why do you have to sell all your secrets to another brewery?"

"For one thing, it takes a lot of money. For another, it just seems, I don't know, *disloyal* maybe, to start over again without Robin. The company had been her idea. She financed it."

"But you actually made the beer, am I right?"

Wade nodded.

"I see no reason why you shouldn't be making beer again. From all you've told me, Robin was a very level-headed young woman. Certainly you don't think she'd have wanted you to leave the business behind forever."

"Probably not," Wade admitted.

"Who's the fellow you're going to work for?"

"A guy I met at a couple of brewers' conventions."

"Oh? A former rival?"

Wade grimaced. For someone who'd momentarily appeared not to have followed a conversation a few minutes ago, she was right on point now.

"I guess you could call him that," Wade conceded, recalling the time when he and Robin had called Ted Billingsly that and more. "The guy made me a good offer, and like I said, I need a job."

"Maybe you should take more time off to think things over a little more carefully. You've been through a lot over the past few months, you know. Decisions made in haste, and all that."

"In all fairness to Ted, he has a business to run. He

can't wait indefinitely for me to show up. He wants to get this new line of beer into the stores for the holidays."

"He wants to get *your* beer into the stores for the holidays. With his labels on the bottles."

Wade nodded.

Berry poked him playfully on the arm. "You know, St. Dennis has never had its own beer. You could call it 'Berry Beer.' "

He laughed in spite of himself. "I'm afraid Berry Beer doesn't have a particularly manly ring to it."

"Perhaps not." Berry smiled. "But I still wish you'd stay awhile longer in St. Dennis." She sat back in her chair and gazed out toward the Bay. "I haven't had nearly enough of you or of that boy of yours."

"Don't you miss having your house to yourself? With Dallas and Cody here, and now Austin and me . . ."

"Bite your tongue. I wasn't aware of just how quiet things were around here until they no longer were. Frankly, I'm enjoying it. And look at it this way"—she leaned over to confide—"it's keeping me young. Why, it's almost like having Ned back again."

"Ned? You mean my father?"

Berry nodded, a faraway look on her face. "What a delightful boy he was. From the moment of his birth until the day he left us, he was the greatest joy of my life."

"Were you there, when he was born?" Wade asked.

"What?" Berry slowly turned to him.

"Were you there with your sister, when my dad was born? You said, from the moment of his birth . . ."

"I meant, from the time he was a newborn, of course." Berry turned her face back toward the Bay.

"I guess you and my dad were really close. I remember seeing pictures of him here in this house when he was really little."

"He stayed with me from time to time, when I was between pictures. Sometimes I took him to California with me, and several times to Europe."

"But not so much his sisters?"

"They were a pair of twits." Berry dismissed them with the wave of her hand. "Neither particularly smart nor interesting as children, less so as adults. Unlike Ned."

"How did your sister and brother-in-law feel about that? About you taking their son on trips but never their daughters?"

Berry shrugged as if it mattered to her as little now as it must have back then.

"So, in other words, you didn't care what they thought about that."

"Not in the least." She slanted a glance in his direction. "Why all the questions? Why the sudden interest in your father's early days?"

"I'm just curious. And it's not so sudden. I've always been interested in my dad. I was only seven when he died, remember?"

"I remember. Your mother brought you and Dallas here in the middle of a thunderstorm—at night—and essentially just dropped you off before she headed back to New Jersey." She smiled at Wade and added, "Which was perfectly fine with me, since Roberta and I never got along all that well."

"Why was that? I mean, I know my mom can be difficult at times . . ."

"Truthfully, I just never thought that she . . ." Berry paused, as if remembering that this was Roberta MacGregor's son she was talking to. "I never felt that she and I were on the same page much of the time. Conflicting personalities, and all that."

"How did she get along with Grandma Sylvie?"

"About what you'd expect," Berry sniffed. "My sister wasn't involved as much with Ned as she was with her daughters."

"You and Grandma Sylvie were twins, right?"

She nodded. "Physically, we were identical, but our temperments, our personalities, couldn't have been more different."

"How about Grampa?"

"Duncan went along with pretty much whatever Sylvie wanted, as far as the children were concerned. I believe he thought that taking care of the children was her realm."

"Even when it came to having his only son spend more time with you than he did with them?"

"Even then." Her eyes narrowed. "What brought this all on today? Has someone said something to you about your father that you'd like to discuss with me?"

"No." Puzzled, he shook his head. "What would someone have said?"

"Nothing of any consequence, I'm sure." She turned her wrist to check her watch. "Oh, look at the time. I told Dallas I'd pick up the sale papers for the warehouse she's buying from Hal Garrity when I was in town today. I'm meeting a friend for lunch at Captain Walt's, but I wanted to get the paperwork on the property resolved. It's going to make a fine movie studio for Dallas. I suppose I needn't tell you how thrilled I am that she's formed her own production company and she's going to be making her own movies."

"Would you like me to drive you?" Wade asked.

"Why on earth would I want you to do that?"

"I just thought maybe you'd like the company." He couldn't bring himself to say the words, that he was concerned about her. This morning had been the first time since he'd been home that Berry's memory had seemed a bit short-circuited. He'd have to ask Dallas if she'd noticed anything similar since she moved back.

"Dear, these days, I have all the company I need." Berry stood and stretched her back, then called Ally back from the dock. "Besides, one would almost get the impression that you think I might not be capable of driving myself." Her eyes narrowed. "I may get distracted from time to time, Wade, but I am not getting senile. Please feel free to ask Dr. Harmon, who keeps a close eye on such things. It may be hard to believe, but I have a number of things on my mind right now, any one of which would distract—dare I say it?—even someone *your* age."

"I'm sorry that the kids and I—"

"Oh, pooh on that." She shot him The Look again. "I'm talking about real distractions. For one thing, I'm preparing to return to the screen in my first film in . . . well, in more years than I like to think about."

"*Pretty Maids*. The film Dallas is going to make."

Berry nodded. "There's going to be a tremendous

amount of pressure on me. Everyone in Hollywood will be looking to see if I screw it up."

"You won't screw it up, Berry."

"Well, of course I won't, but it takes a lot of focus to get into a character like Rosemarie." She rested her arms on the back of her chair and looked toward the Bay. "I don't want to let Dallas down."

"You won't."

"And we're having a huge party here for Dallas's birthday, and then I suppose we'll be planning a wedding at some undisclosed future date. And there are . . . other things. Things I don't need to be discussing with you here in the backyard." She tried to smile. "At least, not yet."

"Are you okay? You're not sick or anything . . . ?"

"No, no. Nothing like that. Just . . . things I have to work out for myself. Decisions to make." She turned to the dock. "Ally, leave those poor geese alone. Come along, pup. It's time to go in."

The dog flew to her side, the geese apparently forgotten, and Berry bent over to stroke her head.

"You are such a good girl, Ally. Such a good and obedient girl. Let's go inside and see if we can find a treat with your name on it."

She tapped Wade on the head before starting toward the house. "And you're a good boy. A bit misguided at times, but a good boy all the same. Perhaps we'll find a treat for you in the kitchen as well."

Wade laughed in spite of himself, and set off for the carriage house to fix the ladder.

"Oh, and Wade?" Berry called to him. "Please don't make dinner plans for tomorrow night. We're having a guest. Someone I'd like you to meet."

"Sure. Who's coming for dinner?"

"My beau." Berry smiled and continued on to the house.

"Your *beau*?" Wade repeated, then called to her retreating form, "Did you say, your beau?"

Whether Berry had not heard him, or had heard and was ignoring him, he wasn't sure, but she never acknowledged his question.

"Berry has a beau," he muttered as he picked up the hose. "Does anyone even say 'beau' anymore . . . ?"

Chapter 8

BERRY was still on Wade's mind when Dallas came into the kitchen while he and Austin were eating lunch.

"What's this about Berry having a beau?" Wade asked.

Dallas grinned. "Oh, so she told you about Archer."

"Who's Archer?"

"Archer Callahan, who, I suspect, was the great love of Berry's life."

"How come I never heard of him?"

"I hadn't heard about him until this summer. I think she kept that part of her life to herself, but once he retired—he'd been a judge and then went back to practicing law and then I believe his wife died—anyway, he and Berry have gotten back together."

"You've met him?"

"Oh, sure. He comes for dinner every week, spends a day or two, then goes—"

"Spends a day or two where?" Wade frowned.

"Well, here, of course."

"Where does he sleep?"

"Anywhere he wants," she replied playfully, and poked her brother in the ribs.

"Seriously. Does he stay in the guest room?"

"Of course not. He stays with her."

"With Cody in the house? You think that's okay?"

Dallas stared at him. "Excuse me while I go into the basement and check for pods."

"Dallas . . ."

"Ha!" She snapped her fingers. "They're in the carriage house, aren't they?"

"Stop fooling around," he said. "You think it's okay for her to have a man sleeping over and staying in her room? With her?"

"Don't try to change the subject, Pod Person. Somehow you've changed my wild child brother into a prude."

"I'm not a prude, I just think she—"

"Should do exactly as she pleases because (a) she is an adult"—Dallas held up one finger—"and (b) this is her home. I don't comment one way or another because of *a* and *b*, and because it's none of my business."

"All good points." He nodded. "Still, what do eighty-year-old people . . ." He paused. "Never mind. I don't want to know."

Dallas laughed and went to the sink to fill the teapot with water.

"I did want to talk to you about Berry, though," he said. "She's going to be eighty-two on her next birthday, right?"

"Right." Dallas grinned. "Good luck getting her to admit it, though. Why do you ask?"

Wade related the conversation that he'd had with their great-aunt earlier that morning.

"You're saying that she had a problem following the conversation?" Dallas proceeded to make herself a cup of tea.

"You've been here much longer than I have this year. Have you noticed her having any memory lapses or forgetting things, that sort of thing?"

Dallas shook her head. "Well, nothing out of the usual."

"What's the usual?"

"You know, coming into a room and forgetting what she came in for, but I do that myself."

"Does she do it often?"

"Just occasionally." Dallas took the chair across from Wade at the table. "I haven't noticed anything that gave me pause, though. Nothing that's been a red flag."

"Do you think maybe we should have her make an appointment with her doctor, have him check to see if she has any other symptoms."

"Symptoms of . . . ?"

"Well, you know. Forgetfulness. Confusion."

"Oh, for crying out loud, Wade. Don't you think you're overreacting just a wee bit?"

"I don't remember her being forgetful like that before."

"You haven't really been around her very much these past few years," she reminded him.

"True enough. But she is past eighty, whether she wants to admit it or not."

"Are you sure it's really a problem? Maybe you've just forgotten that the elderly sometimes do things like that if they're not focused on the conversation. Did you call her on it this morning?"

"She said she was just distracted, that she has a lot on her mind."

"Of course, she has a lot on her mind, Wade. She's planning on making a film—a film in which she will be the big star name—for the first time in decades. She and I have been rehearsing lines every afternoon, she's so determined to give the exact right performance." Dallas went to the fridge and took out some cheese and an apple. "Sweetie, you have no idea how difficult it is to give a great performance—and Berry has always prided herself on being great. 'Good enough' has never been good enough for her, understand?"

Wade nodded.

"And she probably is distracted," Dallas continued, "with the kids and you and me here. She's used to a quiet life, she's lived alone for years. I know that she says she loves having us—and I'm sure she does—but maybe it's too much for her," Dallas said. "But of course, that won't be a problem in another few months. Grant and I will be getting married, so Cody and I will be moving into his house."

"So he's really the one? No more Mr. Hollywood?"

Dallas made a face. "I can't believe how lucky we are to get a second chance. When I think of all the years we've wasted . . ."

"So now you can make up for lost time." Wade patted her hand. "Grant's a terrific guy. I couldn't be happier."

"Me either." She opened the flatware drawer and searched for the cheese slicer and a paring knife.

Finding both, she returned to the table. "I feel like the luckiest person in the world right now. I really am the woman who has everything. A great guy, a great kid, a great opportunity to make films of my choosing right here in St. Dennis."

"You forgot to add, a great brother."

"You are a great brother. I can't even begin to tell you how happy I am that you are here with us, you and Austin."

"Thanks. We're happy to be here, aren't we, ace?"

Austin grinned through a mouthful of mac and cheese.

"Well, as far as Berry is concerned, I do think you're overreacting. I believe her when she says she's distracted, but if it makes you feel better, how 'bout if we both keep an eye on her." Dallas cut the apple into wedges and offered a piece to Wade, who declined. "But keep in mind that on top of everything else, she's excited about the big party we're having for my birthday—she's gotten involved with the planning and she's looking forward to seeing everyone who's coming from the West coast. She knows we're going to be planning a wedding soon, so she's looking forward to that. You know how she loves social events. Let's see how things are when everything dies down."

"Dallas, you know that I'm leaving in two weeks for Connecticut."

"You're still planning on going to work for that other guy?"

He nodded.

"Well, I don't understand why you couldn't start your own company here," she pointed out. "You don't have to go to Connecticut to make beer for someone else."

"Have you been talking to Berry?" He eyed her suspiciously.

Dallas shook her head. "Not about this. Why?"

"Because she and I just had this conversation this morning."

"Well, that proves my point," she said smugly. "There's obviously nothing wrong with the way Berry's thinking if she recognizes that you'd be better off here in St. Dennis."

"Look, like I told Berry, there's a lot involved. It's a little more complicated than merely deciding to do it. I don't have any equipment and I don't have any capital nor do I have any collateral to obtain credit," he said. "What I do have is a really good job offer from an up-and-coming brewery. All I have to do is show up every day and make beer. I don't have to run the business, I don't have to deal with the problems, and I get to leave at the end of the workday. All pretty appealing to a single parent."

"Well, let's think this through." She sliced off a thin rectangle of cheese and took a bite. "Say you go to work for this other guy, and you make your beer for him." She paused. "Did he make you sign a noncompete clause? And if you leave there, do all of your recipes stay with him? Can you open another brewery and use those same recipes elsewhere?"

"I haven't signed anything yet. It was a verbal offer and accept." He thought it over for a moment. "Though a contract was mentioned."

"Get a copy of that now, before you leave St. Dennis."

"I did request it. But I'll call him again and remind him that I'm still waiting for it."

"So say you go to work for him, and in three or six months you decide you hate working for someone else. If you've already signed away your brewing secrets, you're screwed, Wade."

"True enough. Though Ted didn't mention that that would be part of the deal, that whatever I bring with me has to stay with him if I leave."

"It will be in there, once his lawyers get their hands on it." She cut another paper-thin slice of cheese. "So let's talk alternatives. You mentioned the expense. I could loan you the start-up money."

Wade watched Austin drop a handful of macaroni onto the floor.

"Thanks, Dallas, but I don't know that I have the mental energy to start another business from the ground up. Ted's offer is appealing because everything will be set up by the time I get there, and I won't have to invest anything except my talent for brewing beer." He smiled. "Which I admit is considerable."

"Oops." Austin leaned over the side of high chair to point at the mess. Wade cleaned it up with a napkin, which he tossed into the trash.

"Besides, I'd feel like I'm taking advantage of you."

"Please. You're my brother. Only one I have. And note I said 'loan,' not 'give.' Then again, maybe I'd rather be a silent partner."

"I'll think about it."

"Please do that."

"I'd think you'd have your hands full with starting up your own business."

Her eyes danced. "My own production company.

My own creative team, my own films. I do believe I have died and am on my way to heaven. But I digress. Why not draw up some figures for me and we'll talk about it?"

"That's very generous of you." He sliced a piece off her apple and handed it to Austin. "But I've already pretty much committed."

"Oh, like you'd be the first person ever to change your mind about a job." She rolled her eyes. "Besides, you haven't seen the contract yet, so you couldn't have agreed to all the terms. Wait and see what kind of commitment he's talking about."

"I'll be real surprised if there's something in there that we didn't discuss, but I see your point. Like I said, I'll call and remind him that I'm still waiting for the contract."

"Did you like it? Making beer?"

"I really did. It was interesting and it was fun experimenting with different grains to make different flavors."

"Sort of the way Steffie makes her ice cream," Dallas noted. "She likes to experiment, too."

After a momentary lull, Dallas asked cautiously, "So, have you seen Steffie? Other than the day we all went into Scoop for ice cream."

"Just here and there around town." He shrugged, averting his eyes.

"Berry tells me she's now the proud owner of one of the old places off the Square."

"Yeah. It's a pretty cool house."

"Oh? You saw it?"

"Austin and I got a quick tour the other night while we were out on our walk."

Another bit of silence, again broken by Dallas. "So, have you talked to her? I mean, about Austin?"

He shook his head. "There hasn't been much opportunity. I did stop in for a moment at the shop the other morning, but one of her staff came in, and it just didn't seem appropriate. Besides, I don't know what to say to her."

"How about the truth, from start to finish?" When he opened his mouth to protest, she said, "I don't know what the relationship is between the two of you. Frankly, I don't think you do either. All I know is that you both get this look when you're in the same room at the same time, and neither of you can keep your eyes off the other. Don't interrupt me," she warned when he appeared about to do just that. "Even if she's no more than a friend to you—a friend you do have a bit of a history with, if what I've heard is true—then I think you owe her the truth, because you know this is a small town, and sooner or later she's going to hear some things that might be nothing more than idle gossip. If she hears the story—the entire story—from you, she'll know what the truth is. Wade." She tapped him on the arm. "It's the least you could do for a friend."

"You're right." He nodded slowly. "I guess I could talk to her tonight when I drop off the ladder." He looked at his older sister and said, "Thanks. I appreciate the advice. But you realize it's tough to have a serious conversation with Himself here running around. Which means you'll probably have to babysit tonight."

"Oh, that's such a hardship, isn't it, Austin?" Dallas ruffled her nephew's dark curls. "Poor Aunt Dallas has to spend time with her little guy. We always have fun, don't we? You and Cody and Berry and I?"

Austin nodded enthusiastically and craned his neck to look toward the front door. "Cody?"

"Not yet, pal. But you can come with me when it's time to pick him up from school," Dallas told him. "Maybe we'll stop and get some ice cream."

"Steppie." Austin clapped his hands.

Dallas shot Wade an amused glance. "Well, it looks like Steffie has more than one friend on River Road. I guess you wouldn't want to come with us?"

"Thanks but no." He pushed his chair back from the table and stood. "I have a ladder to fix."

The entire time Wade was tying the ladder to the roof of his Jeep with rope he found in the carriage house, he was trying to rehearse what he was going to say to Steffie.

"Listen. About Austin . . ." *Nah.*

"So maybe you're curious about Austin . . ." *Uh-uh.*

"Maybe you're wondering if I was married the night you and I . . . I mean, the night of Beck and Mia's wedding." *Ouch.*

By the time he arrived at the Olive Street house, he'd pretty much decided that this was one of those times when it would be best to wing it.

He'd been thinking about Steffie a lot since he left Texas, and he was coming to the conclusion that the less he thought about her, the better off he was going to be. There was something about her that drew him in. Dallas was right about that.

"Moth to flame," he muttered as he stopped in front of her house.

He untied the ladder, hoisted it onto his shoulder, and headed toward the front door. Her car was in the driveway and there were lights inside and music coming from somewhere. He rang the bell, and hoped that it worked, and that he wouldn't have to wait too long for her to answer it. His hands were sweating, and he told himself that was because he'd been reliving the past six months in his mind all afternoon in anticipation of talking to Steffie about Robin.

The door opening suddenly startled him. He took a step back and almost went down the porch stairs backward.

"Are you okay?" Steffie swung the door open wide.

"Sure. Fine. I just took a little misstep." He moved the ladder slightly to balance it.

"Hey, you really didn't have to—"

"I said I would."

"I didn't want you to go to any trouble."

"No trouble. Where would you like it?"

"I guess you can just leave it here in the entry." She stepped back and held the door for him. She was wearing a tank top, cutoff jeans, and bright orange flip-flops, and she had what appeared to be plaster dust in her hair. Wade's heart caught in his chest.

He leaned the ladder against one wall and glanced around at the strips of wallpaper that littered the floor.

"I hadn't planned on pulling it all off," she explained. "But there was a strip hanging, and once I pulled it, the piece next to it sort of sagged. Next thing I knew . . ." She pointed to the floor and shrugged. "Well, one thing led to another. Besides, it's therapeutic."

"You've got the whole entry almost stripped, though, so that's a good thing, right?" Wade opened the ladder and set it up next to the front wall where paper was still affixed to the top near the ceiling.

"I couldn't reach that," she said.

"That's why God invented the ladder." He reached up and pulled at a strip of paper. It came loose but left glue marks on the wall. He looked down at Steffie and asked, "You wouldn't have a scraper, would you?"

"I do, but you don't have to—"

"Maybe I could use a little therapy myself."

"I'll get the scraper." Steffie disappeared into the kitchen. A moment later she returned, unwrapping the new tool. "Here you go." She handed it to him.

"Thanks. Maybe you could go ahead and finish the lower part of the wall, and I'll do the area nearest the ceiling."

"This is really nice of you." Steffie pulled a long piece of paper and it peeled from the wall with ease.

"I'm a nice guy."

She let that pass without remark.

A moment later, he moved the ladder, removed a stray piece of paper, then climbed down.

"I think we're finished."

"Great." She turned and smiled. "Thanks. I appreciate your—"

"How 'bout this room?" He carried the ladder into the dining room. "Looks like you got a good start on this one, too."

"I just pulled off the stuff that was hanging. Look,

Wade . . ." She sneezed, then coughed. "I guess the dust is starting to get to me." She cleared her throat. "I have water in the fridge. Can I bring you a bottle?"

"That would be great, thanks." He hadn't wanted to mention it, but the dust was getting to him, too.

He turned on the dining-room light, then whistled. He was pretty sure he had his opening line down. He'd start out telling her about Robin, how they'd been best buds. Not lovers, they'd never been that. But best friends. He'd say, *I want to tell you about Robin.* And she'd say something like *Okay.* He'd take a deep breath and say, *Robin Kennedy was the first person I met when I arrived at school my freshman year—*

"What do you think of that dining-room wallpaper? Does anything say 'Welcome to 1943' like little pink flowers on a taupe background?" she called from the kitchen. "It's been there for as long as I can remember."

"It's good to get rid of all the old paper before you start to paint." He grabbed a loose strip and pulled it, releasing a cloud of dust and crumbling plaster. He paused. "You weren't planning on painting tonight, were you?"

"No, I wasn't."

"Good. It's better to get all the paper dust out of the way first. Otherwise, it can settle into the fresh paint and it will look like . . ." He peeled another strip of paper and let it drop to the floor.

He stared at the wall. Removal of the paper had revealed a large heart drawn directly onto the plaster. Inside the heart had been written HORACE LOVES DAISY.

"Stef, was your cousin Horace married?"

"Nope. Lived and died a single gentleman. Why do you ask?"

"You're going to want to see this."

"What?"

He went into the kitchen, and she turned to look over her shoulder.

"I can't get the cap off." Stef held up the water bottle.

Wade took it from her hand and gave it a good twist, then reached around her to sit it on the counter. She was still turned toward him, as close to him as she'd been when they'd danced. For a moment he was tempted to put an arm around her and lead her into a slow dance there in the kitchen. Instead, he smoothed her hair back from her face. One long strand had pulled from her ponytail, and he tucked it behind her ear.

"You're coming undone," he told her.

"You can say that again," she said wryly.

His hand skimmed along the contour of her face, his thumb tracing her cheek to the corner of her mouth. For that one moment, he wanted nothing more in life than to kiss that mouth. Her eyes held his and he knew he couldn't look away if he'd wanted to. His thumb followed the full curve of her bottom lip and she turned her head toward it. He lifted her chin and leaned in to kiss her, telling himself just one, just to see what he'd been missing, to see if kissing her would be as good as he thought it would be, even though he knew that was a lie. His lips brushed against hers lightly, but she made no move to pull away. Her hands slid up his chest, grabbing the fabric of his shirt and pulling him closer. He kissed her for real then, a long-drawn-out kiss that could have lasted forever, would have certainly lasted longer than it did had they not heard the front door slam.

It took a moment for either of them to react. Stef looked up into Wade's face quizzically, as if not quite sure she'd heard anything at all.

"Steffie?" a male voice called from the front hall.

"Were you expecting someone?" Wade asked as she disengaged herself from his embrace.

"No. I don't know who—"

"Steffie, are you here?" the voice called again.

"It's Jesse Enright," she told Wade.

"Who's Jesse Enright?" He frowned.

"My lawyer." She cleared her throat and called, "In the kitchen, Jesse."

"Good timing, Jesse," Wade muttered.

"I saw the lights and thought I'd stop in and see if you needed any help." A dark-haired man about Wade's age and height came into the kitchen.

"Hey, Jesse," Steffie greeted her visitor.

"Wade, this is Jesse Enright. My lawyer." Steffie looked up at the new guy. "Jesse, this is Wade MacGregor, an old friend."

"Nice to meet you." Jesse extended a hand to Wade.

"Likewise." Wade shook Enright's hand and wondered why the lawyer was calling on the client at ten at night.

"Am I interrupting . . . ?" Jesse asked Stef.

"We were just taking a little break," Steffie said, not really answering the question.

"Are you sure? I know it's presumptuous for me to

just pop in like this. But I worked late wrapping up a case and was taking a walk to clear my head and the lights were on when I passed by—"

"It's perfectly fine, Jesse."

"This is a terrific house. Nice high ceilings, nice large rooms, lots of windows, lots of light." He nodded appreciatively. "Very nice, Steffie."

"Thanks."

"Are you sure I'm not interrupting something?" he asked again.

"Actually, I was just about to show Stef what I found in the dining room," Wade said.

"You found something in the dining room?" she asked. "What is it?"

"You have to come see for yourself." Wade took her by the elbow. "You, too, Enright. You'll want to see this."

Steffie and Jesse followed Wade into the room, and he turned up the lights on the chandelier to better illumine the wall.

"Remember I asked you if Horace had been married?" Wade pointed to the wall. "This is why."

Steffie looked positively dumbstruck.

" 'Horace loves Daisy.' " She stared at the wall.

"Who's Daisy?" Jesse asked.

"I have absolutely no idea." She touched the plaster with her hand, running her fingers around the outline of the heart. "I wonder if Mom would know. Though it is strange that she never mentioned it."

She dialed her mother's number on her iPhone.

"Mom," she said, "did Horace have a girlfriend named Daisy?"

She explained their find.

"Yes, I'm sure that's what it says. It's big as life. I'll send you a picture . . ."

Stef disconnected the call, snapped the picture with her phone, and sent it to her mother. Moments later, her phone rang. She spoke briefly with her mother, then hung up.

"Mom is as mystified as I am." Stef stuck the phone back into her pocket and moved closer to the wall. "She has no idea what this means."

"I think it means he and Daisy had a thing going on," Jesse said.

"Why do you suppose he wrote that, then covered it up?" she wondered aloud. "It's big as life. It almost covers half that wall."

"Probably because he wanted to hide it," Wade said.

"But why?" Steffie frowned. "He had to know that sooner or later, someone would see it. Maybe I'll ask around," she said. "Maybe someone knows." She snapped her fingers. "Miss Grace! Miss Grace knows everything that ever happened in St. Dennis."

"There's always the possibility that Daisy wasn't from St. Dennis," Jesse noted.

"Or maybe she wasn't his girlfriend," Wade reasoned. "Maybe she was his secret crush."

"Maybe we'll never know." Stef continued to stare at the heart. "It's such a romantic gesture, to leave something like that for posterity. I was going to paint the walls. Now, though, I think I should repaper. Paint would cover that forever."

"I wonder if Daisy—whoever she was—knew how Horace felt about her," Wade mused.

"I hope so," Steffie replied. "It would be so sad

to . . ." She shook her head and the words trailed away. She turned to Jesse. "So I guess you wanted a quick tour of the house?"

"Actually, I need to get going. I have court in the morning." Jesse checked his watch. "Some other time, though."

"Sure. Anytime you see the lights on, stop in." Stef walked him to the door.

Jesse looked back over his shoulder to where Wade stood near the arch that led into the dining room. "Nice meeting you."

"You as well. I guess I'll see you around town."

"Sure." Jesse waved and went through the open door, and Stef followed long enough to be hospitable.

"That was nice of Jesse to stop in," she said when she came back inside and closed the door behind her.

"His timing could have been a little better," Wade said as he walked to her and wrapped his arms around her.

Steffie looked into his eyes and asked, "Wade, who was Austin's mother?"

The silence was so complete that they could have heard a pin dropping on the second floor.

Wade sighed. He'd planned for this. He'd even rehearsed it, but now all he could say was, "Her name was Robin Kennedy."

"That's a good start," Steffie told him. "I'm assuming there's more?"

"The main reason I came by tonight was to tell you about her. Well, that and to bring the ladder." He cleared his throat. "Mostly, I wanted you to know about her. It's a long, complicated story, Stef."

"I'm not going anywhere."

He nodded, and with his heart in his throat, he took a seat on the hall stairs. He wanted Stef to know everything, but it wasn't an easy story to tell.

"Wait one second." Stef disappeared into the kitchen, then returned with their water bottles. She handed one to him and said, "Okay, now you can start."

"Robin was the first person I met when I arrived on campus my freshman year. We were in the same dorm. She was pretty and lively and just so smart and so much fun." He smiled at the memory. "Did you ever meet someone you had an instant connection with?"

Steffie nodded.

"Well, that was how it was with Robin. We were best friends. All four years. We shared an apartment for three of those years." He glanced down at her and thought he saw her flinch. "It was never a romantic relationship, Stef. When I say we were best friends, that's exactly what I mean."

He took the top off the water and took a sip. Talking about it was so hard.

"When Robin was a senior in high school, her parents were involved in an auto accident with some big country-music star who was driving drunk. Both Robin's parents were killed. There was a huge insurance settlement—eight figures. Robin was an only child."

"So the entire settlement went to her."

Wade nodded. "So four years later, senior year, it's getting close to college graduation, and neither of us knows what we want to do. We talked about going into business together, and to make a long story short, we decided we were going to make beer. Of course, neither of us had a clue about how to go about it, so we had a lot to learn. But we both studied up and we talked to other people who'd started their own breweries, and KenneMac Brews was born."

He began to peel the label from the water bottle.

"But your company did well, right? I heard your beer won awards and was written up in magazines."

"Yeah, we did. We made a great product, we made a profit, and we were having one hell of a good time."

"So what happened?"

"Robin had been dating this guy toward the end of senior year. He seemed nice enough." Wade picked at another strip of paper from the label. "But after graduation, he just sort of disappeared. Then about three years ago, he popped up. Said he'd been in the navy. Anyway, he and Robin started dating again; the next thing I know, she's madly in love and asking me if I have any objections to bringing him into the company." Wade shrugged. "He said his degree was in business management, so it seemed like a good fit. I was spending more and more time actually brewing beer and Robin was doing the marketing and selling, so it seemed like the right time to bring in someone who could keep the books and pay the taxes. Besides, who was I to stand in the way of her happiness? And she was happy, Stef. She really loved this guy. She was talking about marrying him. Even asked me if I'd give her away at the wedding."

Stef turned all the way around to look up at him. "I'm sensing something really bad coming right about now. Tell me he didn't—"

"He did. Sucked the company dry. He'd even

talked her into letting him 'invest' some of her personal money."

"I'm guessing the only thing he invested in was himself."

Wade nodded.

"That bastard. Poor Robin." Stef frowned. "Damn. That just sucks."

"It gets worse. A few weeks after she realized he'd embezzled from the company and had taken off with a good-size chunk of her personal funds, Robin found out she was pregnant."

"Austin."

"Yes, Austin. Right from the start, she wanted to keep her baby, but she was bothered about what to put on the birth certificate. She didn't want to put the real father's name on it. She didn't want this guy to ever know that he'd fathered her child. But at the same time, she didn't want to put 'unknown' on it either. So we decided that she'd put my name down as Austin's father."

"So you're on Austin's birth certificate as his father?" She seemed to mull that over. "Wade, that's really huge."

"She was my best friend," he reminded her, as if that explained everything. To his mind, it did. "Our plan back then was to regroup and restart the business. We figured we'd made a go of it once, we could do it again. And then, when Robin was eight months pregnant, she found out that she had a really rare, aggressive cancer. The doctors wanted to put her into the hospital and begin treating her that day, but when they told her that the treatments would kill her child, she refused. They'd told her the treatments would only buy her an extra couple of months—maybe a year—and she didn't think her baby's entire life was worth a few months of hers."

"Dear God." Steffie shook her head. "I can't even imagine what it's like to have to make that kind of choice. Did she get any treatment after Austin was born?"

He nodded. "She hung in there for as long as she could, but it was pretty clear to everyone that it was too little too late. She went down pretty fast."

Wade's throat hurt from the strain of trying to maintain control, but he'd gone this far, he might as well tell her everything.

"The week before Beck's wedding, they decided to stop her treatments. As sick as she was, all she could think about was her son. There was no question that Austin would stay with me, but she became obsessed with the idea that somehow the guy who fathered him would find out and come for him and take him away. She was literally terrified that Austin might have to live with this creep someday. So I told her I'd marry her so they'd both have my name and there'd never be any reason for anyone to think that he wasn't my son. This was the week after I got back from St. Dennis. The day after we got married, she began to slip away for good."

Steffie got up and went into the kitchen. When she came back, she was wiping her eyes with a tissue and carrying the box under her arm. "That's the most selfless thing I've ever heard of."

"Stef, Robin was dying and she needed to be able to die in peace. She'd made a huge sacrifice so that

Austin could be born. She needed to know that I'd always take care of him."

"That's a hell of a commitment for a single guy to take on." She blew her nose. "One hell of a sacrifice."

"I'd been taking care of Austin since he was born, so it wasn't any big change. And, Stef, the one thing you need to know is that I really do love him. As far as I'm concerned, he is my son. There's no sacrifice here."

"This other guy, where's he now?"

"I have no idea, and frankly, I don't care. I don't believe in looking for trouble."

"He never knew about Austin?"

"No. The shit hit the fan when she realized he'd cleaned out the company. I don't know who she was angrier with—him for his duplicity, or herself for making it so easy for him. By the time she found out she was pregnant, he was gone."

"But you reported it to the police, right?"

"Yes, but Robin was running out of steam fast. We gave the police all the information we had, but since this guy hadn't used his real name, they weren't able to track him. I'll probably never know who he really was. Everything he'd told us about himself was a lie, all fabricated so he could get close to Robin."

"Why?" she asked, then rolled her eyes. "Oh, duh. Robin was the beneficiary of a very large insurance settlement. I'm guessing that because of the high profile of the driver of the car, the whole thing made the news."

"Right."

"So all along he'd been setting her up. That son of

a bitch." Steffie's hands fisted. "To think he could just walk away like that. Damn."

"Yeah. By the time the police came back and told us they'd hit a wall, Robin had no interest in looking for the guy. Actually, she was praying they'd never find him."

"Because of the baby."

Wade nodded. "At that point, she didn't care about the money or the company. All she cared about was keeping Austin safe."

"So he got off scot-free, and Robin died." Stef frowned, her anger apparent.

"That pretty much sums it up."

"You lost your company and everything because of this creep?"

"We sold all our equipment to one of our competitors so that we could pay the taxes that he'd never paid. Robin insisted on liquidating so that there wouldn't be any medical bills left for me to deal with."

"That just stinks, Wade. Sometimes I just can't believe that there are people in this world who are so horrible. Who just go through life destroying other people and not giving a damn."

They sat on the steps without talking, Steffie's arm still resting on his knee.

"Anyway, that's why I had to leave Beck's wedding reception so abruptly," Wade told her. "Our upstairs neighbor had been taking care of Robin and Austin that weekend, and she called me around eleven that night to ask me to come back."

"I remember you had a call."

"I didn't want to leave, because . . ."

She looked up at him. "Because . . . ?"

"Because being with you that night . . . you were so beautiful and so . . ." He tried to find the right word to describe what she'd been to him that night. Finally, he had to settle for, "Steffie."

She smiled. "So is 'Steffie' an adjective now?"

"You were just so you. Fun and lighthearted and so beautiful . . . did I say 'beautiful'?"

"You did, but it's okay if you repeat yourself."

"Well, you were. I felt as if I'd been transported to another planet that night. Music and dancing and a beautiful woman to share them with." He bit his lower lip. "I hated to leave, Stef, but I had to get back to Robin. I felt guilty enough for having left her, and I felt guilty for having such a terrific time with you when she was suffering so much."

"I bet Robin would have been very happy to know that you had a good time, even for just those few hours," Stef said.

"Yeah, but still . . ." His voice trailed off.

"I'll bet if she were here, she'd be really pissed at you for thinking so little of her." She moved up a step to sit next to him. "I'll bet she understood how much you'd sacrificed for her even more than you did."

"It never felt like a sacrifice, Stef."

"I wonder whatever happened to the Wade MacGregor I knew when I was a kid," she mused. "You know, the one who almost got kicked out school about five times every year from elementary school right through twelfth grade? The one who used to race his aunt's Mercedes on the road to Ballard in the middle of the night? The one who broke more hearts in St. Dennis than—"

"All right. Enough." Wade laughed in spite of himself.

"It was a wonderful thing you did for your friend." She paused. "What you're still doing for her."

"Stef, can you please keep this to yourself? It isn't something that I want out there. Dallas and Berry know, of course, but no one else."

"Grant?"

He nodded. "Right. Grant knows, but Dallas has threatened him with all manner of terrible things if he tells anyone."

"He wouldn't tell," she said softly. "Your secret is safe, Wade."

"I know. I wanted you to know what really happened, but I don't want it to get around."

"Got it." She pretended to zip her lips.

She rested her head against his shoulder for a moment.

"Thank you," she said simply. "For telling me about Robin. I'm sorry I didn't get to meet her. I think I would have liked her."

He nodded. "She would have liked you, too."

"Well," she said, "I don't know about you, but I feel as if I've had my guts ripped out. How do you walk around with all that inside you? It must hurt like hell."

"It's what is," he said simply.

"Thank you." She leaned over, kissed him softly on one side of his mouth. "Thank you for trusting me."

They sat with her head on his shoulder for a few long moments, Wade too wrung out to say much more. Finally, she said, "I just heard the church bells from St. Mary's. They ring out the hour. It's eleven, and I have a very early morning."

"I'll help you close up the house," he told her, but made no attempt to move.

"That's not necessary, I can—"

"I'm not going to leave you here alone. You never know who's going to be passing by and see the lights on . . ."

"That didn't bother you, that Jesse stopped by . . . ?" She stood and brushed the dust off the seat of her jeans.

"Nah." He dismissed the thought.

She smiled as if she knew it for the lie that it was.

They gathered up the pieces of wallpaper that had been stripped and filled several large plastic bags. Wade waited in the front hall while she turned off the kitchen and dining-room lights.

"All set?" she asked when she came back into the foyer, and he nodded.

They walked out together and he waited while she locked the front door. At the end of the walk, he pushed open the gate and it creaked loudly, as if it were complaining.

"I'll do something about that," he told her. "It sounds like it's screaming in pain."

"You don't have to—"

"I want to."

He saw her to her car, and kissed her before she got in. He stood at his own driver's-side door and watched her drive away, her hand emerging from the window to give a little wave. He sat behind the steering wheel in the Jeep and felt raw inside. He wondered if there would ever come a time when thinking about Robin didn't make him feel sick.

He'd said her name aloud tonight, which was something he almost never did anymore. It felt as if he were invoking the dead, and after all Robin had been through, he wanted nothing more than for her to rest in peace.

His mind went back to that moment when his lips brushed against Steffie's. He'd felt a spark, he could swear he had, a quick little charge that had gone right through him. He reminded himself that kissing her had not been part of the game plan for the night. Talking—*explaining*—that had been the plan. But once he'd found himself that close to her, there hadn't been any conscious thought or any decision. He'd just been drawn to her, and while his brain may have been thinking *I want to talk to you about Austin's mother,* his mouth had been thinking *kiss.*

Moth to flame . . .

He turned the key in the ignition and drove back to Berry's on all side roads, meandering around town because he needed a little time alone. He sensed that he'd taken a step in his relationship with Steffie that night on more than one level. He just wasn't sure he knew where they were heading. In another week, he'd be off to Connecticut. So where, he asked himself, did that leave her?

Chapter 9

"So how'd it go last night?" Vanessa knocked once on Scoop's back door before letting herself in and making herself at home.

"How'd what go?" Steffie frowned, her concentration broken. "Here. Taste this and tell me what you think. Too much vanilla? Not enough?"

She handed Vanessa a spoonful of ice cream the color of buttermilk.

"Oh, yum!" Vanessa's eyes widened. "What is this?"

"You like it?"

"Love it. What's in it?"

"Honey and lavender. I've been having a devil of a time balancing the flavors." She picked up a spoon and swiped a bit for herself. "I've been experimenting with different flavors of honey and different strains of lavender, and I don't know which I like best."

She tasted again.

"Still not right," she mumbled.

"Lavender? As in the herb? The flower?" Vanessa asked.

"Right."

"No wonder it smells so good."

"I'm more concerned with the way it tastes."

"It's delicious, Stef. It's not like anything I've ever had before. You're not going through all this for the ice cream for Saturday's run, are you?"

"Nah. That's strictly a vanilla and chocolate day. If I tried to do something too complicated for that many people, I'd have a breakdown. It's been stressful enough trying to come up with this." She held up her plastic spoon and took one last lick before tossing it into the trash.

"Well, what's this for? Flavor of the month?"

"Dallas's birthday. Grant asked me to make a special ice-cream flavor just for her. What do you give the woman who has everything if not her own ice-cream flavor?"

"How romantic is that?" Vanessa leaned on the end of the counter and sighed. "And you just invented this, just like that?"

"Not really invented. I found a ton of recipes on the Internet. What I'm doing is modifying what I found." Stef grinned. "Perfecting, if you will."

"And I will." Vanessa picked up a clean spoon and took another swipe at the container. "It's a beautiful idea—not to mention an extremely tasty one."

"Well, I hope she likes it. It took me forever to come up with the concept. I mean, when you look at Dallas, what do you notice first?"

Vanessa mulled over the question for a moment, then began to nod her head. "Her eyes. Lavender eyes. Lavender ice cream." She grinned broadly. "Genius!"

"Thanks. I still want to tweak it a bit, but I have a

little time before I have to start making enough for the party. Grant said she's invited a ton of people, but he doesn't have the count yet. I told him this morning he really needs to pin this down for me so that I know how much I have to make."

"Why don't you just call her and ask?"

"He wanted it to be a surprise."

"So speaking of MacGregors, we saw a certain Jeep parked in front of your house last night." Vanessa helped herself to a bottle of water from the refrigerator, then pulled a wooden stool closer to the worktable and sat.

"Wade dropped off a ladder."

"And . . . ?"

"And . . . we stripped wallpaper." She shrugged nonchalantly. "And we made out a little."

"Nice of him to help . . ." Vanessa blinked. "Run that last part past me, would you?"

"You heard me." Steffie grinned.

"Whose idea was that?"

"I guess it was his, but I think the spirit probably moved us both at the same time." Steffie made a face. "And this after my vow to keep my distance from him. I was going for immunity but that didn't work out so well. I caved at the first opportunity. Gotta work on that willpower thing."

"So?"

"So what?"

"Don't make me hurt you." Vanessa poked Steffie on the arm with the blunt end of her spoon.

"So it was . . ." Stef paused to search for the word. "It was one perfect kiss."

"Just one?" Vanessa frowned.

"Hey, no one was more disappointed than I was," Steffie shot back. "And there would have been more—probably a lot more—if Jesse Enright hadn't arrived on the scene."

"Jesse Enright? The guy we figured out was the handsome stranger we saw around the docks a couple of weeks ago?"

"Right. He's my mom's family lawyer, and now he's mine as well. He handled all the paperwork on the house. His grandfather actually wrote the will for Horace."

"So wait . . . I need to picture this." Vanessa closed her eyes. "You and Wade are getting it on in the kitchen and Handsome Stranger rings the doorbell—"

"Didn't even ring. Knocked, then walked in," Stef corrected her. "My own fault for leaving the front door wide open."

"Oooh, how'd the Brew Meister like that?" Vanessa's eyes popped open.

Stef shot Vanessa a look that clearly said, *Not much*.

"Fancy that," Vanessa replied.

"Jesse only stayed for a few minutes. He made some polite comments about the house and then he left. I think he realized he'd walked into a 'situation.' "

"Nice of him to stop by, though. So you think he's interested?"

"Maybe." Steffie paused. "Yeah, I think he might be."

"You?"

"I feel so conflicted about Wade." She grimaced. "I've spent half my life conflicted about Wade. I've waited forever for him to put a lip-lock on me like he did last night, but . . ."

"But . . . ?"

"But he's been breaking my heart since I was a kid." Stef put down her measuring spoons. "Jesse, on the other hand, is really a nice guy. Not the heart-breaker type."

"I am a fan of the nice guy myself, since I happen to have snagged me a truly nice guy who also happens to be a very hot guy."

"A nice, hot guy." Stef nodded. "What every girl wants."

"So true."

"Oh!" Steffie remembered the heart on the dining-room wall. "Horace drew a huge—I mean huge—heart on the dining-room wall and wrote 'Horace loves Daisy' inside the heart, then covered it with wallpaper. Wade found it when he was stripping the paper in there."

"Who is Daisy?"

"We don't know. Mom doesn't recall ever seeing Horace with a lady friend." She measured cream for a new experimental batch in a clean ice-cream container. "We're assuming that Horace drew it, anyway. You need to see it. It's very cool."

"I bet Miss Grace would know who Daisy was, if Daisy was from St. Dennis." She took a sip of water. "Stef, I know this sounds off-the-wall, but you know my Ouija board?"

Stef nodded and measured sugar and added it to the mix, muttering, "Maybe another egg, maybe make this more like a French vanilla . . ."

"Well, maybe the spirit's name isn't Daz, as in 'dazzle,' but Daz, as in 'Daisy.' "

Stef looked up. "Huh. Horace's Daisy could be your spirit guide?" She shook her head as if to clear it. "Listen to me, I'm starting to sound like you." She laughed and went back to her recipe.

"What? You don't think I have a spirit guide?"

"No, I don't. I think at this point you're subconsciously directing that little plastic triangle to spell out 'D-A-Z.' "

"Stef, I swear, I am not."

" 'Unconsciously' means you're not aware you're doing it."

"I know what the word means. And consciously or unconsciously or subconsciously, I am not pushing that little . . ." She paused. "I wonder what that little triangle is called . . ."

"I have no idea. But your Daz and Horace's Daisy can't be the same because 'D-A-Z' doesn't exist."

"Well, the next time you're at my house, I will hand over the board and the little thingy and you can try it yourself and then you'll see." Vanessa screwed the cap back onto her bottle.

"I know who Austin's mother was," Stef confided. She'd known she wouldn't be able to resist telling Vanessa something—not everything that Wade had told her, but she couldn't lie to Vanessa and she couldn't withhold everything.

"We are sitting here talking about ice cream and Ouija boards and all this time you've known about Austin's mother?"

Steffie took Vanessa by the arm and led her out the front door to the tables outside. There was no one in sight, but still, Stef lowered her voice as she and Ness took seats.

"Listen, if I tell you something, you have to promise—you have to *swear*—not to tell anyone. Not even Grady." Stef was certain that Vanessa would tell Grady every word, but she had to impress upon her the importance of not passing it on to anyone else and definitely not sharing over coffee.

"I swear." Vanessa's eyes were large with anticipation. "So spill already."

"Her name was Robin Kennedy and she was Wade's business partner, but we knew that part from Miss Grace." Steffie took a deep breath. "She was also his best friend, but they'd never been more than friends. Wade married her because she was dying. She had an affair that turned out badly and then she found out that she was pregnant and then she found out that she was terminally ill. Wade married her before she died because she was so afraid of what would happen to Austin."

"Oh God, that's so sad." Vanessa's eyes filled with tears. "And that's so noble of him, why—"

"Vanessa, you can't tell anyone."

"I know, I said I wouldn't, but . . ." She sighed deeply, then sat up straight and asked, "You don't think Wade was making that up about them just being friends so that he could make a fancy move on you and not look like a tool?"

"No. You had to see his face, Ness. It was obvious that it was killing him just to talk about it."

"That is just the saddest thing I ever heard." Vanessa took a tissue from her bag and dabbed at her eyes. "So I guess he sold their business and came back to St. Dennis because he couldn't bear to stay in Texas after she died."

"I guess." Steffie knew better, but she wasn't telling that part.

"Poor Wade. Poor Austin."

"I saw a picture of her," Steffie said softly.

"He showed you a picture?"

"Uh-uh. I looked her up."

"What do you mean, you looked her up?" Vanessa frowned. "Looked her up where?"

"On Google," Stef admitted.

"You Googled Wade's dead wife? Didn't that feel a little creepy?"

"A little, yeah. It did."

"So what did she look like?"

"She was very pretty."

"Very dark hair, dark eyes, I imagine."

"You're thinking of Austin's coloring. I expected that, too, but no." Stef shook her head. "She was sort of fair, light brown hair. I couldn't tell what color her eyes were."

"Anything else?"

"There were several articles about an accident her parents were in years ago. They were both killed."

"That poor girl really had the worst luck, didn't she?" Vanessa's eyes reflected sympathy. "I'm sorry she had such a bad time of things."

"I am, too," Stef agreed. "My heart just aches for her, and for Austin, and for Wade. The whole thing is just beyond tragic."

"Tragic." Vanessa agreed as she glanced at her watch. "I have to get back to my shop. I left Nan in charge and told her I'd be back in a half hour so she could leave, and I'm late."

"Did you want anything special?"

"Yeah, I wanted to pump you for information about Wade." Vanessa smiled. "Mission accomplished."

"But you won't forget and you won't tell . . ."

Vanessa shook her head. "Never. We won't even speak of it again."

Steffie seriously doubted that but she let it pass.

"As long as you're here, take a little of the butter brickle for the road. I made it earlier this morning and it totally rocks. You need to try this flavor." They walked back into the shop.

"Well, in that case"—Vanessa grabbed a small container from the top of the counter—"don't mind if I do . . ."

Steffie was interrupted four more times that afternoon: once by a teacher from the local nursery school wanting to arrange for a class field trip to Scoop; once by several old friends of her parents who stopped in to let her know that they'd registered for Natalie's Run and how wonderful it was that the family had found such a nice way to honor Nat, who they remembered as a "precocious little thing" before she fell ill; Jesse stopped in right after lunch, and later in the afternoon, Clay Madison popped in.

"Hey." He poked his head into her workroom. "Am I disturbing you?"

"Why, yes, you are, but since it's you, I'll overlook it." She looked up from the cutting board where she was painstakingly chopping lavender buds. "Thanks for the apples last week. I know how annoying those last-minute, drop-everything-and-take-care-of-me phone calls can be, because I get them, too."

"All in a day's work."

"I appreciated it."

"I heard the apple sundaes you made for the Historical Society were amazing."

"From . . . ?"

"My aunt Emma's on the board. She hasn't stopped talking about it since."

"Good." Steffie grinned. "Best advertisement is word of mouth."

"Right." He placed a brown paper bag on the counter. "Which is why I wanted to thank you for noting on your chalkboard that the apples were from Madison's Farm."

"These days, people like to know where their food comes from." She shrugged. "Particularly, they like to know that it's from a local source. Can't get more local than Madison's."

"We appreciate it. I was trying to think of a way to thank you." He handed the bag to her. "This was the best I could come up with, this late in the season."

She opened it and peered inside, but even before she could look, the scent of fresh mint wafted upward.

"Oh, mint!" she exclaimed. "I love the smell of fresh mint. Thank you, Clay."

"My sister mentioned that you were making ice cream for after the run. I thought maybe you'd like to toss some mint into the chocolate."

"That's so thoughtful of you." She closed the bag. "I'll put this through the food processor later."

"Great. Glad you can use it." He smiled at her, a smile that went all the way to his warm brown eyes. "Well." He slapped on hand on the table lightly. "I need to get on back to the farm. I'll see you on Saturday."

"Oh, you're running?"

He nodded. "I've run every year. This year, I'll be running with my nephew, Logan—my sister Brooke's son—so I don't know how much actual running we'll be doing, but it's for good cause. Logan saw the signs around town and he wanted to participate, so we'll see how he does."

"Good luck to both of you." Steffie walked Clay through the front of the shop to the door. "I'll make sure we save some of the chocolate mint for you and Logan on Saturday."

"Great." He opened the door halfway, stopped, and said, "It's good to see you, Steffie. It's been a while."

"It has been. Fourth of July, maybe."

"That long?" He frowned. "We'll have to do better, make up for lost time."

She smiled as he closed the door behind him, the bell tinkling softly. She turned to walk back to her workroom when she realized that Tina was leaning on the refrigerated case, grinning.

"What?" Steffie asked.

"Nothing." Tina shrugged.

"What?"

"Oh, it's just that any number of good-looking men seem to be popping up right and left around here. The MacGregor guy one day, then today that cute lawyer, then that hunky farmer. Wonder who's going to turn up next?"

Steffie stared at her for a long moment, then shook her head as if to clear it, and went back to work.

The next morning, when she and Vanessa were leaving Cuppachino together, Stef mentioned that she was making chocolate mint ice cream in addition to plain chocolate, compliments of Clay.

"Oh, where'd you run into Clay?" Vanessa asked.

"He stopped into the shop to bring me the mint. Wasn't that nice of him?"

"Hmm." Vanessa looked thoughtful. "And wasn't it just the other night that Wade brought you a ladder and put a move on you and Jesse stopped in?"

"Yeah, so?"

"So, you can thank me now, or you can thank me later." Vanessa beamed.

"Thank you for what?"

Vanessa sighed with apparent exasperation. "Don't you see? It's working."

"What's working?" Stef frowned. "What are you talking about?"

"The spell. It's working." Vanessa looked triumphant. "It's bringing all these wonderful options to your door. One of them," she confided, "is your soul mate."

"Oh, dear God, give me strength." Stef rolled her eyes heavenward. "You did not just say that."

"How else to explain the steady stream of eligible—and dare I say hot?—guys less than a week after I—"

"—after you read some random words from a dusty old book that an old woman stashed in her attic a million years ago. Come on, Ness, you don't believe in any of that."

"Well, I admit I didn't use to. And I certainly didn't last week. But you have to admit it's strange timing."

Stef held up one finger. "Wade stopped over to bring me a ladder because he wanted to help and because, well, because there's some unfinished business between us." She held up a second finger. "Jesse stopped over because I'm his client and because he doesn't know many people his own age here in town and he figures friendship with me could lead to some sort of social life for him because I know everyone within a fifty-mile radius of St. Dennis." A third finger went up. "Clay stopped over to thank me because I gave his orchard a little free advertising last week."

She wagged all three fingers in front of Vanessa's face.

"No spell, Ness. Just coincidence."

"Grady always says there's no such thing as coincidence."

"Grady was in the FBI for a long time. He learned to interpret things logically. Which is exactly what I'm doing."

"You say logic, you say coincidence, I say spells." Vanessa fought a smile, then closed her eyes and waved one hand slowly back and forth in front of her face. "I see . . . I see another tall, handsome man in your future . . ."

"I see . . . one bat-shit crazy woman." Steffie laughed and headed for Scoop, thinking that Vanessa's occasional wackiness aside, having a best friend who could almost make you believe in magic wasn't necessarily a bad thing.

Chapter 10

"It's one thing to be in demand," Steffie told Tina "but it's something else entirely to be overextended. There's just too much going on right now. If I'm lucky, I may get some sleep by Halloween."

"So bring in a few more part-timers," Tina suggested. "You already have Claire, and I'm available for full time for as long as you need me."

"You're hired." Steffie pulled up the shades in the windows that faced the Bay. "How 'bout your daughter? What does she have going on after school?"

"Not a whole lot right now. She's off the field hockey team since she injured her knee, so she's free in the afternoon. How many extra hands do you think you'll need?"

"Maybe two or three, and I'll only need them for ten days."

"I'll check with Heather and see if she and one or two of her friends could come in."

"Great. As long as I can get a few hours each day." Steffie turned the "Closed" sign to "Open." "I leave it in your hands. I've been so busy these past few days,

I haven't even gotten to stop at my house." She smiled dreamily. "My glorious house . . ."

"Bit off more than you can chew?" Tina opened the cash register for the day.

"Well, you make the call." Stef opened one of the windows to let in some fresh morning air. "We have chocolate, vanilla, and chocolate mint for the run on Saturday, and the lavender honey for the one hundred fifty or so guests who'll be attending Dallas's birthday party the following week. My brother wants that to be a surprise, so I'm not supposed to tell anyone I'm making it." She rolled her eyes. "And I still have to make my daily supply for the shop."

"I'm almost afraid to remind you that you agreed to make chocolate monster mash for the annual St. Dennis Halloween Parade."

"Arrgghh! Someone just take me outside, stand me up against the wall, and shoot me." Steffie pretended to pound her head on the cooler.

"Oh, can I have Scoop?" Tina's sister, Claire, asked brightly as she reported in for the morning. "Waterfront anything is so pricey these days."

"And if you'd leave me your new house, I'd be really happy," Tina added. "I could sell it and use the proceeds to pay the tuition bills. Did I mention that my daughter Amanda wants to go to law school?"

"Sure." Steffie tossed a container of vanilla beans onto the work station. "And feel free to dance on my grave after the will is read."

"Will do." Tina grinned, then added with due solemnity, "Respectfully, of course."

* * *

Stef had wisely moved her alarm clock into the bathroom on Friday night so she'd be forced to get up and turn off the noise, which grew ever louder between the time it began as a soft buzz until it was silenced with a smack. By the time she made it to the bathroom, it had reached jackhammer level. Grumbling and groaning, she showered and dressed in a T-shirt that had RUN FOR NATALIE on the front, and a picture of Nat before she began treatments screened onto the back. According to Grant, they'd made several hundred dollars on the sale of the shirts during the two weeks since they'd been selling, and he expected to double that by selling them at the registration table.

"By the end of the day, we should have a very nice check to donate for leukemia research," Grant told her when he called her on Friday night. "Did you know that Sips is donating half their profits tomorrow? When Carlo at Cuppachino found out, he said he'd match it."

"I did hear that." Steffie had nodded. "I also heard that Olivia is having a 'Buy a Rose for Natalie' special all day. She's selling single pink roses and donating all the receipts. I love the way everyone has taken to this fund-raiser. Mom and Dad are really touched that so many people in town have stepped up to participate."

"So, got enough ice cream?" Grant asked.

"Only by the skin of my teeth and the help of Tina's daughter and one of her friends."

"Training the competition, are we?"

"Only in the basics, like cleaning the machines between batches and making sure there are cold canisters and chopping mint and vanilla beans and stuff like that. For the actual brewing, you need the master's touch."

"Since when do you *brew* ice cream?" She could almost see him smirking.

"I'm hanging up on you now. But be warned that I plan to take you tomorrow," she told him. "I'll be waiting for you at the finish line when you crawl across it."

"You wish," he snorted, and hung up.

Stef *was* waiting at the finish line on Saturday when Grant crossed it, but not because she'd beaten him. As it turned out, she was only ten minutes into the race when she remembered that she hadn't unlocked the back door at Scoop. The volunteers who were going to set up the ice-cream tables would need to get into the storage room to bring out the boxes of plastic spoons and paper cups and napkins. Reluctantly, she jogged back down Kelly's Point Road to her shop. By the time she'd opened the building, helped to bring out the supplies, and took a shortcut back to Charles Street, the first runners were just crossing the finish line. She took a bottle of water from the table that was set up to supply the runners and twisted off the cap, poured a bit into the palm of one hand, then with her fingers, spritzed her face, arms, and neck.

She was in the process of trying to make herself look sweaty when Wade crossed the finish line.

"Hey," he said as he doubled over momentarily to catch his breath.

"Hey back."

"You showering or are you trying to cool off?" he asked, his breath ragged from exertion.

"What?"

"The water." He gestured toward the bottle. "I saw you sprinkling it all over you."

"Oh. That." She bit the inside of her lip and tried to think fast.

He walked off to cool down and get his breathing under control.

"Wow, you really did it," Grant exclaimed when he finished the race. "I can't believe it, but there you are. How'd you do it?"

"Training and superior athleticism," she told him.

"When did you have time to train?" He grabbed a bottle from one of the volunteers. "And when did you become an athlete?"

"I'd have expected you to be a more gracious loser," she said solemnly.

"I smell a rat." Grant narrowed his eyes. He saw Wade leaning against the table, a grin on his face. "Were you here when she crossed the line? Did you see her finish?"

Wade shrugged. "She looks pretty sweaty to me."

"You will never stop underestimating your little sister." Stef smiled and poked Grant in the ribs. "I'll see you down at Scoop."

"Did she cross that finish line?" she heard him asking one of the volunteers as she walked away. "Did you actually see her . . . ?"

"Stef, wait up," Wade called to her, and she half turned to see him walking toward her. "What are you up to?"

"What do you mean?"

He laughed and gestured toward Grant, who was still trying to find someone who saw Stef finish the race.

"Just a little sibling fun. Thanks for not blowing the whistle on me."

"Anything to get in your good graces." He came closer, close enough for Steffie to see the beads of sweat—real sweat—on his forehead.

"You mean you're sucking up to me?"

"Right."

"For what purpose?" Her eyes narrowed and she tried to ignore just how good he looked in running shorts, a tank top, and sweat.

"I'd think it's obvious." He folded his arms across his chest. "Ice cream, of course. I crave it. You've got it." His expression was solemn but his eyes danced.

"Which flavor?" she deadpanned.

"I kinda liked the stuff I had that first night I was here."

"Ah, yes. Chocolate monster mash." She nodded. "The favorite of little boys everywhere."

He laughed and she told him, "Stop down at Scoop sometime. I'll see what I can do for you."

She knew he was watching her as she walked away, could feel his eyes on her back and her legs and her backside. She wondered if he liked what he saw, and she wondered it he'd lost as much sleep these past few days thinking about kissing her again as she'd lost thinking about kissing him.

"Stef."

She paused at the sound of her name, and turned to see Wade jogging down the path toward her. "Wait up."

She took the cap off her water bottle and took a long drink.

"I'll walk down to Kelly's Point with you." He met

up with her on the path where she waited. "So this is the back door between Scoop and the end of the race."

Steffie laughed. "I'm surprised Grant didn't figure it out. The path runs right behind the police station and comes out at the top of the hill. Everyone in town knows it's there."

"I didn't."

"That's because the municipal building wasn't there when you lived in St. Dennis. It's only about six years old."

"When I was growing up here, the police station was at the end of Charles Street on the way out to Cannonball Island."

"I remember."

The path narrowed, forcing them to walk a little closer. Their hips grazed as they made their way down the hill, their hands brushing against each other's. Where the incline was steepest, she stumbled slightly, and he grabbed her hand to keep her from falling.

"You all right?" he asked.

"Yes. Sorry. I need to watch where I'm going."

She had righted herself, but he hadn't let go of her hand. That small gesture, the casual mingling of their fingers, felt like a promise yet to be fulfilled.

"Where's the little guy?" she asked.

"He's with Berry and Dallas. Cody was going to try to run with Clay and Logan. I doubt they made it to the finish line."

"Bring Austin over for ice cream later."

"Will do."

They'd reached the end of the path, and when they rounded the municipal building, a line had already formed for ice cream. It snaked from the tables set up near Scoop right along the edge of the parking lot.

"Holy crap," she exclaimed.

"Looks like you're going to be busy for a while." He stopped at the end of the parking lot. "Do you need any help?"

"I think I'll be all right, thanks. I brought in extra hands for today."

"Guess I should let you go, then."

"Guess so."

"I'll see you later." He released her hand.

She nodded and made her way through the crowd to the tables, where her employees were already hard at work.

"Wow, do you believe this crowd?" Stef said as she approached the table.

"People have been lining up for the past ten minutes," Tina told her. "This is going to be a long day."

"Won't be if we run out of ice cream," Stef said from the corner of her mouth.

"I think next year we go with three tables," Tina whispered, and headed back to the freezer for another container of chocolate.

"I think next year we go to Jamaica," Stef muttered, and picked up her scoop. "I hope we have enough to finish out today."

Forty minutes later, there were still people in line.

"How's it going?" Jesse Enright appeared at her left elbow.

"My wrist is killing me, if you want to know the truth," she told him.

"Here, let me spell you for a little while." He stashed a water bottle and a T-shirt under the table, and then reached for the scoop she was holding and took it from her hand. "I worked in a deli when I was in college. I sling a mean scoop. Give yourself a little break."

"Maybe just for a few minutes." She handed over the scoop gratefully and rubbed her wrist, and watched him dish out the next few cups of ice cream. Satisfied that he was up to the job, she excused herself for a moment and went inside for some ice for her wrist. She knew that a minute wasn't near enough time to do much good, but the ice felt really great while she held it on there and she popped a few Advil before grabbing an extra scoop and going back outside. She stepped next to Jesse at the table and shared the duties with him for the next forty minutes.

After they'd served up the last of the ice cream, she said, "Thanks, Jesse. I never would have asked a friend to pitch in, but I'm really glad you did. Otherwise, there'd still be a line and I'd still be wondering when it would end."

She looked beyond Jesse to scan the crowd, wondering if Wade was around, but didn't see him. Cody and Logan had come for ice cream earlier—chocolate mint—but they'd been in Tina's line and she hadn't seen them since.

"I was happy to give you a hand." Jesse stood with his hands on his hips. "Looks like you had a great turnout for the run."

"It exceeded every one of our expectations. We never would have guessed that so many people would show up. Not just people from St. Dennis, but a lot of day-trippers came. I'll bet my mom and dad were pleased to see how many were wearing these T-shirts today." She pulled at the front of her own red shirt. "I'm sure we raïsed a record amount of money for research, and that's the bottom line."

"You must be exhausted," Jesse said as he gathered his things from under the table.

"I admit I'm a bit tired."

Steffie heard her name called and turned to see her parents making their way toward the shop.

"Oh, damn," she told them when they drew near. "I'm just about out of ice cream."

"Not to worry," her mother told her. "We'll just sit inside while you make more."

"Oh. Okay," Stef replied almost feebly.

"Just kidding, sweetie." Shirley Wyler kissed her daughter's cheek. "What a wonderful day you and Grant put together. We're so proud of you."

"Very proud," her father, George, greeted her with a bear hug.

"Don't give us all the credit, please," Stef protested. "We had a committee this year, and Grant did most of the organizational work. And remember that you two started this whole thing years ago."

"Well, I'm betting you raised a much bigger bundle than we did back then. And love the shirts, by the way." Shirley turned to Jesse. "So, it looks like you ran today, too."

"I did," he told her.

Shirley took her husband's arm. "Dear, this is Jesse Enright. He handled Cousin Horace's will for us."

"George Wyler." Stef's dad extended his hand. "Good to meet you."

"Nice to meet you." Jesse shook the older man's hand.

"I made dinner reservations tonight at Captain Walt's for all of us, but Grant can't make it. He just found out that he'll be getting a van full of dogs from Georgia for the shelter and he and Dallas will be tied up most of the night with them." Shirley turned to Jesse. "Our son runs an animal rescue shelter in addition to his veterinary clinic and apparently last-minute deliveries are quite common."

"I don't know if that's accurate, Shirl," George noted. "I think he said something about the place they'd intended to take the dogs had an outbreak of kennel cough and they didn't want to expose them."

"Whatever the reason, he just found out and he and Dallas have had to cancel dinner." Shirley dismissed the matter with a wave of her hand. "I still find it hard to picture Dallas MacGregor working alongside Grant with all those dogs. I always picture her as that delicate flower in *Silver Mornings*."

"Mom, Dallas made that movie about fifteen years ago," Steffie reminded her.

"I know, but there was something in her performance that stayed with me," her mother told her. "It's one of my favorite films of all time."

"I hope you told her," Stef said. From the corner of her eye, she caught sight of Wade standing on the boardwalk in conversation with Clay Madison. Dallas had just joined them with Austin in the stroller, though that appeared to be temporary, as he was busy climbing out.

"I did." Shirley turned to Jesse. "So it seems we have two extra seats at our table tonight. Why don't you join us if you don't have other plans?"

"Great idea, Shirl. Hope to see you then, Enright."

George looked over his shoulder and waved to someone. "Oh, there's Hal Garrity. I want to say hello before he gets lost in the crowd. Excuse me for a moment . . ."

"So, we'll see you tonight, Jesse?"

"Ahhh . . ." Caught off guard, Jesse appeared unsure as to how to answer. He glanced quickly at Steffie.

"What a good idea, Mom." Stef sensed his discomfort and turned to Jesse. "If you're free, of course."

"I don't have other plans," he told them, "but if you're sure I won't be intruding . . ."

"Nonsense." Shirley smiled. "We'd love to have you. The reservations are for seven. If that fits your schedule, we'll see you then."

"Seven is fine. Thank you."

"Stef, we'll see you then as well." Shirley hugged her daughter. Her voice lowered, and she added, "And thanks again for putting so much time into this. I'm sure wherever she is, Natalie is very proud of her little sister."

"Thanks, Mom," Stef whispered.

"Well, then, I think I'll go and try to catch up with Grace. I want to thank her for all the ink she's given to this project and to her thoughtful, personal remembrance of Natalie."

"I didn't see that." Steffie frowned. "Where did you see that?"

"She sent us a copy of the paper that came out on Wednesday. Didn't you see it?" her mother asked.

"I haven't seen much of anything over the last three or four days. I think I still have the paper, though."

"Make sure you read it, Stef. Grace wrote about

how difficult it was to explain to her own child why she wouldn't be seeing her friend anymore."

"How who . . . ?"

"Oh, Grace's daughter. Of course you were just a baby then, but Lucy and Nat shared a birthday. They were in the same play group together and became fast friends from the first day. They really were best buddies. Grace would bring Lucy over on days when Nat was feeling up to company, and the two girls would play with their dolls." Shirley swallowed a lump and looked away. "When Natalie was too sick or too weak to play, Lucy read to her. She was inconsolable when Natalie died. For years after, Grace said, Lucy didn't want to celebrate her birthday because she couldn't celebrate it with Nat." She blinked several times as if to blink away the tears that welled in her eyes. "Anyway, Grace wrote a piece about the girls and their friendship and it was very touching. And now"—she looked around—"where did your father get to?"

"He's over by the walk talking to Hal," Steffie told her. And closer to the water, she noticed, Wade and Clay had been joined by Clay's sister, Brooke, who was chatting with Dallas.

"No doubt giving Hal a full report on the condition of the Bay, environmentally speaking. I should go save Hal." She turned to Steffie and Jesse. "I'll see you both at dinner."

"My dad's working on an environmental study of the Chesapeake," Steffie told Jesse as her mother rushed off. "He's concentrating on the Susquehanna Watershed, what pollutants the river dumps into the Bay, and how best to combat them. He's become quite militant."

She looked back toward the water, where Dallas was just walking off with Austin in the stroller.

Jesse followed her gaze. "Isn't that your friend from the other night? Wade?"

Steffie nodded. "The other guy is Clay Madison."

"Who's the woman with him?" Jesse's eyes narrowed slightly.

"Clay's sister, Brooke Bowers."

Jesse stared for a moment, then turned back to Stef and said, "Listen, I know your mother put you on the spot, asking me to join your family for dinner. It's okay if you don't want me to do that. I mean, I won't be offended."

"Don't be silly. Of course I want you to join us." She smiled. "But if I'm going to make it by seven, I need to get to work now."

Wade, Clay, and Brooke began to make their way toward the marina.

"Well, I guess I'll see you there." Jesse started to walk away. "Unless you want me to pick you up?"

"No, but thanks." She shook her head no. "I may run a little late. If you get there before I do, just ask my dad how his efforts to clean up the Bay are going. That should keep everyone busy until I arrive."

"Will do."

Steffie went into the shop through the back door. Surprised at the number of customers awaiting service, since the ice cream they'd given out earlier had been free, she grabbed an apron and went to work.

"So, how's your new helper working out?" Vanessa came up behind her. Along with Grady, she'd stopped in to see if Stef needed any help cleaning up outside.

"What new helper?" Stef frowned.

"I noticed Jesse Enright helping you dish a while ago. Very cozy, you two." Vanessa leaned in to whisper in Stef's ear.

Stef smiled, handed over her customer's order, and turned around. "He was here when the crowd built up and my wrist was giving out. He offered to help, and I was desperate, so I let him, since my wrist was killing me."

"Did he ask you out?" Vanessa asked. "And what's wrong with your wrist?"

"We're having dinner tonight with my parents, but no, it wasn't his idea. It was my mother's. Grant and Dallas had to cancel, so there was space at the table," she explained. "And my wrist just got a bit overworked today. It'll be fine."

"Hmm . . ."

" 'Hmmmmm' what?" Steffie asked

"Oh, nothing." Vanessa retied the strings of Stef's apron in the back, where they were coming undone. "Just that, well, could be a coincidence, or, it could be because of—"

"Do not even pretend it has anything to do with your . . ." Stef lowered her voice, eyeing Grady who was on the other side of the counter talking to his sister, Mia, who'd just come in the front door. "Does he know that you're practicing spells? Or pretending to?"

"No, and do not tell him. He'll think I'm flaky."

"Gosh, ya think?"

"And don't be so smart-alecky about it. Had he asked you out before I . . ." Vanessa stole a glance at Grady. "Before . . . you know."

"I hadn't even met Jesse . . . *before*. And," Stef reminded her, "he didn't ask me out. This is not a date. I repeat. This is not a date. My *mother* asked him."

"Same difference." Vanessa walked to the other side of the counter and checked out the ice-cream flavors. "I don't suppose there was any of the mint left over."

"There was, but I put it aside for Clay. I promised I'd save some for him, but I didn't see him after the race." She scanned the containers, then put two scoops of pineapple coconut into a dish.

"He and Wade were talking outside for a while," Vanessa told her. "And Brooke. The three of them took off together a while ago."

Steffie put two spoons into the dish and passed it over the counter to Vanessa. "On the house."

"Thanks. I suppose the two spoons means I'm to share. And I will, as soon as I can get Grady's attention."

"Clay and Wade are old friends," Stef told her. "Brooke's all right. She had the hots for Grant for a long time, but now that she's worked that out of her system, she seems okay. I don't know if she'd dating anyone, but Jesse sure did give her the once-over."

"Why wouldn't he? She's really pretty."

Stef nodded in agreement. "Her son, Logan, is a doll. He and Dallas's son are BFFs. They do everything together. Two peas in a pod, Miz Berry always says."

"I know. Dallas had both of them with her one day last week when she stopped in to pick up a top she'd ordered." Vanessa leaned on the counter. "I still can't get over the fact that Dallas MacGregor buys her clothes from me." She paused. "Well, not all of them, of course, but some."

The bell rang and a new group came into the shop.

"I'll get out of your way. Thanks again for the ice cream. One day I'll come in here and actually buy something from you." Vanessa stepped away from the counter.

"And one day I'll let you. As soon as you stop giving me those fabulous discounts in Bling."

Vanessa smiled. "What are friends for?"

"Ice cream and deep discounts on cool clothes."

"Exactly," Vanessa said before making her way through the crowd to Grady.

At five thirty, Steffie hung up her apron and tapped Tina on the shoulder. "If you and Claire are all right here, I'm going to head home. I'm meeting my mom and dad for dinner at seven, and I'm a mess."

"Go," Tina told her. "The next few hours should be fairly light."

"Call me if you need to." Stef grabbed her bag from the back room and made her way to her car in the municipal lot. Lately she'd been walking to work more frequently, but today she'd driven. She'd had a feeling she'd be tired by the end of the day, and the long walk back to her apartment would have felt endless.

Fatigue tempted her to fall facedown across her bed, but she forced herself into the shower. By the time her hair was dry and she'd dressed and put on some makeup, she had just enough time to get to Captain Walt's by seven.

She wasn't sure how she felt about her mother's invitation to Jesse. On the one hand, she almost wished he'd said no. Oh, he was a nice enough guy, and it had been so thoughtful of him to pitch in this morning. She really had appreciated it. But frankly, she'd just as soon skip dinner and paint cabinets in her kitchen, which was, she had to admit, a sad commentary and a sure sign that her interest in him was nothing more than platonic. Now, if it had been Wade . . . well, that would certainly have put a little extra bounce in her step.

If it were Wade, she'd be obsessing over what to wear, how to fix her hair, and her palms would be sweating with anticipation of seeing him. She hadn't been thinking about Jesse when she pulled a plain black knit dress from the closet, or when she decided to leave her hair down, or when she leaned over her makeup mirror to put on mascara. She barely thought about him at all until she arrived at Walt's and ran into him in the parking lot.

"Hey, good timing," Jesse called from the doorway.

"What?" She looked up. "Oh, right. Thanks for holding the door."

Jesse followed her into the restaurant, through the short lobby, past the long horseshoe-shaped bar that ran along one side of the dining room. Seeing her parents, Stef turned her back on the bar and headed straight for them. It was only after she was seated that she looked across the table at her father and realized that she had a perfect view of the bar, and the two men seated directly in her line of vision.

Clay and Wade sat a mere thirty feet away, deep in conversation, no doubt enjoying their burgers and beers. This was the second time today she spotted those two with their heads together. What, she couldn't help but wonder, were the two of them up to?

Chapter 11

WADE swiveled slightly on his bar stool just in time to see Steffie walk into the dining room at Captain Walt's. He was so busy watching her—he hadn't seen her in a short skirt and high heels, her hair down, in a long time—that he almost missed the guy who was following her. His eyes narrowed. Enright, the guy who broke up a big moment the other night.

He tried to tune back in to Clay, but it was tough to keep his eyes off her. He turned his head back to the bar and made another attempt to catch up with whatever it was that Clay was saying. Their conversation had started earlier in the day, when Clay asked about KenneMac and Wade started to tell him what had happened to the company.

Of course, he didn't tell him everything. He'd left out the part about Robin and Austin, but there'd been enough that Clay got the gist of it. Wade agreed to meet Clay at Captain Walt's for dinner because Clay wanted to finish the conversation. Wade wasn't sure what else there was to say, but all the same, here he sat, drinking beer and picking at a pile of buffalo wings in Walt's bar with Clay.

It had irritated the hell out of him when he saw that Enright had been one of Steffie's helpers that afternoon. Wade suspected that the lawyer was just that kind of guy, the guy who's always handy and dependable and thoughtful. What a suck-up . . .

What irritated Wade the most was that she hadn't asked him to help her.

"So does this mean you're out of the brew business for good?" Clay had asked after they sat down at the bar.

"Not really. I'm leaving after next weekend to work for a guy who has a microbrewery in Connecticut." Even as Wade spoke, he reminded himself to call Ted about that contract he still hadn't seen.

"Working for someone else?" Clay's eyebrows had risen. "Won't that be tough after having been your own boss?"

Wade shrugged. "Hadn't really thought about it."

"Have you given any thought to starting up another brewery?"

"It's a complicated process." Wade tried to brush it off.

"How complicated can it be?" Clay had asked. "What-all do you need?"

"Besides a lot of money to buy equipment and a place to set it all up?"

"How'd you do it last time?"

"I had a partner who had money to invest in the building and the equipment and the ingredients. We thought we'd be in business forever . . ." Wade's voice trailed off. He and Robin had been planning on expanding KenneMac Brews right before the shit had hit the fan. Even now, it saddened him to remember the goals they'd sketched out for the company they'd both loved.

"You just made a face," Clay noted. "Why'd you make that face?"

"Just thinking about hops." Wade tried to smile. "We used to buy them from a guy out near Seattle, but right before we had to close down, we'd been looking to expand. We'd even been talking about finding some land and growing our own. We were thinking about starting a line of organic beer." He could have added, *That was right before we found out that our third partner had cleaned out our accounts and left us practically bankrupt,* but he didn't feel like going into all that tonight.

"Organic beer." Clay nodded. "I like the concept."

"Yeah, so did we."

It had been right about this time that Steffie, all legs and just the slightest sway to her hips, walked past to join her parents in the dining room. She was a knockout in a simple black dress with all that honey-blond hair curling around her face and over her shoulders. He felt his heart thud in his chest.

"I've gotten into a lot of organics myself over the past few years," Clay was saying. "You know I took the farm over from my dad before he died?"

"I think I heard someone mention that. How's that working out for you? I thought farming was a tough row—no pun—these days." His eyes kept returning to the dining room. Stef had just arrived at her parents' table and was kissy-kissy with Mom and Dad.

Enright was all smiles and shaking hands with Stef's father . . . but did he just actually hug Mrs. Wyler?

Seriously, Enright?

"Farming has always been tough," Clay conceded, "but I never considered anything else. My parents insisted I go to college—and I did—but there was never been anything else that interested me and no question that I would farm. These days, a lot of farmers have it tough because it's so profitable to become part of the 'big agribusiness' culture, you know? Grow corn or soybeans for one of the big conglomerates, but that restricts you in what you can do. Plus the whole genetically-modified-seed thing bothers me. I know there are pros and cons, but it just doesn't sit right with me."

"So what do you grow?" Wade asked, one eye still on the dining room.

"We've always grown corn, but it's harder to find seed that hasn't been genetically modified, so this may have been the last year I'll do corn. We have the orchard, and we do a good business there. Plus, I've started to develop a solid business in organics." Clay took a sip of his beer. "Which is why I was interested in your idea of making organic beer."

"It's an idea whose time has come," Wade told him. Across the room, Steffie was taking off her hot-pink jacket and Enright was draping it over the back of her chair. Wade eyed him suspiciously.

"I've done a pretty good job getting the chemical fertilizers out of our soil these past few years," Wade heard Clay say. "Lola down at the café asked me a couple of years ago to grow some organic herbs and lettuces for her. Then she wanted tomatoes. Then a couple of the other restaurant owners got wind of it, and asked me to grow for them, too, so I've been building up that business steadily over the past few years. It's a lot of work, but it's better than sitting behind a desk all day."

"I hear you." Wade's eyes wandered back to the dining room, where everyone at the Wyler table was laughing. It appeared that Enright was telling a story that everyone thought was pretty damned funny. Ha ha. Wade scowled.

Clay turned on his stool to see what Wade was looking at.

"Yeah"—Clay nodded—"little Steffie grew up real good."

Wade turned the scowl on Clay.

"Oh, so that's how it is." Clay raised his glass to his mouth, a knowing smile on his lips.

"We were talking about farming," Wade reminded him flatly.

"The future's in organic." Clay took a long drink from his glass before signaling to the bartender for another.

"I thought the future was in plastics." Brooke breezed into the bar. "Oh. Sorry. That was 1967."

"You weren't even born in '67." Clay got off his stool and offered it to his sister.

"True, but the movie was a classic." Brooke tossed her hair over her shoulder and smiled at Wade.

"And here's to you . . ." He tilted his glass in her direction and she laughed.

"The point I was trying to make is that organics are here to stay." Clay resumed the conversation. "The locavore movement is coming on strong; more and more people are becoming interested in eating locally grown foods, and I'm one of them. Not just because it makes a great business for me or that the food's better—that's a whole 'nother discussion—but frankly, it's more interesting to grow a variety of produce to sell locally than it is to sell one or two crops for the large agricompanies."

The bartender brought his beer and took Brooke's order.

"It's gotta be more labor-intensive," Wade pointed out.

"Backbreakingly intensive," Brooke said. "My brother's addicted to pain."

Clay nodded. "Like I said, organic farming keeps my interest."

"So what did you grow this year?" Wade glanced back at Stef's table and caught her eye as she looked up. For a moment they gazed at each other from across the room, and for a moment it was as if they were alone there, just the two of them. Until her mother tapped her on the arm and brought her back into the conversation.

"Peppers—eight or nine kinds this past year; next year I'll add a few more," Clay was saying. "Cucumbers. Summer and winter squashes—seven or eight varieties there, too. Swiss chard. Eggplant. Tomatoes—fifteen varieties including a couple of heirlooms. More to come for next year. There's a huge market for heirlooms. Oh, and I had over twenty different herbs."

"Madison growing herbs." Wade shook his head. "Somehow that's just wrong."

"Actually, I kinda enjoyed it." Clay grinned. "But

even if I tripled the organic crops next year, that would still leave me with a hell of a lot of fallow acreage and two barns filled with a bunch of unused farm equipment and a whole lot of air."

"And?" Wade wasn't sure what the point of all this was.

"And I have to find something to fill those empty acres."

Brooke's eyes wandered first around the bar, then across the dining room.

"Who's the guy with the Wylers?" she asked. "I've seen him around town a couple of times."

"Jesse Enright. He's their lawyer," Wade said, refusing to give voice to the possibility that Jesse could be anything else.

Clay turned around. "He's Mike and Patti's nephew. Joined the firm a while ago. Why'd you ask?"

"Just curious." Brooke shrugged.

"I've had offers to rent out my fields," Clay said, "but I hate that idea because I never can be sure what others are putting on their crops. And if they're using GMO seed, it can cross-pollinate with what I grow. If they put crap fertilizers on their plants, it can blow onto mine or get into my soil, neither of which I want if I want to be certified as an organic farmer."

"What are your options?" Wade asked because he knew he was expected to, but it was hard to concentrate when he could see Steffie's face so clearly.

"I've been thinking about grapes," Clay said. "As in wine grapes."

That got Wade's attention.

"Grow to sell to wineries?" he asked.

"Maybe, to start. Or maybe to start up my own vineyard, who knows."

"It takes a while before the vines mature and the grapes are wine quality," Wade told him.

"About as long as it takes hops to mature?" Clay countered.

"You can get hops the second year if you're lucky, but from year three on, you're good." Wade studied the glass of beer the bartender had placed before him. "As long as you don't get hop beetles or some other pest, and if you can stay disease-free."

"So the hop vines have to mature, too," Clay pointed out.

"They're called 'bines,' by the way, but yeah, they need a year or two." Wade paused for a moment, then asked, "Why the interest in hops?"

Clay shrugged. "Seems to be a good business to get into right now, if you have the time and the patience and the place to grow them organically. All of which I have plenty of." He picked up his burger, but before he took a bite, he added, "I figure now's as good a time as any to explore my options. Microbreweries are doing well. I think a brewery is just what St. Dennis needs. Yeah"—he nodded—"I might want to try my hand. Maybe I can pick your brain while you're here. Since you're not interested in sticking around and doing it yourself, it's not like we're competing, right?"

Before Wade could respond, Clay went on: "And the more I think about it, the more I think St. Dennis needs its own beer."

"That's what Berry said. She suggested it be called 'Berry Beer.' "

Clay nodded. “I like it.”

Wade frowned. “Guys are not likely to drink a beer named ‘Berry.’ ”

“The ladies would, though,” Clay noted. “Nothing wrong with focusing on the ladies.” He followed Wade’s gaze across the room. “Which you don’t seem to have a problem doing.”

“She’s just in my line of vision, that’s all,” Wade told him, then wished he hadn’t. Clay wasn’t stupid, and it was obviously a lie.

“I say go for it, Wade.” Brooke patted him on the back. “Haven’t you and Steffie always had a thing of sorts going on?”

“Of sorts,” he acknowledged.

“Just something else you’re going to leave behind when you go,” Clay pointed out. “Don’t be thinking you’ll lure her up north with you. Steffie’s got Bay blood in her veins and a damned fine business that she built for herself, by herself. No way that girl’s going anywhere. If you’re thinking about making a move in that direction, you’d best be thinking about sticking around, because right now she’s fair game, and you’re not the only guy in town who’s interested.”

“Obviously,” Brooke said. “And who could blame them? Stef’s a doll, and a very successful one, at that. And hey”—she poked Wade—“the two of you are almost family now.”

“Almost.” Wade tried to smile.

“Well, if you want my advice—” Brooke began.

“If he did, he’d ask for it,” Clay interjected.

Wade smiled and nodded to Brooke to go on. He’d take any advice he could get right now.

"Like I said, go for it." Brooke's expression changed, her eyes somber. "Life is short, Wade, it's unpredictable. Don't think there's always tomorrow, because sometimes, there isn't."

Clay put down his beer and rubbed his sister's back, and Wade knew that Brooke was thinking about her husband, who'd been killed in Iraq a few years back.

"I'm all right," Brooke told Clay, "but thank you for the comfort." She turned back to Wade. "I just want you to understand that it can all turn on a dime. You always think there's time, but you—"

"Hey, guys." They'd not seen Steffie's approach.

"Oh, hey, Stef." Brooke reached out a hand to her and Wade hoped Brooke wouldn't tell her that she'd been the topic of their conversation for the past five minutes. He needn't have worried, though. "You look terrific, girl. All that ice cream is doing you a world of good."

"I walk it off." Stef smiled, then turned to introduce Jesse to Brooke and Clay.

"I was just saying to my mother the other day that I needed to get a will made," Brooke told Jesse.

"Stop in at the office anytime," he told her. "I'd be happy to draw one up for you."

Brooke launched into an explanation of how she wasn't sure of the best way to protect her son's interest in a business that had been owned by her late husband and one of his brothers.

"So," Wade said, tugging on Steffie's hand to get her attention, "did you have a good dinner?"

"We did. Walt's chef does the best seafood in town." She eyed the plate that was next to his elbow on the bar. "Who orders buffalo chicken in a seafood restaurant?"

"I guess I lost my head." *Looking at you,* he could have added, but he was afraid the corn factor might be too great for even Steffie to handle. Instead, he said, "So, what's with you and Enright?"

He hadn't meant to be quite so blunt, but there it was.

"My mom asked him to join us," she explained. "He is her lawyer, you know."

"And yours."

"Yes, and mine." She leaned forward just enough so that her leg was touching his, and whispered, "If I didn't know you better, I'd think you were just a teeny tiny bit jealous."

"Maybe," he whispered back, "you don't know me as well as you think you do."

"Apparently not." She stood back, looking pleased.

"Stef," Clay was saying, "can I get you a drink?"

"No, but thanks, Clay," she declined. "I had a glass of wine with dinner and I think that was my limit tonight. I am flat-out exhausted."

Her parents were leaving and they stopped at the bar to chat with everyone for a few minutes. After they left, Stef said, "I think I'm going to call it a day as well."

"I'll walk you out," Wade said. "Unless you came with . . ." He pointed to Jesse, who was engrossed in conversation with Brooke.

"I drove."

They said good night to the others, then walked out into the parking lot.

"It's a beautiful night," Wade said as they walked to her car.

"Chilly, though."

He put an arm around her and pulled her close. "Better?"

She nodded. They were almost to the car, and she searched her bag for her remote. She unlocked the doors, and the lights blinked. Wade walked her to the driver's side and leaned against the door, thinking that it would be a shame to waste all this moonlight.

He pulled her to him and covered her mouth with his. Her lips were soft and full, and she tasted faintly of wine and smelled like lavender. He felt that jolt he always felt when he was close to her, a shot straight to the gut, and he drew her closer and kissed her again, his tongue exploring the inside of her bottom lip. Her fingers dug into his shoulders and she leaned back against the car, and he eased into her body. There was no question as to where this could lead if she were willing.

Wade was pretty sure she was willing.

Clay's words—*Steffie's got Bay blood in her veins . . . no way that girl's going anywhere*—stuck in Wade's head, because he knew they were true.

He kissed the side of her face and very slowly stepped back.

"We should call it a night," he said as he opened her car door. "Be careful driving home, Stef."

The look of surprise on her face was followed by one of confusion, but she covered up well.

"You, too. See you around." She angled behind the wheel and he closed the door.

He stepped back from the car and watched her drive from the parking lot and up around the bend until her lights disappeared, and still he stood there.

He drove back to River Road and found Austin and Cody asleep across Cody's bed and Dallas and Grant in the kitchen going over the RSVPs for Dallas's birthday party and making last-minute changes on the menu the caterer would serve their guests. Berry's friend Archer's car was in the driveway, but neither was to be seen. Wade chatted with Dallas and Grant for a few minutes before wandering out onto the dock, where he stood at the end looking out toward the Bay.

It was so quiet and peaceful on the river, especially now that the summer people were gone. The night air had a definite chill, an augury of the frosty nights just ahead. He lowered himself to the wooden deck and leaned back against one of the pilings and looked up into the night sky, much as he had done when he was a child and newly come to St. Dennis, a child who wasn't sure where he belonged.

Some things never change, he told himself wryly. Even as an adult, he still wasn't really sure.

When he was younger, he'd moved back and forth between St. Dennis and Dunellen, New Jersey, the town his mother called home. She'd fallen apart after his father died suddenly, and Berry had insisted that the children, Dallas and Wade, come to stay with her for that first summer. And Berry being Berry, she'd wanted them to return the next summer, and the one after that, until spending the summers in St. Dennis became the routine. Then Roberta met a handsome polo player and eloped with him to South America.

Dallas was already out of high school and Wade just about to begin. Berry insisted Wade should go to school in St. Dennis, not in a foreign country, and Berry, as always, got her way.

Up until then, Wade had gone back and forth between Dunellen and St. Dennis. In Dunellen, his father's loss was felt most keenly: the empty chair at the dinner table, the newspapers that were delivered to their door every day but went unread, the chores that Wade took on because his father was no longer there to do them. The heart had gone out of their family, and the house where they'd lived together was never the same. It never again felt like home to Wade.

It had taken him a long time to feel that he belonged in St. Dennis. He'd made friends with some of the local kids, but it was understood that he was a temporary resident, not quite a townie, not quite one of the summer people. He long understood that the fact that he was a really good athlete as well as the grandnephew of the town's only celebrity gave him a status he otherwise would not have enjoyed. The year Wade started high school in St. Dennis was the year that Dallas moved to Hollywood. By his junior year, she'd made several films, and was on her way to becoming an icon in St. Dennis, much like Berry had been years before. Wade's identity was now Dallas MacGregor's little brother, Berry Townsend's nephew. There didn't seem to be a place in town for him without them. With high school graduation came freedom, and he headed for the farthest college that accepted him, which was, as fate had it, in Texas.

He thought about those first few days after he arrived on campus, meeting Robin, becoming such fast friends. Without her friendship, he wouldn't have felt like he belonged there, either, for all his sports and his involvement in campus life. After college, he built a career for himself in Texas, but deep down, he'd not been at home.

Now a person like Steffie, he told himself, has always known where she belonged. She had deep roots here and had no intention of pulling them up. Clay was right about that.

Wade had tried to be objective about Steffie, but it was becoming increasingly more difficult.

There was no denying that what he'd felt earlier in the evening watching Stef with Jesse was jealousy, pure and simple. Jesse could fit seamlessly into her life in the way that mattered most to her—her business and her family—and knowing that made Wade just a little bit crazy. Jesse was likely to stick around. His law office was in town and he had relatives there. Roots, however shallow, were still roots.

On the other hand, every time Wade and Steffie almost got together, Wade left town.

He looked back on all the holiday parties they'd both been at over the years, where one or both of them had dates with someone else. One Christmas a few years ago stuck in his mind. Steffie had arrived late wearing a memorably short, silky red dress that looked more like a slip than evening wear. She'd worn her hair down, much as she'd done tonight, and silver shoes with very high heels. Wade hadn't been able to take his eyes off her, and neither, apparently, could her date, since they left the party after a mere hour. Wade had felt an unexplainable urge to pick a fight with that guy, which was laughable because Wade had never picked a fight with a stranger in his entire life.

Jealousy, he admitted.

He'd vowed right then and there that the following Christmas, he'd skip the date, and hoped she would as well, but that was the year everything had begun to fall apart in Texas and leaving Robin to deal with it alone was out of the question. Last year, it had become clear that the holiday season would be Robin's last, and Wade was determined that she and Austin have that one great Christmas together.

Walking away from Steffie tonight had been tough, but it was probably the best thing he could have done for her sake. He was pretty sure that whatever it was he felt for her, she felt the same, but Clay was right about Steffie not going anywhere. St. Dennis was her home, always had been, always would be. What would be the point in complicating things for either of them?

Chapter 12

"Too strong," Stef muttered, and screwed the lid back onto the jar of honey she'd tasted, then crossed it off the list in front of her. Reminding herself that the darker the honey, the stronger the flavor, she looked through her samples for something lighter. She tried the lightest in color that she had.

"Still not right. Back to square one."

She turned on her laptop and searched the web for a source of honey that might be lighter. She knew she was just about out of time. Dallas's party was on Saturday. That gave her five days, not counting Saturday, though conceivably she could be making ice cream right up until the party, which was to begin at six.

"This place looks promising." She reached for the phone, but a glance at the clock reminded her that it was only four in the morning on the West Coast, so she sent an e-mail instead to the website that was advertising the finest lavender honey money could buy. Okay, Stef thought as she typed, let's put our money where our mouth is . . .

She'd made test batches of formulas that she'd thought were pretty darned good, but after she'd tried them a few days later, she found the honey flavor stronger than she remembered and the texture of the ice cream was too crumbly. Panicking as Saturday drew closer, she'd gone back to her recipe file to start again.

She'd abandoned her idea to add edible lavender flower buds to the mix. She'd tried that, and while the batch right out of the ice-cream maker tasted pretty good, once the flowers froze solid, they were like tiny flavored balls of ice in her mouth and the flavor of lavender was, well, odd.

"Pity." She sighed. "The ice cream looked so pretty with all those purply specks in it."

She put Dallas's birthday ice cream aside and made what she'd need for Scoop that day plus two batches of her homemade cones. She was halfway through the cones when the owner of Lavender Hill Farm in Shelter Bay, Oregon, called and assured her that their lavender honey was indeed light in color and delicately flavored. Once Steffie told her what she needed it for, the owner, Sofia, offered to overnight a sample.

"That would be perfect, thank you so much. I've really gotten myself into a jam here."

She hung up the phone after three more "thank-yous" and returned to the task at hand: deciding which flavors to feature that week. The chocolate monster mash was still popular, so she chopped some solid chocolate and put it in the double boiler to melt over a low heat. She checked the fridge and found she had enough eggs for only a few batches, so she sent Tina to the farm where they usually purchased their eggs to pick up the week's supply plus extra for the weekend.

All of the ice creams with maple flavor were also a hit this time of the year, so she checked her supplies before adding maple walnut to the menu board. Because of its high water content, pure maple syrup had a tendency to dilute the butterfat, so she needed to make sure she had enough of the cream with the highest butterfat content for more than one batch. She had just enough for three or four batches, so she made a note to call her supplier—an organic dairy farm three miles outside of town—and request an early delivery this week. She felt like an idiot calling him again—she'd already called once this week to triple her order in anticipation of the ice cream she'd be making for Dallas's party, and that was before Grant had called to let her know the guest list had grown.

"It's the damnedest thing," Grant had told Stef. "Everyone who got an invitation must have told other people about it, because Dallas's agent has been fielding calls from people asking to be invited."

"I guess the fact that she's starting her own production company and will be making her own films is incentive enough to make the trip east," Stef said. "Maybe people think they'll have a better chance at scoring a role in one of her films if they come to her birthday and bring a big present."

"Uh-uh. No gifts. Dallas put that on the invitations. She asked for donations to 'an animal rescue shelter near you' instead."

"That's nice. I like that. But of course, the no-gifts thing doesn't apply to you."

"What do you mean?"

"Well, she can tell everyone else not to bring her something, but you're her honey. You have to give her a present."

"I arranged for her to have an ice-cream flavor created just for her," Grant reminded Stef.

"Yes, but I'm the one who's making it. I'm the genius who's doing the creating, so it could be said that the ice cream really is from me."

"It was my idea," he protested. "And I'm paying for it."

Steffie smiled sweetly. "I'll be sure to mention that when she's thanking me."

"So how's the ice cream coming along, anyway?"

"It's coming. And don't change the subject."

"I just want to make sure it'll be ready for Saturday night."

"It will be. Now, back to her gift . . ."

"You really think that no-gift thing doesn't apply to me?" Grant sounded worried.

"Yup. You're going to have to come up with a gift, and it's going to have to be good."

A very long silence followed.

"What should I do?" He sounded pathetically flummoxed.

"Two words, sport. Nana's ring."

"You're sure about that?"

"I told you, it's perfect. Unless, of course, you decided not to ask her to marry you. Which could be a break for her . . ."

"Very funny." Grant sighed. "All right. I'll call Mom and see what she thinks."

"Go for it." Steffie hung up and stuck her phone back into her pocket.

She checked the chocolate and found it had melted, so she turned off the stove and set the pot on a trivet to cool, then checked the freezer to make sure she had enough canisters chilling.

"Hey, we missed you at coffee this morning." Vanessa came through the back door with a paper bag in her hand. "I brought you lunch since I figured you'd be too busy to stop to get something for yourself, and knowing you, you didn't bring anything from home."

"You're right, I didn't. Thank you, Ness."

"Aren't you going to ask what it is? Maybe it's something you don't like." Vanessa held up the bag and swung it in front of Steffie.

"I'm so hungry, I almost don't care what it is," Steffie told her. "And you're my best friend. You wouldn't bring me something I don't like."

"True." Vanessa opened the bag. "It's grilled chicken, Swiss, and tomato from the new place around the corner from Book 'Em."

"That's one of my two most favorite sandwiches."

"I know." Vanessa handed over the bag and Steffie peered inside.

"And an iced tea. How did you know I was dying for iced tea today?" Steffie hugged her, then turned to wash her hands at the sink.

"Daz told me," Vanessa deadpanned.

Steffie shot a quick glance over her shoulder and Vanessa laughed. "Kidding. It just seemed to go with the sandwich."

Stef dried her hands and unwrapped the sandwich, then looked back into the bag.

"There's only one sandwich in here," she noted.

"I know. I ate mine on the way down here. I had a really busy morning, so I had to multitask if I wanted to eat." Vanessa rested her elbows on the worktable.

"I had one delivery after another this morning, which was a good thing because I sold out of so much stuff on Saturday. The charity run was good for business, Stef. Everyone was talking about it this morning."

"Good. I'm glad. I love a win-win. Money for research, business for the merchants."

"And we're all looking forward to another big weekend coming up, with all the Hollywood people coming for Dallas's party. Grace was saying this morning that her son told her they were totally booked from Thursday right through until Monday," Vanessa told her. "Barbara heard the other two inns and all the B-and-Bs were booked as well. And Carlo told us that every table at every restaurant in town is reserved for Friday and Sunday nights. Someone booked Let's Do Brunch for Saturday and Sunday—both days, for the entire time they're open." Nessa's eyes were shining. "Of course, that's only from ten in the morning until two in the afternoon, but still, that's a lot of guaranteed business." She sighed. "I hope there will be lots of those Hollywood types stopping in at Bling."

"There will be if Dallas tells everyone that she shops there." Steffie took a bite of her sandwich, thinking that she should make extra ice cream as well. The forecast was for unseasonably warm weather. She knew from experience that the warmer temperatures alone would increase her business. Add an extra hundred people to the mix and she would run out early if she didn't prepare in advance for the increase in foot traffic. "This is delicious, thanks. I appreciate it."

"What are friends for?" Vanessa paused before adding, "Besides, I promised everyone I'd pump you for info on Saturday night."

"I told you, I didn't have a date with Jesse. Didn't you tell everyone that?"

"Yes, but apparently half of St. Dennis was in Walt's on Saturday night. The other half was in the parking lot."

"Oh. That." Another exercise in frustration that she didn't feel like reliving right then.

"So . . . ?"

"So he walked me out to my car and he caught me in a lip-lock."

"And . . ." Vanessa rolled her eyes. "Am I going to have drag every little detail from you?"

"Depends."

"On what?"

"On what you've already heard."

"Brooke stopped in at Bling this morning, and she said that her brother and Wade were eating at the bar and they saw you with Jesse, and Wade looked put out about it."

"She said that? Wade was put out because I was with Jesse?"

Vanessa nodded.

"So what else did she say?"

"She said that you and Jesse stopped at the bar on the way out, and she got into a conversation with him about something to do with her will, and that when she looked up, you and Wade were gone."

"True enough. Brooke did seem interested in Jesse, and he sure seemed interested in her," Stef told her.

"That's not the way it's supposed to happen." Vanessa frowned.

"The way what's not supposed to happen?"

"Unless . . ." Vanessa bit her bottom lip. "Unless somehow Brooke was walking past the house . . ."

"What are you talking about?"

"The"—Vanessa looked around, then lowered her voice—"incantation wasn't intended to draw anyone into Brooke's life. It was supposed to draw them into yours."

"I'm having a really hard time keeping a straight face right now, Ness." Steffie looked up from measuring ingredients. "I just thought you should know."

"Skeptic."

"Well, at least you can feel vindicated that Brooke and Jesse really hit it off." Stef bit back a grin. "So even if your . . . incantation went haywire, at least you know it hit home somewhere."

"Very funny."

"I guess it was the universe that brought everyone together at Walt's on Saturday night," Stef said. "Clay and Wade were at the bar after I sat down at my parents' table, then Brooke joined them. I wondered what they were talking about. They had their heads together for a long time."

"Beer." Vanessa took another swipe at the chocolate. "They were talking about beer."

"Why?"

"Brooke said Clay might be interested in starting his own brewery here in St. Dennis."

"And he wanted to hire Wade to work for him?"

Vanessa shook her head. "He wanted Wade to tell him some of his beer-making secrets, I think. Since Wade will be leaving next week to go to his new job, he and Clay wouldn't be in competition."

Steffie put her sandwich down on the paper it had been wrapped in.

"He's leaving next week?"

"So he told Clay, and Clay told Brooke." Vanessa and Stef stared at each other. "He didn't tell you, did he." It wasn't a question.

Stef shook her head.

"Crap. I'm sorry. I thought you knew." Vanessa frowned.

"No big deal." Stef waved it off. "What difference does it make if he goes next week or next month? The bottom line is that he's going."

"Still . . ."

"It's okay. Really." Steffie took a sip of iced tea and checked her watch just as the timer went off.

"What's the timer for?"

"The chocolate's ready." She removed a cold canister from the freezer.

"I have to get back to the shop and you're busy." Vanessa hiked up her shoulder bag. "Stef, I'm really sorry."

"Ness, it's fine."

"Maybe some night this week we could have that sleepover we talked about," Vanessa said from the doorway. "Grady took a group hiking in Idaho and he won't be back until Friday afternoon."

"Sounds good to me." Stef looked up and smiled. "The sleepover, not the hiking."

"I'll talk to you later."

Steffie nodded. "Thanks again for bringing me lunch."

"Anytime." Vanessa looked about to say something else, but apparently had second thoughts. She closed the door behind her without another word.

Stef put the pot of chocolate on a trivet on the table and wondered how long she'd feel as if she had a stake through her heart. She heard the bell ring in the shop several times and was glad that Claire was there to serve her customers, because she really didn't feel like seeing anyone right then.

Get a grip, she told herself. *You had no reason to believe he'd be sticking around.*

She almost wished there was something to that spell of Vanessa's. It would certainly make life easier, one way or another. Either Wade would be falling at her feet, or else she'd be able to wave good-bye to him knowing that something better was right around the bend; and it wouldn't hurt so much that he was leaving. And it did hurt that he hadn't told her himself that he'd be gone soon. Just as it had hurt when he'd pulled away right as she was thinking about dragging him home with her, though now she was beginning to think she understood why.

Secretly, she'd thought that maybe this time, he'd stay around for a while, at least long enough for her to get him out of her system once and for all. And secretly, in her heart of hearts, she'd harbored the belief that he was the one. Somehow she must have projected that, he'd picked up on it, and he'd decided to put the skids on things before they went any further. She supposed she should thank him for that.

"Time to say good-bye to my Wade fantasy for good," she muttered. "I may have obsessed about him when I was a kid, but I haven't pined for him since high school. I'm not going to start now."

The wall phone rang and she rose from the stool to answer it.

"One Scoop or Two. This is Steffie. How can I help you . . . ?"

Diary ~

You'd think that once the season had ended, we'd have seen the last of the tourists, but no! Not this year! Dallas MacGregor is celebrating her birthday here in St. Dennis next weekend, and the guest list is a veritable Who's Who in Hollywood. Why, on Monday evening, I happened to answer the phone at the inn's reservation desk—don't ask me where Becky was, she wasn't at the desk when I walked by—and who was on the other end but Sidney Warren! At least, that's how he identified himself! He wanted to book a suite of rooms from Friday through Sunday, and I had the disappointing task of telling him that not only do we not have suites, but that we were totally booked for the weekend. Oh, the pain of having to turn away a genuine heart-throb (and my heart was throbbing!). I did, however, direct him to several other establishments and I told him to check back later in the week in case there were cancellations (fat chance, but one can hope!). He left his phone number for us to call in the event that something opened up.

And it's been like that all over town for the past two weeks—stars and superstars and famous directors and producers, and yes, even tabloid reporters all calling for rooms.

Well, we all—the hoteliers here in town, that is—got together and decided not to book rooms for anyone who worked for one of those sleazy papers. Dallas deserves to have a happy birthday in the company of her family and friends without the rest of the world watching.

So who's next? The paparazzi??

Oh—and Vanessa stopped in on Sunday afternoon and dropped off all of Alice's journals. Some, but perhaps not all. I imagine as she finds others, she'll pass those along to me as well. I admit that I do feel better now, knowing they're safely in my keeping. Bless the girl for remembering that I'd asked for them.

~ Grace ~

Chapter 13

"HEY, buddy, where are you going?" Wade followed his son's toddling steps across Berry's backyard.

"Geeses." Austin pointed a chubby finger in the direction of the river.

"Yes, those are geese. Did Cody teach you that?"

"Uh-huh." Austin's head bobbed up and down. "Cody."

Austin continued down to the dock with Wade close behind. When he came to the end, the little boy lay down on his stomach and peered slowly over the edge.

"What's down there?" Wade lowered himself to the deck beside his son.

Austin looked up, and with one finger across his mouth, he whispered, "Fishies."

Wade craned his neck and looked over the side of the dock.

"See?" Austin pointed into the water. "Fishies."

"I see," Wade said, earning a "shhhh" from his son.

Wade stretched out alongside Austin and watched the river below.

"Crabbies," Austin said softly. "See?"

Wade nodded. "I see."

From the opposite side of the river, a great blue heron rose, startling them both.

"Ooh!" Austin exclaimed. "Big bird!"

"That's one big bird, all right," Wade agreed. "That bird is called a heron. They like to walk along the edge of the river and eat the little fish."

"My fishies?" a horrified Austin asked, and Wade nodded.

"Bad bird." Austin scolded the heron whose wide wingspan had taken him to the mouth of the river, where he set down and began to troll the waters at the edge of the Bay. "Bad, bad bird."

"Hungry bird," Wade corrected him, then realized that his son was probably a little young for the food-chain talk. "Let's see what else we can find out here on the river today."

They resumed their places, both on their stomachs watching the river slowly roll by, and soaked up a bit of sunshine. The morning was tranquil, and for a quiet while, father and son simply enjoyed time in each other's company. Several boats went by, one speeding by earning an emphatic "shhh" from Austin.

Wade turned onto his back, folded his arms behind his head and closed his eyes, and took a deep breath. It smelled like autumn again today, like falling leaves and the last of the summer annuals and the pine needles that had dropped to form a soft carpet beneath the branches. The nursery on the highway already had hay bales and pumpkins and mums for sale, and he'd heard Dallas telling Berry that Olivia the florist was carving out pumpkins and filling them with flowers for the centerpieces on the tables for her birthday party.

With Austin curled up next to him, Wade moved one arm to hold the child close to his body. Within minutes, Austin was asleep, his head on his father's biceps, his breathing warm and gentle on Wade's skin. Wade was aware now that Austin was not just an important part of his life, but a necessary one, and that every decision he made and would make for the next eighteen years or so would be done with Austin's interests in mind. That reality had been waking Wade in the middle of the night for the past week. For one thing, it hadn't been something he'd fully comprehended when he'd promised Robin he'd raise her son as his, but it had become a fact of his life. No regrets, but still, for someone who'd pretty much winged it for most of his life, having a constant was somewhat heady. The responsibility overwhelmed him when he thought about it, so he'd tried not to think about it very much. He'd long since come to believe that some things were better off left alone.

But along with the responsibility had come a sense of purpose he'd not expected, and he'd found that he enjoyed Austin more and more as time went on. He was pretty sure that most parents felt that way, but since he'd not had much preparation for becoming a father, so much had come as a surprise. Like the way his heart bounced just a little when Austin's face lit up when Wade came home from being anywhere for any amount of time, be it several hours or fifteen minutes. Or the way Austin's laughter made him smile every time he heard it, or the pure and simple love Wade felt when, every night before he went to bed, he checked Austin's crib to make sure he was covered and that his favorite stuffed giraffe was nearby.

To say that the child had blindsided him might be an understatement.

Austin was so happy here in St. Dennis that Wade was starting to wonder how leaving would affect him. His son had grown so close to Cody, and he was doted on by both Dallas and Berry. How would it affect him to lose them as part of his daily life so soon after having lost his mother? And what if he couldn't find anyone in Connecticut who could provide the kind of child care Austin had always had? Ted had made his offer to Wade long before they came to St. Dennis, before Wade saw how the growing child adapted to his new environment and how quickly he'd bonded with the new people in his life. Before St. Dennis, for the most part, Austin's inner circle had consisted only of an increasingly ill Robin, and Wade. Occasionally their upstairs neighbor, Mrs. Barker, watched Robin and Austin when Wade had to be somewhere else, like when he'd made the trip to St. Dennis for Beck and Mia's wedding. It had been Mrs. Barker who'd called Wade that night to let him know that he needed to come home, that Robin had taken a turn for the worse, and that she didn't want to be there alone with the little boy if his mother passed that night in her sleep.

Child care was only one of the things Wade would need to investigate when he arrived in Connecticut on Monday. He hated to admit it to Dallas, but he was becoming increasingly concerned about the contract that Ted kept promising to send him but that hadn't arrived. The day after Dallas had raised questions—good questions, issues that hadn't occurred to Wade—he'd called Ted and asked to have the contract overnighted so he could take a look at it. That was last week, and it still hadn't come. He'd e-mailed Ted two days ago, but despite the promise, Wade had yet to receive it. So what, he had to ask himself, was this guy hiding? And wasn't it a bad sign to begin a business relationship with someone you were starting to think of as "this guy"?

Well, soon enough Wade would know what was what. He planned on touring the brewery on Monday and the town of Oak Grove on Tuesday, look for child care and living accommodations on Wednesday. He knew the day-care center at the plant was an option, but he wasn't sure how Austin would fare in a group setting after having lived with adults—very few adults—for his entire life. Yes, there was Cody, but he was older than Austin and wasn't exactly a peer. Austin had never been around a lot of other kids his own age, and Wade didn't know enough about parenting to tell when a kid like his, who was pretty shy, would be ready to join such a group.

Did all parents anguish over this stuff, or was it just Wade? And how did moms always seem to manage, anyway? Maybe he should talk to Dallas before he left on Monday. Then again, he had the feeling that any doubts he might express would likely raise her hopes that he'd changed his mind.

And then there was Steffie.

Nothing in his life had ever created as many conflicted feelings in him as Steffie. Deciding to claim

Austin as his own had been a piece of cake compared to figuring out where—if anywhere—he fit into Stef's life, and where she fit into his. When it came to her, the only thing Wade knew for certain was that he didn't have a clue. Oh, yeah, and that his body temperature rose and his ability to think clearly diminished in direct proportion to his proximity to her.

Bottom line: he'd been a fool to think he could stand that close to the fire and not feel its heat.

Like it or not, he was beginning to suspect that his concerns about the new job—the contract and about the move being too upsetting for Austin and the child care maybe not being what he wanted it to be—maybe it was all a smoke screen for the fact that more and more he was beginning to think that there was more for him in St. Dennis than he'd realized.

A shadow fell across his face, and he heard a soft clicking sound.

"You'd best put that camera away," Wade said without opening his eyes. "I know guys who've tossed their sisters into the river for less than that."

"Sorry. I couldn't resist. You and Austin look so peaceful sleeping there together." When Wade looked up, Dallas was staring upriver. "It sounds as if someone's cutting down trees."

"Berry said the other day that one of the lots near the warehouses was sold. Maybe the new owner is going to be building there." He eased up onto his elbows, trying not to awaken the still-sleeping child.

Dallas was frowning. "I hope it's not the lot closest to the properties I just bought. One of the reasons I found those warehouses so perfect for a movie studio was that they were naturally shielded from the public. Those woods are a big part of that shield."

"Why don't you give Hal a call, see if he knows anything about that?" Wade suggested.

"Good idea." She turned toward the house.

"Did you come out here for any reason other than to disturb my sleep?" he asked.

"Oh. Yeah." Dallas took a few steps back in his direction. "Berry wanted to know if you could move that trailer that you brought all your stuff in so the caterers can start putting up the tent tomorrow."

"Where would she like me to put it?"

"Someplace other than in her yard."

"Any suggestions?"

Dallas appeared to be thinking. "You could probably leave it in one of the warehouses. Or maybe you could leave it over at Grant's, back by the shelter. Either way would work. And it's only for a few days."

"I'll think it over."

"Think fast. The tent's going up in the morning." She waved and answered her ringing phone as she returned to the house.

Wade carefully lifted the sleeping boy and held him against his chest and shoulder. The trailer held everything he and Austin owned other than the things they'd needed here in St. Dennis. All the photographs Wade had taken of Robin that he'd saved for Austin, all of Austin's baby toys, including the things Robin bought for him before he was born, before the combination of cancer and pregnancy rendered her too weak to do much of anything except sleep. And Wade's notebooks, where he'd jotted down the formulas for some of the best beer he'd ever tasted. He hated the thought of leaving those precious items anyplace where he couldn't see them.

He wondered if he'd have time to clean out enough of the carriage house to fit the trailer inside.

Austin stirred, then snuggled. Wade hesitated for a moment, then went up to the house. By the time he got there, Austin was awake and ready for his morning snack.

"Why, you're just in time," Berry declared. "I'm having some yogurt with fresh pineapple. Who'd like to join me?"

"Me would." Without prompting, Austin climbed into his chair, and Berry took the chair next to him.

"You hold the bowls for me, and I'll do the scooping," she said.

"Scoop." Austin laughed. "Steppie."

"Ah, you clever child." Berry beamed and turned to Wade, who stood in the doorway. "See how he quickly he made that connection?"

"He's clever, all right," Wade agreed. "Especially where ice cream is concerned."

"Eem." Austin's word for ice cream.

"After your nap we'll go for ice cream, ace," Wade told him. "Right now, have a snack with Aunt Berry." He turned to Berry. "Would you mind if I tried to make some room in the carriage house for the trailer? I hate to leave it anyplace off the property."

"If you can do so by tomorrow, dear. The caterers—"

"Dallas told me they'd be here in the morning." He frowned. "Why do we need tents for the party, anyway? Why don't we have the party in here, in the house?"

Berry burned him with The Look. "Seriously, Wade? Picture several hundred people—most of them strangers to me—running amok in this house."

"I doubt if Dallas's friends would be running a—"

"My house, my rules. No strangers in the house. Which is why I insisted on hiring security for the weekend." She turned back to the task of preparing yogurt sundaes for herself and Austin.

"Security? As in guards?"

"Absolutely. You haven't been in the business, dear, so I forgive your naïveté. With the guests will come the reporters—print and TV—and with them will come hordes of paparazzi and every form of gate-crasher you could possibly imagine. I won't have those people trampsing all over my property."

"Do you mean trampling?"

"No, I mean *trampsing*, as in 'trampsing about.' "

Wade smiled. It must be a Berryism. "So how do you intend to keep the interlopers out?"

"Invitations must be shown at the door, and they will be scrutinized for authenticity and the names checked against the final list. No invitation? Name not on the list? No admittance."

"How do you determine whether or not the invitations are authentic?"

Berry smiled. "Dallas personally numbered them in a most discreet manner. On the back of the invitations there's an ink sketch of the Chesapeake with a boat heading toward the sunset. The side of the boat bears a number. That's the number of the invitation."

"What about the river?" he asked. "Have you

thought about people who might try to sneak in from that direction?"

"Yes, dear, but there will be security around the dock area." Berry smiled. "Besides, if anyone tries to sneak in from the river, their wet clothes will give them away."

"Seems like a lot of trouble to go to just to have a party." Wade got a fork and stabbed a piece of pineapple. "I'd never have a party if I had to go to all that trouble."

"When you're world famous for making your beer, and people are clamoring for your attention, we'll have this discussion again."

"Don't hold your breath." He ate the pineapple and went out to the carriage house.

Once inside, he started taking a mental inventory of its contents. Old tractors, once used for cutting the grass, he supposed, before Berry hired a lawn-care service. A couple of canoes, a rowboat, garden implements, old sleds, and several pairs of old ice skates—men's and women's—that hung upon one of the vertical beams. Old furniture—chairs, tables, Victorian-era settees that had been stripped of their cushions and upholstery—sat in stacks throughout the large space. It was a stunning array of accumulated stuff that no one had used in at least a quarter century if not more.

"I don't know what she's keeping all this stuff for," Wade muttered as he maneuvered around.

Toward the back wall he found some empty space, enough to contain a lot of the items closer to the door. He debated whether it would be easier to simply move the front items to the back or move everything back by ten feet. In the end, given the amount of time he had to work with, he'd carry the canoes and roll some of the wheelbarrows—really, Berry? Five of them?—and hopefully, he'd have enough room to back the trailer into the carriage house.

He'd stood one of the canoes up against the wall and was returning for a second when his shirt was snagged by a skate blade hanging from one of the posts. As he carefully disengaged the fabric from the blade, he noticed the carving on the post: A B C. Funny, he thought. Was someone practicing writing the alphabet or practicing their skill with a knife?

It took him most of the afternoon, but he succeeded in clearing the way with room to spare. He was in the process of detaching the trailer from the back of the Jeep when Berry showed up with Austin at her side.

"I hope you didn't break anything," she said as she peered inside the building. "Or bury things so that I can't get to them if I need something."

"Berry, when was the last time you needed something out of there?" he asked.

"Immaterial." She dismissed the thought with a wave of her hand. "If I want something, I need to be able to get to it."

"If you want something that you can't get to, I'll get it for you," he promised.

"Easy for you to say, since you won't be around."

"When you need something from the carriage house that you can't find, I'll come back and find it for you."

"Damn right you will."

He was about to ask Berry if she'd learned her alphabet by carving letters on the post, but Austin interrupted by reminding him of the promise of ice cream after his nap.

"Let me get cleaned up and I'll take you," Wade told him.

"I'll come along, if you don't mind," Berry said. "I'd love to see what Steffie has this week. You know she's making something special for Dallas's party, and Grant says . . ."

Berry chatted all the way to the kitchen and all the way into town and while Wade parked the Jeep in the big lot behind Scoop. Something about all the upcoming social events must have loosened her tongue, Wade thought as they walked into the shop, because he couldn't remember her ever talking so much.

". . . and so I told Olivia that I thought the pumpkins were a lovely idea." Berry tapped Wade on the arm. "Don't you agree, dear?"

Wade nodded. "I do."

"You fake. You haven't heard a thing I've said since you locked up the carriage house." Berry walked past him and went directly to the cooler. "Well, then, Austin, what shall it be today . . . ?"

Wade held Austin up to the counter while trying to see into the back room when someone, abruptly, closed the door from the inside.

"What looks good to you, Ms. Townsend?" Tina asked.

"Everything looks good, Tina. It always does." Berry scanned the contents of the case. "I think the young master here will have a small scoop of chocolate in a dish. I'll have the maple pecan." She turned to Wade. "And for you, dear?"

"I'll go with the chocolate."

After they'd been served and Wade was at the cash register, he asked, "Is Steffie around?"

"She's tied up right now," Tina replied without looking up from the register. "Did you need to speak with her?"

"Just wanted to say hi."

"I'll let her know." Tina handed Wade his change with a smile.

"Thanks."

Odd, he thought, when he stopped in the following afternoon, that she was still tied up. He made sure to include Olive Street on his nightly run, but there were no lights on in Stef's house. Odder still, she was not available the following day when he took Cody and Austin for ice cream.

"Is Stef in?" he asked Claire.

"She's in but she doesn't want to be disturbed," Claire told him.

"Could you just tell her that Wade was asking for her?"

"Sure." Claire smiled.

She was busy again on Thursday when he called and left a message, and she wasn't around Friday after dinner, either. Too busy to return a call? Too busy to stick her head out the door and just say hi? What the hell?

He almost caught up with her on Saturday. He was in the kitchen giving Austin lunch when he looked out the window and saw her talking to one of the caterers. He watched as several of the young guys on the crew helped her unload coolers from the back of her car and place them into one of the portable freezers on two of their trucks. He wanted to run out to catch her before she left, but by the time Austin had finished eating, she was gone.

It wasn't until he was getting dressed for the party that it occurred to him that she was avoiding him. He tried to dismiss the thought, but it wouldn't leave. Why would she be annoyed with him? It wasn't as if he . . .

He paused, thinking back to the previous Saturday night. Forgetting for a moment that he was acutely aware that he hadn't seen Steffie since he'd closed the car door and watched her drive away that night, he went over the scene in the parking lot. The chitchat. The embrace. The kissing before his conscience got the best of him and reminded him not to start something he wasn't going to be around to finish. What, he wondered as he looked out the window and saw the first of Dallas's guests arrive, had been wrong with that?

Chapter 14

STEFFIE could hear the band from the street, and it was really rocking. She wondered what the neighbors must be thinking. But of course most of the neighbors had known Dallas since she was a girl and were probably all partying just as she would be in another moment or two.

It was so odd, she thought as she passed through security, to see so many people standing around outside Berry's fence on River Road, many with cameras trying to catch a glimpse of this actor or that actress. A well-known entertainment-show hostess interviewing the arrivals apparently thought that Steffie was "somebody," as she'd momentarily attempted to interview her before realizing the mistake. The crowd of locals had booed when the microphone was turned from Stef to a famous director who was just alighting from his limo.

Times like this served as a reminder that, as much as Dallas fit into St. Dennis, she was one of them only because she chose to be.

The first person Stef recognized when she walked down to the tent was Grace.

"Hi, Miss Grace." Steffie waved. "Are you here as a friend of the family or as a reporter for your paper?"

"Both." She leaned toward Steffie and confided, "Dallas left word at the door that I was to be allowed to bring in my camera. I don't believe anyone else is being permitted."

"I think you may be right. Dallas didn't want a lot of candid shots popping up on the Internet. I know Grant has his camera because he's asked me to take a picture when he asks Dallas to—" Steffie tried to stop herself from letting the cat out of the bag, but it was already too late. She tried to cover by adding, "When he surprises Dallas with a special gift."

But Grace was having none of it.

"Oh, my, is Grant thinking about proposing tonight?"

"I could just shoot myself," Steffie mumbled.

"No, no, dear. Not to worry. I won't say anything." Grace laughed.

"Thank you, Miss Grace. Grant would just kill me if he got word of this." Steffie gave Grace's arm an affectionate squeeze.

"Oh, I've kept more secrets for more people in this town than anyone could ever imagine," Grace said.

"Well, then, we just added one more." Steffie took two glasses of champagne from a passing tray and handed one to Grace. "Here's to the keeper of the secrets."

"I'll have just a sip to accept the honor." Grace barely touched her lips to the rim of the glass. "I need to stay sharp to get lots of good shots tonight."

"I'm sure you will." Steffie glanced around the crowd that milled about the lawn and under the one big tent that the caterer opted for instead of the several smaller tents they'd originally planned on having. At the last minute, a tent they felt would be large enough to hold the entire group was found to be available from another caterer in Annapolis and was borrowed for the occasion.

"It certainly is festive, isn't it?" Grace nodded to the scene under the tent, where the band was playing, a few couples were dancing, and dozens of round tables for ten were draped in brown cloths and decked with flowers in shades of purple and orange and touches of red. "It's just beautiful. I think Olivia has outdone herself with the flowers. I'll have to seek her out and compliment her on her work."

"She always does beautiful work. I love to walk past her shop and just look in the windows and at the displays out front. It always picks up my spirits."

"Oh, look, there are Vanessa and Grady. Don't they make a stunning couple?" Grace pointed them out in the crowd.

"They do," Steffie agreed.

"I must say, though, that you look quite stunning, too, dear. That shade of green is so lovely with your coloring."

"Thank you." Steffie pushed back the shrug she was wearing to show off the thin straps of the dress. "I bought this from Vanessa's shop, but I wasn't thinking about how cool it would be tonight, so I had to add the shrug. I hate to cover up the top of the dress because it's so pretty, but I hated the thought of shivering all night even more." Steffie continued to scan the crowd from her vantage point near the house. "There's Barbara." She noticed the bookseller in the crowd. "I know she was looking forward to this. She said she came to a lot of garden parties here when Berry was younger."

"Oh, yes, I remember. Berry was quite the social butterfly back then." Grace nodded. "She was every bit the hostess. Back in the day, it wasn't at all unusual to have Hollywood types about. Speaking of which, isn't that Cindy Sims, the actress?"

"Where?" Stef squinted. "Oh, over there near the tent. Yes, that's her. Everyone says she's the next big thing."

"She's lovely, and she's talented. I saw her in something not too long ago, and I said to myself—"

"Hey, kiddo. Glad you could make it." Grant appeared through the crowd in the tent and hugged his sister and planted a kiss on both her cheek and Grace's. "And you're looking lovely, Miss Grace."

"Thank you, Grant. You look quite handsome this evening."

Grant laughed. "Wait till you see Berry. And Dallas."

"Beauty definitely runs in the family," Grace told him.

"Gee, Grant, this is pretty heady company you're keeping these days. I see movie stars, directors, producers . . ." Steffie looked around the tent. "And half the guests haven't arrived yet."

"I know, it's crazy, right?" He shook his head. "All friends of Dallas's."

"But I see friends of yours, as well," Grace pointed out. "I see the Madisons are all here. Brooke, Clay, their mother . . ."

"Oh, yeah. Dallas couldn't have a party without her St. Dennis buddies."

"Steffie." Grace grabbed Stef's arm, "Isn't that Victoria Seymour, the writer? The author of *Pretty Maids,* the book that Dallas is making into a movie?"

"I don't know what she looks like, so it could be." Steffie turned to Grant. "Do you know?"

"I think it might be." He watched Berry approach the woman with both arms out in welcome. "I know Berry's been talking with her on the phone on and off for the past couple of weeks and they've been looking forward to meeting each other since Berry's going to be playing one of the leads in *Pretty Maids.*"

"And that would be Laura Fielding joining them," Grace noted. "She's to play the role of Charlotte, Dallas said. It's so exciting to see the three of them there together. Oh, and there's Dallas, joining them. I must see if I can get a picture. If you'll excuse me . . ." Grace sped off.

"Dallas looks gorgeous, as always." Steffie watched Dallas glide across the lawn in a beautiful deep plum dress.

"She is the most beautiful woman on the planet." Grant was clearly still mesmerized.

"So are you all ready to get down on one knee and propose in front of all these people?" Steffie teased, thinking that would be the last thing her brother would ever do.

He shocked her by nodding solemnly.

"Get out." She laughed. "You'd never . . . Grant? Really?"

"Really." He nodded. "I started thinking about what you said the other day, about giving Dallas something that no one else could. And I talked to Mom about Nana's ring and she thought it was perfect. Then I was thinking about how much Dallas loves a little bit of drama."

Steffie rolled her eyes. "Duh. Actress?"

Grant smiled. "So after she's finished welcoming everyone, and Brooke brings in the cupcakes and we sing 'Happy Birthday,' I thought that would be the time."

Steffie's eyes misted. "I never thought of you as a romantic soul, but I have to hand it to you. That's just beautiful."

"Unless, you know, she says no . . ." Grant's voice trailed off.

"You are just so . . ." She gave him an affectionate whack on the arm and he laughed. "Dallas isn't going to say no. She loves you. God knows why but she does."

"I know. I can't believe it either."

"And how great was it that Krista let Paige come for the long weekend?" Steffie pointed out Grant's teenage daughter, who was walking across the lawn with Cody and Austin.

"I really am grateful to my ex-wife for that," Grant said. "Paige is delighted that Dallas is going to be her stepmother and that Cody will be her brother."

"I don't imagine having a movie star as your stepmother damages your social standing," Stef observed.

"Probably not." Grant watched his daughter for a moment, then turned to Stef and asked, "So what's with you and Wade?"

"What are you talking about?" Steffie frowned. "There's nothing with me and Wade."

"That's what I mean. What's going on?"

"Nothing." She felt her voice rise slightly in defense, and tried to tone it down. "We're friends."

"Friends return friends' phone calls."

"I've been busy. I had a boatload of ice cream to make for tonight and another boatload to make for the Halloween thing in a couple of weeks. There are only so many hours in the day." She folded her arms across her chest. "Besides, Wade's a jerk."

"I think you need to have that conversation with him." Grant lowered his voice. "And it looks as if you're going to be able to do exactly that in about twenty seconds. Since I have enough to deal with tonight, I'm just going to fade away and see if I can catch up with Paige."

"Coward," she said from the corner of her mouth.

"Damn straight." Grant snagged a glass of beer from a waiter and took off in search of his daughter.

Steffie took a sip of champagne and tried to keep her temper in check. For two cents, she'd have let it rip, but this was an important social event not only for Dallas, but for Grant as well, and the last thing she'd ever want to do would be to embarrass them. Still, it took most of her control.

"Hey, Stef." Wade came up behind her and she turned to him. "You look . . . you look . . . beautiful." He stared at her for a moment, then frowned. "And pissed off."

"Oh, gosh," she deadpanned. "What on earth could I be pissed off about?"

"I don't know. I'm the one who's gotten the brush-off this week. I've called you, left messages, stopped in. Haven't heard a word from you."

"And you can't figure out why?"

He shook his head. "No, I can't."

"Perhaps it has something to do with a little bit of information that you neglected to share."

Several people walking by turned to look at the two of them. Wade took Steffie by the hand and said, "Let's move this out of the entrance to the tent, shall we? No need to—"

"No need to tell me that you were leaving the day after tomorrow for a job up north someplace and you weren't coming back?"

"I was going to tell you—"

"When? When you got there and got settled?" She shook her hand from his. "When you came home for Christmas?"

"When you returned my phone call from Wednesday. Or Thursday. Or Friday. Oh, that's right." He snapped his fingers. "You didn't call back any of those times."

"I didn't see any reason to, after you left me hot and bothered in the parking lot last Saturday night. Which was, I might add, the second time you've done that to me." Her eyes all but shot fire. "Well, you know what they say: Fool me once, shame on you. Fool me twice . . ."

"Stef, I wasn't trying to—"

"Your loss, buster. You would have gotten lucky." She pushed him away and started past him. "It would have been a night you'd never forget."

"Stef, I was only trying to—"

"To what? Screw up the local girl? Again?"

"That's exactly what I was trying to avoid. Look, I know what happens every time you and I get too close." He reached out and tried to take her arm, but she pulled away. "You know it, too. Knowing that I was going to be moving away, I just thought I should . . ." He paused.

"You thought you should what?" Her eyes narrowed. The tone of her voice all but dared him to continue.

"I just thought I should . . . back off. Protect you," he said. "From, you know, getting hurt because I was leaving."

"Oh, wait. Let me get this straight. You were protecting me because if we'd gotten involved, I would have gotten hurt."

Wade nodded and almost looked relieved for a moment, but the moment didn't last.

"You are the biggest ass I have ever known in my life." Her voice rose. "How dare you presume to make that choice for me?"

Before he could respond, she went on. "And what makes you think I can't protect myself? Do you really think I'm so helpless and so stupid that I can't take care of myself when it comes to you?"

Wade appeared stunned.

"Say something," she demanded.

"I . . . I'm sorry," he started, but she cut him off.

"For insulting me?"

"For . . . whatever it was . . ." He ran his fingers through his hair, a look of sheer confusion on his face. "Stef, I never meant to . . . to do any of those things I've obviously done. It just seems like I'm always leaving you, Stef."

"You *are* always leaving, Wade," she shot back.

"You've been leaving since you were eighteen years old. But you always come back."

"I'd think you'd be tired of it by now."

"Aren't you?" she asked.

"When I took this job, I didn't think about coming here or leaving here. The only thought I had was that I needed a job to support Austin and me. I didn't think about how it would be to see you, or what it would feel like to kiss you." He tried to force a smile. "You might recall that I've tried to avoid kissing you for a long time."

"My high school graduation party. I tricked you into coming out to the grape arbor with me and I made you kiss me."

This time he did smile. "Even then I knew how hard it would be to resist you, Stef."

"Is it?" She took a step closer to him. "Hard to resist me?"

"Gets harder all the time," he admitted.

"Then why do you? And if you say it's for my own good, I will kill you right where you stand."

He hesitated, then said, "It's because of the look."

"The look?" she frowned. "What look?"

"The look you get on your face when you're disappointed. I keep seeing the look on your face the night of Beck's wedding. You looked so crushed and so hurt . . . Let me finish. You asked, so I'm going to assume you want the truth. I never wanted to see you look like that again. I never wanted you to feel like that again. I hurt you that night when I left."

"You did hurt me that night, but I understand now why you left, and I'll give you the benefit of the doubt and say that I think you were so blindsided by your neighbor's phone call that you wouldn't have had time to explain the whole thing about Robin that night. I understand that you thought there was a good chance that Robin would die before you got back and I'm sure the prospect terrified you. I can accept that."

"Thank you."

"And I appreciate that you did tell me about Robin."

Wade nodded.

"What I don't appreciate is you deciding for me that I can't handle whatever would come next. After this." She stepped closer again, and wrapped her arms around his neck. She drew his face to hers and kissed him on the mouth. He seemed to hesitate for the briefest moment before his arms tightened around her.

She pulled back from him and looked into his eyes. "Because I can handle it, Wade. I can handle going wherever this leads. Can you?"

"You're not a love-'em-and-leave-'em girl, Stef," he protested.

"What kind of girl do you think I am?"

"A forever girl," he said softly.

"Then treat me like I'm one. Take a chance tonight, Wade. It might be your last. Then again . . ."

Applause from the tent seemed to roll across the lawn like thunder.

"Oh, hell. I forgot about Dallas. . . ." She grabbed his hand and headed toward the tent.

"We can see Dallas later," Wade told her. "We can see Dallas tomorrow."

"But not this . . ." She turned to him at the entrance

to the tent and smiled. "We need to see this." She leaned forward and whispered, "I'll make it worth your while later."

"In that case . . ." Wade followed her into the tent.

Dallas stood on the bandstand with a microphone in her hand and the crowd hushed.

"Thank you all so much for coming to celebrate my birthday with me," she began. "I know many of you traveled quite a distance to be here tonight, and I appreciate it. I'm happy that you all got a little taste of our beautiful town, and I hope that tomorrow you'll visit our shops and our restaurants and you'll understand why the longer I stay in St. Dennis, the harder it is for me to leave. If you enjoyed the ice cream you had for dessert, stop in at One Scoop or Two down near the marina and sample some of Steffie Wyler's ridiculously delicious flavors—all made right there, by Steffie, from scratch. If you like my dress"—Dallas twirled around to give everyone a good look—"you might want to stop at Bling up on Charles Street and see what other goodies Vanessa has to offer . . ."

Dallas went on to give shout-outs to other merchants and to invite her guests to stay through tomorrow to tour the site where she'd be building her studio.

"I know you've heard the rumors, and yes, they're true. My first project will be *Pretty Maids* . . ."

Dallas introduced Victoria Seymour and the two leads, shocking everyone with her choice of Laura Fielding, an old friend of Dallas's who hadn't been particularly successful but who Dallas believed was the perfect Charlotte. The most enthusiastic applause was saved for the announcement confirming that Berry would be returning to the screen as Rosemarie.

Then a table holding Brooke's cupcakes was wheeled across the floor and the candles on thirty-eight of them were lit. The birthday song was sung, the candles were blown out, but before Dallas could begin to hand out cupcakes to those closest, Grant turned her around and went down on one knee and took her hand.

"Dallas, you know that I've loved you since I was eleven years old. I . . ."

A stunned Dallas turned the mike off so that only she could hear what Grant had to say. But the entire crowd had grown hushed, and when he slipped the ring on her finger and Dallas pulled Grant up to kiss him, the whoops and hollers could have been heard across the Bay.

"Wow, he really did it," Steffie said.

"Let's go congratulate them." Wade tugged her hand and they made their way to the bandstand.

"You really went down on one knee in front of all these strangers." Steffie marveled when she finally reached her brother.

"I barely saw them," Grant admitted. "All I could see was Dallas."

"Aw, that's so sweet." Steffie kissed his cheek, then turned to Dallas and hugged her.

"You knew this was coming tonight and you never said a word." Dallas hugged Steffie back. "And Grant said this"—she held up her left hand and wiggled her ring finger—"was your idea."

Stef nodded.

"It's perfect. It couldn't be more perfect. I love it.

And I thank you for thinking of it. Nothing would have meant more to me." Dallas had tears in her eyes. "And oh! The ice cream! I can't believe you did that for me! My own flavor!"

"That was Grant's idea," Steffie told her. "Well, the idea was his, the flavor was mine. He thought I should make something just for you and then throw away the recipe and never make it again . . ."

Dallas and Grant's discussion about the ice-cream flavor's exclusivity—or not—was interrupted by well-wishers, and the congratulations went on and on.

Steffie and Wade stepped farther and farther back from the crowd. When they reached the edge of the tent, Steffie asked, "Who's watching Austin tonight?"

"Paige brought Cody and Austin out to say good night earlier, so I imagine both boys are in bed by now. We did hire an older woman, much to Paige's annoyance, but once we explained to her that she could come to the party for a while, she was all right with it."

"So, then, Austin is covered for the night."

He nodded.

"Good. Then we've covered all the bases. We said our congrats to the happy couple, we made nice with our friends, so I suppose our work here is done."

"I suppose it is."

She stepped closer, her hands on his waist.

"Come home with me," she whispered. "Stay with me."

He took her by the hand and they walked out through the front gate, then realized that his car was in the driveway in front of the caterer's.

"It's okay," she told him. "Mine's out front."

But when they got to her car, they found it blocked in by a news van and the driver was nowhere to be seen.

"Oh, damn," Stef complained. "It's a long way to walk in these shoes. Talk about a mood killer."

"I have an idea," Wade told her. "Wait here."

Moments later, a stretch limo pulled up next to her car and the driver hopped out and walked around the car.

"Miss Wyler?" he asked.

"Yes . . . ?"

Wade pushed the back door open.

"What are you doing?" She laughed and got in next to him.

"It's ours for twenty minutes," Wade told her as the driver closed the door. "Long enough for him to drive to your house and back again. You'll have to give him directions."

"Go straight to the stop sign, then on through the center of town," Steffie said, and the car began to move. "Then make a left when you get to the third light."

"That's not how you get to Olive Street," Wade noted.

"It's how you get to my apartment," she told him. "I haven't moved yet."

Steffie's apartment was in a three-story house that had two units on each floor. There were lights on in one of the downstairs apartments and one on the third. The entire second floor was dark. The driver opened the door and helped them out, and Stef looked for her keys while Wade paid the driver. Steffie was still searching through her bag as they walked to the front door of the building.

"Here they are." Stef pulled a long chain of keys from her bag and unlocked the door.

"How could you have missed that? How many keys are on there, anyway?" Wade followed her through the door and up the steps to the second floor.

"Well, there's the shop, and the car, and the house, and the front door here and this door . . ." She reached the landing and took three steps to the door on the right. She unlocked it and stepped inside, waited for Wade before closing the door behind him and turning the lock.

She'd barely turned to him when she found herself in his arms. She dropped her bag and the keys onto the floor and raised her face for his kiss. His mouth demanded and she complied, his tongue filled her mouth and she took it in. He moved her back against the door, his hands on her waist, and he pulled her body closer until she was melting into him. Then his hands were in her hair and on her arms and her breasts and her thighs, everywhere at once and nowhere long enough. He slid his hands under the hem of her dress, pulling the soft fabric to her waist. His mouth moved along her throat, his lips trailing a hot line of kisses until her head began to swim. Her hands moved up his chest to the buttons of his shirt, which she began to undo, one by one, as quickly as her eager fingers could move. She pulled his shirttail from his khakis and pushed against him with her entire body.

"Bedroom," she gasped. "To the right."

He took several steps backward, still kissing her,

forcing her to move along with him. He lifted her from the floor, his arms around her hips, and she pushed the bedroom door aside with one foot.

"Straight back," she whispered.

She guided him to the bed, and pushed on his shoulders till he reached the edge. She straddled him, then grabbed the hem of her dress and pulled it upward. His hands were on her breasts before she had it over her head, and she arched into him, offering more, offering everything she had. Her hands found the buckle of his belt and she undid it, tugged at the waist of his slacks until she could slide them down. She repositioned herself so that when she moved her hips she ground against him, and he groaned deep in his throat. She undid her bra and tossed it and his mouth found her breast, his tongue almost driving her over the edge. He somehow managed to shed the rest of his clothes and she eased herself onto him until he was inside her. She rocked her hips back and forth, setting the pace, and he followed her lead. Surrendering to the hot licks of sensation that flooded and filled her, Stef gave herself over to the night and the man she'd waited a lifetime for. She'd craved his touch everywhere, and tonight, he fulfilled every desire she'd ever had. She closed her eyes and whispered his name as the world around her exploded and unbearable pleasure all but broke her in two.

Wade fell back, taking her with him, his arms wrapped around her, his heart pounding so close to hers, his breathing ragged, his eyes closed as he sought to recover from what had felt like a long fall over a steep cliff. Stef felt his chest rise and fall beneath hers, and watched his face in contented silence until her own breathing returned to normal.

She nibbled on his chin and smiled to herself.

"Wade," she whispered, "that was round one, right?"

"Huh?" His eyes partially opened, and she smiled to herself.

She pushed herself up slightly. "That was first-time sex, right?"

"Call it what you want, Stef, it was terrific."

"We still have to have makeup sex."

"What?" His eyes were wide-open now.

"I was really angry with you earlier, but then we talked things out and we made up. Hence, makeup sex follows."

"Perhaps you could give me a minute to catch my breath."

"Perhaps a minute." She lowered her mouth to his. "Then again, perhaps not . . ."

Chapter 15

WHAT time do you have to have to be at Scoop today?" Wade lay on his back, Stef curled in the crook of his arm and covered by a light blue blanket. Whatever response she'd made was unintelligible.

"Say that again?"

"I said Tina is opening for me today." She yawned. "I told her I'd come in after the brunch my parents are having for Dallas and the family." She covered a second yawn with her hand. "So I'll see you and the little guy in about four hours or so."

She burrowed back under the blanket. It had turned cold during the night and cool air had seeped in through the partially open window on the opposite side of the room.

Wade tried to check the time, but he couldn't quite see the face of the clock on Stef's bedside table. He wanted to be at Berry's when Austin awoke. He hadn't told anyone he was leaving or that he wasn't coming back last night, and he didn't want his sister's active imagination conjuring up scenes of his body floating downriver toward the Bay.

He eased himself out of the bed, with as little disturbance to Stef as possible, and turned the clock around. It was later than he'd thought. He gathered his clothes and made his way to the bathroom. When he came back into the bedroom, ready to leave, he found Stef still all but passed out.

"You're a lightweight, Wyler," he whispered in her ear. "You went out cold after three rounds."

"I'm not the one who's dressed and ready to flee the scene," she replied without opening her eyes.

"I'm only leaving because—" he began to explain.

"I'm teasing you." She emerged slightly from the covers and smiled. "I know you have to get back to Austin. It's all right. I'm all right with it. Actually, I'm surprised you stayed all night."

His fingers caught in the tangle of her hair and he watched her eyes, still smoky with sleep. "Best night ever," he told her.

"Really?"

He nodded. "I always knew it would be like that between us, you know?"

"You mean, damn near perfect?"

"Yeah. Damn near."

"You know what they say about practice." She sat up and placed a hand on either side of his face, drew him close and kissed him. "Now go take care of Austin. I'll see you in a few hours."

"Are you getting up?"

"Are you crazy?" She snuggled down onto the pillow. "I'm not the one with a child . . ."

He laughed and pulled the covers up to her chin, then let himself out of the apartment. It was almost a mile back to Berry's, but the cool air felt good and the walk served not only to wake him up but to clear his head as well. He *had* known it would be like that with Stef, and it *had* been pretty damn near perfect. He wondered if that was the reason he'd avoided her for so long. Maybe somewhere deep inside he'd known that if they ever got that close, they'd fry each other to a crisp.

Moth to flame. He'd been right about that, too.

Back when he was eighteen, with all the world before him, he'd had to leave. Now he wasn't so sure that what lay ahead was going to be worth losing what he'd be leaving behind.

He'd wanted to talk to her about the job, thought they'd spend some quiet time talking last night, but that hadn't happened. Maybe today, he thought, there'd be time.

Or maybe tonight, if she'd let him stay again tonight. He hoped she would. Maybe another night, and he'd have her out of his system.

"Yeah," he muttered. "Let me know how that works out for you . . ."

Stef heard Wade's footfalls on the steps, listened to them descending, heard the front door open and close, his footsteps leading down the walk, then nothing. She pulled both pillows under her head—his and hers—and propped herself up. She grabbed the remote control from the table next to the bed and mindlessly began to channel surf, hoping to find something that would help her drown out the thoughts that were running through her head. On Sunday morning there were about a dozen televangelists doing their thing and about an equal number of news shows. Mostly there were infomercials for makeup—four different kinds; skin-care products—another three; exercise equipment, all guaranteed to effortlessly reduce the size of your thighs, hips, and butt—there was an endless number of those. She clicked off the TV and stared at the blank screen.

She'd finally had what she'd wanted for so long, and it had been more than she'd even dreamed of.

"So you'd think you'd be satisfied," she said aloud. "But no. You want more. You want all of him, but you can't have him. No surprise there. He never pretended otherwise."

She got out of the bed and went into the bathroom for a shower.

"What part of 'leaving tomorrow for Connecticut' do I not understand?" she asked herself while she dried her hair. "What part of 'job in another state' is a foreign phrase?"

She dressed and put on makeup and tried to put on a happy face to go with it. She *was* happy. She wanted to be happy again, stay happy for a while. Tough to do with Wade leaving the next day.

Her bravado the night before aside, she wasn't sure she could handle saying good-bye to him again. She'd believed it when she said it, and at the time, it had probably been true. After spending one long magical night with him, she had to reconsider.

"But this time," she told her reflection as she put on her earrings, "if I'm sad, that'll be on me. If I hurt—and I probably will—I can't blame him since last night was my idea. I was the one who pushed."

She paused. "And I'm not saying it wasn't a good idea. I just want more. Lord help me, I want more . . ."

She strapped on high heels and grabbed her bag and her keys. She got as far as the front walk when she realized her car was still parked on River Road. Unless, of course, the police towed it because of the overnight parking restriction.

Nah, Beck wouldn't do that to her.

She strode off toward town and hoped that her feet wouldn't be crying the blues by the time she got there. She knew she was going to be late because she hadn't planned on having to walk from the apartment to Let's Do Brunch, which was several doors down from Bling on Charles Street. But the walk was invigorating and she was flushed by the time she arrived. The other guests were all seated, and she tried to sneak in the side door.

Wade rose when he saw her, and he pushed back from his chair and went to her.

"I saved a seat for you." He took her hand. When she looked into his eyes, she saw something that she hadn't seen there before. She wasn't sure she knew what it was, but she liked it.

"Great." She smiled and let him lead her to the table where his family and hers were seated together.

"I hope you don't mind that we started already, sweetie." Her mother appeared to be ignoring the fact that Wade still held her hand. "We weren't sure what time you'd be arriving."

"No apologies." Stef glanced around the room. "Lots of folks here from last night. Lots of business for the little town." She smiled broadly. "I like it."

They talked about the party, what big-name star had been wearing what and which up-and-comer had embarrassed himself by making a blatant—and drunken—move on a well-known director; who seemed to really enjoy St. Dennis and who was paying lip service to Dallas in the hopes of being cast in her first picture; and how Berry had been the showstopper.

"I need to get down to Scoop," Stef announced as the morning faded into afternoon. "I can't leave Tina there all day by herself after I had her open this morning for me."

"Scoop!" Austin clapped his hands.

"What do you say we walk Steffie down to the shop?" Wade lifted his son from the high chair.

"Yay!" Cody got up and tugged on Paige's hand. "Let's go with them."

"Hold up there, Cody," Dallas called to him before he could open the door. "We'll all walk together."

"Speak for yourself, dear." Berry stood, Archer holding the back of her chair. "We'll drive. My knees, you know. The old girl isn't what she used to be."

"Couldn't tell that by the applause you got last night," Archer reminded her. "You're still a star."

"Of course I am." Berry smiled.

The group trailed out onto the sidewalk, where Wade stopped to lift Austin onto his shoulders. Paige sought Stef's company, and arm in arm, they strolled along.

"Are you having sex with Wade?" Paige whispered in her aunt's ear. "I think you and Wade are having sex. You look like you—"

"Paige Wyler . . ." Steffie sputtered. "That's totally inappropriate and none of your business. And how would you know what it looks like when . . ."

Paige laughed and pointed ahead to her father and Dallas.

"You're too young to think about things like that." Steffie tried to keep a straight face.

Wade turned around and asked, "What's she too young for?"

"Driving," Paige piped up. "I was saying I couldn't wait until I could drive."

They'd crossed Charles Street and were halfway down Kelly's Point when Stef saw Dallas turn to Grant and say, "Paparazzi on the left. Do you mind?"

"Nah." Grant shook his head. "Everyone's been talking about your birthday weekend for weeks now. A couple of pictures aren't going to hurt anyone."

Scoop was crowded and it seemed that many of the customers had been at the party the night before and were hoping for another taste of honey lavender.

"Sorry," Stef explained as she stepped behind the counter and tied on an apron. "That was special for Dallas. But we have some other really yummy flavors . . ." She directed their attention to the cooler and the containers of chocolate monster mash, apple walnut, maple walnut, pumpkin raisin, and spiced pear.

She served Cody and Austin and sent Paige to one of the tables out front with the boys. Dallas and Grant mingled with some of last night's guests and Berry and Archer arrived as some of the crowd were beginning to disperse.

"Goodness," Berry said, watching others leave as she arrived. "Was it something I said?"

"We offered to give a tour of the warehouses to

anyone who's interested," Dallas told her. "So everyone can see where my new studio will be."

"Right now all they're going to see are empty warehouses," Wade pointed out.

"True. But anyone with any vision will be able to see how fabulous it's going to be."

"Whatever." Wade shook his head and his sister laughed.

From the corner of her eye, Steffie saw Wade standing at the end of the cooler. Between customers, she took a few steps sideways and asked, "Did you want me?"

"Again and again," he told her, and she laughed.

"That kind of talk is for later. Right now I'm working."

"I'm going to take Austin back to Berry's and get him settled while I try to get things organized for tomorrow."

"All right."

"Can I stop over later?" he asked as if he wasn't sure how she'd respond. "It might only be for a little while. We have to leave early."

"I'll be home after I close up. You know the way." She touched his hand, then went back to work, reminding herself that a little while was better than no while.

It had only been a little while—less than three hours, but they'd used every minute of the time they had together. He'd wanted to talk about his job, but she had other plans.

"We can talk some other time," she told him as she unbuttoned his shirt. "We can talk on the phone. Or text. Or send e-mails. But we won't be able to do this . . ." She drew herself up to kiss his face and then his lips, and whatever it was he'd wanted to talk to her about had had to wait.

"What time will you be heading out tomorrow?" Steffie asked while she watched Wade dress. She tried to sound casual but wasn't sure she pulled it off.

"Early. I had planned on driving, but then I got to thinking about things, and decided maybe we should fly instead."

"What about all your stuff?"

He zipped his jeans and sat on the edge of the bed.

"What if it isn't a good situation for Austin?" he said.

"What are you talking about?" She moved closer, the sheet wrapped around her.

"Ted said there's a day-care right there at the plant."

"That's good, though, right?"

"I guess. Austin's never been around a whole bunch of kids at the same time before. He's always been with adults. Except for Cody, but they're like brothers now. What if Austin doesn't like being part of a group all day? Eight or nine in the morning till six at night is a really long day for a little kid. What if he doesn't like it? What if he doesn't like the people who work at the day-care center? What if he misses Cody and Berry . . . ?" He stopped and turned to her. "I'm beginning to obsess, aren't I?"

"Uh-huh. But those are the things parents have to deal with every day. Not that I know from experience, but that's what I've read. You do what you have to do."

"True enough. I've just never had to think about it until now, and once I did, I realized that it's going to be a big change for him. He's already had one big change in his life, you know?"

She nodded. Losing his mother had certainly been a big change.

"Anyway, I need to make sure things will be right for him." He took her hand. "And then there's this contract issue."

"What contract issue?"

After he explained, she said, "So you've asked to see it but this guy hasn't sent it yet?"

"Right. I still haven't seen it. Which makes me wonder what he's hiding. Like maybe the fine print."

"Could he really do that? Make you sign away your rights to your beers?" Stef frowned. "That would be like someone else laying claim to my ice-cream recipes."

"Exactly."

She shook her head. "You can't give up your brewing secrets, Wade."

"That's what I'm thinking."

She rested her head on his shoulder.

"Wade?"

"What?"

"If I didn't know you better, I'd think you were looking for reasons to not stay in Connecticut."

"The thought's occurred to me."

"But maybe you'll get there and everything will be just skippy. The day-care thing and the job and the contract and you'll find a great place to live."

"Will you come see us?" he asked.

"Sure. Will you come back and see me?"

"Absolutely." He smoothed her hair with his hand. "We'll see how far this goes, okay?"

"We'll be okay," she told him, and prayed she sounded more convinced than she felt.

She managed to keep a smile on her face and a positive attitude as they said good-bye, even until the door closed behind him and she turned the lock.

Then, from somewhere deep inside, a little voice whispered that some things never change. Wade would leave and get on with his life, and she'd still be here, in St. Dennis, alone, until next time.

Diary ~

My, what a time we had on Saturday night! It reminded me of the days when Berry would fly in from California with some of her Hollywood friends and throw one of her fabulous cocktail parties. What fun to see so many celebrities up close and personal. All those designer dresses and fabulous jewels! Our little town is still buzzing. And why not? Dallas's party made it to the cover of every entertainment publication on the market. Why, almost every one of the tabloids and the glossy gossip magazines had pictures on their covers. We had a grand time passing those around at Cuppachino these last few days. Everyone was tickled to see that even Steffie and Wade made several of the covers. Oh, not by themselves, of course, but in photos of the birthday girl and her new fiancé! Yes, Grant went down on one knee to pop the question at the party. Who knew he was so gallant? He gave Dallas a ring that had belonged to his grandmother. Some of us—I and a few others—are old enough to remember when his grandmother, Helen Kay, received that ring on her wedding day. Dallas, who I hear has some very lovely diamonds of her own, seemed genuinely touched to have received this special piece, and showed it off to absolutely everyone. Ah, true love . . .

Speaking of which, I can't say that I was surprised to see Berry on the arm of my cousin Archer once again. Now there's a romance that goes way back. I had seen them out to dinner on several occasions, and even more telling, had noticed his car parked right out there in the open in her driveway for several days at a time over the past few months. I daresay they could be a tad more discreet—but I am happy to see them together again. I know he loved his wife all the years they were married, but I don't think he ever quite got over Berry. Berry never did marry, and I always wondered if it had something to do with the way she and Archer had parted all those years ago.

Oh, of course, I took lots and lots of photos at the party—Daniel is going to print them for me and I cannot wait. I had my picture taken with so many celebs, I can't even remember them all! Now, these will be something to put in the family archives! I told Daniel to make extras so I could send a few to Lucy so she can see what she's missing! She seems to think that nothing fun ever happens in her old hometown.

~ Grace ~

Chapter 16

HEY, wake up!" Vanessa thumped on Steffie's worktable with a rolled-up newspaper.

"Oh. Sorry. I didn't hear you come in." Steffie swiveled around on the stool she'd been sitting on.

"You look like you're a thousand miles away."

"Close enough." Stef held up a piece of paper. "Recipe for Mexican chocolate monster mash. Adding cinnamon and . . ."

She stared at the cover of the tabloid Vanessa was holding. "That's me." She reached for the paper. "Me and Wade and . . . oh, how cute does Austin look! This was taken right out front." She held the photo up and pointed. "See, there's the shop right there in the background. I guess one of those guys taking pictures yesterday sold them." She grinned. "That was fast."

"These publications pay a lot of money to get this stuff, like, pronto. I bet there are a half-dozen more publications on the stand today with the same kind of coverage. This article is pretty accurate, as far as tabloids go," Vanessa pointed out. "It's all about Dallas's party and who was there and talks about her getting engaged. There's a close-up of her ring on page three."

Steffie read the front-page photo's caption: " 'Superstar Dallas MacGregor on a stroll with fiancé, Grant Wyler, after celebrating her birthday in St. Dennis, Maryland. With Dallas and Grant is (left to right) her son, Cody Blair, and his daughter, Paige Wyler'—how crazy will Paige be when she sees her face on the cover of a national newspaper—'Dallas's brother, Wade MacGregor, and his son, Austin; and Steffie Wyler, Grant's sister and owner of One Scoop or Two, the ice-cream shop and the group's Sunday afternoon destination.' "

Steffie looked up from the paper and laughed. "My name is in a tabloid. My picture is on the front page. How insane is this?"

"That much fuss for Dallas's birthday, imagine what the coverage of the wedding is going to be like."

"Do you think I look fat in this picture?" Steffie held up the paper.

"No. You look hot." Vanessa looked closer. "So does Wade. The three of you—you and Wade and Austin—look like a happy family."

"Yeah, well, whoever said that the camera never lies wasn't aware that Wade and Austin would be on their way to Connecticut this morning to check out the new job and look for a place to live." She glanced at the clock. "Actually, they've been there for a while. They left early this morning."

"How are you feeling about that?" Vanessa asked.

"How do you think I feel?"

"That bad, huh?"

Stef nodded. "I'm trying not to, but I can't help it."

"Maybe you should tell him, Stef." Vanessa sat on the other stool. "Maybe he should know how you feel."

"Oh, he knows." Steffie laughed. "Believe me, he knows."

Vanessa's eyes narrowed as she studied Stef's face. "You slept with him."

Steffie grinned and took a mallet to a hunk of dark chocolate, tapping it gently so that the pieces didn't fly all over the table.

"You did."

Gathering up the smaller chunks, Steffie nodded.

"When did this happen, and why am I just finding out about it?" Vanessa demanded.

"Because it just happened last night . . . oh, okay, and Saturday night. But I haven't seen you and didn't have time to call you." Steffie smiled at her friend. "And I knew you'd be here today, if for no other reason than to talk about the party. Which, face it, was a once-in-a-lifetime event. Did you see Derek Manheimer? Oh, my heart. He looks good on the screen, but damn! In person, he—"

"Don't even try to change the subject, missy. I want details. I demand details." Vanessa snagged a chunk of chocolate that Steffie missed and nibbled. "Like, how was it?"

"Amazing. Incredible." Steffie sighed. "Life changing."

"Seriously?"

"Seriously."

"I don't know whether or not that's a good thing." Vanessa reached into the bowl where Stef had dumped the chunks. "This is ridiculous chocolate, by the way."

"It's Mexican. High butterfat content. Like, eighty-four percent."

"So, talk to me. Tell me what's going on."

"Wade's taking a job up north and I have a business here."

"That was terse."

"I don't know what else to say. That's what's going on."

"So it's, like, nowhere?" Vanessa frowned.

"I guess." Stef swallowed the lump in her throat. "Oh, I know he'll be back. Once he finds a place to live, he's going to have to come back for all his stuff."

"All what stuff?"

"All the stuff that's in the trailer he had hooked up to his car when he got here. All his stuff from Texas, I guess. And his Jeep," she added. "He'll need that."

"I don't understand. If he knew he was moving, why didn't he just take everything with him today?"

"I'm not really sure, but I think he's worried that Austin won't adjust to the child care."

"I think it's more likely that Wade's worried that you'll adjust to someone else." Vanessa wagged a finger at Stef. "I think he knows that the universe is bringing others into your orbit."

"How can you say stuff like that with a straight face?" Stef asked.

"Because I—"

"Yeah, yeah. You cast a spell." Steffie rolled her eyes. "Notice the path that's been beaten to my door."

"Hey, I did my part. Just because Jesse doesn't do it for you or Clay—"

"Jesse and I have a professional relationship. And besides, I think he has his eye on Brooke. And Clay and I have known each other forever and he's more like a brother to me."

"Maybe I should try—"

"No. I know what you're thinking, and no. Do not do it again. Whatever it is that you think you did the first time, don't bother doing it again."

Vanessa muttered something under her breath.

"What was that?" Stef asked.

"I just said, you deserve to be happy. If not with Wade, then with someone else."

"I agree. I do deserve to be happy." Stef bit her bottom lip. "But the thing is, I don't want anyone else. I've tried—God knows that all my adult life I have tried—but it's always been Wade. Especially now that we . . ." She shook her head. "Look, if you're going to be saying some kind of mumbo jumbo—not that I want you to, and not that I'd ever ask you to, because, you know, I don't believe in any of that—but if you were to do it, just don't make it nonspecific, okay?"

Vanessa nodded. "Got it."

"So. With the party behind me, I get to go back to work on my house. I haven't even been inside in almost a week, except to meet with Cam one day for about twenty minutes to go over what the plumber and the electrician did."

"How's it going?"

"I can probably move in sometime next week. I'll need to air out the place a little. The dust from all the work they've been doing is enough to choke a horse, but my bathroom is ready and the kitchen is pretty much operational."

"That was fast."

"It's been about a month, and since I didn't make any major changes—no walls moved or anything like that—they were able to stay pretty much on schedule. I do want to have a powder room built on the first floor, but the room is already there and Cam said the pipes are in line with other pipes, so it won't be a huge project."

"So what are you going to do first?" Vanessa asked.

"Finish painting my kitchen cabinets and the woodwork in there. And paint my bedroom. And maybe the bath and the upstairs hall. And the—"

"Slow down. Focus on one room at a time."

"Right. The kitchen and then my bedroom." Stef forced a smile. "I won't be entertaining a whole lot, so I'm not in any hurry to do the downstairs rooms. I'll get to them."

"So what night this week can we do our sleepover?"

"What?"

"The sleepover. You promised me popcorn and ice cream and s'mores. Grady's away until the end of the week. I was thinking it would be nice to have company and do some girly things."

"Promise not to paint my nails 'Pretty in Pink' while I'm sleeping?"

"How did you know . . . ?"

"You're the ultimate girly-girl. You love the froufrou. Me, I'm more the 'Paint Me Plum' type."

"I'll stock up." Vanessa picked up her bag and hopped off her stool. "So which night?"

"Wednesday's good."

"Great. Bring your pillow and the previously mentioned snacks." She hesitated at the door. "What kind of wine goes best with s'mores?"

"I'd guess a dessert wine."

"Champagne." Vanessa brightened. "Perfect."

Stef closed Scoop up for the night at seven on the nose and headed for Olive Street and a long night of painting. She stopped at the market and bought copies of all the papers and magazines that had coverage of Saturday's party, then at the Checkered Cloth for take-out pasta and a salad. When she arrived to the house, she got out all her brushes and her paint, then she sat on the front hall steps while she ate. She told herself she was being just a wee bit morbid—sitting where Wade had sat the last time he was here—but feeling a little depressed, she decided to wallow in it. By the time her phone rang at almost eleven, she had the inside of all the cabinets painted. A record, she thought. Then again, when you're anxious and worried, you do tend to move a little faster. So what if she dripped a little paint here and there. She was going to replace the counters anyway, so neatness, she decided, didn't count. Except for the streak she got in her hair when she answered the phone.

"Stef, it's Wade."

"Hey, hi." She tried to sound chipper. "How was the trip?"

"Good. Austin mostly slept on the plane, and Ted had a car waiting for us when we got into Hartford."

"That was nice of him."

"Yeah, it was."

"So, did you get to tour the plant?"

"The brewery, yes. It's amazing. Top-of-the-line, everything up-to-the-minute in terms of technology. He's very forward thinking. I have to hand it to him. He's doing a few things I hadn't thought of."

Her heart sank with every word.

"Sounds like quite the operation," she said.

"It is. I'm really impressed."

"So did you sign the contract?" Was she really holding her breath?

"Funny thing, Stef. He gave it to me to look over, and when I started questioning certain clauses, he said those were things his lawyers insisted on putting in there and for me to just go ahead and cross out anything I didn't like."

"So you signed it."

"That's the funny part. When I told him I wanted a little time to look it over, he ripped it up and said the hell with it, that we'd work things out between us. Crazy, huh?"

"Crazy," she agreed. "Where was Austin during all this negotiating?"

"He was in the day-care center with Mrs. Worth."

"Mrs. Worth?"

"She runs the center. Think Angela Lansbury in *Bedknobs and Broomsticks*."

"How do you know *Bedknobs and Broomsticks*?"

"It's Cody's favorite movie. We must have watched it fifty times while we were at Berry's."

"So the child-care situation looks pretty good."

"It looks very good. There are only seven other kids and most of them are older than Austin, and Mrs. Worth has two assistants." He paused for a moment. "Tomorrow Ted's hooking me up with a Realtor to look at a couple of houses that are available."

"Great." The enthusiasm was becoming more difficult to maintain. "So it sounds as if you're all set. The job is right, Austin's happy, and you'll find a great new house. Congratulations, Wade. It sounds as if you caught the brass ring."

"I guess."

"So what's your schedule there?" she asked, when what she wanted to say was, *When are you coming home?* Her heart sank to her knees when she realized that St. Dennis wasn't his home. His home was going to be in Connecticut before too long.

"Well, tomorrow I'll be looking at houses. I guess if I don't find anything, I'll look again on Wednesday and Thursday until I do."

"Well, good luck with finding a place."

"Thanks." Another pause. "Look, I'll be back there before the weekend. Maybe we could go to dinner or something."

"That would be great."

"I'll give you a call and let you know when."

"Good. I'll wait to hear from you."

"Okay, then. Talk to you."

She wanted to say, *Wait, don't hang up. I miss you. Talk to me for just a little longer.* But she knew that wouldn't do. Instead, she said, "Right. I'll talk to you . . ."

She disconnected the call, then opened a bottle of water and sat on the kitchen floor.

"This totally sucks," she said aloud. "And it's going to suck more and more as time goes on."

Holding her fist to her gut to stop the sick feeling in her stomach from spreading all through her, Stef tried to figure out why she'd put herself in this situation when she knew how it was likely to end.

"Because it's always been Wade," she said. Just like she'd told Vanessa. It had always been Wade.

She finished cleaning her brushes and started to close up the house when she found the magazines on the counter. She'd meant to tell Wade that they'd made the cover of *Celeb Today,* but she'd forgotten. They had magazines and tabloid papers in Connecticut, she reminded herself. If he'd already seen it, he, too, had forgotten to comment. She took a long look at the photo before tucking it into her bag to take home. Just as Vanessa had pointed out, she and Wade and Austin did look like a happy family, like two people who were deeply in love and their little guy who was basking in their glow.

"Fantasyland," she mumbled, and turned out the lights.

Stef wasted a good part of Tuesday morning trying to decide what to make that day, but nothing intrigued her. She was done with chocolate for a while, and she'd done the usual fall flavors with apples, walnuts, maple, and pumpkin. She was tired of fall. She wanted something . . . fun. Unfortunately, she'd gone through her recipe box twice already and nothing said "fun." She checked her freezer and found she had enough there to get her through the day. Maybe tomorrow she'd feel inspired. Today, she just felt tired.

"Stef, mind if I run out to the post office?" Tina stuck her head into the back room. "I want to get my sister's birthday present mailed today."

"Go on. Take your time. We're slow today anyway."

"I can stop and pick up lunch for you on the way back."

"Great."

"What do you want?" Tina stood in the doorway.

"Whatever you're having will be fine." Stef shrugged.

"I'm having PB and J that I brought from home."

"Oh. Well . . ." Stef tried to think of something that she wanted, but nothing came to mind. "Skip it. I'll run out later."

"Are you sure? 'Cause I don't mind . . ."

"I'm sure. I don't know what I feel like eating, but thanks anyway."

"I won't be long." Tina hung up her apron and took off out the back door.

"Maybe a milk shake. Vanilla." Stef nodded as she went into the shop. She got as far as the ice-cream case when the bell over the door rang. She looked up just as a tall, good-looking guy with curly dark hair came in.

"Hi," he said brightly.

"Hi," she returned the greeting.

He walked to the counter and smiled. "The sign says all your ice cream is made on the premises. Are you the ice-cream maker?"

"I am." She returned the smile and slipped her apron over her head.

"What's good today?" he asked.

"Everything's good." She tied the apron strings behind her back. "Depends on what you're in the mood for."

He gazed into the case and seemed to look over each container. "Salted caramel. I never heard of that."

Stef grabbed a plastic spoon and scooped some up, then passed the spoon over the top of the cooler. The man tasted the ice cream, then grinned.

"That's pretty amazing stuff. I'll have a bowl. Two scoops, like the sign says." He leaned on the counter near the cash register.

She dished the ice cream. While he was pulling out his wallet he asked, "So what do people do around here for a good time?"

"Not a whole lot during the week in the off-season." She took the bill he gave her and handed back his change along with his purchase. "But this coming weekend there's going to be a haunted house tour. Are you staying in town . . . ?"

"Just for another couple of days. I saw an article about what a nice place St. Dennis is, so I decided that the next time I could take a few days off, I'd come down, check it out for myself."

"Well, if you're looking for peace and quiet, you should get plenty of that this week."

"If you were here for a couple of days, what would you be doing with your time?"

She thought it over for a moment, then said, "If I had nothing to do for a few days, I'd probably go to

Book 'Em and pick up something I've been wanting to read, then I'd hole up someplace and read. I'd only come out for walks along the Bay at dawn and at sunset, and meals." She added, "Fortunately, we have some excellent restaurants in town. There's Café Lola, if you like fine dining. There's the Checkered Cloth for casual stuff—soups and sandwiches and takeout. They're both up on Charles Street. Captain Walt's down on the other end of the boardwalk, past the marina, if you like seafood."

"I guess I'll have a chance to try a little bit of each while I'm here. Thanks for the suggestions—" He paused. "Can I ask your name?"

"It's Steffie."

"Steffie. That's nice." He smiled back at her. "I'm Greg."

"Nice to meet you, Greg." She watched him take a seat at one of the tables. "So what do you do that keeps you from taking time off during the summer when everyone else is vacationing?"

"I have a boatbuilding business up near Chestertown."

"I guess summer would be your busiest time. Hence the fall vacation."

"That's the way it goes." He ate for a moment. "You know what, this is the best ice cream I ever tasted. You should sell it to supermarkets. You'd make a fortune."

Stef grinned. "Too much trouble. Besides, I like my shop. I like coming to work every day. I like seeing all my friends." She shook her head. "I don't want to change the way I work or the way I do things. I built this business by myself, for myself. I'm happy the way things are."

"But think of all the money you could make."

"I do just fine. Besides, money isn't everything."

"Well, I admire a woman who can do what you've done."

"Thank you."

He appeared to be about to say something else when Grace bustled in.

"I just picked up the pictures I took at the party from my son. He has one of those printer things at the inn and I couldn't wait to show you." Grace waved a small white bag.

"Oooh, would I. Hand 'em over, Miss Grace." Steffie took the bag and peered inside. "You were a busy lady. Look at all these."

"Daniel said to pick out the ones you want and he'll run off duplicates. You can share them with your parents and Dallas and Grant."

Steffie and Grace were poring over the photos when Tina returned.

"Oh, pictures from The Party. Let me see what I missed." Tina nudged between the two women. "Oh, my, how gorgeous is that dress? And who's this over here?"

"Excuse me." Greg approached the counter. "If I could trouble you for a glass of water . . ."

"Oh, sure. Sorry." Steffie got him a bottle from the cooler and handed it over.

"I heard you mention Dallas . . . that wouldn't be Dallas MacGregor?"

When Stef nodded, her customer said, "I heard there was a big party here over the weekend."

"Yes. She lives in St. Dennis now."

"You were there?"

Stef nodded.

"Wow, I met someone who knows Dallas MacGregor. I'm impressed."

"You'll be even more impressed when I tell you that Steffie's brother is engaged to Dallas," Grace told him.

"Unbelievable." He shook his head as if he was finding it hard to believe. "So was the party as much fun as the magazines made it look?"

"Every bit," Steffie said.

"I think there was something on one of those entertainment TV shows, too," he mentioned.

"There were cameras everywhere," Grace told him. "News crews, you name it."

"Well, nice that you had a good time." He turned to Steffie. "Good luck to your brother and his fiancée. I think I'll take your advice and stop in at that bookstore and pick up something to read, then later hit one of those restaurants you named for dinner."

"They're all up on Charles Street—that's the main street," she told him. "Except for Walt's."

"Right. You said earlier that's down near the marina."

She nodded.

"What do I owe you for the water?" He held up the bottle.

"It's on the house." She waved him away.

"Thanks. Maybe I'll see you again before I leave town." Greg moved toward the door.

"Stop back anytime." Steffie smiled, then turned her attention back to the photos.

"Who was that guy?" Tina watched Greg leave.

"Just some off-season tourist looking for a few days of R and R."

"Was it my imagination, or was he flirting with you? Maybe just a little?" Tina asked.

"Your imagination." Stef held up the next picture in the pile. "Oh, look at Cody and Paige. How cute are they . . ."

Chapter 17

To Steffie's surprise, Greg was back the following afternoon.

"I couldn't stay away," he told her. "I had to come back for more of that salted caramel ice cream."

"I'm glad you enjoyed it." She dished up another couple of scoops for him. "It's a gorgeous day. We don't get too many late October days this warm. You might want to sit outside in the sun and enjoy the scenery."

"I like the scenery in here just fine." His eyes held hers as he took a seat near the door.

Tina kicked Stef in the shin lightly as she headed to the back room. "Flirting," she whispered.

Stef pretended to ignore her.

"By the way," Greg called to her, "I took your suggestion and tried Captain Walt's last night. Best tuna I ever had. Thanks for the tip."

"You're welcome," Stef replied. "Glad you enjoyed it."

"I did. As a matter of fact . . ." He got up and started toward the counter when the door flew open and Brooke Bowers came in with her son, Logan, and a few of his friends, including Cody.

"Hey, why aren't you guys in school?" Steffie asked. "I know it isn't three o'clock already."

"We didn't have school today," Cody told her.

"Our teachers are all being serviced," Logan added.

"In-service day," Brooke clarified for Steffie. "And it's such a nice day, we decided to have lunch in town. Which, of course, includes dessert at Scoop."

"That's why we like to have lunch in town," Logan said, and Cody nodded enthusiastically.

"You boys do know how to flatter. So what will it be today?"

By the time Stef finished serving Brooke's group and the two groups that came in after, she noticed that Greg had slipped out.

"Who was the guy sitting over near the wall?" Brooke asked.

"Guy taking some R and R for a few days," Stef said.

"He was cute." Brooke wiggled her eyebrows.

"He was that," Stef agreed.

"He was here yesterday, too," Tina piped up. "He's been flirting with Stef."

"Has not." Stef brushed off the remark.

"Has too," Tina told Brooke.

"So word has it that you and Wade . . ." Brooke left the rest unspoken.

"Where's the word coming from?"

"Clay said he saw you and Wade leave the party together the other night," Brooke confided.

Steffie made no response.

"So you think he'll stay in Connecticut for long?" Brooke asked.

"That's his plan."

"Too bad. Clay's still hoping to talk him into starting up a brewery together. He's been reading up on how to make beer and growing crops you make beer from and all that." Brooke paid for the boys' ice cream. "He even had a name picked out for their brewery."

"And that would be . . . ?"

"Mad Mac."

Stef laughed. "That certainly fits the two of them."

"That's what I thought." Brooke was herding the boys out the door when she turned and said, "Clay hasn't given up, you know. I'm hoping for everyone's sake that Wade has a change of heart."

"I wouldn't bank on it," Stef said.

Before she left Scoop for the night, Stef stocked a small portable cooler with the ice cream she'd promised Vanessa, then stopped at the market for the other snacks. She took the ice cream inside and put it into the freezer when she stopped at her house, where she hoped to finish painting the kitchen cabinets. Bling was open until nine on Wednesday, so she had a few hours before Vanessa closed up, and she didn't intend to waste them. The sooner the kitchen was finished, the sooner she could start painting her bedroom.

Painting was the kind of work you could lose yourself in, she was thinking as she applied the first coat to one of the cabinet doors. It could be as mindless as you wanted it to be. Sort of like watching an ice-cream machine do its thing after all the ingredients had been added, she mused. You could go on autopilot and—

Her phone was ringing in her pocket. She put the brush down and checked the caller ID.

"Hello, Wade," she said.

"Hey. How's it going?"

She could have said, *Better now that I hear your voice,* but she settled for, "Just doing a little painting here at the house. You?"

"Just got Austin to sleep. These past few days have been long ones for him. He's not used to quite so much activity."

"How's he doing with Angela?"

"Angela?" Wade laughed. "Right. Lansbury. He's doing really well. He keeps asking for Cody and Berry, but I told him that he'd see them soon." He paused. "Like, tomorrow."

"You're coming back for your stuff?" she asked. Before he could respond, she said, "I guess you found a house that you like."

"Actually, there were several that I liked. One more than the others, but they're all in the same really nice neighborhood. Lots of kids Austin's age, it's not too far from the brewery, the elementary school is just three blocks away."

"Great." She tried to sound enthusiastic. "So it sounds like everything's a go for you. The job, the child care, the housing situation . . ."

"Yeah, everything's even better than I could have hoped."

"I'm glad things are working out the way you need them to. You deserve a couple of breaks after, well, after everything that's happened over the past couple of months."

"Thanks, Stef. I appreciate hearing you say that. Hey, maybe we'll stop down when we get home. Austin needs his ice-cream fix. There's nothing up here even remotely like Scoop."

"Of course there isn't."

Wade laughed. "We have an early flight, so I'll see you soon."

"You know where to find me."

She hung up and put the phone on the counter, her heart still beating a little faster at the sound of his voice and the prospect of seeing him tomorrow. No matter what, she told herself, she was not going to let him see her cry. She'd thought long and hard over this, thought about what it would be like if for some reason she lost Scoop and had to go to work for someone else. It would be hard enough to leave her business behind without having someone she cared about getting all weepy on her. She knew exactly what it was like to work your butt off to build a business that you loved, one you were proud of, one you'd given everything to. She was pretty sure she could figure out what it would take from her if it was lost to her. She understood all that. But she didn't have to like it or the hole Wade's absence was going to leave in her heart.

She heard the front door open and she jumped. She tiptoed to the doorway and peeked into the hallway.

"Ness, you scared the crap out of me." Steffie exhaled the breath she'd been holding.

"Sorry. I saw the lights on and thought I'd come in and help you clean up so that we could get over to my house and change into our pj's and get our little party started."

"And you're how old?"

"Chronologically old enough to legally buy a very nice bottle of champagne to share with my BFF," Vanessa told her, "but mentally, I'd have to say thirteen tonight." She reached into her shoulder bag. "Wait till you see the movies I picked up. Horror classics."

She pulled out several DVD cases from her big leather tote. "*Night of the Living Dead. Scream. Psycho. Nosferatu.*"

"Have you seen that last one?" Steffie frowned.

"No, but my sister-in-law said it was really creepy." Vanessa grinned. "Actually, they were all highly recommended by Mia, and after nine years in the FBI, she knows horror. But I also got *Ghostbusters* in case we wimped out."

"Any one of those will make you afraid to close your eyes, so we'll probably be up all night." Stef put the lid back on the open paint can.

"Good. More time to eat junk food."

"And soon we shall. As soon as I clean this brush."

Stef finished cleaning up while Vanessa wandered through the house.

"The heart on the dining-room wall is just killing me." Vanessa strolled back into the kitchen.

"I know, right? Old Horace was a romantic. Who knew?" Stef dried off her brush.

"And you have three fireplaces! You expect one in the living room, but I love that there's one in the dining room. And in your bedroom, too—woo-hoo! At least, I'm guessing that's the room you're going to use, the one with the fireplace and the bathroom."

"Good guess."

"That's the one I'd pick, too."

"I'm done," Stef told her. "Let's just get the ice cream and we can lock up."

"What kind did you make?"

"Butter brickle . . ." Stef removed the containers she'd earlier placed in the freezer.

"One of my favorites." Vanessa smiled.

". . . and s'mores."

"S'mores ice cream?"

"Yup." Out of habit, Stef checked the back door to make sure it was locked.

"Genius." Vanessa followed Steffie out the front door. "Stef, seriously. That's sheer—"

"Hey, Steffie, is that you?" A man called from the sidewalk.

Stef looked up from the lock. "Who's there?"

"It's me. Greg. From Scoop?" He stepped out of the shadows near the sidewalk. "Sorry. Did I frighten you?"

"No, I . . ."

"I did. I'm sorry. I was out for a walk and saw you coming out the door . . ." He appeared much chagrined. "I'm really sorry."

"It's okay. I just wasn't expecting to see anyone," Stef told him.

"Is this your house?" he asked.

"Uh, no. It's my mother's cousin's. I was just doing a little painting for him."

"That's nice of you." He gave Vanessa the once-over.

"Well, I guess I'll see you around . . ." Stef said as she went to her car.

"Right. I hope so." He smiled at Vanessa as he walked on.

"Ness, I'll meet you at your place," Steffie said under her breath, as if afraid of being overheard.

"Are you all right? You look rattled." Vanessa looked after the departing figure. "Who was that guy?"

"Tourist. He's been in Scoop a couple of times this week."

"Has he been, like, stalking you?"

"No."

"Then why'd you lie? Why'd you tell him this wasn't your house?"

"I don't know. It just came out."

"Do you want me to say something to Beck? Because he can—"

"No, no. The guy just startled me. He was sort of just there when we came out of the house. I overreacted. He really seems like a nice guy." Steffie slammed the back car door and opened the driver's side. "I'll follow you to your place."

"Okay."

They decided to forgo the sleeping bags in favor of the sofa.

"Grady said we could use a couple of his sleeping bags, but they smell like pine and, I don't know, bears, maybe, to me." Vanessa stood in the living room in her bare feet. "Which end would you like?"

"Either is fine."

"You're the guest, so you get to choose," Ness told her.

"In that case, I choose the end closest to the fireplace."

"Good choice." Vanessa plopped her pillow on the opposite end of the sofa and curled up. There was a big bowl of popcorn drizzled with melted chocolate on the coffee table and two wineglasses. "So what about that guy freaked you out?"

"Greg?" Steffie shrugged. "He didn't freak me out. Like I said, it was just that he sort of popped out of the darkness. It was just sort of creepy."

"He was awfully cute, though. Maybe the universe sent him, you know, in response to my . . ." Vanessa pondered.

"Stop it. This is going to be a woo-woo-free night." Steffie reached for a handful of popcorn.

"Boring," Vanessa told her. "Besides, if you believe, as I do, that everything happens for a reason, you'd know that the universe brings you what you need."

"True enough there. Hence, popcorn and wine."

"He—Greg—is here for a reason, Stef."

"Right. It's called vacation. Now pass the bowl over and slip one of those movies in so we can get the crap scared out of ourselves."

"I want ice cream first."

"Of course you do, my little thirteen-year-old friend." Steffie got up and patted Vanessa on the head. "I'll get it."

A few minutes later, when Stef returned with two bowls, Vanessa asked, "What kind to start with?"

"The butter brickle. I thought we'd save the s'mores for when we have—ha-ha—s'mores."

"I do like the way you think." Vanessa held up a hand and Steffie placed a bowl in it as she walked past. "Oh, hey, I almost forgot. I found Alice's diary." She leaned over and grabbed a leather-bound volume the size of a paperback book from the table. "I called Miss Grace to let her know I had it and I was going to give it to her, but she got talking about her daughter and the diary got lost in the shuffle."

"What about Lucy? Is she all right? Last I heard, she was an event planner in California."

"She still is. Miss Grace was just saying how she doesn't understand why Lucy won't come back to St. Dennis and do the event thing at the inn, because they've lined up some heavy-hitter weddings and Daniel doesn't have anyone who he thinks can handle them. She said Lucy gets testy whenever she brings it up." Vanessa placed a throw pillow behind her back and leaned against it. "I told her maybe it was just, you know, the normal mother-daughter thing that everyone goes through."

"I didn't. I've always gotten along with my mother. And Lucy's what, thirty-five now? You'd think she'd be over whatever issues she might have had with her mother by now."

"I don't know her, so I can't say. But anyway, I forgot to give Miss Grace the diary, which is why I still have it."

"So what's with the diary?"

"It seems Alice had a lover. Listen to this: 'He came to me again last night. I cannot put into words the love I have for him and the joy he brings me. But even that great love fails me when I try to imagine myself joining him out in the world as he begs me to. The thought of leaving my own walls terrifies me to my soul. I would do anything—anything—to be released from this fear that grips my soul and my mind. What dark forces have inflicted this evil on me?' "

Vanessa looked up. "Alice was agoraphobic; you know that, right?"

Stef nodded. "What's the date on that entry?"

"April 1934."

"I wonder if people understood agoraphobia then? Did they even have a name for it in 1934?"

"I don't know. Doesn't it sound as if she thinks she's under some sort of spell?"

"I think you're under some sort of spell."

"Seriously. 'I would do anything to be released from this fear.' 'What dark forces have inflicted this evil on me?' Doesn't that sound like someone who thinks she's been cursed?"

"Maybe." Steffie thought it over. "If she did, maybe that's why she started studying . . . oh, listen to me. I'm starting to sound like you."

"Think for a minute. If you don't know what agoraphobia is, and you're afflicted with it, how would you explain it, even to yourself?"

"That's a reasonable question."

"Why, thank you," Vanessa said drily.

"It would be interesting to know when Alice first started to be fearful of leaving her house." Stef ignored the sarcasm. "Was this the only diary you found?"

Vanessa nodded. "But there could be more. There

are so many trunks in that attic, Stef. I've gone through maybe half of them, but there are more."

"Maybe I'll ask Miss Grace if she remembers how old Alice was when she stopped going outside."

"I'll try to remember to take this"—Vanessa held up the diary—"to the shop tomorrow."

"Well, give it here. Daniel's making copies of some of the pictures that Miss Grace took at the party. She said she'd drop them off in the morning."

"It'll be interesting to see what she has to say about Alice's mystery lover." Vanessa passed over the diary and Steffie dropped it into her bag.

"It may not have been a mystery to Miss Grace."

"True enough," Vanessa agreed.

"So how should we scare ourselves silly?" Stef pointed to the stack of DVDs.

"Let's do the scariest one first and get it out of the way."

"Which one would that be? They're all pretty scary. Do we want to be up all night, too terrified to sleep? Or do we want to be able to get into our respective shops on time tomorrow?"

"Hmm. Good question. One I hadn't thought through. Usually scary movies are okay during the week when Grady's here, which is generally the only time I watch them." Vanessa pondered their dilemma. "He won't be back until tomorrow, though."

"Wade either."

Vanessa's head swiveled in Stef's direction. "Wade's coming home tomorrow?" Vanessa's foot gave Stef's thigh a punch. "You didn't tell me that."

Stef shrugged. "I'm trying not to make too much of it. He's coming back to pick up all his stuff."

"What did he say about the job?"

"The job's perfect, the child care is perfect, and the house he found is perfect."

"Oh, well, *damn.*" Vanessa frowned. "Well, we can skip the scary for a minute and we'll just make a fire and snack and drink. You decide." She got up and searched the mantel. "Grady laid the fire before he left so that all we had to do was light it."

"Grady's a hell of a guy." Steffie looked through the stack of movies and settled on *Ghostbusters.*

"Isn't he? I don't think I ever loved anyone in my life the way I love him, you know?"

"I do." Steffie hugged her pillow to her chest and watched Ness start the fire. "I think I do . . ."

"Is the L-word rattling around in your brain?" Vanessa stopped and turned around to stare at Stef.

Stef nodded. "I'm beginning to fear it might be so."

"Wow. Just . . . wow."

"Yeah." Stef nodded and reached for the champagne bottle to open it. "Wow."

"Did you tell him that while you were . . . you know, the other night?"

"Are you crazy? You don't tell a guy who's leaving town that you're in love with him. It's against the rules. Everyone knows that."

"So you're just going to let him go off and make a life for himself someplace else, without you?" With the fire going, Vanessa returned to the sofa and plopped down. "Without telling him?"

Stef nodded. "I don't have much of a choice."

"I'll bet a guy made up that rule." Vanessa studied a fingernail. "So what are you going to do?"

"Well, you have a fire going, so I'm going to make s'mores." Stef handed the bottle to Vanessa and went into the kitchen. "And then I'm going to get drunk on champagne and watch *Ghostbusters* till I pass out."

"I like it." Vanessa nodded and filled both glasses with champagne. "Count me in."

"My, but don't we look a tad ragged this morning." Tina studied Steffie's eyes.

"Stop shouting." Stef opened the refrigerator in the back room. "No Pepsi. Tina, if you'd run up to Sips and get me a very large Pepsi—lots of ice—it would save your job."

"How do you figure?"

"This headache is going to kill me. Without me, there is no Scoop. No Scoop, no job for Tina."

"You told Claire she could have it if you died. She's my sister. She'll have to hire me."

Steffie gave her a withering look.

"Okay. One very large Pepsi, lots of ice."

"Run like the wind, T."

"I'm on it." Tina put on her jacket. "By the way, what were you drinking?"

"Champagne. It looked so benign in those pretty girly glasses that Vanessa has, you know?"

Tina laughed and left the shop, Steffie calling after her, "Hurry back."

Steffie couldn't remember the last time she flat-out did not feel like making ice cream. She checked the freezer and thought maybe she had enough to hold her over till tomorrow. She felt like absolute death, but Vanessa had had her sleepover, and truth be told, a headache was a small price to pay to have heard her friend say, "I don't feel at all bad about not having been invited to any sleepovers when I was a kid, because no one I knew back then was as much fun as you are."

"Nicest thing anyone ever said to me," Stef muttered, and looked out the front window.

A few sailboats had braved the morning's chill to head into the Bay, and they skipped briskly across the water. The sun erupting from behind the clouds all but blinded her, and she fumbled in her bag for her sunglasses. She was still wearing the shades when Tina returned.

"Thank you. You may have saved my life." Stef reached for the paper container and took a long drink.

"Better?" an amused Tina asked.

"It will be," Stef told her. "Give it time."

By eleven, Stef felt almost normal, and since they'd served exactly one person all morning, she told Tina she could take the afternoon off if she wanted.

"Normally I'd stay," Tina told her as she gathered her things, "but I do have a few errands I'd like to run, so I'm just going to say thank you as I head out."

"Enjoy the afternoon."

The shop was very quiet with Tina gone and no customers and not even the sound of an ice-cream maker running in the back room. Stef was thinking maybe she'd make something after all when she remembered Alice Ridgeway's diary. She took it out of her bag and flipped through it as she searched for Grace's phone number on her cell. Something fell from the back of the book and landed on the table. Stef put the phone down and carefully picked up the dried bit of vegetation. Once upon a time, it had been some sort of flower. She stared at it for a long moment, then realized what it was, and what it meant.

Son of a gun.

She was just about to call Vanessa to tell her what she found—and what it meant—when the bell over the door rang. She turned just as a small voice called, "Steppie!"

"Why, Austin MacGregor, is that you?"

"Austin." He nodded, then pointed to Wade. "Daddy."

"Hello, Austin." She smiled. "Hello, Austin's daddy. That must have been one heck of an early flight."

"It was. Crack of dawn. We came right here from the airport. Austin couldn't wait to see you." He ran one hand up her arm. "And neither could I."

"I'm glad." She forced the words out, not totally sure how they'd be received, but Vanessa was right. She needed to speak her mind. "I missed you, Wade."

"I missed you, too."

"Eem!" Austin stood on his tiptoes and tried to peer into the case. "Steppie, eem."

"What kind would you like?" She picked him up so he could see into the cooler, and couldn't resist smoothing down his dark curls.

"That." He pointed to the chocolate.

"Chocolate it is." She carried him to a table, one hand snagging a child's seat. "Let's sit you down here with your daddy and I'll get your ice cream."

"Yay!" Austin clapped his hands.

Wade settled Austin into his chair, then took the seat next to him.

"Wade, do you want something while I'm back here?" she called to him.

"I'm good for now."

Stef brought Austin his ice cream, a spoon, and a pile of napkins, which she handed over to Wade. "Just in case."

"Do you have time to sit with us for a few minutes?" Wade asked.

"Sure." She pulled out the chair next to Wade. "We're really slow today."

"I guess you saw the photos from last weekend," he said.

Stef nodded. "I couldn't believe all the newspapers and magazines and TV pieces that were done on that party. Though I must say, I'm happy the photographers got my best side."

"You have no bad side." He reached for her hand and covered it with his own.

"Now, if I didn't know better, I'd think you were coming on to me."

"I am coming on to you."

"Too bad you couldn't have brought Angela back with you." Stef ran a finger up the side of his face and he caught it with his hand.

"What are you doing tonight?" he asked, his eyes watching hers.

"Painting. Feel free to join in."

"I'll do that."

"So tell me all about Oak Grove and your new job," she said. "It sounds like everything is going perfectly for you."

"It's a dream job. All of the fun of brewing and concocting new beer flavors and none of the headaches because all Ted wants me to do is brew. He does a lot of things the same way I used to do them. Actually, he said he studied our business model while setting up his company."

"That's quite a compliment," Steffie noted.

"It is." Wade nodded. "And Mrs. Worth couldn't be more perfect if Dallas had cast her. She loves the kids and has all kinds of fun activities for them. Her assistants are a couple of college kids who are majoring in early childhood education. Maizie and Fern. They're really energetic and the kids seem to have a great time. Austin had a ball both days he spent there."

"Did you find a house that you loved?"

"Oh, yeah. Stone, four bedrooms, three baths, a big kitchen, big fenced-in lot. And like I said on the phone, the neighborhood's terrific."

"Well, then, it sounds as if you're all set." Stef tried really hard to smile.

The bell over the door rang, and Stef looked up as Greg came into the shop. She smiled and waved, and Wade looked over his shoulder to see who was coming in.

Later, in retrospect, Steffie wasn't sure if Wade's first reaction had been one of shock or of fury. His face had gone white, then his jaw clenched and his eyes went dark.

"Well, hello there, little guy." Greg went right to Austin, who was feeding himself chocolate ice cream sometimes with the spoon, and sometimes with his hands.

"Get away from him." Wade's voice was low, but

there was no mistaking the deadly threat. “Don’t touch him.”

“Wade, what’s going on?” Stef stood up. “How do you know Greg?”

“Greg?” Wade laughed out loud. “His name’s not Greg. And I think the real question is how do you know him?”

“He’s been in the shop a few times . . . ,” Stef answered.

“Well, let me introduce you to Hugh Weston. At least that’s what he called himself when I knew him.”

“I don’t understand,” she said, looking at Hugh. “Why’d you tell me your name was Greg?”

“Because he was afraid I’d told you about him,” Wade replied while Hugh stood by looking smug. “Which I did. I just hadn’t mentioned his name.”

Without taking his eyes off the man, Wade said, “Stef, meet the man who drove KenneMac Brews into bankruptcy.”

Chapter 18

"I THINK I'd rather be known as this little guy's daddy." Hugh squatted down next to Austin's chair. "What do you think, Steffie? Doesn't this boy look just like his papa? And we both know we're not talking about Wade."

Hugh slid a chair back from the table, turned it around, and sat.

"You have ten seconds to get up and leave before I call the police," Wade told him.

Hugh laughed. "I don't think so."

Wade started to stand, but Hugh locked his gaze and said, "Sit down, Wade. I'm going to outline for you the way I see this thing playing out."

"Stef," Wade said coolly, "do me a favor and take Austin in the back room."

She lifted the child from his chair. "Come on, Austin. Let's go see what we can find back there to play with."

"Pretty girl." Hugh's eyes followed Steffie to the door. "Real pretty girl. You always did have pretty girls around you. I always thought you were cool that way."

"Aren't you going to ask how Robin is?"

"No, because I know she's dead. Shame, isn't it? Smart, beautiful thing like her, wasting away like she did." Hugh leaned on the chair back. "I did my homework, Wade. I know that you married Robin just before she died. I figured out that's why you have the boy."

He took a folded piece of paper from the inside pocket of his jacket.

"Must be nice to be a celebrity, get your picture on all the magazine covers." He unfolded the paper and tossed it onto the table in front of Wade. "If it wasn't for this"—he tapped a finger on the photo—"I'd have never known about the little guy. What a tragedy, huh, never to know about your own flesh and blood? But thanks to . . ." He turned the page around and glanced down. "Thanks to Todd Litchfield, who snapped this picture, I've found my son."

"Are you crazy? You're wanted for embezzling millions of dollars in Texas, I have copies of the books you cooked, the police have all the records, and you—"

"I don't think you're going to be calling the police, Wade."

"What's going to stop me?"

"The DNA test I'm going to ask the courts to order to prove that the boy is my natural son. I never signed away my parental rights, Wade."

"Because you left Robin as soon as you finished stealing from her. You never even knew she was pregnant. If you'd stuck around—"

"I would have been arrested." He shrugged. "Still might be in danger there, to hear you tell it, but even so, first-time offender, with a good lawyer, most I'll get might be a couple of years. In the meantime, my mama will be raising her grandson. And when I get out of prison, I'll still be his father. And you?" He chuckled. "You'll be nothing to him." He leaned forward. "By then, he won't even remember you."

Wade fought to keep a tight rein on his emotions. The last thing he wanted was a fistfight that could demolish all of Steffie's pretty chairs and tables, and would accomplish nothing more than to scare Austin. Though, he had to admit, there would be a certain amount of satisfaction on oh so many levels in beating the crap out of Hugh. Still, it wasn't the time and it wasn't the place to exact retribution for everything the man had done.

Patience, grasshopper.

"So what it is you really want?" Wade asked with outward calm. "Because we both know you don't really want a child."

"Maybe I do, maybe I don't. Maybe I spent foolishly and need a big infusion of cash."

"Seriously? After you cleaned me out down in Texas, what do you think I have left?"

"Seriously?" Hugh parroted. "Don't insult me with that crap. Start with your sister, why don't you? How much do you think her 'nephew' is worth to her? I'm willing to bet she's just dotty over the kid. As a matter of fact, I'm betting she's gotta be, oh, I don't know, five million dollars' worth of dotty."

"There's no way in hell I'm going to—"

"Of course you are. This is where free choice comes in. You get the money, or you can wave bye-bye to . . . what's his name?" He glanced at the paper before refolding it and putting it back in his pocket. "Austin. Did Robin pick that out?"

When Wade didn't respond, Hugh pushed up from the chair. "So how 'bout we get back together right here in about"—he paused to look at his watch—"oh, let's make it around seven tonight. We can make this little transaction smooth and easy. Or I can have the state's child services down here to look into this little mess." Hugh looked toward the back room. "Take good care of my son for me. And tell pretty Steffie I'll see her later."

Hugh got to the door and stopped. "Oh, and don't even think about leaving town with him, MacGregor, because I *will* go to the police and tell them you kidnapped him. Can you imagine how embarrassing that's going to be for Dallas? Can you imagine the scene, cop cars screaming all around you, the boy being wrenched from your hands? That'd be enough to scar that kid for life, don't you think?" He shook his head as if genuinely concerned about Austin.

"What a dilemma to be in, right? On the one hand, I can tell that you'd like nothing more than to kill me right here and now and just dump my body in that Bay out there. I can't say that I blame you, all things considered. But the way I see it, you're going to have to decide what means more to you. Revenge could be very sweet, I know. On the other hand, I figure you have to have grown attached to the boy. You can't have both, Wade. You can pay the money and keep him, or you can blow the whistle on me and spend the rest of your life wishing you hadn't."

Hugh went out and quietly closed the door behind him.

Wade sat at the table for a moment, trying to push through the cloud of anger that completely filled every cell of his body and consumed him until he literally saw red.

"Wade?" Steffie stepped out from the back room, Austin in her arms.

"You heard?" he asked without turning around.

"Yes. What are you going to do?"

"I don't know." He stared at the opposite wall, trying to gain control.

Stef sat next to him, Austin on her lap playing with an empty ice-cream bowl and two spoons.

"Daddy, eem." Austin leaned over to offer his father an imaginary treat and Wade almost lost it. There was no way in hell he was going to hand over this child to Hugh Weston or whoever he was. There was no power on earth strong enough to take him away. And yes, Wade acknowledged, he could have killed Hugh this morning. Clay had a boat; they could take him far out into the Bay and toss his evil body overboard.

But that would, of course, lead to other problems.

"I have an idea . . ." Stef told him. "Let's see if Dallas can keep Austin company for a while. Then we're going to take a walk."

Thirty minutes later, Wade and Steffie were sitting in Jesse Enright's office.

"Start from the beginning," Jesse told him.

Wade told him everything.

"Let me make sure I've got this right: this guy embezzled your company into bankruptcy and stole personal funds from your partner, and now he's back here to extort money from you to keep quiet about Austin's paternity." Jesse tapped a pen on his desktop.

"That sums it up." Wade nodded.

"Is there any chance that he is not Austin's father?"

Wade shook his head. "None."

"This is a really tough place to be in," Jesse told him. "I'm assuming he never signed away his parental rights."

"He didn't know about Austin, never knew that Robin was pregnant. He still wouldn't have known if it hadn't been for those damned photographs." Wade ran an anxious hand through his hair. "Doesn't it matter that he robbed Austin's mother blind, destroyed her company, and then bolted out of town without looking back?"

"Not as far as establishing paternity is concerned. There's no way anyone could predict the outcome of a case like this. A lot will depend on the judge." Jesse was clearly giving the problem some thought. "Though I'm not sure if the law is more favorable in Maryland or in Texas. I'm going to have to research that in case we need to file some quick motions. Unfortunately, he didn't give us much time."

Jesse opened his laptop. "I'll see if I can get my sister, Sophie, to work on that." He typed for a moment, then turned back to Wade. He was about to speak when his intercom buzzed.

"Jesse, Chief Beck and Mr. Shields are here to see you and Mr. MacGregor."

Jesse looked across the desk at Wade. "Were you expecting . . . ?"

Wade shook his head no.

"Send them in, Liz." Jesse shrugged. "Let's see what's up."

Beck and Grady Shields came through the door as it opened, and immediately pulled up chairs to join the conversation.

"How can we help?" Grady asked.

"Officially or unofficially, whatever it takes, Wade," Beck assured him.

"How did you . . . ?"

"I called Vanessa while you were dropping off Austin at Berry's," Stef admitted. "I knew she'd call Beck, and when we were talking, Grady walked into Bling. We thought it was a sign." She paused. "Well, Ness thought it was a sign."

"It was the right thing to do, Wade," Beck told him. "From the little my sister told me—damn, but that woman can talk fast when she's revved up—there's a lot at stake here, and you're only going to get one chance with this guy. Once he goes for the DNA test, that part is over. If he can prove he's Austin's father, things are going to get real complicated real fast. Let us help you."

"I appreciate the thought, guys, but I don't know what either of you can do."

"Start by filling in some blanks for me," Grady said. "When I was in the Bureau, I was real good at working my way around tough situations. Let's see if I've lost my touch . . ."

"I feel like we're in a remake of *High Noon,*" Steffie told Wade as she watched out the window. "Like we're waiting for the gunslinger to show up."

Moments later, the doorknob turned and Steffie

cleared her throat, then stepped back as the bell rang and Hugh entered. When he smiled at Stef, she pretended not to have seen him. She turned the OPEN sign to CLOSED and locked the door.

"Maybe you should leave," Wade said to her.

"I'm not going anywhere," she replied.

"Well, suit yourself." Hugh sat opposite Wade and smirked. "Hey, maybe I'll walk out of here with your girl and the five million."

"What makes you so sure I'm going to pay up?" Wade asked.

"Well"—Hugh looked around the shop—"I don't see the kid."

"You don't have any interest in Austin and you know it."

"Not beyond the pleasure I'll take in knowing how much it's going to hurt you every day for the rest of your life not to know where he is. How he is. Is he still alive, even. You never know what can happen to a kid these days. I don't live in the best of neighborhoods."

"I'd think you'd be able to afford a great neighborhood. You stole what, two million dollars from Kenne-Mac? Plus whatever you stole from Robin."

"The easiest three and a half million I ever made—plus what I got from Robin—but who's counting." Hugh laughed.

Grady and Beck came out of the back room.

Pointing to Grady, Beck said, "He's counting."

"Who the hell are you?" Hugh demanded.

"Some interested friends." Beck sat on one side of Hugh. "Interested in that three and a half million dollars you stole from Wade's company. Plus the money from Robin's personal account."

"I don't know what you're talking about." Hugh shook his head.

"You got that little recorder I gave you?" Grady asked as he sat on Hugh's other side.

Wade nodded and took it from his pocket, sat it on the table, and pushed play.

"You stole what, two million dollars from Kenne-Mac? Plus whatever you stole from Robin."

"The easiest three and a half million I ever made—plus what I got from Robin—but who's counting."

"You think blackmail is going to work?" Hugh turned to Wade. "Like I said, you can send me to prison for that one job in Texas; first offense, I won't spend much time there. I don't really care how many people know that Austin is my son, but I'd have thought you'd have wanted to keep it quiet." He looked first at Beck, then at Grady. "And I'm not impressed with your posse."

"Maybe you'll be impressed with this." Grady opened his briefcase, took out a folder, and began to read. " 'Hugh Weston. Aka Henry Willis. Aka Harry West. Wanted in four states—' " Grady looked across the table at Wade. "I guess that's five now—for embezzlement. He's made a career of ingratiating himself with women who have come into large sums of money and finding ways to separate them from their cash." Grady turned to Hugh. "That 'first offense' was long ago and far away, my friend." He went back to his file. "All those nasty little embezzlement charges pile up, you know? Enough to put you away for a good long time. But you know what's going to do you in, Hugh?"

Grady slid a piece of paper from the bottom of the pile.

"There's this assault case up in Maine that's been hanging around for the past five years. You picked up a woman in a bar—Christine Davenport; let's not be cavalier and forget who she was. You smacked her around in the parking lot, drove her to New Hampshire, where you kept her in a motel for three days. I don't suppose there's any doubt as to what you were doing with her for those three days, right?"

Hugh sat back in the chair, his arms folded over his chest, his expression lethal.

"Now, here's the thing. You take someone anywhere against their will and hold them—again, against their will—and that's pretty much the definition of kidnapping. You take them across state lines, and it becomes a federal case. Add in the fact that she was coerced at gunpoint, and we're looking at . . . well, shall we add it all up?"

"Who is this guy?" Hugh pointed to Grady and tried to look amused.

"Sorry. I forgot my manners. Meet former FBI Special Agent Grady Shields," Wade told him, then pointed to Beck. "Our chief of police here in St. Dennis, Gabriel Beck."

Hugh tried to look indifferent, but Wade knew the exact moment that he began to realize that the sand might be shifting.

Grady took his iPhone out of his pocket. "I love these gadgets that multitask, don't you?"

He whistled. "Wow, that many?" He turned the

iPhone in his hand to show Hugh the number on the screen.

"I don't know what kind of a clever game you guys are playing here, but I'm done with it." Hugh looked across the table. "You know what the deal was."

"The deal's changed, Hugh," Wade told him. "It might be different if embezzling from KenneMac had really been your first offense. Nice bluff there, by the way. But we all know that KenneMac wasn't anywhere near being the first, and we know—thanks to Grady's family and friends at the FBI—that it wasn't your last. You may have been slick about getting out of town, but you always left prints behind."

"You can leave now—just walk away and don't look back. Or you can keep going with this and I can guarantee you won't live long enough to serve out all your time," Beck told him.

"You're forgetting something real important here, MacGregor." Hugh's bravado was beginning to wear thin. "I can prove that boy is mine. I can go to court and get an order for DNA testing that will prove he's my son. I can still—"

"You can still save your ass," Beck told him. "Or I can take you into custody right now, hold you till the FBI gets here." He turned to Grady. "What time did your brother say he'd be here?"

Grady turned his wrist to look at his watch. "He said he'd be here in time for dessert. So any time now."

Hugh looked from one face to the next, trying to decide, Wade figured, whether or not they were bluffing.

"No five million dollars, Hugh," Wade said. "Just

one long prison sentence. Oh, sure, it would just about kill me not to know where Austin is; you're right on the money there. But just how much satisfaction will that give you when you're spending every day in a five-by-eight cell with some guy who calls you 'Peaches'?"

Grady took one last sheet of paper from the folder. Wade reached across the table to pick it up.

"Now here's the only deal you're going to get, and I'm only going to say it once, so listen up. You sign this and then you walk out of here. These"—Grady held up the reports he'd been reading from—"will go back into those cold-case files they've been sitting in for the past couple of years, and as far as I'm concerned, I never heard your name."

"If you think I'm going to sign a confession . . ." Hugh scoffed.

"It isn't a confession." Wade handed him the paper.

Hugh scanned it, then glanced at the faces of the other three men at the table. He appeared to think for a long while before finally asking, "Got a pen?"

Grady signed as witness, then tossed the pen on the table. "As someone who spent a good part of my life in law enforcement, it makes me sick to say this, but go ahead and leave."

Steffie, silent throughout the entire scene, got up and unlocked the door, held it for him. Hugh left without a backward glance and Stef closed the door behind him.

"Guys, I don't know how to begin to thank you." Wade looked from one man to the other, both his friends. "I know it has to go against everything you believe in to let him walk out of here."

"I'm not gonna lie, Wade," Beck told him. "I can't believe I let him leave. The only consolation I have is in knowing that Austin is staying where he belongs."

Grady nodded, then added, "And the fact that every move he ever makes from here on will be very carefully watched. The next time—and there will be a next time—he won't go free."

"I feel terribly conflicted about that woman from Maine, though." Steffie sat next to Wade. "She deserves justice for what he did to her. Not that the others don't, but there's a difference between what he did to the others—the money he took—and what he did to her. I would have liked to have seen him pay for that."

"He will, but not in this lifetime, I'm afraid," Grady told her. "Christine Davenport died in a car accident two years ago. I wouldn't have let him go on that if she was still alive." He looked at Wade apologetically. "I don't know how we would have handled it, but I couldn't have let him walk."

"I understand." Wade nodded.

"And I feel confident that he's going to pay for it all anyway," Beck said. "All those notes that Grady has were compiled by a friend of his at the FBI."

"My father always told me to never burn a bridge behind me when I left a job," Grady said.

"Who are you kidding?" Beck laughed. "You called your brother who's an active agent."

"No, I didn't. I called a friend of mine who is the best computer geek the Bureau has. He called the police department in Texas that investigated Wade's case. They had Hugh's prints and they'd gotten them into the system. By the time I called my buddy, all these other matches had popped up, all cases similar to Wade's. Then we found the case in Maine, and I knew we had a guy who is a serial offender. He's going to steal again. It's his nature. He's slick, I'll give him that, but next time, he'll be caught."

"And when that time comes, and he points back to tonight?" Steffie frowned. "How are you going to explain your part in this when he talks about how you two law enforcement types went along with this deal?"

"What deal?" Grady got up and stretched his legs. "I just came in to witness Hugh's signing away his parental rights to Austin."

"I just came in for ice cream." Beck walked to the counter. "Stef, you got any of that stuff left over from Dallas's party . . . ?"

Chapter 19

"WHAT just happened here?" Steffie sank into the chair next to Wade. She'd stayed quiet through the entire ordeal, but now she was starting to shake. "Seriously? Did those two just . . . ?"

"Yeah. They did." Wade nodded, his face still unreadable.

"Has it occurred to you that you might not have heard the last of him?" Even her voice was shaking. "What if he comes back and threatens you all over again? Then what? Aren't you worried?"

"It has occurred to me, but Grady feels pretty sure they'll have him in custody for something else by the time he decides to try again. He studied behavior when he was in the FBI and I believe he knows what he's talking about, but it doesn't take an FBI profiler to see that this guy has made a living off of conning people out of their money one way or another. Given his history, it isn't likely that he's going to go into some legitimate business now. Both Beck and Grady think he'll go on from here to extort money from someone else. The difference now is that he's being watched but doesn't know it."

"But what if he comes back and says that he was coerced at gunpoint or something into signing that waiver of his rights?" Stef bit a fingernail, something she hadn't done since she was in her early teens.

"I think he'd be hard-pressed to prove that with four witnesses who'd testify to the contrary, one a police chief, the other a former FBI agent." Wade shook his head. "I'm all right with this for now. I have to be all right with it."

"How can you be sure Hugh really left?"

"Beck was going to have a couple of cruisers follow him all the way to Route 50. I think just seeing a cop car next to you and another one in your rearview would be enough to keep you going for a while."

"I still don't trust him."

"Neither do I, but I'd have agreed to anything to keep Austin safe. The thought of my boy being raised by that bastard makes me sick. I'd never have handed him over, you know that, right? Not even by court order. I would have taken him and run. That was Robin's biggest fear, but I never believed she had anything to worry about. I never really thought he'd come back."

Stef shifted uncomfortably in her seat. At one point over the past week, she'd thought that maybe Hugh—or Greg—had been drawn to St. Dennis because of the spell Vanessa had cast—or thought she'd cast—to find Stef's soul mate.

Note to self: Remind Vanessa to be careful when she tosses that net out into the universe: you never know what might get caught in it.

He reached over to take her hand. "Stef, I don't know how I'll ever be able to thank you for being here for me through this. Not to mention the fact that you did what I should have done."

"All I did was tell Vanessa."

"Knowing she'd pick up the phone and call Beck. I should have done that the minute Hugh walked out of here this morning."

"I imagine having him show up like that must have been a bit of a shock."

"For a moment, when he first walked in, I thought I was hallucinating. A couple of times over the past few months I wondered what I'd do if somehow he found out about Austin and came for him, but like I said, I never really thought it would happen."

"It was just one of those really bad coincidences: the photographers following us around the day after the party, the photos all over everywhere, Hugh seeing them, and seeing himself in Austin." She averted her eyes. "I hate to say it, but there really is a strong resemblance between Hugh and Austin that's pretty hard to miss."

"That, and knowing what happened to Robin, and given Austin's age, I guess it was inevitable that Hugh would put two and two and two together and figure out that this was . . ." Wade grimaced. "I can't bring myself to say 'his son.' "

"What are you supposed to do with that paper Hugh signed?" she asked.

"Jesse said under ordinary circumstances, you'd use it in adoption proceedings. But he thinks we should just sit on it for now and only go that route if we ever have to. In the meantime, my name is on Austin's birth certificate and I was married to his mother. We're going to leave it like that." He ran a hand through his hair. "God, Stef, I don't know how I'll ever be able to tell Austin that I'm not his father. That his real father is a criminal who used his mother—"

"Wade, Hugh is not Austin's 'real' father." She took his face in her hands. "You are his father. Someday, when he's old enough to understand, you'll tell him the truth, but do not ever refer to that man as Austin's real father, because he isn't. He hasn't done a damn thing to deserve that honor."

"I wonder if Austin will ever be able to understand what happened."

"You'll know when the time is right. Besides, you're going to raise him with love, and he'll be a confident, strong boy because of you. He'll understand that what you did was the right thing."

"I hope you're right."

"Of course I am." She forced a smile. "And look at it this way. The worst has happened and it's behind you. You met Robin's biggest fear and you and Austin survived. Now you can start your new life in Connecticut."

"I need to talk to you about that." His phone began to ring in his pocket and he pulled it out to check the caller ID. "It's Dallas," he told Stef.

"Hey, Dal . . . what? Oh. Right. I can explain that." He looked slightly chagrined. "I'll be home in fifteen minutes and I'll tell you all about it. Just . . . stop shouting, okay?"

He disconnected and slid the phone back into his pocket.

"Hal just called the house and told Dallas that Austin was asking for his daddy and while he—Hal—

didn't mind keeping him, he just thought I should know that Austin was getting antsy," Wade said. "Needless to say, she wanted to know why Austin was at Hal's and what the hell was going on and if I needed someone to watch Austin, why didn't I ask her."

"I guess you should go get him and take him home." Stef glanced at the wall clock. "It's late anyway, past Austin's bedtime, I guess. You go on. I'll close up here and—"

"You're coming with me," he told her. "We'll get Austin and put him to bed. And then maybe later you can put me to bed."

"Would you like to explain why you took that baby to Hal's instead of leaving him here with us?" Dallas demanded.

Stef and Wade had arrived with a sleeping Austin at the house on River Road, and Dallas had met them at the front door.

"For one thing, you weren't here when Austin and I got in today from Connecticut. I drove past the house and there were no cars in the driveway, so I went straight to Scoop. Then Hugh showed up and everything sort of snowballed from there."

"Hello? Phone?" Dallas reached across the kitchen table for her cell. "And who is Hugh?"

"Austin's birth father."

"What . . . ? You mean the guy who embezzled . . ."

Wade nodded. "Things happened so fast, Dallas. One minute, Stef and I were sitting there and Austin was eating ice cream; the next minute, Hugh was coming through the door," he explained. "When I stopped back here this afternoon, Berry was here alone with Cody and she wasn't sure what your schedule was. Besides, if something had gone terribly wrong, I didn't want you or Cody or Berry to be caught in the cross fire. Besides, I thought he'd be safer at Hal's. It was bad enough that Stef was—"

"What are you talking about? What cross fire?" Dallas interrupted. "Damn it, Wade, start from the beginning."

Still holding Austin, Wade sat on the edge of a chair and told his sister everything.

"You're telling me this guy wanted five million dollars to just go away and never come back?" Dallas stood and began to pace the length of the kitchen.

"Right." Wade kept his voice low, with Austin asleep in his arms. "But Beck and Grady thought the chances of him not coming back were—"

"You didn't even tell me about this? Someone is threatening to take Austin and you don't even tell me?" Dallas appeared to be just winding up.

"What would have been the point?" Wade frowned.

"The point would have been that I'd have gone to the bank and requested the withdrawal, which would have taken more than a day because you can't walk into a bank and say give me that much money and have them just hand it over and you walk out with it. There are regulations about such things. There'd have been an investigation. And he'd be behind bars right now."

"Behind bars and demanding a DNA test to prove that he's Austin's birth father," he whispered his reply. "He'd have taken us to court, Dallas. Jesse said there's a very good chance he'd win."

"I could call on a posse of lawyers who could—"

"Who could have pounded on their chests all they wanted, and he still probably would have won. He has the matching DNA and has not surrendered his parental rights. He held the cards, Dallas. Grady said he could have made allegations that Robin and I conspired to withhold the knowledge that he had a son—which frankly, we did."

She sat as if stunned, as if it had never occurred to her that "this guy" had any rights or any points in his favor.

"The only way to get around him was to get him to sign the waiver of his rights and make him leave town. The only way to do that was to muscle him with his own criminal past. And I could not have done that without Beck and Grady," Wade explained. "Grady had a friend of his from the FBI run Hugh backward, forward, and sideways through the system, and they found enough on him under different names that he was facing a lifetime behind bars. I had to make the decision to let the two of them set him up. Hugh had to make the decision to walk."

"You could have told me."

"It all happened so fast. He only gave us a few hours. You weren't around when I got back here today and I didn't know if you were in meetings or something, and I didn't want to tell Berry."

"I don't know how he thought anyone could have gotten their hands on that much cash in a few short hours," she said, "unless it was in a wall safe or under a mattress."

"I don't think he was thinking of the logistics. All he was thinking was 'Hey, rich movie-star aunt will fork over the money.' "

"Rich movie-star aunt would have." Dallas gently stroked the sleeping boy's back. "In a heartbeat. No one's going to take him away from us. He's our little guy."

She patted her brother's shoulder and said, "We've missed you this week. You and Austin both. It's not right around here without you. Cody's been very unhappy."

"We've missed you, too. As a matter of fact . . ." Wade appeared about to say something else, but Austin stirred in his arms. "I'm going to get this guy changed and into bed. Stef, want to give me a hand?"

Stef, who'd wisely kept out of the family discussion, nodded. "Sure," she said, and followed Wade up the stairs.

"He sleeps in here." Wade pointed to the door, three down from the second-floor landing. Wade changed Austin and got him into his pajamas by the faint light of a lamp on Wade's bedside table. When Austin stirred, Wade picked him up and held him for a moment to settle him, then placed him in his crib and covered him.

He turned to find Stef sitting on the side of his bed.

"You didn't need me for that," she whispered.

"I needed you to be here with Austin and me so I could just savor the fact that we're together. I came very close to losing him. It's just starting to sink in how close. This day could have ended in a total nightmare, but instead, I'm here with my girl and my son, and I can't remember ever feeling that my life was more right than it is at this moment."

"I can make it righter." She played with the buttons on his shirt.

"I'm counting on it." He pressed his lips to her throat.

"But not here," she said.

"No, not here. Dallas will be in to check on Austin, and when Berry gets home from her dinner date, she'll check in."

"Berry has a date?"

"Archer Callahan. Her old boyfriend."

"I know that name. Archer Callahan." Steffie sat up. "The book. Alice wrote about them in her book."

"What book? Who's Alice?" He frowned.

"Alice Ridgeway. She lived in Vanessa's house for about a hundred years and she left these journals." Stef caught herself before elaborating. Did she really want to get into all that?

"What kind of journals?"

She debated whether or not she should tell him about Alice.

Nah.

"Just journals about people she knew in St. Dennis back in her day."

"Like a diary?"

"Sort of." If one kept a diary full of spells and a list of names one taught them to.

"And she wrote about Aunt Berry and Archer? What did she say?"

Stef shrugged and tried to appear nonchalant. "I don't remember the particulars. I just remember that I noticed the names there."

"So Alice knew Berry before she went to Hollywood? I'm intrigued. Where are those journals now?"

"I think Ness gave them to Miss Grace."

"I'll ask her about them the next time I see her."

Since Wade was moving to another state, Stef didn't think this was likely to happen anytime soon. But that reminded her to ask, "So I guess you'll be moving this weekend."

"That's something we need to talk about." He took her hand. "I think Dallas is in for the night, and she's good about listening for Austin, though he almost never wakes up at night. Any chance we could go to your place? I don't want to wake up Austin, and we have a lot to talk about."

"If Dallas is okay with it, sure."

Wade was softening her up for the news, Stef could feel it. Well, she supposed it had to be done. Sooner was better than later, and she did want one more night with him. He'd say something like, *We can still see each other. You can come visit us, and we'll be home from time to time. We'll be back for holidays. Blah blah blah*. Nothing he hadn't said before.

And then she'd say—

"Stef?"

She looked up and he was standing at the side of the bed, holding his hand out to her.

"Oh." She took his hand and he pulled her up and put his arms around her. They were a step away from Austin's crib, his breathing sweet and even in sleep.

"You did the right thing," Stef whispered. "There's no way you could have let Hugh take him, regardless of what the law might have said."

Wade nodded and reached a hand into the crib to cover the sleeping child, and Stef's heart melted.

"Come on." She tugged at his hand. "Let's go see if Dallas feels like babysitting . . ."

"Stef, we need to talk." Wade had his hand on her bare back.

She tried to pretend to be sleeping, but he apparently wasn't buying it. He'd been trying to have his say all night and she'd been finding ways to divert him. When they arrived at her apartment, he'd headed for the living-room sofa—she assumed for "the talk"—but she pulled him straight into the bedroom before he could get a word out and she'd kept him well occupied for most of the night, attacking him with a fervor that had probably had his head spinning. She knew hers had been.

When he said, "Stef, we need to talk," she'd mumbled, "Later. I'm exhausted." and he'd let her sleep, or pretend to.

Now, with dawn closing in, she couldn't keep him at bay any longer. She rolled over, braced herself for what he was about to say, and said, "Okay. I guess you want to talk about your move to Connecticut."

He nodded.

"Everything sounds so perfect." She sat up and pulled the sheet with her and tried to be supportive. "The job. The child care. And you found a house, right?" She tried to brighten. "You found a house that's as perfect as the job and the child-care situation?"

Wade nodded. "Actually, I saw several I liked, but I did find one that would be perfect."

"Tell me about it. What's it look like?"

"It's light gray clapboard and it has black shutters and a red door. The previous owner did a lot of renovation and it's just been painted inside and out. Even the hardwood floors have been refinished and it has a new deck. It's in that terrific neighborhood I told you about on the phone."

"It really does sound perfect." Even to herself, she sounded wistful.

"That's exactly what I thought the minute I first walked through the front door. We went into the backyard and Austin ran around for a while. Then we went back inside and went from room to room, just trying to get a feel for the house, and all the time I was thinking, 'This could be it. This could be home.' And it almost was. It was almost home, Stef. But there was something missing, and as soon as I realized what it was, I knew if I bought that house and moved there, it would never be more than *almost*."

"So what was missing?" She frowned.

He raised her hand to his lips and kissed her palm. "You were."

She tilted her head to one side, not sure she was understanding.

"If you're not there with us, any place is always going to be *almost*. That's not good enough for me, and it's not good enough for Austin."

For a moment Stef was certain that her heart had stopped beating. Had he just said . . . ?

"What exactly are you saying?"

"I'm saying that there's no home for me—not there, not here in St. Dennis—without you."

She took a deep breath and tried to slow the rapid

beating of her heart. "Just because I helped you today doesn't mean that you have to change your plans. You're not obligated to me because of anything that happened here tonight."

"I changed my plans before I left Connecticut, Stef. I already told Ted that I was passing on the job."

"Huh?" She wished her response had been more gracious, more eloquent, but her mind had gone mostly blank. She recovered enough to protest, "But . . . but it was all so perfect for you there."

"The perfect job for me is having my own brewery. I can start over. It won't be KenneMac, but it can be damned good. Actually, it can be great. Clay mentioned he was interested in working with me if I ever wanted to start up again. I called him last night to see if he still thought it was a good idea, and he does. He's got the fields to grow whatever we need and he has a large unused barn that can be retrofitted with equipment. Clay's interested in organics, so we talked about what he'd have to grow next year—barley, hops, and so on—and what we'd need in finances. Then I called Dallas because she'd said once before that if I wanted to go into business for myself, she'd fund it as an investment, so we talked that out."

"So you'll be back in business?"

"It's going to take a while to get set up, but yes, I'll be back in business." He nodded happily, then added, "But the best part is that I'll be back in business right here in St. Dennis."

"That's really good. Great. I'm sure Dallas and Berry will be happy to hear that you're staying."

"And how 'bout you, Stef. Are you happy that we're staying?" He pulled her to him.

"Oh, well, yeah. Sure. If that's what you want, if you're sure. But you're passing up on a lot. I mean, what about Angela Lansbury? And the perfect house in the perfect neighborhood?"

"I'm sure we can find some good child care here in St. Dennis. And as far as the house is concerned . . . Stef, did you hear anything I said about that house? About why we couldn't live there?"

"You said . . . you said it wasn't home . . ." She could barely get the words out. Had he really said such a thing?

"I said it wasn't home because . . ." He prompted her.

"Because I wasn't there." She thought it over for a moment. "You really meant that? That it wasn't perfect because I wasn't there?"

"I can't believe it took me all this time to figure it out, but there it is. There isn't anyone else for me, Stef. I think it's always been you."

"Oh." The small word squeaked out.

"Aren't you going to say something? Like, 'Wade, it's always been you for me, too.' "

"I . . . I can't seem to get . . . I mean, you were. You are. You always have been. But hearing you actually say it . . ." She pinched herself. "Ouch. I guess I'm not dreaming."

"We have a lot of time to make up for, you and I." He nuzzled the curve of her neck.

"Let me get this straight." She tried to ignore the little flame that was igniting inside her again. "You passed on the job because of me."

"Right." His lips moved across her throat.

"You gave up perfect child care and the perfect house because of me."

"Right again." And across her shoulder.

"Any chance that someday you're going to regret—"

"None," he said adamantly. "Not gonna happen. As soon as I realized it, I knew it was right. I know this is where I belong. I know that I want Austin to grow up here and I know that I want to make my home here."

"With me," she said dreamily. "You want to make a home with me."

"Yes," he replied solemnly. "I want to make a home with you. If you'll have me."

"Oh, well. I'll need to think about that. After all, I already have my own home." She tried to appear solemn, thoughtful. Inside, she was positively giddy. "I've lived by myself for a long time, you know. I'm going to have to think long and hard about whether or not I want to give up my independence."

"Well, while you're thinking . . ." His lips found their way back to her skin.

"Stop." She tapped him on the back. "If you want me, you know what you're going to have to do, don't you?" Finally—finally!—she'd hear the L-word from his lips. Finally, she could tell him exactly how she felt.

"I'm trying to but you keep interrupting me."

"Not that."

"All right." He laughed. "I get it." He paused. "Should I get down on one knee?"

"As long as you don't take the sheet with you." She grinned and started to sit up, then realized what he was about to do, and her smile faded. One knee . . . ?

Did he really say, "One knee"? The thought took her breath away.

It was the moment she'd waited for since she was thirteen years old.

He took her hands in his and she held her breath.

"Stef, I've been falling in love with you for more years than I can remember. You're the woman I want to spend the rest of my life with. I've never thought of saying those words to anyone else, because there's never been anyone like you. I want to marry you and—"

He stopped.

Damn. Just as he was getting to the good part. "What?" she asked. Was he having second thoughts?

"I don't have a ring." Even in the dark, she could see that he was frowning.

"Don't stop now," she told him. "You can get a ring later. Keep going."

"Okay, where was I?"

"You want to marry . . . oh, you're teasing me."

"I am." He laughed softly. "I want to marry you and live a long and happy life with you. I want to spend every new morning and every new night with you in my arms. I want to plan vacations with you and worry over our kids with you. I want to celebrate birthdays and Christmases with you. I want to have brothers and sisters for Austin. Here, in St. Dennis, where we both belong."

"That's all I ever wanted, Wade." She was almost too overcome to get those few words out.

"You didn't say yes," he pointed out.

"You didn't ask me."

"Oh. Right. Will you marry me, Stef?"

"Yes, of course I will marry you," she squealed, and threw her arms around his neck. "I don't remember a time when I didn't love you. I would marry you tomorrow. I would marry you right now, this minute."

She felt tears running down her cheeks, but she didn't bother to wipe them away.

"This minute might be tough to pull off," he whispered. "Tomorrow . . . that might be tight, too."

"But we can't get married before Dallas and Grant anyway," she told him.

"Why not?"

"It's the rule. They got engaged first."

"So?"

"So they get first shot at choosing their date."

He shook his head. "I don't want to know where that rule came from, but when I get back to Berry's, I'll ask Dallas if they have a date. And since the sun is just about up, I will need to get going." He looked out the window at the light that was just starting to spread across the bedroom floor. "But I think we might have just enough time . . ."

"I think so, too." She lifted her arms and her mouth to his, and welcomed him home.

Chapter 20

It was a glorious morning. Wade stood on the dock with his son and smiled just because life was so damned good. He had everything that mattered to him. He had Austin, he had Stef, he had a place in St. Dennis that was just his, not one that was dependent upon his sister or his aunt or anyone else. And soon he'd have his own brewery again. Well, his, Clay's, and Dallas's. But he was going to be the brewmaster. All of this good fortune made his head spin, like someone who'd been living on the bare edge of poverty who'd just won the lottery. There seemed to be almost too much goodness in his life. Could there be such a thing, he wondered, as too much good fortune?

"What are you grinning about, silly boy?" Dallas came up behind him and pretended to push him toward the edge of the dock.

He told her. Life was overflowing with an embarrassment of riches.

"Don't you think you deserve it after the two years you've had?" She sat on the dock and swung her legs over the side. Austin lay down next to her to see what he could see in the water below. "Your life was on a mean streak there for a while, bud. I think it's time you got a little break."

"Thanks." He sat next to her. "Actually, I got a big break. Several big breaks."

"Name three things you're thankful for this morning."

"Austin and you, of course," he replied without hesitation. "And Stef."

"Oh, so she's made it into the top three, has she?"

Wade nodded.

"That's nice, sweetie." She smacked him on the arm. "It shouldn't have taken so long."

"I know. I don't know what I was thinking."

"Me either. But at least you've seen the error of your ways." Dallas smiled. "What is it about those Wylers that we MacGregors find so irresistible?"

"Speaking of the Wylers, when are you and Grant getting married?"

"We can't decide. On the one hand, I'd love to be a Christmas bride, and get married at the inn." Dallas's eyes were shining. "On the other, a summer wedding is always so lovely. All the flowers I most love are only available then. But a winter wedding, with everything white and sparkly . . ."

"So the answer is, you don't know."

"It's still under discussion. Why the sudden interest?"

When he didn't respond, she said, "Wade? Why do you want to know?"

He cleared his throat. "Because, um, I . . . ah . . . asked Steffie to marry me and she said you and Grant had to get married first because you got engaged first. That it was some sort of rule. Not that we're engaged yet, not formally. I mean, I didn't buy her a ring. But I will." He paused. "Buy her a ring, that is."

"You! You knew this and you're sitting out here in the sun like a big fat old toad and you didn't think to tell me?" She smacked his arm again.

"I just did tell you."

"This constitutes Very Big News, brother."

"I know. I was just sitting here thinking about it and thinking how lucky I was." He turned to his sister. "I was going to tell you this morning, really. I just came outside with Austin because it's such a beautiful morning and he likes to watch the little fish swim under the dock. But I was going to come back in, in a few minutes, and talk to you and Berry."

"That was all so lovely, I'll probably have to forgive you." She smiled. "But Berry isn't here. She went to Archer's last night and didn't come back."

"She drove all the way to Annapolis last night in the dark? And you let her?"

"He has a place out near the inn, right before you go onto the bridge that goes over to Cannonball Island. It's on the road that winds toward the Bay, so she didn't drive to Annapolis. And since when has 'letting' been involved when Berry wanted to do something?"

"You have a point." Wade nodded. "I didn't know Archer had a place here in town."

"He sold the Annapolis house last month and bought a smaller place here. To be closer to Berry, I'm sure."

"He has kids, right?" Wade asked.

"Three or four, I think."

"How do they feel about their father's relationship with Berry?"

Dallas shrugged. "I don't know if they even know that he's seeing her. His wife has been dead for a few years, though, so it shouldn't come as a complete shock that he'd want the company of a gorgeous, vibrant woman like Berry."

"That's your second good point of the morning," he told her. "You're on a roll."

"I will be in about two hours. I'm meeting an architect at the warehouse at eleven to go over my plans for the studio." She grinned. "We are just digging our heels in, aren't we, the two of us? Me with my studio, you with the brewery. Your phone call made me very happy."

"I'm glad you're happy. But hey, you just reminded me. I have a meeting this morning, too." He stole a look at his watch. "Clay and I are going to go through his barns and see which is best suited for conversion into a brewery. Then we're going to look into the equipment we need to order."

"I'm delighted that you're moving ahead immediately with this. But what are you going to do with Austin? I won't be here to watch him."

"Clay's mom recommended a sitter, some friend of hers who's looking for something she can do at home. I thought I'd give her a call. I need to find someone local anyway, if I'm going to be working here."

Dallas stood and brushed off the seat of her jeans. "I'm really happy for you and Stef, Wade. I couldn't be happier. I think it's wonderful. I'll have to give her a call later and tell her so."

"Good idea," he said. "Maybe you and she can work out the whole date thing."

* * *

Steffie could barely contain herself all day. Her arm was almost black and blue from pinching herself every other minute to see if she was still awake. Having your best dreams come true was nothing short of awesome. That they did so unexpectedly made the reality even sweeter.

She couldn't wait to tell Vanessa.

Calling on the phone wouldn't do, and when she stopped at Bling around noon, Vanessa was taking delivery of some merchandise she'd ordered for the shop. She'd just realized that the order was short and was going back and forth between the vendor and the delivery guy.

"I'll stop back later," Stef told her.

Vanessa put her hand over the phone. "I have three more deliveries scheduled for this afternoon, and if this is any indication of how things are going for me today, you don't want to be around to witness the aftermath."

Steffie was keeping the shop open until seven, but Wade had brought her dinner—Chinese takeout—at six. Dallas had a meeting, and Wade had both Austin and Cody to feed and put to bed.

Cody had homework, which meant Wade needed to get the boys back to the house by six-thirty so that he could help Cody with those all important spelling words.

"Dallas called me this afternoon," Steffie told him. "She said she was thrilled that you'd finally come to your senses and that she and Grant wanted to get together with us to celebrate really soon. Which I already knew because my brother stopped in this morning and I told him. I was going to tell my mother but

I thought I'd wait until we were together. Dallas and Grant are still talking about a date, though."

"I have to ask your father for your hand."

"I'd have thought there were other parts you were more interested in."

"Ha-ha. That's not part of the tradition. If I'm going to do this, I'm going to do it the right way," he said.

"Did you tell Berry?"

Wade shook his head. "She wasn't around today, at least, not when I was. Of course, I was at Clay's for most of the afternoon." He ruffled Austin's hair. "And Austin got to meet his new babysitter, right, ace? Mrs. Lindstrom," he told Stef.

"Cathy Lindstrom's mom?" Stef asked.

Wade shrugged. "I don't know. Clay's mom recommended her and she seems really nice and Austin really had a good time at her place today, didn't you?"

Austin nodded and picked up a piece of overcooked broccoli to lick.

"Nice manners," Wade noted.

"He's just a little guy." Stef leaned on the back of Wade's chair, her arms around his neck. "But if he eats his dinner, he can have ice cream."

Austin nodded again and stuffed the broccoli in.

"I don't know what time Dallas is getting home tonight," Wade said when they were leaving. "I don't know if I'll be able to make it over to your place."

"Give me a call if it isn't too late when she gets home." Stef helped Austin on with his jacket then handed Wade a carton of ice cream. "Or just call me. I want to stop at Vanessa's on my way home and I might be there awhile."

"Okay. I'll talk to you later." Wade kissed her, then picked up Austin and, taking Cody by the hand, went out into the cool night air.

Steffie stood at the window and watched them disappear around the bend. "My guys." She sighed happily, then closed the door.

She packed a few containers of ice cream to share with Vanessa in between waiting on the two customers she had after Wade left. At ten after seven, she grabbed the bag of ice cream, locked up the shop, hopped into her car, and headed for Vanessa's house on Cherry Street. She all but danced from the car to the front door, where she rang the bell in three or four spurts.

"Hey, Stef," Ness said as she unlocked the front door. "I wasn't expecting you. Come on in."

"I have something really huge to tell you." Stef followed Vanessa into the living room. "Last night . . ." she began, then seeing the woman seated on the sofa, she stopped. "Miss Grace. Hi. Am I interrupting . . . ?"

"No, dear. Of course not." Grace sat back slightly on the cushions as if to distance herself from the coffee table, where, Stef realized, the Ouija board had been placed.

"I hope that's ice cream in that bag," Ness was saying as she tugged off Stef's jacket.

"Duh." Stef swung the bag back and forth. "I'll put it in the freezer for later."

"Or we could have some now. I'll come with you and get bowls. Miss Grace." Vanessa turned to her guest. "You'll have some, won't you? I'm not sure what flavors we have tonight . . ."

"If Steffie made it, I don't even need to know the flavor. Of course I'd love some. Could I help . . . ?"

"No, no. You just sit there and and relax and we'll just be a minute." Vanessa smiled, and grabbed Stef by the arm and pulled her into the kitchen.

"I am so glad to see you," Vanessa whispered when the door closed behind them. "You are not going to believe what is going on out there." She took a deep breath. "Miss Grace stopped over to pick up a few more journals that I found in the attic, and she asked about the Ouija board. Well, I had it here, so I took it out and said something like, 'Let's see if it will say something besides DAZ with someone else playing with that little triangle thing.' "

"Did it?"

"Did it ever! It's the strangest damned thing. It keeps spelling out 'Hello, Gracie. Hello, Gracie!' Like it—the spirit—recognizes her! It's totally creeping me out."

Vanessa pulled back the left sleeve of her sweater and held out her arms. "Look at the hair on my arms. It's standing straight up."

Stef looked. Vanessa wasn't exaggerating.

"She's got to be controlling that thing," Stef told her. "She's playing with your head."

"This is Miss Grace we're talking about," Vanessa reminded her. "She doesn't play with anyone's head."

"Well, she's playing with yours."

"Stef, you have to see it. That little triangle was flying across that board like nobody's business. Zip zip! Like it was excited. It was so weird, even Miss Grace was getting tense. We could hardly keep up with it."

"Was there a message from beyond?"

"Just 'Hello, Gracie.' "

"Let's dish up the ice cream and we'll go back out there and we'll see if she'll do it with me here. I think she was just trying to spook you."

"Why would she do that?"

"Maybe so that you'd let her take the Ouija board home with her."

"I'd already offered it to her, and—"

"Do you girls need a hand?" Grace stuck her head through the door.

"No, thank you. I just need to get a few spoons. Stef, grab those two bowls and I'll take this one." Vanessa smiled. "Miss Grace, if you could just hold that door . . . thank you."

The three women returned to the living room. Vanessa and Grace sat on the sofa, and Stef took one of the floor cushions and tossed it next to the table.

"Oh, a Ouija board," she said as she sat on the pillow and placed her bowl on the table.

"We were just . . . testing it," Miss Grace told her.

"And did it work?" Stef asked innocently.

"I'm afraid so, dear." Grace put her bowl down next to the board. "It's been most puzzling."

"What's the puzzle?" Stef asked.

"I'd thought we might be able to contact Alice, but it appears the spirit isn't hers."

"How can you tell who the spirit is?" Stef frowned.

"It . . . whoever . . . keeps calling me 'Gracie.' " She looked from Stef to Vanessa then back again. "Alice never called me Gracie. Never."

Stef's spoon stopped halfway to her mouth. "Seriously? You're not playing with Vanessa? Please say so if you are. And if you are, please stop."

"Steffie, I do not 'play' with things such as this. In most hands, the Ouija is a harmless toy. In the hands of someone who might have some . . . *sensability,* it can become a channel of sorts. That's what's happening here. Someone is contacting me and I'm very confused because I do not know who it is."

"Stef, why don't you try it with Miss Grace?" Vanessa sat on a nearby chair, as if putting as much distance as she politely could between herself and the coffee table.

"It's okay with me, as long as it's okay with Miss Grace." Steffie looked across the table at Grace. "But you have to understand that I don't believe in this stuff."

"That's quite all right, dear. You don't have to."

"You just put your fingers on the little planchette," Vanessa said. When Stef looked up questioningly, Vanessa smiled smugly. "That's what the little triangle thingy is called."

"Did you look that up yourself?" Stef asked.

"Nah." Ness loaded her spoon with ice cream. "Miss Grace just told me."

Grace reached across the table and took Steffie's hands and placed them on one side of the triangle. But even before Grace added hers, the triangle began to move, as if quivering.

"Holy crap," Stef whispered. "I swear I'm not—"

"Hush, dear," Grace told her softly as her fingertips touched the triangle. "Let's see where it goes."

"It's spelling out *HS* over and over." Stef watched as the small triangle sped back and forth between the two letters."

"What word starts with *HS*? I can't think of a

one," Vanessa said. "Unless it means *his*. Which makes no sense at all."

The three women watched as the same letters were touched over and over again.

"I don't get it." Steffie shook her head.

"Wait, it's doing something else now. Look." Grace pointed to the board.

"What's the word it's spelling?" Vanessa leaned forward.

"H-S-T-E-P . . ." Steffie's jaw dropped. "Oh, my . . ." She held her breath. "H. Stephen."

"What?" Vanessa frowned.

"H. Stephen. I used to call Horace 'H. Stephen.' " Steffie's eyes filled with tears. "Horace?" she whispered.

The triangle went around and around in circles, as if doing cartwheels, and Stef laughed out loud. "Horace. How can this be happening . . . ?"

"Steffie, your cousin Horace *always* called me Gracie."

"Can you tell him thank you for me?" Stef asked Grace. "And can you tell him I miss him?"

"You just did, dear."

Stef took her hands off the triangle and placed one over her heart. "I can't believe this just happened. I don't believe in this stuff. I think somehow you made this happen, maybe even unconsciously, but I don't believe it."

She thought for a moment. "But why would Horace be here, in Alice's house?"

"You'll have to ask him," Grace replied.

Stef sat for a moment, her hands in her lap. "All right. Let's ask it something. Something none of us knows the answer to." She put her fingertips onto the triangle. "Will this work with just me?" she asked Grace.

"I don't know. Give it a try."

Stef thought about the dried flower that had fallen out of Alice's diary. "Horace, is Alice your Daisy?"

The triangle went still for several seconds, then slid across the board to *yes.*

"Oh, my stars." Grace stared at Steffie as if she'd sprouted a second and a third head. "Horace and Alice . . . ?"

"How did you know to ask that?" Vanessa frowned. "Oh, you're the one who's goofing with this thing. Honestly, Stef, you had me going there for a minute."

"I swear to you, I was only guessing. Why else would Horace be here, in Alice's house, if there wasn't a very close connection between them?" Stef stopped to consider what she'd said. "I don't believe in any of this, but I can't explain what just happened."

She placed her fingers on the triangle again, but nothing happened.

"Miss Grace, you try it," she said.

Grace did, but . . . nothing.

"They're gone," Grace said simply.

"*Gone* means they were *here.*" Vanessa looked around the room. "Swell. I've got ghosts."

"Not ghosts, dear. Just spirits." Grace patted her arm.

"Right. Just a couple of the undead." Vanessa looked at Stef. "I wonder what they do all day . . ."

"Vanessa, would you mind if I took the board home with me?" Grace asked.

"Oh, would you?" Vanessa looked relieved. "I mean, of course, take it. I won't be touching it again, believe me." She looked at Stef. "You?"

"Nope." Steffie shook her head. "I'm done."

"Well, then, thank you, Vanessa, for the journals and the board and the . . . interesting evening." Grace stood and gathered her things. "Yes, indeed, this was a very interesting evening." She shook her head. "Horace and Alice. Who knew?"

Both Stef and Vanessa walked Grace to the door, but once she was gone, Ness turned to Stef. "Now tell me the truth. Were you pushing that little thing?"

"Uh-uh."

"Oh, come on. Just a little tiny bit, maybe?"

Stef shook her head.

"How am I going to explain to Grady that we are not alone here?" Vanessa bit the inside of her lip.

"I wouldn't bother. He won't believe you and then you'll have to explain the whole Alice-and-the-spells thing."

"Good point." Vanessa stood in the middle of the living-room floor. "I say we have more ice cream and forget that this little incident ever happened."

"Amen." Stef picked up the bowls they'd already used and followed Vanessa into the kitchen, where she placed them in the sink. "Let's do cones this time. I brought two. They're in the bag."

"Okay. And you can tell me what's on your mind."

"I had an interesting night last night," Stef told her.

"Oh? Why didn't you call me?"

"Because it's the kind of interesting thing you want to tell your best friend in person. I was going to tell you when I stopped at Bling today, but you were busy."

Vanessa stopped scooping the ice cream and stared at Stef. "You're not sick, are you? It's nothing bad, is it? Please tell me you aren't sick."

"It's not bad. It's good." She grabbed the scoop and took over. "Like, really super good."

"What's super good?" Vanessa frowned.

"Super good is Wade telling me that he loves me and wants to marry me."

Vanessa's jaw dropped. "He didn't."

"He did."

"But what about his job . . . ?"

"He told the guy he changed his mind before he left Connecticut."

"I'm . . . I'm . . ." Vanessa sputtered.

"Speechless." Stef grinned.

Vanessa hugged Stef. "You . . . he . . ."

Steffie laughed out loud. "Yes. Me and he. Him."

"It happened. Just like you wanted." Nessa gave Stef one more big hug before letting go. "I'm deliriously happy for you. This *is* super good. We should have champagne." She looked in the fridge. "No bubbly, but we do have some white wine." She pulled out the cork and grabbed a couple of glasses from the cupboard.

"To you and Wade." Vanessa toasted and took a sip. "May you have the happiest life ever." She took another sip. "Stef, this is just like we planned. The love of your life—your soul mate—has found you."

"Don't start with the woo-woo stuff again." Stef took a sip, then put her glass on the counter. "I've had enough tonight to last me a good long time."

"You have to admit—"

"I'm not admitting anything." She kissed Vanessa

on the cheek. "But I do have a ton of monster mash to make for the kiddies in the morning, so I need to fly. I hadn't planned on staying quite this long, but with Grace here . . ."

Her voice trailed into the living room and Vanessa followed her. ". . . certainly was an experience I won't forget."

"But at least you learned something you didn't know," Vanessa reminded her. "You found out that my Alice and your Horace were lovers. Alice was his Daisy."

"That is something," Stef agreed. "But I think I might have suspected that."

"And now you know for certain."

"Or not. Who knows what really happened here?" Stef grabbed her bag from the living-room floor and headed out. "I'll talk to you tomorrow."

"I'm really happy for you Stef," Vanessa said from the doorway. "The only person I'd be happier for would be me."

Stef laughed, but once in her car, she started to wonder about the incident with the board. When she got home, she turned on her laptop and looked up *Ouija.* She read for a few minutes, then dialed Vanessa's number. The call went directly to voice mail.

"There's something called the 'ideometer effect,' " she said. "It means that somehow you can unconsciously control the movement of the triangle, like, your muscles have a reflex reaction to your thoughts. It's what they call a 'psychophysiological phenomenon.' No spirits. No ghosts. So sleep easy tonight." She paused. "But I gotta admit, it sure did beat a game of Scrabble . . ."

Chapter 21

STEF was still poking around on the Internet, having progressed from the ideometer effect to automatic writing and dowsing when the phone rang at two minutes before eleven.

"Hey," Wade said when she answered, "I have a great idea. Why don't you sleep over here tonight?"

"Won't that be a little awkward? What will Berry think?"

"Berry's still at Archer's. She's been there for the past day or so."

"My, that sounds serious."

"I'm thinking I'll need to have a talk with him, find out what his intentions are toward my great-aunt."

She looked at the clock. "I guess I could throw some things into a bag and drive over."

"Great. We can all have breakfast together in the morning."

"All of us?" Stef frowned. "Who's *us*?"

"You and me and Dallas and Grant."

"Grant's there?"

"Yeah. That's why I can't come over there. When

Berry's not here, Grant stays over, so Dallas isn't really listening for Austin, if you get my drift."

"I can't stay there if Grant is there," she said, horrified.

"Why not?"

"He's my brother. It'd be too creepy. I don't even want to think about it. Him with Dallas right down the hall. Me with you." She shook her head. "Uh-uh. I can't."

"You leave me speechless sometimes, Stef."

"It's part of my charm."

"I suppose that's one way of looking at it."

"Let's plan on tomorrow night," she suggested. "I'll close up at seven and then I'll come over, and after Austin goes to bed, I'll even take you out to dinner."

"And if Berry still isn't back?"

"Then you'd better track Archer down and have that talk."

"Good point."

"I stopped over at Ness's tonight. Wait till I tell you." She related everything that had happened at Vanessa's.

"You really believe that some spirit told you that this Alice was Horace's Daisy?" He sounded incredulous. "Once again, I am almost speechless."

She told him what she'd learned about the ideometer effect.

"Well, that would make sense, that somehow you or Grace were guiding the answers. But even if you were, why would you think that Alice and Daisy are the same person?"

"Vanessa gave me Alice's diary to look over, and

while I was reading it, an old, dried-up flower fell out of the book. It could have been a daisy, and that got me thinking and connected her to my dining-room-wall Daisy. Of course, that made me think about Horace, so I guess it was all jumbled in my head and I suppose that was enough for me to connect the dots and somehow control the planchette."

"The what?"

"The little triangle thingy that you put your fingers on and it moves. Or not."

"I see. And this is the same Alice who you said wrote something about Aunt Berry and Archer in her diary?"

"Her journals."

"Why would she write about them? I wonder."

"Wade, Alice used to practice . . ." Her voice trailed away.

"She practiced what?" When Stef didn't answer, Wade asked, "Law? Medicine? Voodoo?"

"Close."

"Which one?"

"The last one."

"She practiced voodoo? There was someone who lived in staid old St. Dennis who practiced voodoo?"

"No, magic. She . . . Alice . . . she knew how to put spells on people."

Wade laughed out loud.

"Wade, I saw her book." The words spilled out. "She taught some of the girls from town how to cast love spells. Berry's name was in her book, Wade. Alice taught Berry how to do a love spell."

"Stef, there is no such thing as spells."

"I'm serious. I saw the book. One of the girls she taught was my nana Cummings. Another was Grace Sinclair, who just a few months later married Dan."

"I suppose next you're going to tell me that you put a spell on me."

"No," she told him. "Vanessa did."

"Vanessa put a spell on me?" Through the phone, she could hear him chuckle. "That just goes to prove that this is nonsense. I didn't fall in love with Vanessa. I fell in love with you."

"That was the spell. I thought it was all hokey at the time, I never believed it, but here you . . ." Stef felt slightly panicked. "I don't know if she can reverse it."

"Why would we want it reversed? Don't you love me?"

"Well, yes," she said, exasperated. "That was the whole point."

"I don't think I understand the problem."

"The problem is that I wanted you to love me because of *me*, not because of some spell. Which is why I told Vanessa not to—"

"Stef, I do love you for yourself, not because of a spell." Wade paused. "Are we really talking about this? I can't believe we're having this conversation."

"I can't believe it really worked."

"Stef. There was no spell."

When she started to protest, he said, "I don't care what Vanessa did or what she thought she was doing. There's no spell. And the only magic I believe in is the magic we make when we're together."

After a long silent moment, Stef sighed. "That was the most romantic thing I've ever heard anyone say."

"You're going to find that I am a very romantic guy."

"I'm packing a bag and I'm going to ignore the fact that right down the hall from your room, my brother and your sister are . . . never mind. I'll be there in ten minutes . . ."

Stef was already up and out by the time Berry arrived home. From the kitchen window, Wade watched his aunt park her big old Mercedes sedan and walk slowly to the house. Berry looked crestfallen, and he wondered if things had gone all right with Archer.

"Coffee?" he offered when she came in through the back door.

"Oh. Yes, thank you." Berry dropped her overnight bag and her purse on the floor near the table. Having heard her voice, Ally came racing down the steps and flew into the kitchen. "There's my girl," Berry crooned to the dog. "There's my very sweet and precious girl."

Berry sat on one of the chairs and stroked her dog's head. "Finding Ally was one of the nicest things I've ever done for myself," she told Wade. "She always loves me, no matter what. And she's always happy to see me. No matter what."

"Much like Dallas and me." Wade smiled and brought Berry's coffee to the table.

"Where is the little fellow?" Berry asked.

"I took him to the babysitter's for the morning. I have some calls to make about equipment. It's tough to watch him and try to get work done."

"Now you know what mothers deal with every day."

"Are you sorry you never had kids, Berry?" he asked.

She turned her head and seemed to study his face but didn't immediately answer.

"I have a few regrets when it comes to children, yes," she finally told him, "though probably not quite what you meant."

It was his turn to stare. It wasn't like Berry to be cryptic.

"Is your sister here?" Berry asked.

"She's in her office. The library."

"Be a darling and ask her to join us, please."

"Berry, are you all right?"

"That remains to be seen, dear. Now please . . ."

"I'll get her."

What the hell, Wade was thinking as he went down the hall to the room Dallas used as an office. He knocked on the door, then pushed it open.

"Dallas, Berry wants you in the kitchen."

She glanced up from her desk. "When did Berry get home?"

"Just a few minutes ago, but she wants you now."

"Is she all right?" Dallas rose from her seat and placed her glasses on the desktop.

"I asked her the same question, but I didn't get an answer that made any sense. I just got the impression she wants to talk to both of us at the same time."

"Then she shall." Dallas led the way back to the kitchen.

"Hello, Berry." Dallas kissed the older woman on the forehead, then sat next to her. "Wade said you wanted to see me."

"Both of you. I need both of you for this." Berry

took a sip of coffee. With her free hand, she petted Ally, who leaned against her leg.

"What's wrong, Berry?" Dallas put her arm around her aunt.

"Tell us what's bothering you. We can help." Wade sat on Berry's other side.

"Oh, dear. I had my courage up all the way from Archer's, and now it seems I've lost it again," Berry said.

"Why do you feel you need courage to talk to us?" a confused Wade asked.

"It's such a tangled web, I barely know where to begin. Just like Shakespeare said. I have deceived you both—I've deceived everyone—and the web I've woven has finally tangled me up in it."

Wade fought a smile. Whatever was bothering Berry, her sense of the dramatic was still intact.

"Well, why don't you tell us what you're talking about, Berry." Dallas rubbed her aunt's back with obvious affection.

Berry sighed deeply and for a moment, Wade thought she'd changed her mind, that she wasn't about to untangle any of her webs after all.

"I made a mistake—a very, very terrible mistake—a long time ago. I was young and headstrong and vain and self-centered and I was convinced that I should always have my way."

And that's different from now in what way? Wade was tempted to ask, but he thought better of it. Berry was obviously in no frame of mind to be teased.

"Berry, we've all done things in our youth that we've come to regret later. We can't change the past, but we can learn from it and not make the same mistakes today that we made back then."

"My dear, it simply wouldn't be possible for me to repeat *that* mistake." Berry took a deep breath and visibly steeled herself. "You see, I . . . oh, dear. I don't think I can go through with this." Tears pooled in her eyes. "You're all I have, and once you know the truth, I'm afraid you'll hate me, and I won't be able to bear it."

Wade looked at his sister. She looked as confused as he felt.

"Berry, there is nothing—I mean, nothing—that could make us hate you. We love you. You're more than a great-aunt to us. You're more like our beloved grandmother, and I know I speak for Wade, too—"

Berry burst into tears.

"Nothing can be that bad." Dallas turned Berry's face to hers while Wade retrieved a box of tissues from the powder room.

He handed her a tissue and remarked, "Berry, I don't know that I ever saw you cry before."

"I knew this day of reckoning would come, but truthfully, I thought I'd die before it got here. A heart attack in my sleep, perhaps. Or a slip off the dock some night into the river . . ."

She might be distraught, Wade thought, *but she still knows how to deliver a line.*

"Berry, take a minute to relax and collect your thoughts. We're here for you, whatever the problem is," Wade assured her.

"You're such a dear boy. So like your father." Berry began to sob all over again.

Wade shot a what-did-I-say look to Dallas, who shook her head.

"Berry, perhaps you should take a few sips of water

and calm down. Then just start from the beginning," Wade told her as he fetched a glass of water for her.

"Thank you, dear." Berry took a few sips. "All right, then. I suppose I must get through this." She sighed deeply. "Years ago, when I was just a girl growing up here in St. Dennis, I had many admirers. Oh, I should just come out and say it. The truth is, I was the prettiest girl in town. Well, of course, there was Sylvie, but our personalities were so very different. I always had a flair for the dramatic, and Sylvie was always so shy. Everyone told me I belonged on the big screen, and I totally agreed with them. I knew that was my destiny. I couldn't wait to turn eighteen so that I could leave this dull little town behind and strike out on my own. I knew in my heart I was going to be a big star."

"And you were," Dallas reminded her. "And will be again."

"Yes, yes, but you're getting ahead of the story, Dallas."

"Sorry." Dallas appeared to be biting back a smile.

"Anyway. I was young and beautiful and talented and I had the world by the . . . well, on a string, let's say. My future was bright and I knew that my life was going to be glorious." She stopped and dabbed a tissue at her eyes. "There was one thing standing in my way, though."

"What, Berry?" Dallas asked.

"Not what, dear. Who. I was in love with the most wonderful man, and he loved me, too. We had plans to marry, you see. I wanted him to come to California with me and share my dreams of fame and glory. Unfortunately, his dream was to be a lawyer, maybe even a judge someday. But here, on the Eastern Shore, not Hollywood, no. He wanted no part of that life."

"You're talking about Archer, aren't you, Berry?" Dallas said softly.

Berry nodded. "So, off he went to Columbia, up in New York City, and off I went to California. We did see each other, and for a while we did try to work things out, but after a time it became clear that neither of us was going to budge. After one of those weekends in New York—" She stopped again, the words seeming to be almost too painful even now, all these years later.

"Berry, listen, we—" Dallas began. She was interrupted by Ally's mad dash to the front door just as the doorbell rang. Fleur, who'd been sleeping on the second-floor landing, flew down the steps to join her.

"I'll go see who it is," Wade said. "I'll be right back."

He reached the door and opened it to find Archer Callahan on the front porch.

"Ah, Archer . . ."

"Wade." Archer stood in the doorway. "May I come in, please? I'd like to see Berry."

"I don't know if this is really a good time." Wade lowered his voice. "She's upset about something and . . ." He stared at Archer. "Did you do something to upset her? Did you have an argument with her?"

"Dear Lord, I told her to wait." Archer stepped past Wade and went straight into the kitchen.

"Archer, for heaven's sake," Berry said when she saw him. "I told you I would deal with this myself."

"And I told you that I would not let you go through this alone. I wasn't there to stand by you then, but I'm standing by you now."

"Oh, Archer." Berry looked up at him with eyes filled with love.

"Have you told them yet?" he asked.

She shook her head. "I'm working up to it."

"As only she can." Wade's remark earned him The Look.

"Will one of you please tell us what's going on?" Dallas looked from Berry to Archer then back to Berry.

"I was saying, that I came back east to visit Archer from time to time. I was by then quite the hot young thing. I'd made several movies by this time—I'd just turned twenty—and I was very much in demand." Berry averted her eyes from everyone. "And then I found out I was pregnant."

"Oh, my." Dallas sat back in her chair. "That is . . . news."

"It certainly would have been, back then. It was a different time. An unmarried woman having a child was simply not done. Not in Hollywood, and certainly not in St. Dennis."

"What did you do, Berry? Did you have the baby?" Dallas asked.

"Oh, of course I did. There was never any question but that I would. But I had quite the dilemma. I had a career that was just taking off, and I had a man I loved who'd have none of that life. I had to choose. I told myself that if he really loved me, he'd come with me. So, for better or for worse, I chose my career."

"And the baby was Archer's?" Wade asked.

Berry nodded. "I never told him. He thought I just left him because I didn't love him, when of course, that wasn't the case at all. He'd already made it clear enough that he never intended to move to California, and I'd made it clear that I was not about to give up my films to live here while he played country lawyer."

"If you'd have told me then what you've told me this week, I would have come to you," Archer told her. "I never would have let you go through all that alone."

"Berry, you never told him until this week?" Dallas's jaw dropped.

"I know, dear. It was terrible of me. Just one more terrible and wrong decision on my part. But I was very young and I'd had amazing success in a very short period of time. It's a very heady feeling, at so young an age, to feel like the center of the universe." She shook her head. "I see these young girls today and I wish I could take them all aside and tell them to be mindful of the choices they make. I know exactly who they are, because I was them, once. But that's a story for another time."

"Berry, what happened to your baby?" Dallas asked softly.

"He was born in California. A beautiful, healthy little boy." She cleared her throat. "And I gave him to someone else to raise."

"Oh, Berry." Dallas's eyes filled with tears. "Did you ever see him when he was growing up? Did you ever know him?"

Berry lifted a hand and smoothed Dallas's hair. "Of course I did, dear. I'd given him to my sister, Sylvie, and her husband, to raise as theirs. And they did."

For a moment Wade thought he hadn't heard her clearly.

"But our dad was the only boy they . . ." he began,

and then the import of her words struck home. “Dad was your son, Berry? You were Dad’s *mother*?”

Berry nodded, then started to cry again. Archer sat next to her and put his arms around her, and she buried her face in his chest.

“How did you pull that off?” he asked. “I mean, didn’t people around here notice that your sister wasn’t pregnant?”

“I had several months between films, and I stuck close to my house for that time. I had Sylvie come out to stay with me in California for a while,” Berry explained. “When she returned to St. Dennis, she brought Ned with her. Everyone assumed she’d been pregnant when she left here. As far as I know, no one was ever the wiser.”

“Berry, that makes you . . .” Dallas said.

“Yes, dear. Your grandmother.”

“Which makes Archer . . .” Wade was still trying to grasp the concept.

“. . . your grandfather,” Archer finished the sentence.

“Holy shit.” Wade sank onto a chair.

“That’s a lovely reaction, dear.” Berry looked up at Archer. “I told you he was most articulate, did I not?”

“Sorry, Berry, I’m just so overwhelmed.” Wade frowned. “Did Dad know about this? Did you ever tell him?”

“I told him, yes,” Berry replied, “but not until he was grown. And he never knew Archer. By then, Archer was married and had children and, from all appearances, was enjoying a very happy life. Both Ned and I agreed that there was no need for Archer to know.”

"Another mistake on your part, Berry," Archer said.

"Archer, we've been going around and around about this for the past two days. What good would it have done for me to have shown up on your doorstep with Ned? What would the news have done to your family?" Archer started to say something but she cut him off. "I know you like to think you'd have acknowledged him as your son, but it was asking too much of your wife. I know you must have loved her to have married her. I wouldn't have put her through that pain. It was too late by then to change things—I'd made my bed, you see—and Ned didn't feel right about contacting you to introduce himself. We both agreed to let it go for a while. I thought maybe the time might come, that when he got a bit older, perhaps he'd change his mind." Her eyes filled up again. "But then, of course, Ned died so young and so suddenly."

"So you never met our dad?" Wade turned to Archer.

"Not really. Oh, I saw him around St. Dennis from time to time, but I assumed, as did everyone else, that he was Duncan and Sylvie's son. Sylvie and Berry were twins, you know, so it wasn't odd that the boy looked like her. I just assumed he took after Sylvie."

"So there you have it. My deepest, darkest secret. If you want to disown me now for all these years of deceit, I'll understand." Berry looked first at Dallas, then at Wade. "Just please don't hate me. I couldn't bear it."

"How could you think for one minute that we could hate you." Dallas put her arms around her. "I am so very sorry that you had to carry this secret all these years. And I'm sorry you weren't able to acknowledge your son. I'm sorry for a lot of things, but this isn't about Wade and me, Berry. It's about you. And Archer, of course."

"Dallas is right, Berry. This is between you and Archer," Wade said. "And as much of a shock as this has been, it doesn't change the way we feel about you. You're our Berry. We love you."

"That's more generous than I had a right to expect from either of you." Berry reached a hand out to both. "Words cannot express how dear you both are to me. Thank you."

Berry turned to look at Archer. "I did tell you, did I not, that my boy and my girl are exceptional? That you'd be proud of them?"

"You did." Archer nodded. "And I am."

Wade sat and stared at Archer for a long moment. How odd to meet your grandfather for the first time.

"I don't have many memories of Grampa Duncan," Wade said. "Do you?" he asked Dallas.

"Not really. It seems whenever we visited St. Dennis, we stayed here, not with him and Gramma Sylvie." She turned to Berry. "I guess she really wasn't gramma, though, was she?"

Berry shook her head.

"Which explains so many things." Dallas got up and went to the stove. She picked up the teakettle and filled it with water.

"Like what, dear?" Berry asked.

"Like how I always had the feeling she liked the other grandkids better. Like how her affection always seemed forced."

"Yes, I know what you mean," Wade agreed. "I always felt the same way."

"I'm so sorry," Berry told them both. "I hadn't realized . . ."

"It's okay, Berry." Dallas sat the kettle on the burner and turned it on. "I never spent much time with them. We always wanted to stay here with you anyway. You were always much more fun."

"Looking back, I guess it makes sense that Dad always brought us here to stay. We never stayed at our grandparents' house," Wade noted.

"I'm afraid I didn't always appreciate how difficult I made things for my poor sister and her husband. Two mothers in the same family is an absolute recipe for disaster. I can't even begin to understand the amount of chaos I must have caused in that family. Always taking Ned places but never his sisters. I'm embarrassed by my thoughtlessness and how unkind I was to those two girls."

"I thought you said they were twits," Dallas reminded her.

"Well, they were, dear, but I didn't have to be unkind to them."

Dallas laughed. "There's the Berry we know and love."

"Archer, I can't help but wonder how you feel about all this." Wade leaned on the back of one of the chairs.

"I'm adjusting to it, Wade. Finding out that you had a son you never knew—and knowing that you can't get to know him now because he's gone . . ." He shook his head. "It isn't something that you process in a day or so. I'm sorry I never knew your father. I'm sorry that . . . well, I have a lot of regrets. I imagine it's pretty near impossible to live as long as I have and not look back and wonder how things might have been."

"Are you going to discuss this with your children?" Wade asked. "Not that it's any of my business . . ."

"To be perfectly honest, I haven't decided yet." Archer's face showed his conflict. "On the one hand, I want my children to know Berry, and to know you and your sister. I want all my grandchildren to know one another. On the other . . . well, I feel I need to get to know you both a little myself first."

Wade nodded his understanding. He turned to Berry and asked, "Berry, I have to ask—why now?"

"Oh, well, with Dallas and Grant getting married and hopefully having a family, I thought they should know. I saw something on television last week or so about a young girl who was being treated for some very serious condition—I forget what it was. The doctors had difficulty in diagnosing her because whatever it was, it's only transmitted genetically, but no one in her or her husband's family had it. Which is how the girl's parents came to tell her that she was adopted and helped her to search for her birth parents. And it got me thinking that perhaps Dallas needed to know since she's getting married soon and hopefully will be adding to her family."

"I'm not the only one," Dallas told her with a smile. She pointed to Wade. "You tell her."

"I asked Steffie to marry me," he said.

"Oh, my dear," Berry teared up—again. "How wonderful for you. She's a darling girl." Berry froze momentarily. "Please tell me she isn't taking Scoop to Connecticut . . ."

"No one's going to Connecticut." Wade explained his recent decision.

"Perfect! We'll have our brewery after all. Now, does this mean that Berry Beer might someday become a reality?"

Wade laughed. "It could happen."

"Well, this has certainly been a big news day, hasn't it? And it's barely eleven in the morning," Berry noted.

"Eleven?" Dallas blanched. "I have a meeting at eleven."

"I have one in a half hour." Wade glanced at the wall clock.

"Why don't the two of you skedaddle? We can all catch up later. Dallas, be a dear and leave the kettle on. I think I need a nice cup of tea . . ."

Wade leaned down to kiss Berry and she took his hand. "Have you a ring for Steffie?"

"No. I need to do something about that, though." Wade wasn't sure how he'd accomplish that, since he wasn't working and probably wouldn't have any real income for at least a year. Good thing Berry wasn't charging rent, he thought.

"I have several very lovely pieces that I no longer wear. You might want to take a look and see if there's something you think she might like. I have a particular ring in mind that I think she would love, but of course, it's up to you," she assured him. "Looking at Dallas's ring made me think that you might want to . . . that is, if you feel it's appropriate."

"Totally appropriate, and wonderfully generous of

you to offer, Berry." He kissed her cheek. "I know that Stef will be thrilled and honored to wear a ring that belonged to you."

He started toward the back door, then hesitated. Turning to Archer, he asked, "Do you have a middle name?"

"Yes," Archer replied. "It's Bowen. Why do you ask?"

"Just curious." Wade shrugged. "See you folks later."

He smiled to himself as he went through the back door and down the steps.

Archer Bowen Callahan. ABC.

A long time ago, a smitten Berry had carved the initials of her love on one of the posts in the carriage house. Sixty-some years later, Wade—Archer's grandson—had found them.

"Berry is your *grandmother*?" Stef's eyes widened. "Did you say, your *grandmother*?"

"Shhhh." Wade glanced around the dining room at Café Lola's, where he'd met Stef for a late dinner.

"Sorry. But, wow. Just . . . wow." Stef rested her forearms on the table and leaned closer. "You know, years ago there were some rumors about Ned being Berry's son and not Sylvie's, I remember hearing that, but I don't know that anyone actually believed it. There was a lot of speculation about who Ned's father might have been."

He tasted the beer that the waiter had brought just a few minutes earlier, held the glass up, and said, "Not bad for a commercial brew. Not KenneMac quality, and I will go out on a limb here and predict that Mad Mac will be superior, but it isn't bad."

"Go back to Berry, if you please. Did she say who Ned's father was? One of her handsome costars? A foreign director? A famous producer? A prince?"

"None of the above. Archer Callahan."

"Archer . . . you mean . . . Judge Callahan?"

"That's right."

"Oh, man. I should have guessed that. Does he know?"

"He does now."

"How'd he take it?" she asked.

"He seemed to be taking it pretty well. They were in love a long time ago, and apparently still are. That might be influencing his reaction. He still loves her," Wade said. "And it's obvious that she still loves him."

"They had a child together all those years ago." Stef shook her head. "And yet they never married. Tell me everything. Start at the beginning."

He did.

When he finished, Stef sighed and said, "Oh, that's just so tragic, isn't it? To love someone and lose them and just go on with your life?" She sighed again. "I suppose people do that every day, though. They make choices and then they have to live with the consequences."

She took a sip of wine. "It makes me wonder, what if you hadn't stopped in St. Dennis. What if you'd gone right to Connecticut from Texas? We wouldn't be sitting here together. We wouldn't have had a chance to fall in love. We wouldn't be planning a life together. All the chances we had in the past that we never took . . ."

"I don't know why it took so long for us. Maybe other things were supposed to happen. Austin, for one. And maybe if we'd gotten together sooner, there'd be no Scoop."

Stef shook her head. "There was always going to be Scoop. It was part of the plan."

"What plan?" Wade frowned.

"My plan." She held up one finger. "Marry the coolest guy in town." Next finger. "Make ice cream." Third. "Live happily ever after."

"Well, I guess that seals it"—Wade grinned—"since I am the coolest guy in town."

"Well, you were back then," she said over the rim of her glass.

"What's that supposed to mean? I'm not cool anymore?"

"Oh, you're still cool enough," she teased. "But other guys are cool, too. It's tough to know who wears the crown of cool these days."

"Well, then, since it's predetermined that you're to marry the coolest guy in town, I suppose I'm going to have to do something extraordinary to prove that I'm still worthy." He reached across the table and took her hand in his. His other hand dipped into the pocket of his jacket. "Will this help seal the deal?"

He slipped a ring onto her finger, and she gasped.

"What? How did you . . . when did you . . ."

"At least look at it, why don't you?" He laughed.

"Oh, my God. Is that thing real? Look at the size of that thing." She held her hand up to her face and stared at the round Ceylon sapphire surrounded by diamonds. "It looks a little like Princess Di's ring . . . only the big stone is round and the color is prettier." She looked up at him. "Seriously? This is for real?"

He nodded. "It was Berry's. She offered it—well,

she offered my choice of several rings that she had. I liked this one the best, but if you'd rather look over the others, I won't be insulted and she's perfectly fine with it."

"No, no," Stef insisted. "I love this one. It's exactly what I'd have picked if you'd asked me. I just can't believe . . ." She stared at the ring. "But wow. I can't believe Berry offered."

"I think she liked the idea that Grant gave Dallas his grandmother's ring. And while we won't be announcing to the world that you're wearing *my* grandmother's ring, it's given her a certain amount of satisfaction, I think, to know that she's passed on something of hers to you."

"I need to make her an ice-cream flavor. I did Berry Berry but I need something more special. Maybe for when her new movie comes out."

"So you're good with it?" he deadpanned.

"I'm more than good." She grabbed his tie and pulled him closer and kissed him soundly on the mouth. "I'm fabulous."

"You are. But the question remains: Who is the coolest of them all?"

"It would have to be you, Wade. That was the plan." She kissed him again. "And see how nicely it's all worked out? I am making ice cream. I am marrying the coolest guy. And I will live happily ever after."

He raised her hand to his lips and promised, "*We* will live happily ever after."

"Of course we will." Stef smiled smugly. "Like I said—that was the plan . . ."

Diary ~

Well, love is certainly in the air in abundance around here these days! Who came into Cuppachino this morning sporting a huge sapphire-and-diamond engagement ring? Why, Steffie, that's who! And I thought I had my finger on the pulse around here. I can't say that I didn't know there were sparks flying every time she and Wade got within ten feet of each other, but last I'd heard, he was headed for a new job in Connecticut. One minute I was wishing him well at his new job and reminding him that we expected to see him at the inn's holiday party this year—the next, he's going into business with Clay Madison right here in St. Dennis and slipping a ring onto Steffie's finger! The ring is glorious, by the way—Steffie says it had belonged to Berry. Now that's lovely, isn't it? Berry having no children or grandchildren of her own, I'm sure she was delighted to pass something on to her grandnephew's girl.

Dallas spoke to me about possibly booking the inn for her wedding, but I don't know that we have the staff to handle a Hollywood wedding. I've asked Daniel—again—to speak with his sister about coming back to handle this sort of thing for us, but he's reluctant. Every time I mention it to

Lucy, she gets very . . . well, prickly, I suppose, is the word. I don't understand it. Truly, I do not. I understand that she has a very successful event-planning business out there in California, and she's rightfully proud of that. But for heaven's sake, the family business needs her here! We're booking weddings left and right and are in desperate need of someone with her vision and experience. I'm afraid if we can't fill the needs of our brides, we're going to start losing some of the business Daniel has worked so hard to attract to the inn. Oh, not the guests—we rarely have an empty room from April right through the first few weeks of September. But the catering and event planning—we need help! Perhaps if I asked Lucy to come back just to do Dallas's wedding . . . I mean, who wouldn't want to be in charge of that event?

Add to that the fact that my dearest friend, Trula, tells me that she's coming to town next week to discuss possible wedding plans for someone who is very near and dear to her—well, I don't know how Lucy could pass up the chance to do <u>that</u> affair, Trula's "near and dear" being who he is. How could anyone in their right mind turn down two such high-profile, sky's-the-limit weddings—one a famed Hollywood beauty, the other an international business mogul. Goodness, if one were trying to build a portfolio and establish a reputation, either of those events would surely do it! Why, the publicity alone would be priceless.

I think I'll call Lucy right now, before I . . . oh, I almost forgot! I am now in possession of Alice's Ouija board, thanks to Vanessa—and I have to say, it's every bit as lively as it was when dear Alice was alive. And I've learned so many fascinating things from it—not the least of which is that Horace Hinson and Alice were lovers! Just fancy that! How sad for her to have been so crippled with her condition that she couldn't bring herself to come out into the world. Horace, apparently, brought the world to her. A tragedy, yes—but a true love story all the same.

That little board is just full of tales. I can hardly wait to see what it reveals to me next!

~ Grace ~

Read on for previews of the first two books from the Chesapeake Diaries series

Available from Ballantine Books

Book One

Coming Home

At 6:02 p.m. on a Tuesday evening, Vanessa Keaton turned the key in the back door lock of her sweet little boutique on Charles Street and flicked off the lights. Foot traffic had been scarce, and would be, she knew, for another two weeks, at least until the St. Dennis Secret Garden Tour brought the first of the serious visitors to town. And that was just fine with her. Once the tourist season began in earnest, there would be fewer opportunities for dinners with friends or for closing early to enjoy slow walks through the town she had come to call her own.

She turned the dead bolt on the door leading down into the basement, then let herself out through the front and locked that door behind her as well. She paused to take a deep breath of the spring fragrance that she found unique to St. Dennis: salt from the Bay mixed with the scent of the hyacinths, daffodils, and early tulips planted in the wooden barrels—

compliments of the garden club—that stood outside each of the shops along Charles Street. The very colors of the flowers said spring to her: purples and pinks, yellows and whites. Just to see them made her smile.

She stepped back to take a good long look at the window she'd spent most of the day designing. Was it too early to display the tennis whites and the pastels that many of the local ladies liked to sport while golfing at the new country club outside of town? Maybe she should move those items to the smaller windows on the side of the shop, and dress her mannequins in something other than sportswear. Maybe those pretty cocktail dresses she got in from New York last week, and maybe a few of those darling evening bags from that designer she found in Cape May over the winter.

The promise of warm weather put a bounce in her step, and as she crossed the street, visions of all the new items she'd recently ordered for Bling danced in her head.

"Step lively there, miss," the driver of the car that had stopped to let her cross called out. "Or I'll have to arrest you for jaywalking."

"Oh, you . . ." Vanessa laughed. "Why aren't you out chasing bank robbers or car thieves?"

"There hasn't been a bank robbed in St. Dennis for as long as I've lived here." Gabriel Beck—chief of police and Vanessa's half brother—pulled his car to the side of the road and activated his flashing lights. "And the last report of a stolen car we received turned out to be Wes Taylor's fifteen-year-old son sneaking out in the middle of the night to see his girlfriend."

"Slow day, eh, Beck?" She walked over to the car and leaned into the open passenger-side window.

"Just another day in paradise." He hastened to add, "Not that there's anything wrong with that."

"Well, wait another few weeks. Once the tourists start pouring into town, you'll be wishing for a day like this, when you can cruise around town in your spiffy new official police-chief car and stop to chat with the locals."

"Only way to stay in touch, kiddo."

"Well, I admit I like the calm before the storm. I like to be able to close up shop at six and have the evenings to myself. I know it won't last—and I'm grateful that my shop does so well. But it's nice to have some quiet days to enjoy this glorious weather before the crowds arrive." She stood to wave to the driver of a passing car. "So where's the fiancée?"

"I dropped her off at BWI early this morning. She's on her way to Montana to see her brother." He glanced at his watch. "Actually, she should be arriving at his place anytime now."

"Is this her brother the hermit?" *The one I like to think of as Mountain Man?*

Beck nodded. "She's hoping to talk him into walking her down the aisle."

"Your wedding's in five weeks." Vanessa frowned. "Isn't she cutting it a bit close?"

"She already asked her other brother, Andy, and he's on board. But she wants them both to give her away, since their dad died last year."

"Well, I wish her luck with that."

"Yeah, me, too. I offered to go with her, but she thought she'd have a better chance on her own. Mia doesn't think he's left his place for any length of time since their dad's funeral. We'll see." He didn't appear optimistic. "So where are you off to now?"

"I'm meeting Steffie for dinner."

"I don't think she's closed up yet. There was a group in town this afternoon for a lecture over at the Historical Society. From the crowd gathered outside Steffie's, I'd say they all stopped at her place for ice cream before getting back on their bus."

"Thanks for the tip. I'll walk on down and see if I can give her a hand."

"You just want ice cream," he teased, and put the car in drive.

"You know what I always say." She stepped back onto the curb. "Eat dessert first."

She waved good-bye as he pulled away, and glanced back at Bling, the front window dressing still on her mind. She mentally slapped herself on the forehead. *Duh.* The display should reflect the upcoming wedding. Pretty dresses and shoes to wear to the event. Flowers—maybe some terra-cotta pots planted with something colorful across the front of the window. Pansies, maybe. Vases of budding flowering cherry in the corners. Lots of white chiffon, puffed like clouds . . .

It was less than a ten-minute walk from Bling to Steffie Wyler's ice-cream shop. Her arms swinging, Vanessa strolled along, marveling, as she always did, at the twists and turns her life had taken since she first arrived in St. Dennis. It was hard to believe that just three short years ago, she'd been destitute and exhausted mentally and physically from the stress of removing herself from a marriage that had started to go bad even before the petals had begun to drop from the yellow roses she'd carried on her wedding day. Even now, the mere sight of yellow roses could make her knees go weak.

That was then, she reminded herself sternly. *This is now. No need to go back to that place and time. Keep the focus on all the good things that have happened since I came to St. Dennis.*

Finding that she had a half brother—finding Beck—was probably the best thing that had ever happened to her. That he and his father, Hal Garrity, had welcomed her so warmly, had urged her to stay, and had offered to help her start up a business in a storefront that Hal owned just when St. Dennis was emerging as a tourist attraction . . . well, who could have foreseen all that happening?

Timing is everything, she reminded herself. *Everyone knows that.*

She waved through the window of Lola's Café at Jimmy, one of Lola's geriatric waiters, and passed Petals & Posies, the flower shop next door, where tall galvanized steel containers outside held long branches of blooming forsythia and pussy willow, and the windows held the eye with a rainbow display of cut tulips and daffodils.

Next to Petals & Posies was Cuppachino, where many of the townies gathered first thing in the morning for coffee, the latest gossip, and to watch the news on the big-screen TV that hung on the side wall before heading off to their respective mornings. Through the screened door, propped open to encourage the evening breeze to enter, Vanessa noticed Grace Sinclair, the owner and editor of the local weekly paper, the *St. Dennis Gazette,* at one of the front tables. She was deep in conversation with Amelia Vandergrift, the president of the garden club. Gathering tidbits for a piece on the upcoming tour, no doubt, to remind everyone to buy tickets to the event. Vanessa considered Grace, a white-haired septuagenarian with unlimited energy who knew everyone and everything, the town's number one cheerleader. Secretly, Vanessa attributed half of what she'd learned about St. Dennis to Hal, and the other half to Grace Sinclair's weekly editorials about the community.

She rounded the corner of Charles and Kelly's Point Road, and moments later, passed the municipal building, with its new wing that housed the police department. She noted that Beck's car had not yet returned to its designated parking space.

Probably out doing what he does best, she mused. *Reassuring the locals that all is just skippy in St. Dennis.*

At the end of the road, right where it T'd into the wooden boardwalk that ran next to the Bay, stood One Scoop or Two, the onetime crabber's shanty Steffie Wyler had turned into a charming ice-cream parlor. Seeing the crowd gathered around the tables out front of the small structure, Vanessa quickened her step. She excused herself to those patrons waiting patiently in line, smiling as she walked around them and between the two freezer cases to grab an apron off the pegs that hung behind the cash register.

"I can help the next person in line," Vanessa announced. She slipped on a pair of thin, clear plastic gloves as a pleasant white-haired gentleman stepped up to place his order.

"I owe you big-time, babe," Steffie whispered in Vanessa's ear on her way to the cash register.

"Yes, you do. And you'll pay up." Vanessa smiled and turned to the customer. "Sir, did you want the blackberry or the chocolate on the bottom?"

Thirty minutes and four dozen customers later, the crowd had been served and the last cone dipped. When the buses departed, Steffie sank into a chair at one of the small tables that stood along the outside wall.

"Got caught shorthanded, eh?" Vanessa scooped a small ball of rum raisin into a paper cup and took the seat opposite Steffie.

"Did I ever," Steffie groaned. "Who knew that the lectures at the Historical Society would be so popular, or that they'd start so early in the season?"

"Maybe you should get a copy of their schedule."

Steffie rolled her eyes. "I can't believe I didn't think of that sooner."

"Well, it's the first year that they've invited groups from other communities to come," Vanessa reminded her. "Who could have guessed they'd have such a turnout? What was the topic, do you know?"

"No. And at this point, I don't care." Steffie pulled a nearby chair closer and rested her feet on the seat. "Any other day of the week and I'd have had Taffy Ellis with me, but she had a meeting with her prom committee after school and wouldn't have gotten here until after five. I didn't bother calling anyone else in because I figured I could handle things for an hour on my own."

"You probably should always have someone else here with you," Vanessa pointed out. "I don't think you should be here alone."

"This from someone whose only regular employee

doesn't start until Memorial Day? And that one part-time?"

"I'm up on Charles Street and have shops on both sides and a busy restaurant directly across the street. You're down here with a very dark, large parking lot on one side and the Bay on the other. Who knows who could be lurking around here after dark?"

"Well, thanks a heap for putting that in my head."

"Seriously, haven't you ever stopped to think about how isolated you are down here?"

"Not until now." Steffie glared at her pointedly. "But you're forgetting that our fine police department is just a stone's throw down the lane there, right across from the parking lot."

"Not close enough to hear you scream."

"*Au contraire, mon amie.* I have had occasion to scream, and none other than the chief himself showed up."

"I don't remember that." Vanessa frowned. "When was that? What happened?"

"Before you moved here, while I was first renovating this place. I came in one morning and there were bats flying around."

"That would freak me out, too." Vanessa shuddered at the thought. "So did Beck chase them out?"

"Yeah. He opened the windows and they all took off." Steffie fell silent for a moment. "So I guess he's really getting married."

"He is."

Steffie placed both hands over her heart. "Heavy sigh."

Vanessa laughed. "Stef, you would not have been

happy with Beck. If that was going to work out, it would have while you were dating him. As I recall, neither of you really seemed to look back once you stopped seeing each other."

"True enough. But still . . ." Steffie got up and went behind the counter. "Want something else while I'm back here?"

Vanessa held up her empty ice-cream bowl. "I'll take a dabble of cherry vanilla since you're offering."

"You really are an ice-cream hound, aren't you?" Steffie opened the display case and scooped ice cream into another paper cup and handed it to her friend when she returned to the table.

"Thank you." Vanessa smiled and dug in. "You're not having any?"

Steffie held up a bottle of water. "Bathing-suit season is six weeks away. Less, if we get a hot spell near the end of May. I don't walk as much as you do. You're lucky that you live closer to the center of town. I'm out near the point, and that's too far a walk since I run late just about every day. Plus, let us not forget that I make my own ice cream, which means I have to taste-test it as I go along. Believe it or not—and this goes against everything I've ever been told—calories you ingest as part of your job do count."

Steffie dropped into her chair. "So, Mia asked you to be in the wedding?"

Vanessa nodded. "Bridesmaid."

"Any chance I'm on the invitation list?"

"Why wouldn't you be?"

Steffie made a face. "Hello? Old girlfriend?"

Vanessa waved her hand to dismiss the thought. "You're an old friend. Your brother went to high school with Beck and your dad grew up with Hal. That trumps whatever came after."

"Just thought I'd check. I hadn't seen an invitation."

"They're just going out. Since they decided to move the date from June, they're a few weeks off the normal schedule."

"So who else is in the wedding party?"

"Mia's brother Andy's wife, Dorsey, is the other bridesmaid, and the matron of honor is a friend of Mia's from when she was in the FBI. She wants both of her brothers to walk her down the aisle, since their dad died last year. Andy's on board, but she had to fly to Montana to try to talk the other one into coming. Beck took her to the airport this morning."

"I heard the one in Montana is, like, a recluse or something. Barbara and Nita were talking about it in the coffee shop. And they said that there was another brother who had been in the FBI, too, but he was, like, a really creepy guy, into all kinds of really bad stuff."

Vanessa shrugged. "I don't really know. Mia doesn't talk about him, and I don't ask."

"Nice family your brother's marrying into." Steffie tilted her head back and took a long drink of water.

Vanessa glared.

Steffie shrugged. "I'm just saying."

"I've met most of the others, and they're all really nice."

"What happened to the other brother? The creepy one?"

"Oh. Brendan." Vanessa nodded. "All I know is that he's dead, and everyone's okay with that."

"Maybe the one from Montana's hot." Steffie wiggled her eyebrows. "It could make for an interesting day."

"I've met Andy, and I have to say, he is really cute. Mia said once that all the guys in her family look alike, so Mountain Man probably is pretty cute, too. But I'm thinking he's gotta be strange, living by himself all this time. So thanks, but no thanks."

"So what? You've done strange before."

"That's exactly my point. I've met so many guys with issues that I'm starting to believe there's no other kind. I don't care how hot the hermit is. I'm done with all that." She shook her head. "Uh-uh. Give me boring and normal, if you give me anything at all. No baggage, no issues, no drama."

"Doesn't sound like much fun to me."

"I've had fun enough to last a lifetime. If there is a next guy—and I'm not sure I will ever want another one for any length of time and for anything other than occasional sex—he's going to be excruciatingly bland." She held up her empty ice-cream cup. "Vanilla, not rum raisin. Someone who washes the car in the driveway on Saturday morning and who rakes the leaves in the backyard in the fall and reads the newspaper at the breakfast table. He's going to be one of those guys whose idea of a good time is watching a movie at home with a bowl of popcorn in one hand and me in the other."

Steffie rolled her eyes.

"I can't believe I'm hearing this. You've just described my sister's excruciatingly dull life, and it terrifies me to think that someday I could end up like that. It's my worst nightmare."

"Which nicely explains your commitment phobia."

"Don't knock it, since you obviously haven't tried it."

"That was a low blow, Stef."

"Sorry. Really. Damn. I *am* sorry." Steffie looked contrite. "Give me a minute to remove my feet from my mouth."

"It's okay. It's true. At least, it was true, once upon a time. But two really bad marriages have cured me of all that." She finished the last of the ice cream and licked the spoon clean. "Anyway, like I said, Mountain Man is probably as weird as they come after living like a hermit for a couple of years, so it doesn't matter how hot he is. I'll be my usual sweet and pleasant self at the wedding, because he's Mia's brother, but if what she's said about him being antisocial is true, he'll be on a plane back to Montana before his sister even tosses her bouquet. And that's just skippy with me."

"Well, if he gets bored and lonely while he's in St. Dennis, you can send him my way." Steffie lowered her feet to the floor and wearily pushed herself up from the chair. "Do you mind if we do dinner at Captain Walt's tonight? I'm not really dressed for Lola's and I'm too tired to go home to change."

"Walt's is fine. I love their broiled seafood platter." Vanessa stood and gathered the paper cups, napkins, and plastic spoons and tossed them in the trash near the front door, all thoughts of the potentially hot guy already replaced by visions of a few broiled scallops, a piece of rockfish, and one of Walt's famous jumbo lump crab cakes.

Book Two

Home Again

AT the precise moment Dallas MacGregor was picking up her son, Cody, from his pricey summer day camp out near Topanga State Park, the home video starring her soon-to-be-ex-husband and two of the female production assistants from his latest film had already been uploaded to the Internet. By the time she arrived at her Malibu home—she'd stopped once on the way from the set of her latest movie promo shoot to pick up dinner—the one-thousandth viewing had already been downloaded.

The phone was on overdrive, ringing like mad, when she walked into her kitchen.

"Miss MacGregor, you have many messages. Two from your aunt Beryl." Elena, her housekeeper, cast a wary glance at Cody and handed her employer a stack of pink slips as the phone continued to ring. "About Mr. Emilio . . ."

"Would you mind answering that?" Dallas slid the heavy paper bag onto the counter. "And why are you still here? I thought you wanted to leave today by four?"

"Yes, miss, I . . ." Elena lifted the receiver. "Miss

MacGregor's . . . oh, hello, Miss Townsend. Yes, she's home now, she just arrived. Yes, I gave her the message but . . . of course, Miss Townsend . . ."

Elena held the phone out to Dallas.

"It's your great-aunt," she whispered.

"I figured that out." Dallas smiled and took the cordless receiver from Elena. "Hello, Berry. I was just thinking about—"

"Dallas." Her aunt cut her off sharply. "What the hell is going on out there?"

"Not much." Dallas paused. "What's supposed to be going on?"

"That numbskull you were married to." Berry's breath came in ragged puffs.

She was obviously in a lather over something. Not unusual, Dallas thought. At eighty-one, it didn't take much to rile Berry these days.

"What's he done now?" Dallas began emptying the bag, lining up the contents on the counter.

"Not *what* as much as *who*." Berry was becoming increasingly agitated.

"Mommy." Cody tugged at her sleeve. "Why are all those cars out there?"

"Berry, hold on for just a moment, please." Dallas glanced out the side window where cars were lined up on the other side of the fence that completely encircled the gated property, cars that had not been there five minutes ago when they drove through the gates. It wasn't unusual for paparazzi to follow her home, but she hadn't noticed any cars tailing her today. She raised the blinds just a little, and saw more cars were arriving even as she watched.

"I don't know, Cody. Maybe the studio put out

something about Mommy's new movie. Maybe we should turn on the television and see."

"No!" Elena and Berry both shouted at the same time.

"What?" Dallas frowned and turned to her housekeeper, who stood behind Cody. She pointed to the child, then raised her index finger to her lips, their silent code for "not in front of Cody."

Keeping a curious eye on Elena, Dallas asked, "Berry, why don't you tell me . . . ?"

"Are you saying you don't know? Seriously? You haven't heard?"

"Heard what?"

"That idiot ex of yours—"

"Not ex yet, but soon, please God . . . ," Dallas muttered. "And it's long been established that he's an idiot, so anything he's done should be viewed with that in mind."

"—managed to get himself filmed doing . . . all sorts of things that you will not want Cody to see . . ." Berry was almost gasping. "And with more than one person. It was disgusting. Perverted."

"You mean . . ." Dallas's knees went weak and she sat in the chair that Elena wisely pulled out for her.

"Yes. A sex tape. Not one, but *two* young women. I was shocked. Appalled!"

"Wait! You actually *saw* it?"

"Three times!" Dallas could almost see Berry fanning herself. "It was vile, just vile! You know, Dallas, that I never liked that man. I told you when you first brought him home that I—"

"Berry, where did you see this?"

"On my computer. There was a link to a site—"

"Hold on for a moment, Berry." Dallas put her hand over the mouthpiece and turned to Elena. "Would you mind cutting up an apple for Cody? Cody, go wash your hands so you can have your snack."

After her son left the room, Dallas took the phone outside and sat at one of the tables on her shaded patio.

"Dear God, Berry, let me get this straight. Emilio made a sex tape and it was put on the Internet? Is that what you're telling me?"

"Yes, and not just any sex tape. This one had—"

"Wait a minute; they allowed you to download the whole thing?"

"No, no, not all of it, just a little peek. You had to pay to see the whole thing."

"And you did? You paid to watch . . ." Dallas didn't know whether to laugh or cry. The thought of her elderly aunt watching Emilio and his latest conquests burning up the sheets—and paying for the privilege—was horrifying and crazy funny at the same time. "Wait—did you say *three times*?"

"Yes, and it was—"

"Berry, why did you watch it three times?"

"Well," Berry sniffed. "I had to make sure it was really him."

The rest of the evening went downhill from there.

Dallas made every attempt to remain calm lest Cody pick up on the fact that she was almost blind with anger at the man she'd been married to for seven years.

Seven years, she repeated to herself. *Seven years out of my life, wasted on that reprobate.* The only good thing to come out of those years was Cody—and Dallas had to admit that she would have weathered a lifetime of Emilio's amorous flings and general foolishness if she'd had to in order to have her son. When she filed for divorce eight months ago, following the latest in his long line of infidelities, Emilio hadn't even bothered to beg her to reconsider: they'd done that dance so often over the years that even he was tired of it.

She managed to have a normal evening with Cody and ignored the cars that parked beyond the protective fence. They had a nice dinner and watched a video together, then Cody had his bath and Dallas read a bedtime story before she tucked him in and turned off the light.

It wasn't until she went back downstairs, alone, that she permitted herself to fall apart.

There was no love lost between her and Emilio. She'd long since accepted the fact that he'd married her strictly to further his own career as a director. For a time, she'd remained stubbornly blind, insisting that her husband be signed to direct her movies, and for a time, she'd been equally blind to his affairs. Lately it occurred to her that she well might be the last person in the entire state of California to catch on to the extent of Emilio's indiscretions.

For the past five years, she and Emilio had battled over the same ground, over and over until Dallas no longer cared who he slept with, as long as it wasn't her. Looking back now, she realized she should have left him the first time he'd cheated on her, when the tabloids had leaked those photos of Emilio frolicking with a pretty up-and-coming Latina actress on a sunny, sandy beach in Guatemala when he'd told Dallas he was going to scout some locations for a film he was thinking about making, but it had been so much easier to stay than to leave. There was Cody to consider: Emilio had never wanted the child, but Dallas had hoped—for Cody's sake—that he'd come around. Besides, Dallas's schedule had been so hectic for the past three years that she'd barely had time to read the tabloids. She'd had the blessing—or the curse—of having had wonderful roles offered to her, roles that she'd really wanted, so she'd signed on for all of them, and had gone from one set right onto the next, leaving her time for nothing and no one other than her son. It had only been recently that Dallas admitted to herself that perhaps she'd been deliberately overworking herself to avoid having to deal with her home situation.

Well, avoid no more, she told herself as she dialed her attorney's number. This time, Emilio had gone too far. When the call went directly to voice mail, Dallas left the message that she wanted her lawyer to do whatever had to be done to speed up the divorce.

"And oh," she'd added, "we need to talk about that custody arrangement we'd worked out . . ."

While she waited for the return call, Dallas logged on to the computer in her home office. She searched the Web for what she was looking for. The link to the video appeared almost instantaneously, along with a running tally of how many times the video had been watched—all thirteen thousand, four hundred, and thirty-one viewings. Her stomach churning, she clicked on the link and was asked first to confirm that she was over eighteen, then for her credit card number.

"Great," she murmured. "For the low, low price of

nineteen ninety-five, I can watch my husband . . . that is, my soon-to-be-ex-husband, perform daring feats with his production assistants."

The video began abruptly—"What, no music?"—and while the lighting could have been better, there was no question who was the filling in the middle of that fleshy sandwich. As difficult as it was to watch, she forced herself to sit through it, commenting to herself from time to time. ("Emilio, Emilio, didn't anyone ever tell you to always keep your best side to the camera? And, babe, that is decidedly *not* your best side.")

When the phone rang before it was over, Dallas turned off her computer and answered the call.

"Hey, Dallas, it's Norma."

"Thanks for getting back to me right away." Dallas leaned back in her chair and exhaled. Just hearing her attorney's always cool and even voice relaxed her.

"I just got in and I was going to call you as soon as I kicked off my shoes." Norma Bradshaw was not only Dallas's lawyer, she was also her friend.

"So you heard . . ."

"Is there anyone in this town who has not? So sorry, Dallas. We knew he was a colossal shithead, but this latest stunt even beats his own personal best." Before Dallas could respond, Norma said, "So we're going to want to see if we can move the divorce along a little faster. We'll file a motion to revise those custody arrangements we'd previously agreed to."

"You read my mind."

"I'll file first thing in the morning. If nothing else, I think we should ask for sole custody for a period of at least six months, given the circumstances, which of course we'll spell out for the judge in very specific terms."

"Would it help to know that that little forty-two-minute production was filmed in his house? The same one Cody and I moved out of just eleven months ago because he refused to leave?"

"Really?" Norma made a "huh" sound. "Are you positive?"

"I picked out that furniture," Dallas replied. "Along with the carpets and the tile in the bath and the towels that were dropped around the hot tub."

"That was really stupid on his part. Now you can say you don't want Emilio to have unsupervised custody because you don't know who will be in the house or what they'll be doing. Or who might be filming it." Norma paused. "How are you doing?"

"On the one hand, I feel devastated. Humiliated. Nauseated. On the other, I feel like calling every reporter who chastised me for being so mean and unforgiving to poor Emilio when our separation was announced and yelling, *'See? I told you he was a jerk!'* "

"Anyone you want me to call for you?"

"No. I'm not making any statements to anyone. This is strictly a no-comment situation if ever there was one."

"You know you can always refer people to me."

"I'll have Elena start doing that tomorrow. Thanks."

"How did Cody react?"

"He hasn't. He doesn't know what's going on."

"You didn't tell him?"

"Of course not. Why would I tell him about something like that?"

"Do you really think you can keep him from finding out? Isn't he in camp this summer?"

"He just turned six. He's only in kindergarten." Dallas frowned. "How many of the kids at his camp do you think caught Emilio's act?"

"They could hear their parents talking, they could see the story on TV. It made the news, Dallas."

"I don't think it's going to be a problem." Dallas bit a fingernail. "At least, I hope it won't be. But if he hears about it, I'll have to tell him . . . something."

"Well, good luck with that. In the meantime, if you think of anything else I can do for you, you know how to reach me." Norma's calls always ended the same way, with the same closing sentence. She never bothered to wait until Dallas said good-bye. She just hung up, leaving Dallas to wonder just what she would tell Cody if he should hear something.

She didn't have long to wait to find out. When she arrived at camp the following afternoon, the Cody who got into the car was a very different child from the one she'd dropped off earlier that morning.

"How was camp, buddy?" she asked when he got into the car.

He looked out the window and muttered something.

"What did you say?" She turned in her seat to face him.

"I didn't say anything."

"Well, how *was* camp? Did you have your riding lesson today?"

He shook his head but did not look at her.

Uh-oh, she thought as she drove from the curb. *This doesn't bode well . . .*

"So what did you do today?" she asked.

"I don't want to talk."

"Why not, baby?"

"Because I don't and I'm not a baby," he yelled. He still hadn't looked at her.

Oh, God. Her hands began to shake and she clutched the wheel in an effort to make them stop.

She did not try to engage him in conversation the rest of the way home, and once they arrived, she drove in through the service entrance at the back of the property to avoid the crowd that was still stalking the front gate.

"Those cars out there, they're all there because . . ." Cody said accusingly. "Because . . ."

It was then that Dallas realized he was crying. She stopped the car and turned off the ignition, then got out and opened his door. She unbuckled his seat belt but he made no move toward her.

"Cody, what happened today?" When he didn't respond, she asked, "Does it have something to do with your dad?"

"They said he did things . . . with other ladies. Justin's big brother said his dad saw it on the computer and he heard his dad tell his mom." Huge, fat drops ran down Cody's face and Dallas's heart began to break in half. "Justin's daddy said my daddy was a very, very bad man. The big kids said he . . . they said he . . ." He began to sob.

Dallas had never felt so helpless in her life. She got into the backseat and rubbed Cody's shoulders, then coaxed him into her arms. How could she have been so naive as to think he wouldn't hear something from the older kids at camp? And how could she possibly explain his father's actions to her son?

"I'm never going back to camp, Mommy. Not ever. Nobody can make me." He hiccuped loudly. "Not even you. I'll run away if you try."

"All right, sweetie." Silently cursing Emilio for his stupidity and his carelessness, Dallas held her son tight, and let him cry it out. "It's going to be all right . . ."

But even as she promised, Dallas wondered if, for Cody, anything would ever be right again.